I0547580

Ninjalicious:
The Fictional Autobiography of
Richard Lichman

by G.S. Nearing

Love it or hate it, please leave a review for "Ninjalicious" at your favorite retailer.

**When you need to take a break between porn searches,
check out my Smashwords author page at**
www.smashwords.com/profile/view/RichardLichman

or the Ninjaverse Publishing website at
www.ninjaversepublishing.weebly.com

Cover design copyright © 2016 by Cao Wenzhu

ISBN-10: 1-946551-00-7
ISBN-13: 978-1-946551-00-9
LCCN: 2016921527

Table of Contents

Dedication...3
Introduction..4
1994..7
1995...34
1996...65
1997...92
1998..126
1999..172
2000..197
2001..244
2002..267
Epilogue 273
Ninjalicious II: Crazy Corea preview 275
About the Author 278

Dedication

To Dad, for everything he did for us and especially for the tales he loved to share with us. You passed on your love of living, and I can't thank you enough for that!

To Gram Pat, you saved my life once, even if you didn't know it. And for showing me that I could do this. I hope this book doesn't suck too much for you!

To the Christiensens and Hubbards, my two other families took me in at times when I needed it most.

Introduction

Howdy. You have elected to purchase/borrow/download/steal a fictional autobiographical anthology. It has to be. This laundry list of sexual acts, criminal violations, destruction of property, consumption of illicit substances, and general lack of respect for authority contained herein is too extreme, too vulgar and/or too illegal to be real. The following depictions of life in the Bible Belt of WLOTUS (What's Left of the United States) may occasionally scratch the surface of reality in some ways, but I can assure you (especially for legal purposes) that these are mere coincidences. If you believe that you see a reflection yourself somewhere within this tome, I can assure you that you are simply experiencing that lovely feeling of paranoia that accompanies the heavy consumption of tetrahydrocannibinol. We exist in a weird world that's only getting weirder. These kaleidoscopic vignettes depict various points along one small stretch of one man's path.

What exactly is the Ninjaverse? It's a palace of knowledge entered with the realization of the beautiful absurdity of the world around us. To escape into and become a part of the Ninjaverse is no easy task. This accomplishment involves alcohol abuse, drug experimentation, an amazing pair of testicles (regardless of gender), and the overt ability to roll with the ceaseless stream of punches life throws at you regardless of whether or not you deserved them (and you most likely did).

My name is Richard Lichman, and what follows is a collection of tales emanating from a landscape of insanity presented to you as clearly as I can recollect them. They have shaped not only my view of the universe, but also the person that I am today: Buzzard. Student. Drunkard. DJ. Boyfriend. Fuck buddy. Fiend. Juggalo (and gang member, thank you, FBI). Bodyguard/Sous-Pimp. Hasher. Professor. Reverend. Fiancé. Husband. These will reveal themselves to you as you move along through this litany of mostly Midwestern madness.

Decades ago someone probably would have described this as a collection of tales about sex, drugs and rock & roll. Times change.

Most of what follows are simply tails from the trails and trials of life. If you can deduce some higher meaning from them or extract some sort of moral, then hurrah for you. To me, they are simply amazingly odd events that have taken place with amazingly interesting and/or wonderful people that have played various roles in my life.

Some come from the deep and hazy recesses of my memory banks. Some come from my parents. Some come from pieces I wrote for my university's newspaper. And even more from the nearly illegible pages of the 140-plus journals I've filled with my scrawling scribbles since 1997.

The majority of these tales fall between 1994 and 2002. Those who experienced and survived these eight years witnessed an unadulterated freak show as the fabric of Western civilization (and the world in general) unraveled at a rate that likely outpaced any change to which our species has ever been subjected:

The Murrah bombing. iTunes. 9-11. The invasion of Iraq. The Afghanistan blunder. The rise of overpriced coffee shops. The obese-ification of America. Idiotic gun control debates taking place a century too late. Emos. Hipsters. Political correctness. Public school systems embracing the nonsensical notion that "every child is special and always a winner" coupled with the overbearing intrusiveness of helicopter parents creating the most pampered, whiny, useless, confused, and self-involved generation of children the world has ever had the misfortune to suffer. "Reality" television. The "celebrity" byproducts of reality television. "Vintage" clothing stores relieving morons of $200 for pairs of shredded jeans you could pick up for a fiver at a Salvation Army store if they lowered their standards to sell clothing in that poor a condition. Cell phones. Children with cell phones. Addicts who can't sit through a movie, class, church service, meal, or drive without fiddling with their phones. Future proofs of natural selection so addicted to their cell phones that they can't even manage to walk down the street without staring at their screens. Facefuck. Twatter for endorsing and celebrating our increasingly short attention spans. iReporters (internet access does not instantly qualify you to perform jobs that most people spend years studying or training to do). Pop music. Restaurants selling medium and large but no small sizes. The increase in rage. The decrease in manners. The increase in fear. The decrease in responsibility taken for anything by anybody. The evaporation of our rights and those who sit idly by and allow them to be taken. Safe places.

And this barely scratches the surface. Billy Joel's 4-minute, 49-second "We Didn't Start the Fire" covered four decades of twisted headlines. The Piano Man could compose a song that long for each of the past twenty years without breaking a sweat or crashing his car (again).

Outside of this brief introduction, this book does not aim to present a commentary on society or its downfall. It's merely a collection of recollections. That being said, it is important to understand the decade or so during which these events transpire.

1994

Hello, Alcohol

Growing up, I was a fairly innocent/protected child. I refrained from trying booze until my junior year of high school and from everything else until I started college. My first drink came to me courtesy of the Dude during Spring Break '93. Not one to ever go about doing things the normal way, my spring break wasn't spent cavorting on a beach in South Texas or on a cruise ship in the Caribbean - I broke my liver's virginity at a hotel in Oklahoma City on a school trip.

We were members of the Distributive Education Classes of America, a marketing club for high school students. The organization's annual state conference fell during Waterford High School's spring break my junior year (Oklahoma only recently placed its schools on a standardized calendar). This reduced my high school's normal turnout down to eight: five girls, the Dude and I. And our sponsor.

The Dude informed me that if I went on this trip, he was going to get me drunk. I have never known him to bullshit me or anyone else for that matter.

The first day's activities came to a conclusion, and the Dude emptied the contents of his duffel bag onto his bed in the double room we shared. He produced a gallon jug of Hawaiian Punch he had replaced with strawberry Mad Dog 20/20 and a water bottle refilled with Absolut. Only two of the girls were down with the drunkenness, Cathy and a Bundy sister. They came to our room a few hours before curfew to partake with us.

The Mad Dog went down unexpectedly well, as did the Absolut. When our sponsor came round to send the girls to their room at curfew, I was rather jubilant to say the least. It was all I could do to restrain the joy I felt.

The next morning I awoke without feeling my first hangover. That wouldn't come until my third time to drink, fourteen months later.

The family of Mario, a classmate, hosted a giant graduation bash on their land just east of town. They owned the best Mexican restaurant in town at the time and put out quite a spread for us. I paid a gay couple I worked with at our movie theater to bring me three bottles of Mad Dog. My inexperienced ass drank a few beers while waiting for the booze delivery. I proceeded to take down all three bottles on my own. I later experienced a romantic moment with my last bottle, grape, and proposed to it. One of Mario's cousins didn't approve of my burgeoning man-on-glass relationship and heaved my beloved bottle out into the woods. I never saw her again.

I abandoned my car there to jump into the bed of a pickup truck with some older guys to hit an after-party in one of our town's many trailer parks. I ended up throwing up over the side and passing out there for a couple of hours. I did not feel my best the next morning.

Shortly after beginning university in August, I began upping my intake and tolerance to intolerable levels. Thursday nights served as my school's party night. This came to involve me getting a friend and/or coworker to score a fifth of Smirnoff Blue. I would combine the bottle with two gallons of orange juice throughout the night. Even in my haze, I would stay clear of mind enough to leave an inch or so to kick start my next morning.

Minimum Wage, Maximum Weird

I entered the workforce with a paper route at the tender age of ten, young for Americans, old for Indians. I spent six years flinging flimsy small-town journalism and reprinted AP articles five days a week in rain, snow, sleet, dogs, and tornado warnings. My younger brother, Goober, joined the company a few months later. Six years later, with our fellow paperboy, Ron, we organized and threatened a strike of all of the Waterford News' tossers if we weren't given a raise. We'd all been working at the same four cents per paper since before I had come aboard. They gave us the raise, and we three organizers quit within the following few months. Ron and I left because we turned 16. The time to move up into the wonderful world of very minimum wage had arrived.

Quickly bored by most jobs, I usually stuck around for one year and then moved on to something new. I spent a quiet year cooking at Pizza Slut my sophomore year of high school. It opened the door for me to return a year later as a driver at 18. Between my pizza positions, I worked for Dickhead Theaters.

The Dickhead chain had not too recently bought out the triplex outside of town along with the ancient single-screen downtown on Main Street. The company assembled an eclectic group of malcontents to staff its cinemas. The manager, Pablo, sent employees, on the clock, to procure cocaine for him. The second time I got drunk happened while working Christmas night. He mixed a gallon of Jack and eggnog as an apology for bringing me out at the last minute after forgetting to schedule anyone on the concession stand for the traditionally busy night. I danced with my mop as Jackie, the very innocent frizzy-haired assistant manager, watched. A gay couple ran the projection booth when they weren't doing coke or smoking weed with Pablo.

The theaters had large storage areas filled with the kind of clutter you'd expect from a business with decades of a high-turnover product and equipment with little to no resale value by the time it had found its way out to our out of the way part of the world. During a visit from the regional manager, I offered to remove some of their junk for them. Corporate listened to regional and agreed a few weeks later.

I gave Jizzball a case of beer to use his pickup to remove four full-size arcade games the theaters' previous owners hadn't licensed since 1983. I scored two *Centipedes* (one working, one for parts), a working *Amidar* and a *Zaxxon* stripped of its joystick and marquee. These went to my house where I gutted the spare *Centipede* and built shelving into it for my television and Super Nintendo. *Centipede* and *Amidar* found a new home in my living room and later, licensed in my bar.

Learning to Drink

I hated beer when I first started drinking. This was unfortunate, since this was the drink of choice amongst my amigos – mostly because it was the only alcohol they could easily score. Scooby took it upon himself to teach me to consume beer one hot, Oklahoman afternoon. Both of us recently graduated from high school, he scored a case of Old Milwaukee's Best (the Beast) and shoved it down between the rear bench seat of his Wrangler and its tailgate.

It didn't take long for the two dozen cans to reach summer temperatures. It didn't matter to Scooby. He drove us around until we had killed twelve each. His philosophy was that if I could drain a half-case of one of the world's shittiest beers when it was piss-warm, then I could drink real beer. He wasn't wrong.

Matriculation

My university experience began for no better reason than that it was what I thought I was supposed to do after high school. Our little town has a little college which offered me a couple of little scholarships, so I accepted. The best thing to come out of freshman year was moving into the dormitory (courtesy of one of those scholarships) saving me a nearly five-minute commute to campus. It was there that I met many of the people who would forever alter my life and help format this autobiography you have been kind enough to purchase or dickish enough to steal.

Up in Smoke

I waited to partake of the sweet Mary Jane until the Friday before my first day of college. Not much came of it. Never having smoked a cigarette, I ended up pulling a Bill Clinton and didn't inhale. It took another week of puffing away to finally earn a reward for my efforts. Unfortunately, it came minutes before I had my first biology lab.

Driving proved to be a challenge as I crept through campus. The last to enter the room, I had to sit alone at one of the square, four-person lab tables. I was too stoned to figure out the microscope or which slide to look at. My mind didn't straighten itself out until well after I'd escaped that room two hours later.

Dorm Daze

Thanks to one of the aforementioned scholarships, I had the opportunity to participate in one of the great American traditions of youth: living in the dormitory your freshman year of college. Unsure of what I really wanted to study and even less sure of what I wanted to do after school, I decided to attend South Waterford Oklahoma State University. SWOSU offered me more scholarships than any other higher institution of learning, and I couldn't justify going to one of the state's larger/better/pricier institutions under the cloud of cluelessness in which I was to enroll. The people I met that year and the shenanigans that went down introduced me to a future I never believed existed.

Getting in with the K-Town Mafia

Having survived and shed the horrors of high school, I moved into the dorms and was eager to meet people. Not all of these encounters went as smoothly as they could have. My seventh-floor neighbors made a commotion the day we all moved in. They opened their window to find a harrowing hornets' nest hanging outside. I offered my services, grabbing a lighter and a can of their hair spray. Proceeding to torch the nest, a gust of Oklahoma's song-worthy wind blew my impromptu flamethrower's blast back into my new neighbors' curtains. We extinguished the fire and never spoke again.

I had a different roommate for each of my two semesters in the dorms. For the first semester, the school paired me with Tom McVeigh one semester before he blew up a building in OKC. Maybe that was a different guy. My McVeigh didn't build any bombs. That would have made him at least slightly interesting and could have given us something in common. Instead, Tom had a personality that made beige look neon hot pink in comparison. He would remain the most boring person I'd ever met until the Beigian (pronounced "beige-an") came to teach at my university in Korea more than a decade later.

The day the dorms opened, I tossed a pillow and a sheet on my bed, set fire to my neighbors' curtains, introduced myself to my new roommate, and informed him that I was leaving for Dallas to attend Lollapalooza '94. That was one of only five times we were both in the room and conscious at the same time.

To McVeigh's credit, he did quietly endure my almost daily late-night returns. We existed in different time zones roughly four to six hours apart at any given moment. A senior music major (i.e. band nerd), he proudly displayed his first bottle of beer in a place of honor atop his desk. It was a Bud Light from his 21st birthday. One of only five or so Americans who actually waited until they turned 21 to consume alcohol for the first time in their lives, and he whored out his liver's virginity out to a "beer" only meant for easy/desperate female freshmen. His girlfriend visited a few times throughout the semester. I always walked in on them both fully dressed and playing board games on his bed. The scene would have disturbed me less had I walked in on them performing the horizontal mambo.

Many high school students across Oklahoma's numerous small towns form their own little groups to stand against the world...or in the case of Buzzards, just to commit theft.

Buzzards

This tome requires an explanation of some of my numerous personal affiliations. With the release of the 2012 FBI Gang Report, I became a member of a "non-traditional, transient gang" due to having been a Juggalo for nearly two decades. Thank Alvis the FBI never got wind of the Buzzards, K-Town Mafia or Hashers.

Let's kick this off with a look at the people I went to high school with, the Buzzards. My high school graduating class had less than 130 people. Waterford High School's mascot is the Sparrow, so a group of degenerates designated their people the Buzzards. The Buzzards consisted of a rotating group of track team members with off-season footballers sprinkled among legitimate runners and track and field athletes. I joined the track team the final semester of senior year thinking that the stories I'd heard had to have been highly exaggerated. Not only would they prove me totally wrong but, I would witness the team reach the peak of their buzzardry followed quickly by their demise.

The coaches let me on the team as a fluke. I had been a pretty good student and mostly took honors classes. At the end of each sport's season, the state awarded an Academic All-State plaque to the team with the highest average grade point average. Coach Cigar took me in so that I could hang out with my friends and boost the team's already decent GPA. All I had to do was participate at each meet in an event we didn't have filled out with legitimate competitors.

One week I would throw shot, the next discus. At one meet, I ran in the Fat Man Relay, an unofficial relay for the big boys (off-season footballers) who usually threw shot or discus. They had me start in the two-mile a couple of times. They knew that I couldn't finish, but I could throw some elbows or fall into some of the competition to aide our boys. I refused to go as far as some of our guys who spat fat loogies at their competitors' faces.

The legend of the Buzzard's inception goes back to when I would have been in elementary school. We'd always had a good number of middle-class white guys up for some thuggery. Our coaches knew about it and one day made the mistake of encouraging it before a track meet.

"Boys, we're running low on shot puts. It sure would be nice if we had a few extra by the time we got back to town," said Coach Cigar, as the myth goes.

Our team returned with an abundance of metal balls with other school's names written on them in black Sharpie. This soon opened the doors to our guys looting other track teams' unguarded equipment. By the time I joined the team in the spring of 1994, most of our well-stocked equipment supply had our school's name written above a black Sharpie rectangle.

Having permission to ransack for the benefit of the team, it didn't take long for the guys to figure out that if they were going to risk getting caught pilfering for the coaches, they should also plunder a little something for themselves. And thus the thuggery began.

Their method was simple and sound: At any given track meet, most teams staked out a piece of real estate around the track and dropped their bags in a pile. Few of these trusting people ever left anyone to guard their possessions. Buzzards strolled casually by and snatched a bag here and there. They took the bags back to a hidden spot or to our bus to rifle through them for treasure before returning them to where, or in the vicinity of where, they'd initially grabbed them.

Tracksuits from the larger schools, especially rivals, were always favorite trophies. As a joke, Dirty (most of the Buzzards had nicknames, which you will soon find to be a common denominator in the Ninjaverse) proudly sported an Anadarko HS tracksuit to our daily practices. The coaches said nothing.

Returning from meets, the Buzzards held the Waterford Swap Meet on the bus. This was the time when Dr. Dre's seminal *The Chronic* reached its peak. The trip home gave them time to sort through their quickly acquired booty and exchange items they either didn't want, couldn't use/wear or had taken specifically for bartering purposes. Paranoid long before dropping LSD for the first time, I refused to take part in the stealing sessions at each meet, but didn't say "no" to one of my teammates tossing me a pair of Converse that were too large for them or the odd CD already in their catalog.

The Buzzard's long run came to an end after a meet at Oklahoma Baptist University. OBU's track is set into the side of a small hill. The first buses to arrive parked above the track, lining the rim nose to tail. Later buses parked perpendicular to the first, effectively blocked the view from the track. An increase in the boldness of my teammates that season had led to an increase in the amount and diversity of their thieving. As a result, most of the teams at the meet left their bags on their buses.

This created the perfect theft tornado. The setting sun cast long shadows as Buzzards dashed from bus to bus, snatching bags. They delivered them back to our bus where they quickly dug through them for valuables. Many of their owners would later find their bags hastily tossed beneath their buses or aboard a neighboring bus. This went on for hours. I watched them dart back and forth, but Scooby and Honeycomb made the biggest jack move of the day.

Scooby was a fellow senior, while Honeycomb had graduated the year before. Scooby had given Honeycomb the keys to his Grand Prix that morning. The plan was for Honeycomb to drive up to the meet, help Scooby gather some loot and then ride with Scooby to a club for the night. Scooby backed his ride up to the door of a random bus and popped the trunk. Honeycomb hopped on the bus and tossed bags out until he filled the trunk. Scooby, having finished his events of the day, rode off with Honeycomb into the sunset like an ivory and ebony Butch Cassidy and the Sundance Kid.

It would prove their biggest raid. A boom box filled the bus with Dre and Snoop as the Buzzards held their swap meet. Even the bus received a new secondhand first aid kit courtesy of the Mack.

How did this bring about the end of the Buzzards' thuggery? A lowly freshman committed the fatal error that would prove our undoing. The upperclassmen had always done their best to cover their tracks in order to keep their crime empire afloat - the young ones, not so much. The death knell came from a wallet found in our high school's parking lot turned in to the front office. Whoever dropped it had cleaned out everything except for an ID card. The wallet belonged to a student from the tiny burg of Valium, a town of less than a thousand tucked far away in Oklahoma's southeastern corner. The Buzzards had put a hurting on their gear at OBU.

It didn't take long for the two schools to figure out what had taken place that weekend. Valium gave our coaches a list of their possessions which had gone missing. The list and our coaches' anger had the opposite effect they should have had on us. The list gave an estimated value for each item. We lost our shit upon seeing that some idiot from Valium actually blamed us for stealing a jockstrap - a jockstrap valued at $30. The Buzzards were a twisted group, but not even our people would snag a used cock cap for any reason. Crank might have once taken a piss in a girl's Gatorade at a meet. Dirty ate the remnants of burgers thrown into the trashcan at Hardee's on many nights. But none of us were ever going to steal a used penis pouch.

This immediately prompted our coaches to bust us for the very acts they had encouraged for more than half a decade. Our coaches had a very angry meeting with us in the locker room the following day.

They demanded that we promptly return every item we'd ever stolen or been given from other peoples' loot (excluding of course all of the WHS track equipment), especially those items on the VHS list our coach taped up to the office door. They gave us two days, no questions asked. After that, they would give no quarter. One or two Valium items showed up. Dirty dropped off his Anadarko tracksuit. Nothing else turned up, but it ended a dynasty of thievery.

Down the K-Hole

The little hamlet of Kweenfisher produced the K-Town Mafia, a band of drunken brothers to whom I would become inseparably tied. Several members of the K-Town Mafia resided in the same dormitory as I did. We crossed paths early on in Jefferson Hall's cafeteria. The number of interests we shared stunned us: girls, alcohol, guns, cannabis, and video games or any combination thereof. I guess that, in retrospect, it should not have been that big of a surprise that so many of us would have coalesced in those wild days.

Our posse of dorm rats formed. Many came and went in the short span of a year, but it remained, for the most part, the K-Town Mafia, including Jizzball, a Cordellian Hellian whose family had left K-Town in his youth, and Tex, our cameraman from P-town, Texas. High jinks ensued.

I upgraded roommates between my two semesters. I moved into Gokey's room the second semester. I love the scruffy Fidel Castro look-a-like member of the K-Town Mafia as though he was my brother, but he was one messy son of a bitch. His special powers never failed to impress me.

Piles of clothes and garbage ringed his bed and cluttered his desk - the classic artistic type. Every late morning, once he finally got out of bed, it took him less than five minutes for a small mound of random shit to materialize on his bed. I could never deduce where it all came from. The level of his floor garbage never decreased upon the appearance of the bed junk. He liked the leftover pizza from my job at Pizza Slut I stashed almost daily in my dorm fridge. I could tell by the crusts scattered about the room. He would later join the basement dwellers of the Seventh Street Lighthouse.

The Residential Adviser for our floor didn't think too highly of me. Most nights he sat in the lobby, waiting for the return of his wards. I was always the last one to fly back to the nest. Ninety percent of the time, I found him on one of the lobby's stained couches, half dozing or reading in front of infomercials on the big screen projection television, waiting to ride the elevator up with me. Not that it could've helped much, but I still held my breath on the ride up every time in a futile attempt to hide the odor of booze, but he never said anything.

Our little crew even won the hearts of the women working in our dorm's cafeteria, they but were weirded out by our presence. It quickly became our group's custom that when someone got up from the table for any reason, his tray became fair game. We salted and peppered each other's food and drinks. It was a mess and a waste. We didn't get to eat all that much and thus avoided the so-called dreaded "Freshman Fifteen."

The pranks did sometimes go beyond the simple and childish.

Each pair of rooms in our building had a small vanity area in the middle between the closets (the girls' dorm had sinks in their vanities). A large vent loomed above these spaces, linking each pair of rooms. L-Ron and the Shallow End shared a room whose vent connected to Tex and Jizzball's room. One weekend when L-Ron and the Shallow End returned to K-Town, Tex decided to explore the vent. Sure enough, the dusty, neglected crawl space went straight across to L-Ron and the Shallow End's room. Tex crawled through and unlocked the door for Jizzball. Together, they transferred every item to the exact opposite side of the room.

Two of the quieter guys we smoked with, Jesus and the Pharmacist, shared a room. They often got up to their own strange brand of shenanigans. They got stoned one night early on and reorganized the letters on the signboard in front of the Baptist Student Union. Their version read something to the effect of, "THE LORD GAVE US LSD TO USE."

Despite having accomplished their mission late at night and having given us a much more inspirational message than whatever the BSUers had posted, they came home after class the next afternoon to find a shocking message on their answering machine. Someone from the BSU had called and threatened that as long as they changed the letters back posthaste, their cult wouldn't file charges against them. The original message returned within the hour. The pair later joined forces and skillsets to construct a portable rolling meth lab in the trunk of the Pharmacist's Honda Civic.

Like many college students, we blew many of our afternoons rollerblading through buildings on campus or taking turns holding onto bumpers on quieter streets. We kicked a hack around. We partied. We played N64. We drove aimlessly around town. And we learned the glory of sex, drugs and rock & roll. We even managed to show up for the odd class when we had nothing better to do.

Grotesque Gastronomics

For all of you who have rocked the ganja before, you know that we eat, or try to eat, some pretty crazy foodish items while stoned. My people and I were no exception. This brings us to Arab's and the effect it had on my freshman year of college in the dorms.

The Cash 'n Carry was a convenience store situated at the northwestern corner of SWOSU's campus. The city police and campus cops had for years used it as their hangout of choice, sipping coffee and sitting diligent vigil over the city and campus. A trio of gentlemen of Middle Eastern descent bought the place during my senior year of high school and, in a town where most everything and everybody has a nickname, the C 'n C immediately and lazily became "Arab's" to the Buzzards. The new owners kindly requested that the cops no longer use their business as their nightly hangout, as it scared off their customers.

17

The youth in town quickly learned that their customers consisted of under-aged purchasers of beer. It was fate, not a coincidence, that their shop began selling to minors at the same time I began to drink as a minor. Lawrence, Muhammad and Moustafa kept the Buzzards and many others well plied in the tool of our trade: cheap beer. They went one step further and began hiring our friends to work there. Knee-Bones used to toss a free pack of Zig-Zags to every customer he knew. Not much time passed before I had more skins than even Snoop Dogg could twist in a month.

Cases of the munchies became a nightly ritual for me. I tend to eat like fat, middle-aged European men bang hookers while on sex tours of Southeast Asia. I often cured my pot-induced cravings with a last minute walk down to Arab's. During the afternoon shifts, they fried burritos, jalapeno poppers, cheese sticks, and all the other manner of assorted fried stoner snacks normally associated with convenience stores servicing drivers, drunks and dopers. The night clerks always bundled the dried-out remnants of the day's fry basket for a buck or two for me after 1 a.m. Many a night did I sit on my dorm bed, quietly munching neglected bean burritos and crunchy mozzarella sticks with solid innards. None of it ever killed me, for which I am grateful and more than a little surprised.

Lawrence was the only owner any of us ever knew by a name we hadn't anointed him with. He enjoyed partying with the Buzzards and K-Town Mafia. If we were willing to suffer through him strumming his guitar at his apartment, he'd supply us with a few cases of beer and allow us to smoke herb out of his truly sweet hookah. He was odd, but not odd enough that we turned down live music, free beer and a proper Middle Eastern hookah back before hookah bars had gained any degree of popularity in WLOTUS.

The most legendary story to come from our favorite store came courtesy of the Buzzards. The owners used to allow their favorite frequent customers to fill coolers with ice from a machine stuck in the rear next to the beer cooler entrance. Rockman and a few of the other Buzzards would sneak into the room and steal a case or two to line the bottom of their coolers before they covered the cans with ice.

They got away with this for the better part of a year, but the fun ended when Muhammad caught Rockman filling his cooler. Rockman had anger issues back then and beat Muhammad's ass down. Nobody felt like reporting the incident.

D.A.R.E. to Say No to My Front Bumper

During my freshman year of college, I ran over a sweet elderly lady behind Hardon's. Waterford's cruise ran from Hardon's to Scronic on Main Street. For those of you from big towns (or children of the $4.00/gallon age), high school kids in small towns had little to do most nights they were out other than to drive back and forth between a pair of Main Street businesses. We hung out in parking lots until a manager or the police shooed us away. These cruises and parking lots served as our social networking system before MyShit, Facefuck or Twatter. Word of parties, fights and broken condoms circulated from car to car until the last person went home. Jocks. Preps. Greasers. Cowboys. Stoners. Each group had its own parking lot where they'd wile away the night, but everybody cruised the same loop.

In those days, nothing but an empty lot sat behind Hardon's. The arc sodium lights over the outer ring behind the drive-thru lane had gone out one night while I was cruising in my cute little 1985 Buick Skyhawk (not a misprint, the 'hawk was the smaller cousin in size and production numbers to the more well-known Skylark).

I swung the wheel left as I neared the back of the property on the outskirts of the drive-thru lane. Something momentarily distracted me. When my gaze returned forward, I slammed the brakes as an old lady bounced off my front bumper, her two coffees giving my front windshield a late night caffeine boost. Jumping out of my car, her little old husband began yelling. I began yelling. We both continued our incoherent ramblings as I went to check how badly I had mangled/murdered his wife.

She calmly told us both to calm down. It took a minute, but we did. I helped her up. She swore up and down that I had done no harm except to her coffees. I had barely tapped her and just caught her off guard.

"Honestly, child, I'm fine. Just get us more coffee, and we'll be on our way," she said consoling me less than a minute after I believed I'd killed her.

I ran into the fast food joint and ordered a pair of their largest coffees. The clerk asked me if I knew anything about the commotion outside. I told him I had hit an old lady and relayed her condition and desire for their stale coffee. Somebody called the police. I was fine with that. That was the only normal part of this situation at the time.

Back in the parking lot, I handed over the java to the couple, already in their mini-van. I asked her to wait so that we could talk to the police and somebody could take a look at her. She quickly explained that they had a long drive ahead of them to their granddaughter's house, and she didn't feel right bothering the police over such a nonevent. I had hit her, replaced her coffee and apologized profusely. She assured me that she was okay and that I would never do anything like that again. I had learned my lesson, and they had to cover many miles. They left.

A few minutes later, one of Waterford's finest pulled in. Officer Grasshopper had worked with under Mom (as did many of Waterford's future police) back when she was running the local ambulance service. I relayed my tale to Grasshopper who called it in to the station. They instructed him to use Hardon's pay phone for further discussion. Weird. I watched him nod his head and mutter agreement into the heavy black plastic handset as customers squeezed past our strange duo on their way to the toilets. He hung up.

"What did they say?" I asked, my curiosity bubbling over.

"You might have hit a drug dealer," he said, giving me my second big shock of the night.

Apparently, kindly, elderly people make good dope smugglers. When law enforcement agencies are all too happy to profile brown-skinned terrorists and drug-dealing/transporting/using Hispanics and blacks, it makes perfect sense to enlist the services of down-on-their-luck old white people to move large quantities of your product around the country.

Grasshopper said the station had sent along word to state troopers who would look for them and check them out. To my knowledge, they slipped through the grasp of the authorities and made it safely to either their granddaughter's house or to their dealer's den.

My Own Bicycle Day

In case you don't know, Bicycle Day is the holiday commemorating Albert Hoffman's actions of April 19, 1943 in Baden, Switzerland. Hoffman was the chemist who created lysergic acid diethylamide (LSD). He went on the world's first intentional acid trip on that fateful day by ingesting 0.25 milligrams of his brainchild before riding his bicycle home in a trippy haze. My own Bicycle Day began in a friend's apartment on an October night in 1994 and ended the next morning in Dr. Premature's psychology class.

Having studied several of my friends and classmates get into trouble with various drugs and having had an alcoholic grandfather, I have always fostered a good deal of caution towards most substances. This ensured that I never experimented with any drugs without first observing someone else use them. I hung out with friends while they took several acid voyages. My observations in no way whatsoever prepared me for my first trip into the light fantastic.

The plan was simple: I would drive two of my friends, Hawk and Johnny, to El Ghetto, a shithole of a town west of Oklahoma City to score a couple of ten-strips from their guy. Back in Waterford, ten of us would dose at Money's apartment and fry the night away. The plan was so simple that it could only fail in a most convoluted way.

It wasn't until we reached El Ghetto that Hawk and Johnny informed me of our mission's complications. A very paranoid man, their guy didn't like to meet new people. He was playing tennis at his apartment complex's courts when we called him. I had to pull over to let Hawk drive. I also had to scrunch down onto the rear floorboards of my own car and cover myself with an old blanket.

The deal went down at the speed at which these transactions usually take place. Ten minutes later, we were cruising away from the paranoid tennis player/drug dealer. I retook the wheel of my car another few minutes down the road. Having already munched a square apiece with their guy, Hawk was happy to relinquish controls before we hit I-40.

The rest of our crew was quite happy to see us upon our return. We divvied up the paper which would introduce me to a journey into a wondrous new world. I was the only virgin amongst our numbers - everyone else had followed Hoffman close to or more than a hundred times each. Although our host, Money, had to meet his ex-wife and child the next morning and couldn't partake, he was more than happy to let us hang out at his place while he supervised our descent into insanity.

I ate.

The beginning of my trip involved more than thirty minutes of me repetitively asking a limited number of questions:

"Do you feel anything yet?"

"Do I feel anything yet?"

"Is it supposed to feel like this?"

"Does it feel like anything yet?"

I tried to relax in Money's two-bedroom apartment but increasingly found focusing on anything to be a monumental challenge. I became a verbal fountain. The boys asked me to lie down on the living room floor, close my eyes and relax for a few minutes to gather my thoughts. This did not work out well at all. Rather, I found myself transported to the streets of Tokyo - a city I'd never visited - where gargantuan monsters destroyed the metropolis around me in a tremendous throw down. Part of the joy LSD breeds emanates from the utter state of confusion it produces in the mind. I didn't know if I had lain on the floor for one minute or one hour.

I rejoined the party only to find myself sinking deeper and deeper in mental quicksand. Money's stereo and television fought for our attention. Electronic music battled images of Robin Williams inexplicably speaking Russian on television. A scratched CD skipped for a quarter of an hour before any of us could figure out what was happening. Money knew, but refused to spoil our curiosity.

One of the guys went off to use the bathroom. It set off a slasher movie chain of events. Over time, one-by-one, we all disappeared into the bathroom to check on the welfare of those who had yet to return. The next to last to leave the relative safety of the living room, I wondered what had become of my trip-mates. Nine adult men huddled around the bathroom's doorway. What had so captured their attention? Money's shower curtain defied imagination that evening. Its simple design consisted of nothing more than pencil-thin alternating black and white vertical stripes. It wavered just enough to cause tremendous hallucinations. Money shattered our rapt attention once he deduced what was going on and slipped past us into the bathroom where he punched the curtain, sending cascading black and white lines all over the room.

Four hours into the trip, everyone gathered themselves to go home. I couldn't make heads or tails of this move. My cranium was in several different dimensions, but I figured that since they had done so much acid in the past that maybe it went through them a bit faster, or they had a higher tolerance for it. My car magically transported me back to my dorm room.

I crawled into my bed on the far side of the room and waited in vain for sleep to carry me away. I lay there for nearly five hours unable to go under. From a six-foot-long banner hung over my bed, a large vision of Chucky's head from *Child's Play 3* stared menacingly down at me all night long. McVeigh finally got ready for class as I curled up on my side, facing the window while feigning sleep until he left.

For seventeen years, I sported a single haircut: long hair on the top with the bottom half shaved bald all the way around. I called it the "anti-mullet." No more than three or four weeks passed before I had to shave the bottom clean. On this particular October morning, that time had long since come and gone. With an hour to kill between McVeigh leaving and my psychology class beginning, I grabbed a disposable razor and headed for the seventh floor's communal bathroom. Carnage ensued.

Bic never sold its single-blade disposable razors with me hacking at my inch-long hair in mind. I couldn't pull it off. Or shave it off. My classmates that morning stared and whispered as I took my seat. An hour only allowed time to attempt the right side of my head. Tufts of hair stuck out here and there. Blood flowed from multiple gashes. I looked a shock. It didn't help that I was still frying my balls off throughout class. I would have liked to have learned Dr. Premature's thoughts on my spectacle.

I didn't learn until several years later that my friends had not in fact gone home. Money had expressed his desire to catch some shut eye, so the guys decided to move the party to Hawk's apartment. My difficulty in understanding any spoken language at that point condemned me to driving home prematurely.

Around two hundred hits of paper, liquid and windowpane have since followed that first tab over the years. Few experiences would ever rival the intensity of that first bat-shit insane night.

The Great Rape Ape

Jizzball and Grandy's trailer served as the location for some debauchery during the years we partied there. Grandy was GBDKI (Gay But Doesn't Know It). You didn't have to look hard to figure out which decorations belonged to whom in that wheeled home.

Jizzball had beer-sponsored posters of bikini-clad women - Grandy had *Wizard of Oz* paraphernalia. More specifically, he had Judy Garland crap everywhere. Grandy was a nice guy, but was definitely flamboyantly "straight." Jizzball was a highly intelligent computer nerd/farmer who could, and did, put away a smart amount of stupid juice when he put his bladder to it. Partly due to this, he was my favorite drinking buddy for a long time.

Due to Grandy's mellow nature and dedication to his studies, we rarely partied at his and Jizzball's trailer. Jizzball invited Gokey, L-Ron and I over one night during Fall Break when Grandy had gone home. Jizzball was a ladies' man before he settled down. Upon arriving, he made the mistake of pointing out the case of Miller High Life quarts he and Grandy had earlier gone halvsies on. They planned on these seeing them through until the end of the month. We killed the case that night.

Jizzball got drunk. Jizzball got horny. He called up Eazy, a girl from twenty miles away he had boned a few times and invited/told her to come over. She wanted to see him but had a friend in tow. He told her to bring her along.

Gokey, L-Ron and I left to play on Jizz's computer in his bedroom, leaving him to make out with Eazy while her friend, the Horny Horny Hippo, watched. This being the mid-nineties, he was just about the only person we knew with Evilnet access, which caused us to spend a lot of time exploring the ten or so websites up and running at the time. Jizzball and Easy came back to his room after a time, killed the lights, jumped onto his bed, and began getting busy. They messed around as we messed with around Windows 95. L-Ron and I decided to leave them to play with each other while Gokey stayed with the computer. We dramatically crawled along the wall humming the theme to *Mission Impossible*.

When the lovers eventually kicked Gokey out so they could get down to it, we were fairly sauced. The Hippo was easily pushing 280lbs. I'm not against larger women (I've enjoyed my share - Val Holler remained sexy while packing on the pounds), but when you've got more meat on you than I do on my overweight 6'4" frame, I begin to reconsider. Being morbidly obese wouldn't have been so bad had she not also been morbidly obnoxious. The Hippo was drunk enough to grab my ass every time I stood up. She refused to acknowledge my refusals of her advances.

L-Ron and Gokey left, but I had originally planned on passing out on the couch. The Hippo wouldn't allow that to happen. I did my best to avoid her not-at-all subtle advances. I slapped her hands off of my ass a couple more times. Seeking refuge in the bathroom, I went for a piss, but she burst through the cheap door and even cheaper lock. Before I could cut off the stream and re-holster my meat pistol, she had already managed to strip down to nothing but her circus tent panties. I sidestepped her and bolted out to my two-door Olds, which I was in no condition to drive, hoping to pass out in the back seat.

I fumbled for my keys like a ditzy blond coed in some straight-to-video horror flick as the Horny Horny Hippo plowed her considerable heft through the trailer's front door. Scrambling into the back seat, I made a frantic grab for the door handle, only to have one of her meaty paws pry it away from me.

She shoved me down and dove like Pooh into a honey pot. One hand held me in place as the other fumbled with my pants. Brute strength and drunken determination aided her in her efforts. My loose cargo pants fell away only to be quickly followed by my plaid boxers.

Afraid of hurting even this hulk of a woman, I still punched her in the top of her thick melon to no avail. She grabbed my flaccid penis and jammed it into her mouth, her first non-deep-fried meal in many moons. Slurping, she gobbed on my knob. Every time her head rose, it came between my line of sight and the orange glare of the arc sodium light above the street. I had thought I was freaking out before, but this induced a particularly horrid acid flashback. Her head transformed into a rotting jack-o'-lantern, not the kind of hallucination you want going down on your genitals.

Five minutes or so of bobbing her head was the most exercise she'd had in some time. She realized that her attempts to rape-start my dick into a boner were failing. The only positive aspect of a guy being raped by a girl is that while a male rapist might have to deal with a little dryness, a female rapist can't do much without Viagra. She gave up, and I helped get her unstuck from the doorframe with a generous kick. I slept in a curled-up ball on my backseat that night.

Pizza Slut

Turning 16 enabled me to transition from pennies per paper to minimum wage for pizzas. Legally entering adulthood bumped me up to driving jobs, so I returned to Pizza Slut to sling pies from my parents' red 1984 Chevy Celebrity station wagon. I had just entered university and was experiencing a whole new drunken world. Dealing with the husband of the restaurant's married owner team always ruined my day.

"Hello, Richard. Read the Bible today?" asked Todd, an ex-Baptist minister and alcoholic.

"No Todd."

He also liked to ask if I'd visited to church lately, which elicited the same negative response every time.

Waterford Food Network

Any restaurant not run by dickbags gives their employees a meal a shift (or at least a deep discount on one). The Slut allowed us a personal-sized pizza per shift, although we scored small pies under the better managers. I loved to take a small pan pizza, hit it with sauce and toppings and then fill the deep pan with cheese. I dumped so much mozzarella onto it that I had to run my masterpieces through the oven an extra half-cycle to fully convert the cheese to its hot gooeyness.

The Slut's delivery drivers once provided a vital secondary service to our fellow food service workers in other restaurants around town. Having many friends employed at various eating establishments, I set out to establish a network of restaurant people also bored with their joints' offerings.

This network consisted of me visiting other restaurants to trade our allotted meals. It began simply enough with me trading pizzas for sandwiches with a buddy at Subnuts. There I hit on the idea of building something larger. My gastro project expanded with little effort to include McFood's, Hard-on's, Killing Fucking Chickens, Taco Junio, the Nut, and our downtown barbeque joint. In those mostly pre-cell phone days, setting up trades took a little more work to accomplish my meal missions.

I tried to take care of my friends as best as I could. This often involved multiple trades to achieve one meal. One of my longer trades went down like this: I traded my pizza for a foot-long to exchange for a burger set which I switched out for chicken in order to get the Mexican I'd originally wanted for myself. A couple of drivers tried to keep the network up and running after I'd quit, but it didn't last too long.

Hey Mister DJ

My two longest lasting and most personally involved jobs in WLOTUS revolved around one man I barely knew of in high school who would become my best friend and business partner before transitioning into a paranoid drugged-out sex-addicted man I no longer recognized. This is how I got into business with the Herpinator for the first and longest-running venture of the pair.

Hiroshima Music was only one of the Herps' business ventures. While I didn't know him personally until I started working for him, I knew of him from one early endeavor. A local visionary of sorts, he rented out an old pool hall on Main Street, installed a light and sound system and opened a club for high school kids. It didn't last long. The story goes that our upstanding mayor at the time told him to shut it down, because it was going to attract black people from the neighboring town's "ghetto."

A spank-tard I worked with during my second term at Pizza Slut forever altered the course of my life. Scott was a shift manager and not one of the fun ones. He was trying to get work as a DJ with Herps' company. Hiroshima was a mobile DJ business providing music and lighting solutions to proms, homecomings, wedding receptions, and random parties and events throughout Oklahoma and Texas.

In reality, Scott had lied to Herps about what he was willing to do for him and just wanted to subcontract out the gigs he had contracted from Herps for half of what he was receiving. I didn't know this when he offered me my first dance, but I quickly learned the truth and was moved up to take his place at Hiroshima when Herps discovered Scott's snake move.

I began my DJ career in the fall of 1994 with an ill-fated trip to Southeastern Oklahoma to do a high school prom at a resort. My parents let me use their station wagon, but the engine blew out on me near where I was supposed to leave the interstate.

I walked through a light rain to get to a pay phone to call the only contact number I had for the school. The principal drove out to pick up my equipment and myself. In my haste to get to the pay phone, I had inadvertently locked my keys in the wagon. Mr. Principal didn't know what to do when he pulled up in time to see me heft a rock from the shoulder and bust out the front passenger side window. We loaded his SUV and got underway.

I tried to set up the gear the Herpinator had entrusted me with after having been shown how to do it exactly one time while high - the only way he performed any task. The sparking wires of the lighting system repeatedly shocked me as I hurriedly attempted to get the show going, late as I was. Herps started me off with a Teac dual tape deck and a music catalog consisting of a couple cases filled with special five-minute cassette single bootlegs he had copied. This disaster kicked off a five-year career of sorts.

I liked DJing, because it freed up my weekends when it didn't tie them down. Because of the amount of shows I did, none of my part-time jobs ever scheduled me to work nights on weekends. It did present some problems, though.

Vampire Follies

I have always checked the organ donor box on my driver's licenses. While I hope to help people someday, I'd like to do something a little sooner. To that end, I started donating blood in college. I got to help people in exchange for some snacks, the odd gift emblazoned with a Red Cross logo and the ability to get loaded a little more easily afterwards. I reached the four gallon mark (and received a hat pin for my efforts) before I left the country to donate my bodily juices in foreign countries.

My veins pump that red gold fast enough to surprise most of the vampires when they came around to my campus. I liked that, because it enabled me to quickly move on to better part of the process: getting a buzz. I'd usually head over to Jizzball's, as he was always up for some afternoon drinking.

My blood donation motto became: Give a pint, drink two.

I smoked my first full cigarette after a donation. Of course, I had taken a cough-inducing puff here and there, but I had never before burned a coffin nail to its butt. I sat in Jizz's living room sipping a Coors Light when he offered me one of his Camels. Having smoked and hacked to its filter, Jizz asked how I felt. Polishing off my bottle to wash the foul taste out of my mouth, I responded that other than a dry throat, I felt fine. I stood to grab a new beer from the kitchen and promptly fell face down on the worn carpet in one smooth motion, crippled by the most extreme bout of dizziness I had ever known.

I learned the hard way about the truth behind the people who fill their plastic pint bags with my fluids. Nothing seemed out of the ordinary during the start of one of my regular bloodletting sessions until the phlebotomist spat out a surprised, "Oh no!" She explained that not only had she found and hit my vein but that she had gone clean through it. A bruise rapidly spread from my wrist to my shoulder. She freaked out worse than I did.

After getting her supervisor to have a look at my Grimace arm, I asked when she was going to poke my left, un-bruised arm. She responded with a ghastly look.

"Surely you don't want me to try again. Look what I did to you the first time," she insisted.

"Ma'am, you wouldn't be here if you weren't fully qualified to do and be capable at doing your job. We all make mistakes. I have two arms. Let's go another round together," I persisted.

She deftly inserted the 16-gauge syringe into my left arm. I pumped out a pint for her. As she began to withdraw the needle with a renewed confidence, the needle nicked a muscle. A bruise began to spread across this arm in an effort to match that on my right. The woman completely lost her shit at this point. I laughed it off until I tried to raise my hands and found that I couldn't. I wouldn't be able to bend my arms at the elbows to a 90 degree angle for three days.

Talking to Mom later, she expressed surprise at my having forced the woman to stab me a second time. I reasoned that she was a trained professional. Mom, a nurse, explained the not-so rigorous training procedures blood donation workers undergo. My naivety had me believe that these people were nearly on par with nurses. Mom corrected my belief with the fact that blood collectors can be any schmuck off of the street who can draw out your bodily fluids after a short bit of training.

I continued to donate blood until I left the country at which point I began giving wherever I could find people willing to take it. This has led me to great experiences in Seoul, Manila and Hua Hin, Thailand.

Stone Temple Asshole

The early nineties brought about some of the most solid rock music to emerge since Bonham choked on his own vomit. To the chagrin of those of us who had believed that this time period would bring about a renaissance in music harking back to the decades-long careers of Pink Floyd, Led Zeppelin, the Rolling Stones, Creedence Clearwater Revival, and even the Beatles (before drug use and Ono sunk that piss-yellow submarine), we were instead deceived by the complete bad-ass-ness of the first album or two of the supposed bringers of a new musical revolution. We went from *Badmotorfinger* and *Superunknown* (screw you for ragging on its "commercialism") to *Down on the Up Side*, from *Ten*, *Vs.*, and possibly even *Vitalogy* to *Riot Act* and the miasma which followed, from *Nevermind* and *In Utero* to…oh…maybe we should thank Kurt (or Courtney if you're into conspiracies). Then there was *Core* and possibly *Purple* and the drugs after which affected group and solo albums to come.

That's a long, rambling way to say that when you look at the longevity of the greater bands of the sixties and seventies (even after discounting the later disappointments which came from the bands not having the decency to have a member or two off themselves or overdose), one has to wonder why the fudge so few bands from my generation could produce more than one or two properly listenable albums.

This all brings us back to me getting to see Stone friggin' Temple Pilots at the Oklahoma City Zoo Amphitheater. The show was great. Weiland wasn't too far gone by this point. The audience was a whole other matter.

Known simply as the Zoo, the outdoor venue is set into a stone-terraced hillside. The rock ledges of each level were fun in my youth but now only provide opportunities for the lawsuit-happy times in which Americans suckle from the twisted teat of reality television.

Tall and somewhat slim back then, I could always weave my way to the front few rows of any concert. Being a quality rock 'n roll show, it was sponsored by the OKC's big rock station. They tossed out a couple of beach balls for us to bat around, as it was part of the late summer concert season. One of the balls came towards my long-haired way. I grabbed it and twisted to throw it to those behind me when a pair of hands snagged it from behind and a tinier, more powerful hand punched my stomach.

"That's Marty's, motherfucker!" said the snagger, Marty being the puncher.

Marty was the kind of wife-beater-wearing white-trash trailer park honkaloid thug people who hated Eminem's earlier albums thought he was describing. The major difference between the two being that Eminem can ride roller coasters. Marty was a Smurf-sized critter who got his kicks out of beating random people at concerts. Little people can grow muscle mass faster than taller, longer-limbed folks, in case you didn't know. This one used his major mass to beat down no less than three people that night that I saw. I'm not counting my singular gut-punch. He actually smashed a trio of STP fans into the Zoo Amphitheater's ground.

The STP show was one of the very few where I ended up being quite happy that my hallucinogen connection fell through. I don't know how well I could've handled schrooms coupled with Marty's violence.

I did enjoy one spectacle that night. Let's call him the "Amazing Rubber Spine." As I've said, the Zoo is a venue with terraced with rock ledges. The Spine was an anorexic twig compared to Marty's compact, muscular frame. The Spine had ten inches on Marty and still weighed forty pounds less. The Spine desired nothing out of life that night but to be launched up to crowd surf. This dream does not go over well around rock ledges and a not-so compacted crowd. The Spine continually sought out the tallest people around him wherever he landed to re-launch him in the sad hope that he would land on a group of people willing to send him on to crowd-surfing heaven. Instead, I just saw him dropped time and time again. At the end of the night, I passed by the first aid tent where I saw the Spine on a backboard wearing a neck brace.

Ratallica

Metallica, yet another band to slide downhill in the nineties, came to the OK State Fairgrounds. I joined some metalhead friends of mine in the show. Before we could leave town, we had to score some booze. The oldest of our group at 18, I was useless in this regard. One of the Indians with us suggested that I drive my station wagon over to Bill's Motel, because he knew someone there.

Knowing someone at Bill's Motel is not necessarily a good thing. Bill's was a dive among dives. A 1950's ramshackle building

31

home to a ceaseless flow of down on their luck locals, it was finally razed more than a decade ago. With weekly and monthly room rates, it was the kind of place that would make a person long for homelessness.

My amigo's Uncle Alchy kept house there for several years, providing us with a convenient booze buyer until we finally had people of legal age in our crew. He agreed to let me give him a lift to the liquor store for a fiver and our change. He filled a sack with Night Train and MD 20/20. Nothing was too good for his 17-year-old nephew and his buddies.

Not the largest Metallica fan, I actually passed out standing up less than twenty feet from a speaker stack. The combination of wino booze and too many newer shittier songs did me in. On the plus side, I felt well-rested for the drive home.

Get a Grip
(On MTV's Cock)

Aerosmith once stood as one of the powerhouses of rock. Aerosmith's only redeeming value during its descent in the nineties was a trio of mutable and spankable videos featuring a scantily clad Alicia Silverstone in her prime. As a capstone to his career, front man Stephen Tyler sought out a non-drug-related low by transitioning into a 90-year-old woman and getting a job judging hopeful morons on a singing competition show.

I drove a carload of friends down to Dallas' then Coca-Cola Starplex on Halloween night 1994. Before we could leave, we had to make a pit stop at Bill's Motel so Uncle Alchy could stock our cooler.

I forced myself to smoke enough weed and chug enough Thunderbird to get me through the lackluster performance during their most regrettable *Get a Grip* era.

Skilled at drunk driving, although not so much when stoned, I handed my keys off to my pal, Underwear, for the ride home and lay down in my wagon's cargo area to intermittently conk out for the ride home. I wish I had managed to crash out for the entirety of the ride. It would have made it less uncomfortable for the hitchhiker we picked up along the way despite my very vocal, albeit slurred, objections.

"NO!" I raved. "Don't stop for him! He'll fucking kill the lot of us! Death I tell you! Death for us if we let him in here!"

"Richard!" Underwear yelled from behind the wheel, "Shut up! He's already in the car."

"Death!"

I passed out for good and failed to get murdered.

Neither Rain Nor Sleet Nor Snow…

Oklahoman winters are a confusing time. People routinely find themselves wearing shorts and t-shirts within a week on either side of a five-inch snowfall. We rarely receive more than a few days of snow a year, but they can be really nasty days.

I had to work at the Slut one day when a heavy sleet hit. My station wagon stood as one of the bigger vehicles among my fellow drivers. I took my first delivery of the evening shift and barely survived. I slid downhill across three or four yards, almost sideswiping a couple of mailboxes on the return trip. I entered the restaurant to find our boss, Todd, furious at my fellow drivers for expressing their inability to drive in what was certainly going to be a delivery-heavy night.

Todd had taken a delivery out to judge the severity of the conditions for himself. He returned a little before I did, angry at his pool of drivers. With Jesus as his copilot, our brainless leader drove a full-size extended cab 4WD Chevy Z-74 pickup with plenty of weight tossed in the bed to improve traction. Not really a fair match for our little collection of second-hand beaters typical of small town college kids.

"Get out of here! You're all fired!" Todd screamed at us.

I happened to be standing at the register, so I cashed out my bag as fast as possible and got the hell out of there for a night off in the snow before Todd rescinded his firings.

1995

Val Holler

One of my most mentally confusing experiences related to the dorm came courtesy of Danny the New Mexican towards the end of my second and final semester there. Danny usually kept a supply of THC jell caps he'd scored off of some genuinely sick people in his home state. He shared one with me which I promptly popped and forgot.

I also landed my first fuck buddy that semester.

Val Holler and I hooked up on and off for two years at times we found ourselves both single and horny, which was often enough, thanks in part to my inability to maintain relationships. She earned her name by being the loudest and dirtiest talker in bed I have ever experienced. We had porno sex. The sex was pretty damn good, but she never once shut up. Not even to take a breath. Not even while swallowing my sword.

Holler invited me over to watch her *Sixteen Candles* tape and screw. I had long since forgotten about the THC I'd dropped an hour before when I'd had no clear plans for my evening. Twenty minutes into the movie I found myself chugging a glass of water every few minutes. Hughes' classic '80s romantic comedy made me laugh more than it should have. My words couldn't have made much sense to her. I was too high to remember what had made me high until almost the end of the movie. Holler was not a fan of drugs, even the ones we should legalize, so I couldn't tell her what had me acting so strange. We still had sex. She was still loud. I was still stoned.

Rape Ink

I don't have any tattoos but not because I'm against them. I don't have a tattoo, because I know I wouldn't get one tattoo - I would get my first tattoo. I also know what I would get, which doesn't help much:

- Ween's Boognish logo with my brother

34

- Some sort of self-stylized Psychopathic Hatchetman
- A Hash foot
- A Nut 'n Bone
- One of those tattoos that has a demonic creature ripping through your flesh to escape your body, but instead of the creature, it would be me ripping out of my own flesh

That's why I don't have any ink…yet. However, I nearly received one on a strange night a long time ago behind a Wal-Mart far, far away.

One circle of my friends consisted of many metal-loving stoners from high school. They were mostly a great group of people, whom the cliquey dicks in high school referred to as the "dirties."

A party ensued at Sonny's grandmother's trailer behind our old Wal-Mart. I passed out on a couch and awoke to a nightmare.

"I'm gonna give you the BOMB tattoo! The BOMB tattoo!" Toad drunkenly slurred as two of the group rolled up one leg of my jeans. Toad rubbed my ankle down with a half-used stick of Old Spice to "sterilize" his operating theater for the tat gun he'd pulled from his denim, patched-out backpack.

Toad's older brother had learned the "art" of prison tattooing while doing time for theft or drugs or theft of drugs, or some version of the usual Western Oklahoman golden tickets to lockup for poor white boys. Like any good brother would, he passed his knowledge down to his little brother. Because if there's anything that makes a person feel confident, it's getting a tattoo from a guy named Toad using a homemade prison-style tattoo gun in a trailer park behind Wal-Mart.

I rampaged in my attempt to get people off of me. One flew over a recliner. I dropped Underwear on his ass. They finally realized that corralling me was not going to be a manageable task that night. Toad instead inked Lizzy.

Lizzy had had a cute little one-inch black Playboy Bunny silhouette on her right ankle. Toad decided to super-size it. Unable and unwilling to return to my slumber after their well-meaning assault, I witnessed the butchering of her leg. When his makeshift gun had finally ceased its pulsations, he had left her ankle a bloody, swollen and mangled mess. The smooth, tight lines of her original professionally inked tat had transformed into a three-inch mutant bunny head with mumps, rabies and probably hepatitis.

Brotherly Drunken Love
(and I'd Like to Introduce You to My Brother)

I beat my little brother out of our Mother by a mere sixteen months. Actually, I never had a "little brother." Instead, I had a kid my age living at my house I never really got along with him. After my convoluted naming, my parents had trouble coming up with a name for my little brother. Two weeks before his birth, my Mother heard a voice in a dream that whispered a name. The Grandma from Hell wanted to name him Moses Sydney. Mom's dream name easily beat out grandma's.

When and how my little brother received his nickname, Goober, come later in this saga. Our parents, especially Mom, have always been fond of the truth. "Goober got the looks, and Richard got the brains," I've heard Mom say on more than a few occasions. Neither of us quite knew how to take this "compliment."

We did our best to limit the time we spent alone together. Growing up, we were often our own worst enemies. In the sadly and idiotically politically correct world we now live in, people would say that I was a hefty child. In reality, I was a tubby little fat fuck. My size gave me more strength over Goober than did the 16 month head start I had on him. We fought often and violently. The only reason we are both still alive today is that our parents believed strongly that one parent should always be at home for their children. Even if this meant that they rarely saw each other thanks to night shifts, one of them was almost always home for us. The few random hours they left us to our own devices nearly brought about our demise.

Goober's youthful dickbaggery would instigate battles between us, and my lardassedness would end them. He developed an explosive temper that went off like a string of powerful and illegal Mexican fireworks. I, on the other hand, have a long fuse attached to a briefcase nuke. Early on, he was smart enough to realize that he could not physically defeat me every time his infamous temper sparked (another family issue), so he found other means to take me out of the equation.

This is where I must interject and explain our battleground. Despite my constant yearning for anarchy, I was, and still am to a degree, a stickler for certain rules. Like most kids, I understood the minimum I had to do to keep our parents happy and didn't understand why my brother didn't share the same ability to maintain the status quo. Like all children, we were leeches. We don't necessarily earn our keep. Our only claim to this plane of existence was that we'd exited a vagina and are destined to eventually wrest the world from the hands of those who gave us life. Our parents didn't require anything too difficult from us. We had to rinse our dishes before putting them in sink or dishwasher. We had to put our dirty clothes in the laundry hamper. We had to go to school. We were expected to earn decent grades. Goober and I did not grow up in an overly totalitarian environment. While our family faced the occasional external difficulty, we were mostly able to maintain a degree of internal stability.

That said, Goober and I fought voraciously. He early on realized that he couldn't combat me physically, so he turned his tactics to psy-ops. The rare times when we were left alone, he implemented psychological campaigns that would put America's clandestine operations in Southeast Asia in the sixties and seventies to shame.

He loved to interfere with the missions our parents assigned us. One memorable occasion had us both stuck at home in our double-wide trailer in Mississippi for a few hours one summer day when Dad was called out on an ambulance run, and Mom was working her day shift at the clinic. I had been tasked with vacuuming the double-wide, a job made all the more daunting by the fact that Goober was there.

Goober had plopped down in front of the television for the afternoon and refused to move, despite knowing that I had been instructed to suck dirt - a directive tantamount to being on a mission from god. I warned him several times that I had to clean the shaggy brown carpet beneath him under orders from the 'rents. He refused to move. I warned him that our Kirby was about to suck up his toes. He refused to move.

His refusal faded the moment those spinning brushes scraped his toes. He escalated this into a fist fight which I handily won to my regret. In the first of several battles, he claimed that I had maimed him. I had blinded him after "shredding" his toes. He feigned blindness (this was long before 911 reached those backwoods) until

Dad rolled into the driveway. Praise the lord! As soon as he heard the Suburban pull into the drive, he magically recovered.

Regretfully, this worked several times on me.

Thankfully, we left Mississippi for the kinder, less overtly racist, semi-desert of Western Oklahoma. High school brought forth a constant stream of classmates taking turns kicking my ass. With the exception of a single punch and one knock-down brawl my junior year, Goober was the only person I actually fought back against in high school. For a time, we made semi-regular visits to the principal's office.

Over time, our never-ending war at home taught me how to defeat my brother without getting in trouble myself. His short temper led to many a fight, which I almost always won and then got into trouble for because of his crying. I learned to beat him by not fighting and instead retreating to my bedroom where he pounded and kicked the door until Mom or Dad yelled at him instead of me. It served as a cheap but effective move. The house suffered as he kicked in the bottom third of my door one time and the door frame to his room on another occasion which had come loose from frequent frustrated slammings. Mom and Dad made him pay for the damage he'd caused, which only further pissed him off. My biggest weapon was also my most lethal, as far as the house was concerned.

With two words, I could set Goober off on an intense rampage unparalleled with anything I had ever witnessed. While Mom was earning her nursing degree, she met her classmate, Boozer, who would become one of her best friends. The Boozer left her cat, Mr. Bojangles, with us one Fall Break. This took place towards the end of their studies while Goober and I were in our first and second years of high school, respectively.

We were both newspaper carriers at the time and each had a small wicker basket of rubber bands for rolling newspapers in our bedrooms. Goober was playing with Mr. Bojangles in his room when the cat knocked over his basket while our parents were at work. For reasons no one will ever comprehend, this threw Goober into a frenzy. He chased Bojangles through the house. I heard the commotion and opened my bedroom door in time to see the cat and Goober racing towards me. I let Bojangles in and shut the door on Goober. He pounded away at my door for nearly twenty minutes.

His rage subsided, or so I had thought. I let the cat out of my room and walked outside to get the mail. Turning back towards the house, Goober stood on the driveway holding Mr. Bojangles like Tom Brady ready to launch a hail Mary.

"Goober, put the cat down," I commanded.

"No," he refuted.

"Put. The. Cat. Down."

"No."

"I'm not going to tell you again, put the cat down."

"Okay," he said cocking his arm back farther before letting Mr. Bojangles take flight. The pussy hit the ground running, and we never laid eyes on him again. From that moment on, anytime Goober tried to flip my switches, all I had to do was calmly look him in the eyes and say, "kitty thrower." It's a good thing that a person's thoughts can't manifest themselves and alter reality, or else he would have murdered me a hundred times over.

The last time I deployed my ultimate weapon, our family was in the middle of dinner. Goober said something snarky. I tossed out a "kitty thrower" in response. He shoved his plate forward and stomped off to his room. This was nothing new. The change came when, before we heard him slam his door, we heard a loud "bang." He had punched a hole in the hallway wall. Dad made him purchase plaster and fix the hole. I tried not to laugh too hard.

My brother and I did manage to start spending some good times together once I escaped high school. Goober and I shared our first drink together during Spring Break of my freshman year of college, his senior year of high school. My small university shut down its dorms, kicking out its students during the major holidays. Luckily for me, I only lived one stoplight and five minutes away.

Goober called me one rare night I had planned on not drinking to tell me he was drinking at Grandy and Jizzball's trailer with his girlfriend, Nappy Ne-Ne, and her friend, Roadkill. NNN was good friends with Grandy. Grandy and Jizzball had left town for the week, but Grandy had given NNN the keys to their trailer.

Goober had a redhead fetish for many years. She didn't even have to be naturally red. If the girl had a red top, he was willing, if not eager, to probe his meat thermometer into the middle of whatever color bush lay below it. NNN fell into this category.

I responded to my brother's call by rushing over to receive my first shock of the evening: finding Goober, NNN and Roadkill sitting around Grandy's table getting snockered on wine coolers. Coolers are not and have never been cool. Goober had to learn to respect himself more than that, and I felt it my duty as his older brother to show him the ropes. While Goober began drinking a year or more before me, he had yet to master any suitable drinking skills.

A quick trip to Arab's secured us a couple cases of premium, cheap-as-shit beer. A few games of *Quarters* and *Asshole* were more than enough to get them decidedly more shitfaced and me knocking on drunk's door. A blur of newbie drunken action followed.

Roadkill went to Jizzball's room to lie down. Walking back to check up on her, I met NNN, in the short hallway. She grabbed my face and slobbered something reminiscent of a kiss near my mouth. I pushed her away and went for another beer. Roadkill kissed Goober at one point.

Roadkill recovered a little later. She dragged me outside for a snog session. We ended up in the middle of the nameless trailer park road rolling around until she attempted to remove her jeans. I wasn't against it, but the rough pavement decided for her before I could tap that ass on the asphalt.

The girls planned on staying there that night, but I had to sneak Goober's high school ass back home to Mom and Dad's. Luckily for him, they had gone a little easy on his curfew during the holidays once I had graduated (our previous Cinderella hours having been midnight on any non-school night).

I had just begun to learn how to drive drunk at this point in my life and still frequently feared run-ins with the authorities. Goober did nothing to help relieve the pressure. I drove three blocks down to the first four-way stop where he decided to throw open his door and start a spew trail down Davis Road.

Aware of the amount of police traffic the road has, especially late at night, I yelled at him to shut the door. To this he slurred, "I know what I'm doing." I realized that he must have known what he was doing, because it made a lot more sense to hold his door open at 35mph than to roll down the window and hang out his head.

Dropping Bombs and Scoring Weed

The Goth was responsible for my first proper herbal score. Once I began smoking weed in college, I quickly learned that by the time the Mary Jane reached us in little dime and quarter sacks in Western Oklahoma, we were paying more and generally getting less, depending on from whom we scored our bud. I decided to move a step or two up the drug ladder to get a better price. The Goth assisted me in this by contacting a guy she knew in Oklahoma City in the spring of my freshman year. April to be more specific. April 19 to be very fucking specific.

That happened to be the day some angry hillbillies (quite possibly backed by even angrier Arabs, if you're into conspiracy theories coupled with eyewitness accounts) ignited 7,000lbs of homemade explosives in a Ryder truck in front of the Alfred P. Murrah Federal Building in downtown OKC. I wanted to put off the big buy, but the Goth insisted we not upset her friend. We got in my car and went to score a quarter pound of herb.

Reaching the City that night provided an eerie backdrop for our mission. Few other vehicles shared I-40 with us. The Murrah Building had stood just a few blocks north of the interstate, so we could easily see the activity going down. Emergency vehicle light bars and banks of halogens surrounded the hazy perimeter, while helicopter search beams lent the scene a surreal feel.

The Goth dropped me at an IHOP on the south side of OKC while she drove on to meet her guy with my car and my money. It was uncomfortable to say the least. Members of the various police and rescue agencies resting from taking their turns at the bombing site or waiting to get in there to assist occupied most of the grease factory's tables. Awkward silence reigned at my corner table, as I killed a half hour trying my best not to look like a guy waiting for a girl with a quarter-pound of marijuana to return to pick him up. I think I played the part well.

I don't speed. I've never understood the idiotic idea of people who really think going ten miles an hour above the speed limit will make any sort of difference in their lives, let alone their schedules. Unless you're a long-haul trucker, stick to the limits – they're there for a reason. The police have issued me exactly one warning for speeding, and that came after getting a block away from work one night. I never drive more than five miles over on the interstates. With more Mary Jane than I'd ever seen in one place in my life stashed in my trunk, I put the metal to the pedal for the hour's drive home, averaging 90mph the whole way under the knowledge that the totality of our law enforcement agents had their plates full with the bombing's aftermath.

Double Deliveries

Halfway through my year of pushing pizzas, I became their most requested driver. Actually, I was their only requested driver. Luckily for me, I worked with some semi-innocent people who didn't understand why people who called requesting me as their driver also asked for oregano on their pizzas.

"I'm sorry, but we don't have oregano."

"Okay, but please have Richard deliver our pizza."

"Richard, another of your friends asked for you. And tell them to stop asking for oregano!"

A bad delivery time for such a small town accompanied these requests. Each of these runs required me to dash up to my dorm room and grab a baggie of grass before delivering the pizza and "oregano." I may have had slow delivery times, but I made great "tips."

I moved after a year, my departure coinciding with the end of an era at our Slut thanks to my getting to work with a mostly cool group of nighttime assistant managers. The youngest driver on staff having joined the team just a week after my eighteenth birthday, I was still welcomed into the fold of my coworkers' little clandestine drinking club.

We Slutters spent many nights together at Tracy's duplex tucked away in a Waterford alley. We witnessed a surprisingly open-minded devout Southern Baptist assistant manager who, in his mid-20s, had never before tasted alcohol to sipping wine coolers and later converting to hard liquor and taking the occasional toke of the good weed. I discovered a diverse group of quality friends and a few alcohol-induced hookups.

At work, we had unity most of the time. The assistant managers usually didn't mind people filling 32oz plastic Slut to-go cup with draft beer during a shift. As a driver, most nights found a consistently full beer in my cup holder and a roach in my ashtray. A bit of beer and bud made washing dishes between deliveries quite the enjoyable task. Our cooks made enough "mistakes" each night to ensure that most of us who desired it had a constant stream of pizza in their fridges. One of our managers usually held chugging contests at the end of especially gruesome shifts between the closing cook, driver and himself (the last three to leave at the end of each night). I usually placed second behind him.

While Jason Statham behind the wheel I'll never be, having a steaming bag of pizza riding shotgun in my wagon granted me extraordinary confidence and abilities. For the duration of my Slut employment, I routinely shot across my little town at double or triple the posted speed limits. Stop signs lost their meaning. I graduated from all school zones. I refused to yield. It didn't hurt that I was nearly always drunk and usually a bit high to boot.

Through all of these deliveries, I never had a single accident, nor did I ever face any police entanglements. Ironically enough, the two times the police happened to pull me over during that year, I was on my way home after work and had worked with the one ass hat manager on whose watch we couldn't drink. On both occasions, I received nothing worse than warnings for rolling a stop sign and going 28 in a 25mph zone.

Boning Myself

You should meet my Bone. I frequently wear a bone around my neck and have done so since 1995. It has become an integral part of who I am and even provided me with my Hash name (you'll have to read *Ninjalicious II* for the explanation to that gem).

I found Bone 1.0 at the bat caves southwest of Waterford. L-Ron and I decided to kill an afternoon spelunking the guano-carpeted holes in the ground. I found a small, sundried bone outside a cave entrance. I knew that that bone was put there for me somehow and stuck it in my pocket.

L-Ron and I visited the Waterford High School to see his K-town Mafia buddies who had come down for a basketball game. I don't remember who won. It was the first time I would meet many of the younger Mafia members. Did I mention we were both covered in guano?

Back at home, I boiled and bleached my new tan treasure. Sterilized, I had to devise a method to implement my fiendish plan. I used one of Dad's drills to punch a small hole through either side of what I'd determined to be its top and ran a length of an old leather cord salvaged from something long since forgotten (I inherited some packrat tendencies courtesy of the Grandma from Hell). With a small amount of plaster to cap the bottom, I now had the perfect tool to sneak two hand-rolled "cigarettes" into almost every concert I would attend over the next six years. Who would ever want to check a nasty bone around some long-haired freak's neck anyway? Thus I birthed my talisman.

Together we've attended concerts, parties and classes. It traveled to dozens of countries. Too many mosh pits finally took their toll on my little buddy. The plaster and several pieces of the bottom eventually broke away. I replaced the cord three times. I later added a metal nut to the cord I scored from ICP's stage during the Toledo Gathering's riots. I accidentally committed my battered Bone to the sea in the Philippines, but that's another story altogether for another book.

SCUBA Doobie Doo

I used my time in college wisely. I took classes I knew would forever affect my future: Bowling. Medical terminology. Real estate. SCUBA.

I took a SCUBA certification course the spring semester of my freshman year with Steve. Steve graduated two years ahead of me in high school. One of my two best friends growing up, the Dude finished between us. Steve and I both signed up for the course, while the Dude had signed on to assist the course's instructors in order to satisfy the requirements of some bullshit community service he had to perform.

The class began to follow a pattern each Monday night. We met in the P.E. building at 6 p.m. for instruction in an actual classroom. We then moved to the pool to practice what we'd learned that night. Steve and I stopped going to the pool after the first time we strapped on our tanks a few weeks into the course. When our classmates moved to the pool each week, we simply made a wrong turn in the halls and went out for a beer or many. We didn't suit up again until our certification dive three months later.

SWOSU's diving instructors take their students out to Dirtybird for their YMCA Certification qualifying dive. Lake Dirtybird is considered to be a filthy lake in a state whose cleaner lakes often bear warnings advising the sick, the young, the elderly, and the pregnant not to swim in their waters due to high levels of various pollutants.

The instructors bring out a number of volunteers who have all known each other for a long time and are good friends. They use the weekend to escape from their families to hang at a dingy group of single-story motor court-style motel rooms left over from the 1950s. I'm certain there's alcohol involved the night before, after they deliver a final message to the students. I know alcohol was involved in our room.

Our trio got pleasantly drunk the night before our dive. We didn't want anybody to smell booze on us the next morning, so instead of drinking before our qualifying dive, we smoked a gravity bong McGuyvered from an empty Coke two-liter, some foil and our room's kitchen sink. It worked well. Too well. Fuck Jacques Cousteau and James Cameron!

Unlike with alcohol, I have always been a bit of a lightweight when it comes to the herb. This day was no exception. I got blown out of my mind. The mild Oklahoma spring did nothing to warm the lake's waters or our wetsuits. I nearly froze just trying to pull the neoprene suit on over my shivering carcass. The instructors had enough semi-hungover friends qualified to instruct that they had a partner for each diver. I went down with a local businessman I knew.

Our first of two dives into the murky water had us do no more than go down to twenty-five feet and resurface. I barely survived my first attempt. Losing light as we descended, vertigo infected me faster than *28 Days Later*'s rage virus. I tumbled upwards in the near-weightlessness of the lake. We surfaced. I had gone through almost half of my tank in ten minutes.

"Richard, you don't have to go back down," my partner said, fearful after having witnessed my freak-out.

"No, I'm fine. It just caught me off guard. I can do this. I wasn't expecting the stankness of the water," I pleaded.

"Okay, if you say so. But if you have any problems, just give me the signal, and we'll get out of there," he acquiesced.

We went down a second time and had no issues. We again descended to twenty-five feet, and, at the end of my arm, my hand became a translucent, ghostly image. At forty feet, my hands

45

disappeared unless I held them within an inch of my mask. Or that might just have been the weed talking.

Dirty Bird has hosted countless qualifying dives. The folks running the dive shop there slapped together an obstacle course at the bottom of the lake over the years. Funky algae covers a dilapidated VW Beetle and an outdoor barbeque yard scene complete with lawn chairs and a grill.

I only freaked out one more time. Although it was a fairly major mental mess, I managed to keep it internal, and my dive partner didn't notice anything out of the ordinary this time.

Our instructors hadn't told us what to expect when we hit the obstacle course, only to follow them and explore. Or maybe they had. I was still thoroughly stoned. We passed through most of the murky water's course. I saw my instructor float on ahead of me and turned to my left and exited this world for half a minute. I never thought I would miss the dismal green of the lake. Vertigo crept up on me faster than the tree that killed Sonny Bono. I swished around unable to see anything in any direction I turned. I finally drifted out of the engulfing darkness of a massive concrete pipe which had cut off what small amount of light the filth around me couldn't block out.

I overheard my partner talking to his friends as we stripped out of our gear.

"I never would have believed it if I hadn't seen it. When we went down, the boy shitted himself more than anybody you've had me take down before. I tried to talk him out of going again, but he wasn't having it. The next time down, he handled himself like he'd been doing it for years. I don't know what the hell happened down there."

Let's hear it for skipping class and smoking marijuana!

Laundering My Summer

I took an extra job most summers to supplement my regular part-time gigs and DJing. These were almost without exception the worst jobs I had in college. These summer jobs ended up serving as incredible stay-in-school experiences.

The laundry was by far the most intense of my summer jobs. My old manager at the newspaper had taken a job at a local industrial laundry managing their drivers and their routes. He got me on for the hottest, smelliest and drunkest summer of my life.

I woke up at 4:30 a.m. during the week to drive twenty minutes to a neighboring town to work until the early or mid-afternoon when I returned home to shower and work the night shift at my regular job, a wonderful family-owned barbeque restaurant, until 10 p.m. I showered again, partied until sometime between 1 and 3 a.m. and repeated the process all over again the following day.

I donned my uniform pants and shirt, disposable plastic gloves and a surgical mask every day to sort and count filthy shop towels and rags from 5:30 a.m. until I finished three or four hours later. Our drivers cruised Western Oklahoma in the wee hours of the night to pick up sacks of laundry from our clients: restaurants, fast food joints, beauty parlors, and automotive shops. They dropped them off at my station with a paper ticket pinned to each bag every morning. I opened them and flung the four different types of towels into their appropriate bins. Each towel passed through an electronic beam that counted each break. I scribbled the tallies on tickets.

Grease coated the red automotive towels. The beauty shop towels smelled pleasingly pleasant, permitting me a brief respite in the olfactory assaults to follow.

While I quickly learned that no restaurant can produce rags that smell like roses after sitting in canvas sacks for up to a week in an Oklahoman summer, nothing compared to those we received from Chinese restaurants and chicken joints. Crust-covered and maggot-riddled, handling these was the foulest part of my job.

The laundry provided me with plenty of random odd missions to complete once I'd finished counting my towels and rags. I learned to operate a riding lawn mower, but only after I had dinged a few pre-battered pickups and sedans. I painted most of the building's outside and a lot of the sidewalk. I cleared out decades-old garbage from the antique building attached to ours. I helped unload five and eight hundred pound capacity dryers and carts with hotel bedding to be folded by older Indian women missing impressive amounts of teeth.

The laundry often paired me with Mark, the company's maintenance man. He had a variety of skills, including growing marijuana on the laundry's roof. He planted his little farm below the humid output of a massive exhaust vent. He failed to share this part of his job with me, even though I did spend one afternoon on another section of the roof shoveling dryer lint from a non-pot growing vent.

Mike was my favorite to work with, although I never quite deduced what it was that he did. He often wasn't there to do whatever it was that he did when he was there thanks to what he did when he wasn't. He regularly went to jail, although he didn't get paid for that. I discovered this showing up one morning to find Mike missing and learned something important about the laundry and its crew.

"Hey, where's Mike? Shouldn't he be here by now?" I asked another coworker.

"He's in jail. He'll be back tomorrow."

It didn't matter who said it, because several people said it several times over the summer. Mike had a knack for getting arrested for public intoxication, fighting and/or drug possession.

My summer at the laundry taught me to stay in school, to stay in school and to take care of my cavity-prone teeth.

Tank Tucker and the Birth of Goober

I have come across some amazing people throughout my adventures. I have also come across some truly rotten, scum of the earth bottom feeders. Tank ranks among the top of the bottom, along with the Grandma from Hell, the Herpinator and the Romanian Devil (someone you'll have to read about in *Ninjalicious II: Crazy Corea*), he probably falls between Herps at numero uno and the Romanian at three. Like most of my tales, Tank's is a convoluted twisting narrative that begins with a separate story: my brother's nicknaming.

My friends and I entered our sophomore year of university. We had all left the dorms at the start of the summer. L-Ron and Jizzball rented a house together on Main Street. We couldn't let them move in without a housewarming party. Jizz was out of town, and they had no utilities hooked up yet, but that couldn't stop us. We loaded up our coolers and set candles on them.

Pre-Goober and I ran with many of the same circle of people once he entered university. We more or less had an understood truce between us, although he sometimes played the North Korean half of that truce, introducing a few hiccups along the way.

My brother, pre-Goober at this time, entered my university and entered the same social circle as me. He had met some of them through his ex, Nappy Ne Ne. It was a small party that evening: just

L-Ron, Gokey, pre-Goober, Red II (pre-Goober's girlfriend), and myself.

The night progressed nicely. We drank, played drinking games and talked crazy. Pre-Goober eventually brought up the fact that unlike most of the people in our circle, he had no nickname. Almost all of the Waterford Buzzards and K-Town Mafia had nicknames. He pestered us into bestowing one upon him that night, instead of waiting for a nickname to take its natural course.

We drank and debated, finally arriving at something from *The Andy Griffith Show*. Our booze-addled minds couldn't recall the name of Sheriff Andy Taylor's inept deputy, Barney Fife. We could, however, remember Goober, but since we had gotten way too snockered to be certain whether he was the deputy or not, and this being the days before a smart phone with Evilnet access inhabited every pocket, we rolled with it. Goober was born. Goober was later put into stasis that night, and this is where we get around to Tank.

Someone knocked on L-Ron's door. Who could it be? It was Del, but we wouldn't learn that for another five seconds. A taller man in his late-twenties walked into our new party house.

"Hey, my name's Del. We saw some lights from across the street and wondered if anybody wanted to smoke a joint?"

"Hell yeah!" Gokey and I jumped up in unison, happy to make the acquaintance of our friends' new neighbors.

Goober had a strange relationship at the time. He was under the impression that he had managed to keep his vices a secret from Red II. The rest of us knew that she knew, but nobody really cared. Between Del's entrance and the reactions from Gokey and myself, he had to get rid of her if he were to partake of the sweet Mary Jane with us. He quickly sent her packing for the evening, and we crossed the street to enter one of the lower levels of hell.

Del was not our neighbor. He was Tank's friend. Tank was the devil. A man of decent stature, thick from alcohol and constant, barely suppressed rage and insanity, the majority of his communication consisted of gruff, Neanderthalic utterances. He immediately introduced us to the one person we knew at their little party along with what became a long running gag in our crew.

"This is mah friend, Del. 'Ave you met mah friend, Del?" Tank asked us, throwing one of his tree trunk arms around Del's shoulders. We also met Tran, his Vietnamese-American friend, and Justifiably

Angry Girl, his lone female acquaintance. Del, Tran and JAG turned out to be more or less okay, but the night itself devolved into a horrendous first contact on par with Columbus' "discovery" of the Americas, Hiroshima's discovery of the atomic bomb and Kanye's discovery of the auto-tuner.

Tank instructed us not to touch the pair of whiny dust mop dogs running and yipping throughout the house, because they belonged to his dead wife. She had died from lupus. She has to be the first person you could honestly say was better off for it, as you'll soon learn. Strangely enough, though, our first night with Tank isn't really about Tank.

We were already drunk, as were they. We all got high. Then things got weird. Tank's people played tunes from a small boombox on the kitchen counter. The music wasn't very good, and the newly christened Goober got it into his head that it was his job to do something about it. He repeatedly switched it off and/or tried to change the tunes. JAG got justifiably angry at this point and warned him repeatedly to keep his hands off of their music.

"You might want to be careful about messing with people's music and shit when you just met them. You don't know what they'll do to you," she finally warned Goober. He replied with some slurred weak-sauce rebuttal that she promptly ignored.

This went on for some time. Embarrassment grew. Goober escalated the conflict. We finally removed him and apologized to Tank and his posse. We were so utterly embarrassed that we de-christened Goober. This provided us with a fun game for months to follow at any party we attended together.

"Hi, my name is Goober."

"No. His name is pre-Goober."

This exchange repeated many times over a two-month period. Goober's microscopically short fuse flared every time we denied him the name he'd forced us to bestow upon him. The whole fiasco finally came to a conclusion somewhere down the line when he did something else stupid we were too stoned to remember, and we re-branded him "Goober" as a joke. It stuck and, luckily for him, the joke aspect of it went away over time.

But back to Tank…

As badly as our first meeting had gone, Tank still wanted to hang out with us. It only took one more meeting for us to realize that

50

the feeling was not mutual. He became a plague. Actually, he was more like a case of herpes, appearing and disappearing and never welcomed, only dreaded. He proudly told some outlandish tale about having once bitten off a man's ear while shooting pool at the DUI Bar.

L-Ron and Jizz' (later replaced by another friend, Tee), house was one of our favorite drinking spots, when we could avoid Tank that is. Many nights found upwards of a dozen of our crew and miscellaneous girlfriends/boyfriends at the house. Since Tank had met us once before, he had decided that it was now kosher for him to barge into the house whenever he wanted to scare/piss us off.

No knocking ever accompanied his entrance - he just appeared like an alcoholic slow-moving Kramer. His hands always held a faded 32oz plastic cup leftover from some distant fast food meal. Before 9 p.m., the cup held beer - after 9 p.m., vodka. The caveman was never sober or friendly. He didn't like people. He didn't like our people, except for L-Ron, Jizz and myself. We didn't like that he liked us.

Tank would enter the house, sit next to one of his three favorites, take a long pull from his Hardee's cup, lean over and yell/whisper hate into our ears about the others in the room.

"I hate that bitch," he'd say about any and all of our female friends.

"I'm gonna smack that fag-got," he'd rant about Gokey. To his credit, he proved himself a man of his word by actually hitting Gokey once. We didn't know what to do. He bitch-slapped the shit out of Gokey, turned around and lumbered home.

Sometimes he had Del in tow. Every single time he dragged Del behind him, he spat the same line:

"This is mah friend, Del. 'Ave you met mah friend, Del?"

We met Del dozens of times. Tank wasn't being facetious: he honestly believed we had never before met. Tank's Swiss cheese memory made the myth of a goldfish's six-second retention look Einsteinian by comparison. Del took to rolling his eyes at each meeting but held his tongue.

As much as we despised this intolerant beast, we always found it interesting when first-timers visited the house. I got off on watching their reactions when Tank would yell/whisper diatribes about our new guests. He was our own racist, prejudiced, sexist, homophobic, alcoholic, lonely, angry ogre. But as disturbing as it was for him to come around when we had a group over, it was the events involving only a few of us that created the best/worst stories. Most of us would have gladly traded our roles in these tales for Gokey's bitch-slap.

Pay-Per Hell

Tank randomly came over to drag whomever was home over to his place to drink and partake of his sad brand of madness. Tank dropped a lot of cash ordering pay-per-view sporting events and wrestling (I refuse to call two nearly-naked, oiled-up men rolling around on a canvas mat to a script a "sport" - if wrestling's a sport, then so is gay porn). He "invited" me to his casa for the infamous Tyson-Holyfield fight. A large-screen projection television dominated his narrow living room. Tyson's ear-biting infuriated the drunks in the house. Del threw a throw pillow from the couch at the television. Someone else followed suit, which brought down the wrath of Tank.

"Goddamn it!" he roared. "No one but Del can throw pillows at mah fuckin' TV! Do you know mah friend, Del?" His house rules were not very complicated: Del had free run of the place, while you could do nothing and had no rights or personal space and were most likely a bitch or a fag-got.

He hauled Jizz over one night to watch some pay-per-view wrestling. It was just the two of them. They drank. And drank. And drank. Tank reverted to his childhood (which I can't even begin to imagine, although I suspect it likely involved a lot of animal mutilations) and challenged Jizz to a wrestling match in the living room. By "challenge," I mean that he surprised Jizz by lifting him up and dropping him through his glass-top coffee table. Jizz got the hell out of dodge to tend to his wounds and to try to forget the carnage.

Tank showed up the next afternoon, cup in hand, to demand if anyone at the house knew, "Who the fuck broke mah table?" Jizz told him the story. Tank accepted the hazy truth and returned home to refill his cup.

"Freebird!"

"You're taking me to the Lug-a-Jug," Tank informed me one evening at the Main Street house. He tossed me his keys and walked out the door, automatically assuming that I'd follow him with my beer. Tank was a mind rapist and refused to accept "no" as an answer or to even wait for a response.

I struggled to pull open the driver-side door of Tank's Oldsmobile beater. A rough gash tore through the entire port side of the maniac's maroon machine. He opened up to me on the way to our favorite of Waterford's two liquor stores and told me how his car had received its ugly war wound.

"One day me and mah friend Del. 'Ave you met mah friend, Del? We went to Oklahoma City. We got really fucked up and had to go home. I was drivin' on the innerstate, and Del. 'Ave you met mah friend Del? Del was asleep, and I was drivin'. I passed da fuck out. I heard a horn and swerved into a semi. Fuckin' Skynyrd's 'Freebird' was on the fuckin' radio!"

"Freebird!" he screamed/spat into my face. "I hit the side of the truck and it ripped mah car. I hit the gas and got the fuck out of there. Del, you know mah friend, Del? Del woke up and looked at me and asked if somethin' was wrong. I said, 'No,' an' he went back to sleep again."

Crack Heads

Tank dragged L-Ron and I over to his house one night. He began ranting about one of the few black families living in our little town at the time, who just happened to live a few houses down from him. He paced around his living room ranting about, "those crack smokin' niggas down the street!" He shouted out this fucked-up phrase no less than a half-dozen times over the course of five minutes. He tossed out a final racist rant before telling us that he had something to show us in his spare bedroom.

"Come'ere. You gotta see this. I can't believe those crack head, crack smokin' niggas!" he said as he pushed open a door to reveal the one black guy in my high school class and the one black guy from the year after me. I couldn't figure out which blew my mind more, that they were letting that drunken hillbilly repeatedly call them the "N" word or that they were actually smoking crack! I said, "hi," to my friends, took a couple of hits and got the hell out of there.

Shitilogue

Tank is a beast, a truly unique and reprehensible fringe member of our species. Too stupid to live. Too unbelievable to die. He supposedly found Jesus and converted to the Southern Baptists for a time. I can't imagine him kicking the booze long enough to attend a single episode of church, but at least his racism fit in fairly well.

Basement Bottle Bunker

The greatest/worst/longest torture we put the Main Street house through began one evening when we decided to have a night free from the girlfriends and psychos in our lives. To do this, a handful of us gathered in that poor house's basement, locking the doors and shutting off the lights behind us for a night of cards, drinking and smoking.

We did sometimes smoke ourselves so stupid that we found our well-executed but poorly planned plots foiled by simple follies of reality. One of the women we were hiding from (some of them had their frightening moments) had her curiosity aroused by the number of cars in the driveway of the seemingly empty casa. It only took a short stalker stroll around the house to hear the music and see the light emanating from the rear basement window. Her discovery brought a quick end to the night.

The other event which transpired that night forever changed the house's preferred method of waste removal. A bottle accidentally knocked off the table shattered and started a disturbing trend. Other bottles, cans and butts followed that first broken Natty Light.

It didn't end that night. It became habit to simply open the basement door and toss down our empties. By the time they vacated the dilapidated house, they had created a rubbish pond nearly waist deep.

Cabin Daze

Wahoo and Tex had been high school sweethearts in the fun but dry town of P-ton, TX when they both moved to Oklahoma to study at SWOSU. Wahoo's family owned a cabin in Eagle's Nest, New Mexico. She invited our crew up there for Fall Break '95 and '96. These two trips mirrored each other in many ways, so what follows is more of a combination of the two years with some distinctions between them where necessary.

Preparations and Western Migration

Tee and I represented the ignored voices of reason when it came to packing on both of these excursions. Knowing that we would be out by ourselves in the cabin for four days and three nights, we required a sufficient supply of drugs. When Tee and I laid out our estimations, few believed us and knocked our numbers down to insufficient amounts. Even after we'd consumed all of the lonely ounce of pot we'd taken the first trip, we could still only get the group to agree to double the amount the next year, in spite of the increased number of people joining our party.

Our numbers went from an even half-dozen to nine on the second sojourn west. We caravanned out in a handful of cars each time making a mandatory pit stop in Texas. Our stops couldn't be just anywhere, though. No, we had to swing through a wet county. Oklahoma and Texas are both fucked up states with fucked up liquor laws. Oklahoma doesn't sell beer above 3.2 percent outside of liquor stores, and Texas still has an ass-load of dry counties (of 254, 22 are completely dry and 183 are partially dry). We had L-Ron's sister pick us up a dozen cases of Natty Light to get us through the first expedition but had a couple of us hitting 21 in time for our second outing.

The only area in which we never had a shortage is one I have zero trouble in taking full credit for: LSD. I didn't carry enough either year to have taken care of Woodstock (and by Woodstock, I obviously mean 1969, the only one which counts, including the multiple anniversary ones taking place well before the MTV-sponsored abortion in 1999), but I had more than enough to keep my friends insane for a couple of weeks let alone four days. As a Boy Scout I learned to always "Be Prepared." As an adult, I have taken this motto to heart in my drug experimentations.

In a somewhat wise move, we divided up our substances among each car in the caravan each year. In a somewhat unwise move, we divided up our substances among each car in the caravan each year.

The idea was to minimize the amount of trafficking we were committing. The reality was that each car consumed mucho marijuana getting to New Mexico. It was beautiful in a silly way. Both years, we all agreed that we wouldn't hit any herb until we reached the cabin. Both years we lied and smoked on the highways in our little groups. Every time we pulled over, we found perpetual amazement at the stoned-ness of the riders in the other vehicles. Lord only knows what kind of stoned stupidity went down in our roving Cheech and Chong-mobiles each year. We fell out of our cars giggling at each other at every piss and munchies stop along the way.

Cabin Craziness

Arrival at the cabin kicked off the same level of induced insanity both years. Fall break gave us a chance between the end of the crowded summer season and the onset of the winter ski season to get wild and crazy on the top of a mountain away from all that we thought to be unpleasant about the "straight" people who inhabited these places during the not-so-high high seasons.

We surrendered the concept of time - we were on vacation. Our entry into the cabin at dark-thirty altered our sense of the need to succumb to the yolk of clocks. Instead, we entered the cabin as though we were liberating France from any of the numerous hoards of conquerors they've suffered over the years.

We over-drank and burned through our allotted amount of booze and bud that first night each year. Time lost all focus until Sunday afternoon when we had to begin the arduous drive east. The hours between are when it all fell to pleasantly weird shit. It could've been better if they'd just listened to Tee and I. Running out of drugs on a drug-cation is one of the worst events which can transpire in a college kid's life. Yet it did. Twice.

We shifted our time sense to that of people involved in an international group trip. We busted into the cabin, got fucked up and passed out. The first of us to wake popped Cypress Hill's seminal "Hits from the Bong" into the boom box and blasted it to arouse the rest of us from our slumber. Our numbers slumped down from the second floor bedrooms and up from the couches and floor of the first floor to heed the call of DJ Muggs, B-Real and Sen Dog. This siren song brought us all to convene upon the current bong of choice (the first year it was a converted bottle of Jack Daniels).

The concept of a morning-to-night lifestyle was something we refused to cotton to. Upon waking, we smoked, cooked some food, washed dishes, and passed the fuck back out after a short hike through the woods. Our vacation schedule converted our lifestyle to three eight-hour "days" in which we'd cook, clean, party, sleep, and repeat.

Because this area was really for families who came out during the high seasons, we came out before they turned on the running water. Luckily, Wahoo's cabin had an old outhouse across a dirt road. The outhouse really only mattered when the guys had to drop a deuce or when the girls... Oh never mind, it was always important to them. Luckily for guys in every situation since the beginning of time, we could whip our willies out wherever the hell we were and feel comfortable about having done so. Our penises might get us in a lot of trouble, but they sure are convenient.

The second year, L-Ron brought his girlfriend, Lolla. One night we got really tossed off. Couples received special status at the cabin and were granted the bedrooms upstairs. The tabs of Uncle Cidney I'd brought had really screwed everybody up. While some of us (me) were up for dropping every day of the mountain trip, my people held mixed feelings about this practice.

L-Ron scrambled out into the middle of the night to the outhouse in a fit of mixed intestinal madness. He found himself squatting in the gravel between the cabin and the outhouse with his white-ish Hanes halfway to his ankles as he vomited and shat himself. He made a stab at cleaning himself up and returned to the second-floor bedroom with Lolla. We awoke hours later to the much louder shouts of Lolla. No one can blame her for her freak-out that morning, but it sure as fuck was funny for the rest of us. L-Ron had mistakenly believed that he'd cleansed his undies out of his late night anal mess.

Her morning moans emanated upon the discovery of one of L-Ron's larger turds which had somehow escaped the radar and ended up sharing their mattress with them. This constituted the only time Cypress Hill didn't wake us on either trip.

I had fallen in love with LSD that confusing/confounding night of my first trip back at Money's. It inspired me to concoct and carry around a "trip sack" - a Crown Royal bag stuffed with random toys and trinkets I thought held the potential to entertain my friends and myself when tiptoeing through the tulips with Uncle Cid. A few of the toys I brought along on the second cabin excursion took center stage one night. I had gotten it into my head that wearing an old pair of cardboard 3-D glasses while beaming a flashlight at random reflective objects could provide some fun. Wow. Fuck *Avatar*. We quickly discovered that pointing our flashlights at beer cans held in our hands was quite possibly the most captivating activity in the world. Our tripped-out minds became slightly impatient while waiting our turns for one of the three pairs I'd brought with me. They were left over from *Freddy's Dead: The Final Nightmare*.

The second year's ride home took place without incident, while the first year saw a couple weird acts go down. L-Ron, Lolla, Gokey, and I drove back in Gokey's car. Crossing the Oklahoma-Texas border with Gokey riding shotgun, my blue-haired friend suddenly grabbed the rearview mirror and blindly tugged on it while making strange grunting noises like a chimp masturbating for the first time in public. The pair in the back seat had decided to go at it while partly covering themselves with a blanket. Ever the voyeur and good friend, the Gokstress wanted to make sure I could see the action from my seat of responsibility.

A short time later, we stopped at the Ardmore McDonald's on I-35 for some McGrub and so I could take a McMassive McShit. Reaching the stall just in time, my pants hitting my ankles coincided with my cheeks hitting the surprisingly clean seat as my first anal napalm burst hit the water and rear of the bowl's interior. A most taxing flow of butt bomb blasts blew out of my buttocks. I stood to wipe and immediately doubled over as an anal sneak attack sprang forth from my bowels and made a gooey chocolaty Rorschach Test all over the toilet and the back wall. I got the hell out of there after my second anal Aisle Two cleanup. My sphincter had performed its greatest/worst feat since Mom's claim that I once geysered on her and my nursery walls as a baby.

The Seventh Street Lighthouse

Had it not been for a lack of information my freshman year of college, I can only wonder at what path the following two decades would have taken. Despite going to college in the same town I'd lived in since fifth grade, I was eager to begin a new chapter of my life outside of my parents' house.

During my freshman year, I maintained a GPA above what I had been told I would need to stay in the dorm a second year on scholarship. Nobody had bothered to inform me of a second requirement for renewal: I had to be a registered member of a campus club. I had attended several meetings of the school's environmental club, but had never officially signed up with them. I lost the scholarship and drove five minutes away from campus to stay with my parents for the summer.

Backtracking a bit, among their numerous careers, my parents had been licensed real estate agents in Indiana. They flipped a house our two in their time. They also had grown up in and lived during the end of that time in America when many people knew how to and did make general repairs to their homes on their own. To them, the only people you hired to work on your home were those who did jobs requiring licensing and inspections. Even then, they still managed a few tweaks of their own here and there.

Well aware of my interest in real estate and business, they sniffed out a couple of real estate loopholes I could use to my advantage. Sweat Equity allows a first-time home buyer to purchase an older home with a very discounted down payment under a promise to complete an agreed upon list of improvements and repairs to prove their dedication to the purchase.

We also employed a trick called "Kiddie Condo." This represents a little known but profitable ploy of our government to convince parents to purchase homes for their offspring who have at least one year remaining on their undergraduate degree. When parents rent apartments or homes for their college kids, Uncle Sam doesn't receive much of a cut. But when parents invest in a house for their kids, Uncle Sam gets his cut and the wheels of capitalism crush ever onwards. I was able to land this deal by having my parents cosign the deed with me to make it look as though they were fronting the cash for the place, when in fact I had put up the down payment.

I stayed on at my parents' through the start of my sophomore year and began plotting. It took some time to finally figure out how to make it work. My friends and I went house hunting. My real estate agent chauffeured me around town to check out houses as my friends followed while getting stoned in their cars. Every house we visited had some deal-breaking issue until we visited a very strange home in a great location just two blocks southwest of the university.

One of the four oldest houses in the city, the structure occupied a space set well back into its large corner lot. A half-dozen steps led up to a small front porch which opened into an elongated living room with a nine-foot-tall ceiling and a fireplace. One bedroom sat off to the south of the living room. A tiny hall area opened into the master bedroom in the southwestern corner, the bathroom and a second door into the eastern wall of the first bedroom.

A previous owner had extended the master bedroom by knocking out its eastern wall and adding a sun room. The living room ended with a door to a spacious kitchen with the appropriate large number of drawers expected from the period and a breakfast nook converted into a laundry room.

Originally constructed on a raised base with a coal bin and basement only consuming a quarter of the real estate available below, yet another earlier owner had the idea to dig out the rest of the area below to add two more bedrooms, a combined kitchen/living room, a small bathroom, and an outside entrance that could never be properly sealed against the elements.

A spacious backyard surrounded by a waist-high stone fence held a separated A-frame two-car garage with the second stall forever closed off to the outside.

Entering the living room for the first time on that fall afternoon with my hopeful agent and my baked friends, I knew that I had found the place in which I would soon be living. Negotiations took longer than expected, which was surprising considering how long the place had sat empty.

We signed on December 15. This granted me two weeks to complete the tasks in the Sweat Equity portion of the agreement. Mom, Dad and a few friends came to my aid over the following fortnight to clean, paint the walls, strip the floors, stain the floors, seal the floors, and conduct miscellaneous small repairs around the property.

These two weeks proved to be some of the most eventful of my life.

The day before we began working on the house, I went to Wahoo's to do some celebratory drinking and smoking with her, L-Ron and the D-Man. Later in the evening, with our heads filled with enough substances to make quality life decisions, my trio of companions decided that they wanted to try LSD for the first time. I had become a vocal proponent of Dr. Hofmann's creation upon my first mind-bending experience since the previous year.

I surprised myself by tracking down four hits well after 2 a.m. I was to eat with and guide our little posse on their premiere mental plunge before driving to my parents' five hours later to begin work on my new old house. The trip itself was mellow enough for me. They enjoyed the initial inability to comprehend that they were on their way up. They freaked at times, and they got physical at times. It was all quite nonsensical and normal to the many millions out there who have swallowed that first tab of lysergic acid diethylamide.

Normal, that is, until a dynamic and disturbing outside negative influence injected itself into the equation. I had been quite happy flipping my lid to some Pink Floyd as my compatriots discovered the joy of slathering hand lotion on their bodies (Let's see you try that in an ad campaign, Jergens!).

L-Ron's then-girlfriend, Lolla, drove up to Wahoo's apartment wondering where her boy toy had been all night. Like almost all of L's girlfriends up until he met his future wife, Lolla was a hot ex-cheerleader with the tendency to go completely ape-shit without a moment's notice. Not a one of my three virgin trip-takers could have handled the intensity of her misunderstood madness and misplaced anger she would have brought into Wahoo's cozy one-bedroom apartment. So they sent me out to deal with her.

The sun rose and occasionally set again momentarily as I sat trapped in the passenger seat of her Oldsmobile. I went off on extensive, lyrical, complicated, and rambling explanations as to why it would have been excessively unhealthy and unwise for her to enter our friends' sanctuary while they were temporarily visiting an alternate plane of existence she could not begin to comprehend. My explanations droned on until I realized several times that I actually had no idea as to what the holy fuck I was going on about and had slunk off into random realms of mental mush. I lucked out in that she was too weird in her pissed off state in those days to take note of my departures from reality that morning. Multiple times I ended arguments which had gone sideways and devoid of logic with a statement of conclusion that went something like: "So do you see/understand what I'm saying?" She said that she did more often than not, and I succeeded in giving my friends in the apartment a respite.

I, on the other hand, had to leave immediately after deflecting Lolla. Still in the midst of a proper acid climax, I walked into my parents' kitchen. They sent me back out on a doughnut run to our town's only doughnut shop, filled with crinkled farmers who would never in a million years understand what gateways to the universe spun through my head as I sauntered past them on a mission to pick up a dozen glazed pastries for Mom and Dad.

The first Herculean task of December 15, 1995 completed, I struggled to force down half a bear claw. Mom and I drove to Wal-Mart to pick out paint and have it mixed for our introductory Sweat Equity mission: paint the house's interior. I pulled my pea green Tool baseball cap as low as I possibly could as we walked through the discount retailer's early morning minefield of meth-heads, farmers and insomniacs. Painting supplies secured, we entered my house.

I have never been one to abide silence. I require music or NPR in the background in order to distract the voices in my head, allowing me to concentrate on the task at hand. Consequently, my boombox took up residence at my house long before any other of my possessions or even I did.

Having grown up on my parents' vinyl copies of Steppenwolf; Arlo Guthrie; the Beatles; Peter, Paul & Mary; and the *Jesus Christ Superstar* and *Easy Rider* soundtracks, I was a big fan of quality classic rock and folk music. Oklahoma City's premiere classic rock station had long provided tunes my whole family could enjoy. My early cassette, CD and second-hand LP collection reflected this, while my digital collection continues to hold that lighter aloft.

The LSD far from purging itself out of my system that first morning, Mom and I taped off my future bedroom and began painting to the sounds of the Steve Miller Band's *Greatest Hits 1974-1978*. Standing on a ladder and trying not to freak out as the ancient, neglected plaster literally sucked the paint off of my roller, I did my best to appear normal. I held out well considering the circumstances, until "The Joker" started, that is.

"No matter how I've heard this song - sober, drunk or stoned - I've never liked it," said my Mother, shocking me.

Flabbergasted, I could generate no proper response. At this point we must pause this portion of the narrative for eight months until I recount a concert going experience.

The day wore on. I interlaced the classic rock with some Beastie Boys, Alice in Chains and Ice Cube, all of which helped return me to my version of reality.

Letting the Hammer Fall

I furnished my house with items I had scored at garage sales, estate auctions and SWOSU's semi-annual auctions. The former two provided me with furniture, lamps, cookware, and books. The latter provided me with entertainment and an accidental source of income.

At one point, the school sold off its entire 16mm film collection and a handful of projectors. To me. For a song. I paid pennies for most of them, buying them in lots, my only competition being farmers who wanted the heavy wide metal racks on which they sat. We often struck deals to split the lots so that we didn't have to bid against each other.

The films would supplement my minimum wage income as I tried to keep my house and business afloat. A little Evilnet startup had just begun to secure its place online. I had used eBay once or twice previously, but was about to learn just exactly what could be done with a Sony Mavica camera and my university's computer lab. Home computers and Evilnet connections were lofty aspirations well out of my budgetary constraints at the time.

A moment of inspiration struck me when I decided to bid for the films: I would cut them up and splice pieces together to build trippy visuals for raves. Hiroshima Music was trying to get its foot into the door of Dallas' emerging rave scene. The company had provided sound systems for a couple of shows, and at least one of our guys was honing his mixing skills.

I reviewed hundreds of reels from a collection spanning five decades. When I say "review," I mean that I watched a seemingly endless stream of 16mm educational films in the comfort of my living room and/or garage as I drank and/or smoked heavily sitting next to the roar of a projector older than me.

While I ended up with two large reels of spliced films of various degrees of trippiness, I never got to exhibit them at any venue larger than my home and my parents' garage. On the plus side, I did make several thousand dollars hawking the other films on eBay. I learned much about the site and the United States Postal Service's Media Mail rate. Packages went out around the world.

One auction would further my journalistic career. The school sold me an old Macintosh Performa 636CD for two dollars. I drunkenly pounded the hell out of that keyboard during my time working on the college newspaper. It would be my first and last Crapple product.

My favorite SWOSU purchase was an object I don't believe they should have been allowed to sell to just any random asshole. They auctioned off an old gas spectrometer. The contraption filled a pair of wheeled 12" computer racks I wanted for my DJ gear. Technological antiques, one came equipped with an 8" floppy disc drive, the first I'd ever seen. This drive, along with an array of complex and nonsensical ancient electronics, sat beneath a monitor reminiscent of an early arcade game. The second rack housed a complex piece of equipment bearing labels on it warning of the dangers of the radioactive components contained within. It even had lead shielding around all four sides. The radioactive material I safely and responsibly disposed of in the Dumpster in the alley behind my house. The lead I kept in hopes of a nuclear attack or defense from a Kryptonian.

New Year's Cherry
We easily completed the Sweat Equity list and then some by our December 30 deadline. Mom and Dad gave me a heavier-than-hell fold-out couch we'd had since I was a baby to use as a bed in the living room of my new home until I secured something better. The super single waterbed I had at their place would remain in my old bedroom a little longer.

I threw a party to herald in the New Year. I made up one-third of the attendees. My ex-dormmate and future housemate, Gokey, showed up as did Liza, a cute, but innocent, blond Pizza Slut coworker. Having no cable, we got drunk and angry listening to a local rock station's heinous countdown of the "top" songs of 1995 and their declaration of The Toadies' "Possum Kingdom" as the number one song of the year. It did, however, lead to the smallest party of the house and concluded with Liza and I christening the house all over the kitchen floor.

1996

Beginning of an Era of Errors

The second semester of my sophomore year began. I filled my house with roommates and, in a desire to give the place a name, recalled Stephen King's classic novel, *It*. Mike Hanlon, a member of the self-proclaimed "Loser Club," had stayed behind in the small Maine town where their little posse had grown up to keep the fire in the lighthouse going for anyone needing to return. Thus a name came to me: the Seventh Street Lighthouse. A week later, we threw our second party, beating the three-person head count of the first party by no less than 147 people.

As I mentioned earlier, most of my furniture came from garage and estate sales. Under my parents' tutelage, I outfitted my bedroom and the public areas of my home for less than $75. The consumption of too much alcohol combined with too many drugs would set the tone that first night for years of parties to follow.

As a consequence, I can recall less than ten minutes of the party (and about fifteen of those after). People came. People went. It was the smallest large-scale party any of my roommates and I would throw. Some of the those in the parade of strangers saw fit to break every piece of furniture I owned outside of my bedroom.

It remains a mystery how I didn't overdose at this or any of our parties. I stationed myself at the door to collect cash for the keg while drinking from a 64oz glass beer mug. More than a reasonable number of folks opted for the barter system without informing me ahead of time. In lieu of dropping cheddar into my palm, some partygoers dropped a small galaxy of prescription pharmaceuticals into my massive mug. Whatever drugs people shared with me throughout the night resulted in me hulking out in the wee hours.

I transitioned from clearing out the broken bits of cheap second and third-hand tables and chairs from the living room to smashing them into even smaller pieces in the backyard. I freaked. Thankfully my friends dragged me kicking and screaming to my bed where six of them restrained me until I wore myself down and conked out for

65

the night. I still wish I knew the myriad list of substances people had subjected me to that night (or from any of the parties to follow).

Still, I look back on that first party with a degree of fondness. The naiveté. The lack of preparedness. The police who didn't come. The less than two hours it took to clean the house. The half hour to clear the tornadic debris from the back and front yards.

From this first party evolved a chaotic cycle of monthly parties over the coming years. Thousands of college kids filed through my place to partake of kegs and insanity. The police would bust every party thereafter. One of the county's DEA agents once put in an appearance in my backyard to chase down people smoking weed. That party ended with a half-dozen people in cuffs on the curb across the street, none of them the tokers.

Once the fuzz put a halt to our festivities, my roomies and I ushered out all but twenty-fifty of our closer friends. The cops allowed them to remain once I explained that they were all overnight house guests, knowing that nobody would call them back out to visit us for that small of a number.

Occasionally, party people who weren't known to us wanted to participate in the post-party action. We turned away all but the inner circle. One night a group of cowboys showed up just after the police had departed. They demanded entrance to the Lighthouse. I filled them in on our post-pork party policy and invited them to come back for our next soirée. They announced that they were coming in to play with us. I told their Barf Brooks asses to fuck the fuck off. Those Brooks & Dumbasses snuck around to the front of the house and cut down the middle of three young pine trees blocking my view of the meth house across the street. Thank you, rednecks.

Of course, our worst party also turned out to be one of the smallest. While we generally considered less than two hundred people to be a small party, one of our last parties in the spring of 2001 only managed to draw out forty people before we'd had numerous acts of violence. We got to know the police on duty very well that Friday night.

During the first of several police visits, they informed me of a possible fight involving a gun. Allegedly, some highly intelligent human being pulled a gun on a pair of girls walking to the Lighthouse.

I believe in the NRA and self-defense, but what could have possibly transpired in a matter of minutes to make this "man" feel as though his life needed to be forcefully protected from a pair of drunken college girls on their way to a party.

As if this wasn't enough, I had to break up two near-fights in my living room and remove another "man" who insulted one of my roommates before informing us "you and the cops can't kick me out." Luckily, he was wrong, and we were enough to accomplish the job.

Gokey and His Five-Fingered Dick

Gokey holds a special place in my heart as one of my favorite members of the K-Town Mafia, my roommate from the second semester of my freshman year, one of my roommates at the Seventh Street Lighthouse, and a certifiably insane and loveable man full of mirth, compassion and creativity. Gokey and I occasionally rode around town refusing to enter or exit the car except through the windows, *Dukes of Hazzard* style. We used to joke that he had a crush on L-Ron. When he pulled out his five-fingered dick, it didn't help his cause any.

When Gokey moved out of the Lighthouse, he took with him only what he immediately needed and left behind a room the EPA would have declared a Superfund site: a solid, six-inch pile of garbage spanning the entire room. I found half-eaten meals and a sealed loaf of bread expanded so fat with mold that it had distended the plastic wrapper to its breaking point. He left behind a large neglected aquarium with several fish in it. I had left town for the summer when he moved and returned to find a tank of stagnant water with fish corpses captured in the thick solid moldy layer of funk growing on top.

During our freshman year, Gokey and I dropped in on a theater department party we'd heard about through the usual grapevine. I loaded all of my pockets with as many random cans, bottles and pints I had sitting around. We arrived at the apartment and knocked. The door opened to reveal two dozen strangers sitting around eating cheese and crackers. They asked us what we were up to. Before I could answer, a can escaped its mates from an overloaded pocket and rolled along the floor into the center of their little circle. That was enough for them. We quickly excused ourselves and left.

Unlike the rest of our crew, Gokey wasn't much of a drinker. He'd toss down two or three dollars regardless of what amount or brand of beer we bought and open at least six of them, never drinking one of them as far as the label. The morning after any night we'd all gotten together, we always knew which beers had been Gokey's - they were the nearly full ones left sitting wherever he had grown weary of them.

Don't get me wrong, I love Gokey. He was the fluffy, green-haired teddy bear of our group. He painted and once drew his own comic book (I still have and cherish the first [and only?] issue of *One Time*). I loved riding around in his little blue car, because I never knew when he was going to pull another hit and run. He dented all four corners of his car at least once but never got caught, a feat he could never accomplish in today's world of Big Brother. Every one of us enjoyed him in spite of and because of his quirky ways.

Then there was his five-fingered dick.

This wacky show began the same way every time: with us sitting around one of our homes, amazingly stoned and/or drunk.

"Hey, do you want to see my five-fingered dick?" the Gokestress (as he was also known) nonchalantly asked us.

We always replied, "No," but that never fazed him. He shoved his right arm down into the waist of his jeans, beneath the band of his underwear. With the outline of his arm clearly visible down to his knee, he would then ask L-Ron if he would be so kind as to stroke his five-fingered dick for him. Depending on his altered mental state, L-Ron sometimes reached out to touch the buried arm.

Over time, Gokey unzipped his pants and extended his arm out through the flies of his jeans and tighty-whiteys. This doubled him over a bit, giving him a hunch as he played out his strange performance. He kept it mellow at first, doing little more than using his exposed five-fingered dick to smoke a cigarette. He grabbed a beer and took a pull or two. With this preview out of the way, the real show got underway.

He walked around the room stooped over asking each person in attendance if they wanted to shake hands with his five-fingered dick. Those of us accustomed to this usually ignored him or tossed a crack his way. Most people witnessing the spectacle for the first time didn't know what to make of it.

The show culminated in him trying to find someone to "masturbate" his magnificent five-fingered dick. He never found any takers among his perplexed audience members. Pretending to jerk himself off in front of us, he balled his dick-hand into a fist, exploding his fingers out in a wonderfully crass mimicry of a "climax."

He ended the show by slowly stroking his five-fingered dick to calm it down. He pulled his arm back into the leg of his jeans and rubbed his five-fingered dick for a minute or two to bid it a fond farewell.

With his display completed, we returned, un-phased, to our various conversations and substances, wondering what madness our favorite blue-haired smoker would concoct next.

DM's Bad Drug Days Pt. I

DM was a rarely seen, angry man who randomly made appearances among our people in college. He had bad luck with drugs, and not in the addiction department.

During his freshman year, he paid a visit to his weed dealer. Said weed dealer lived in the dormitory on campus which housed most of the school's male athletes. Universities tend to budget money for their athletic housing so that it corresponds the success of their teams. Our school placed our football and basketball players in a building built in the school's early days and then promptly neglected.

Quarter-ounce purchased, DM prepared to leave his dealer's dorm room. A knock at the door surprised the boys. The dealer moved to crack the door open and see who was paying him an unexpected visit. A man with an athletic build wearing a sweatshirt with the hood pulled so tightly across his face it left only a narrow viewing hole for him burst through the door. Waving a .22 pistol about the room, the dealer's latest guest demanded that he and DM get acquainted with the concrete floor while he unburdened the dealer's dorm fridge of the cash and drugs stowed within its freezer compartment.

Green weed and dollars passed into black hands before the visitor fled a few rooms down the hallway. The dealer dealt his performance un-enhancing drugs to a good number of the school's under-performing athletes. The location of his goodies had become

69

known to too many of his clientele. DM left with his bag of treats once he deemed it safe to bolt.

DM's Bad Drug Days Pt. II

DM's second tragic drug tale is one of his own doing and sees him reaping his rightfully deserved rewards. DM drove a beautifully restored El Camino when he started college. Like many of us, he decided to purchase a quarter-pound of weed to sell in order to reduce the cost of the weed he himself smoked. DM hung around with some shady characters his freshman year of school as he tried to find himself or whatever it is that people claim to do during the time they spend transitioning from high school to college.

His QP came up missing a day or so after he'd bought it. A pierced, green mohawked guy he ran around with had stolen it from him. DM spent the better portion of two weeks telling everyone he came into contact with about the methy Mohawk having looted his bud. I'm certain that his parents and professors were the only people who didn't hear his angry tale. During this time, he never once bothered to confront Mohawk.

Having spread as much anti-Mohawk sentiment as he could, DM took an afternoon off from spreading propaganda to clean his Camino. El Caminos have a storage space behind their bench seats for their spare tires. It was here that DM discovered that his bag of herb had fallen behind his spare. Instead of defusing the situation he'd created with the Mohawk, he went about his daily life, forgetting the shitstorm he'd swirled into life with his people.

This saga ends with Mohawk running into DM a few days later and serving up a well-deserved ass-beating.

In the Mud

DJing non-school events often involved drinking. College bashes, New Year's Eve parties and weddings all featured people getting drunk if not stinko drunk. Many of these people felt the need to share their merriment and booze with their DJ.

I once DJed a friend's wedding reception at the Route 66 Museum in a neighboring town. I was to meet Goober and his best friend, Binky, for a campout nearby and a sweat nearby. I slept under the stars that night but not at Binky's farm.

I partook heavily of the champagne fountain at the reception. Not having ever been to Binky's farm, I was going by a set of hastily written directions on a paper napkin. Turning off of a two-lane farm road, I swamped my hearse on a muddy farm entrance (not Binky's). Weighed down with all of my equipment, the road didn't have to be too bad for Bonnie to sink into it. I had no cell phone and, still drunk, struck out into the night in search of help.

Trying to wave down one of the small number of vehicles passing by on the paved road with a flashlight in the dark didn't help bring anyone but a sheriff's deputy. He informed me that my flashlight was no way to get assistance. He offered me a lift into the west side of town so I could make a call. I had no real reason to go with him, as I had no way to contact Goober or Binky, and I wasn't going to call for a tow. I accepted anyway.

I bought a beer at the gas station and ran into a quartet of crackheads who sort of knew me through some roundabout means. They offered me a ride to…I never did quite understand what they were offering. They got pulled over. By the same deputy I'd met earlier. He knew them and advised me to find a better class of company for the evening. He didn't search them and let us go with a warning for whatever vehicular offense they'd committed.

They dropped me off at the next convenience store, believing me to have brought them bad luck. I wandered the streets with no clue as to where to go. Remembering that, Whale, a family friend from Boy Scouts, lived nearby, I decided I would try to find his house and crash there for the night. What I didn't take into consideration was that I had never visited his home and hadn't seen him or his son in a couple of years.

I walked into the emergency room of the local hospital, figuring that they would have a phone book. They were not exactly happy to see me and wondered whether or not I might require more assistance than their phone book could provide. I escaped the hospital and weaved through some back alleys, unsure whether or not I was being followed.

My goal was met but not until after 3 a.m. Not wanting to wake Whale or his family, I grabbed a piece of firewood from the stack next to what I hoped was his driveway and used it for a pillow on the hard concrete.

In spite of my primitive sleeping arrangements that would have made Fred Flintstone shudder, my hours of consumption and walking conked me out nicely.

The sun had risen just enough by 6 a.m. to wash away most ambiguity a person would have had concerning any object they happen to have been looking at. I for one could easily discern Whale's son, Dolphin, sneaking four of his friends out through their backyard gate. They, however, couldn't tell that my eyes were open.

"Holy shit, Dolphin! There's some guy with long hair sleeping on your driveway," a member of the party announced.

"Shut up…Oh my god…There really is some…wait. I know him!"

Sure enough, Dolphin remembered me. I rustled to let them know that I had roused from my respite.

They secreted me away into the backyard where we climbed through Dolphin's bedroom window. He had snuck his friends into his room the night before to pound a couple cases of Budweiser. With the sun rising, the time had come for them to straggle home. We shared a beer as I explained just exactly how I'd come to use his driveway as my bed. His dually pickup freed my Bonnie in seconds despite having sunk down to her undercarriage.

I thanked him and took my hearse to the car wash. I talked to Goober later that afternoon. He knew just where I had swamped my beautiful Bonnie. I had made my fatal turn one quarter mile too early. At least I got to camp out that night.

Militia Marshall

As evil as Tank Tucker was, we had Marshall as a counterbalance. Goober and I had known Marshall in our youth. He'd dated one of Mom's best friends. They broke up, and he left our lives…until my brother got a house while we were in college. Marshall lived across the street from Goober's Grotto. The Grotto quickly became a regular hangout pad for me as a string of my best friends roomed with him over the years when they weren't living at the Lighthouse.

I got reacquainted with Marshall as an adult after a few strange run-ins at Goober's. It began with our crew sitting around drinking and doing what we normally do one afternoon when we were shocked to see a laser target painted on one of our buddy's foreheads.

Marshall was sighting us from across the street. He came over for a beer.

Marshall was a jack of many trades: Marksman. Gunsmith. Inheritor. Alcoholic. Bomb builder. Dog masturbator. But a slave to fashion Marshall was not. Every day, no matter the season, the temperature or the weather, Marshall invariably wore combat boots, blue jeans, an old Army BDU jacket, and a mesh trucker cap. Below freezing or over 100°F, his attire did not alter. He had some incredible accessories. He always sported a wad of Skoal in his mouth, but never carried a spit cup. He had learned early on during his stint in the National Guard to swallow not only his dip spit but the dip itself.

Marshall joined the Guard in his youth. He spent part of his time in the service piecing together depleted uranium weapons. During a class one day, his instructor caught him brown-toothed and dipping. The officer running the class ordered him to dispose of his wad. Going for his cup, the officer informed him *Full Metal Jacket*-style that he was not allowed to spit in his class. He swallowed his load and never more would he burden himself with spit cups.

Among other things, playing with uranium had screwed his back up pretty properly. This resulted in a lifetime of surgeries and heavy pain medication prescriptions.

Above all else, Marshall was a generous man, especially when it came to his friends. L-Ron, Tex, JeEcHuA, and I enjoyed hanging out with him, while Goober begrudgingly tolerated him. He received monthly pill refills and came over to share his fortune.

"Hey, boys! Hold out yer hands. It's Pill Day!" Marshall exclaimed to announce his monthly self-proclaimed holiday as he distributed drugs to us. Not being a big pill popping person myself, my share usually went into a bottle which I kept at home to celebrate the Four Days of 4/20.

The man ate raw bacon rolled in brown sugar and possessed the insane ability to magically make upwards of ten ounces of tequila disappear in a single go. The latter usually occurred every time he and his wife had a fight, which was often. "You boys got any weed or tequila? Two-Legged Jessica's bein' a fuckin' bitch again!" he cried in fits of wife-induced depression.

Marshall had access to some farm land south of town. We met him down there to shoot guns and blow up shit. We also watched him jerk off his dogs. I fuck you not: WE WATCHED HIM JERK OFF DOGS. He had three big black chows: Bobo, Jessica and Richard. They split their time between the house and the farm, always running out panting and foaming to greet Marshall when he showed up. He'd jump out of his Jeep and greet Richard and Bobo by reaching for their undercarriages and stroking their red rockets.

"The best way to make a dog your buddy is to pull his puddy!" he often told us. We quickly learned not to shake his hand.

He also had something to say about two of the dogs' names. "You and Richard have the same name, but that's just a coincidence. But I named Jessica after my wife, 'cause she's a bitch just like Two-Legged Jessica."

This brings us to the point where I wish this were an audio book. You just can't compose Marshall quotes on paper and hope that people understand them. They need to be uttered in his high-pitched wonderfully nasally twang.

Despite his predilection towards the Jesus juice, Marshall could still center five shots on a nickel from a hundred yards. He was a wizard with anything gun-related. He blued most of our pieces to protect them from rust and offered to convert any and all of our semi-automatics to full auto. Once again, I must interject here.

Western Oklahoma didn't offer a whole lot of activities for its youth back then. Of course we had the dirty lakes and a few crumbling bat caves, but those could only hold our attention for so long. I honestly believe that's one of the reasons Oklahoma and Missouri battle back and forth to claim the national title of the state with the most clandestine meth labs.

If you're not into meth or knocking up drunken high school girls, then your attention naturally falls to weapons. Pistols. Hunting rifles. Shotguns. Assault rifles. Pipe bombs. For my 21st birthday, I treated myself to a virgin Chinese-made paratrooper SKS from a Baptist minister in Oklahoma City I'd found in the *Daily Oklahoman's* classifieds. It came with a 30-round clip, because you never know when those extra twenty-five shells will come in handy. Most of my friends were prepared for a *Red Dawn* (the original, not the shitty remake) scenario. Some even hoped for it.

We had great fun with Marshall on his land. He brought out crazy, high-powered armaments for us to shoot after getting properly wasted. We cut down trees with guns. In colder months we passed bottles and stories around a 55-gallon fire barrel. I almost sliced through one of his arms the first time I used his chainsaw. We were under the snow-laden boughs of a pine tree cutting firewood. I was drunk. Marshall held out a branch for me to cut, but the falling snow had covered and fogged up my glasses. I couldn't see where I was slicing. It was a miracle that we all came out of it with the appropriate number of appendages.

Marshall used to hang out with the Waterford Police Department. He kept a police scanner with him at all times and used another scanner to listen to all of the wireless home phones in town. The police knew him well enough that even when they had to respond to a call at his house because he was out of his gourd and waving guns in the air like he just didn't care in his front lawn, they didn't draw down on him.

Sadly, Marshall died alone in a nursing home in a nearby town a few years ago. Two-Legged Jessica left him once she had finally gotten it through her head that she wouldn't be able to touch the vast quantities of money his mother had left him in an air-tight trust. I appreciate all that he taught me and will never forget the bombings. Much of what we did back then would have landed us on terrorist watch and no-fly lists had we done them post 9/11. I miss you, you crazy son of a bitch.

Bonnie Booty

Without a doubt, my favorite car remains my 1969 Pontiac Bonneville hearse-ambulance conversion. Many people in college or high school knew a guy with a hearse. For folks in Waterford, I was that guy. My station wagon on steroids was a beast to be reckoned with.

Bonnie was one of five hundred, 1969 Bonneville station wagons bought by Comet, a conversion company in Dallas. They extended her to a length of 18'6" feet and raised her roof to the point where I could set a keg in a trashcan in the back and still have room to pump the barrel. They replaced the rear floor with concealed compartments to stash the tools of the ambulance trade along with a jump seat next to the rear passenger side door. This raised the rear section of Bonnie to about eight inches below the top of the front bench seat. Her 24-gallon tank refused to get me as far as most cars sporting 13-gallon tanks thanks to her dismal 10-12mpg. She floated on the road and could do over 100mph despite her age, original engine and size.

As with all of the monster medical wagons of her day, she'd begun her life as an elegant hearse. When her looks began to fade, her owners sold her off to an ambulance barn like a high-class escort getting demoted to a common whores once the ravages of time take their toll.

I used her rear compartments as caches for my camping gear and jury-rigged coolers by triple-lining them with Hefty garbage bags. Bonnie was a source of many adventures, only one of them sexual.

I am not one of those guys who gets car sex. Oh, I understand it, I just rarely have any.

On random occasions in college, I would commit to some sort of cleanse. It might be a week of no solid foods, a month of no beer, a month of no weed, or something really nutty like a weekend without hallucinogens, but I usually accomplished whatever the hell it was I thought I was setting out to accomplish.

Quitting the ganja was one of my more frequent fasts. While I solidly support the legalization of that most useful herb for medical and recreational purposes, I am just not a good smoker - the exception that proves the rule if you will. The end of my longest self-induced pot fast scored me my one and only instance of hearse sex.

I hauled some friends over to the party of a high school friend at her duplex in an alley, pulling into a miraculously empty spot directly in front of her door. My passengers disembarked with the exception of one of my pothead friends and the Streak, a really fun girl that I sometimes hooked up with but hadn't for a while at that point.

The Streak was NOT a smoker but for some reason had decided that tonight was the night she would partake of the good weed for only the second or third time in her life. We had already talked to the pothead about it, and he had agreed to smoke her out for a couple of beers. The Streak didn't want to smoke alone with him, a guy she had only met twice. She twisted my arm to break my nearly two-month fast to join them.

We torched a joint. The Streak proceeded to make out with me. The pothead watched until she and I achieved third base, at which point he left us to our own devices.

The Streak, higher than she'd ever been, and myself, higher than I'd been in months, rounded third base. I slid in to home, so to speak. The way the rear was set up, the Streak's crotch was perfectly positioned so that I could do my duty while standing on my knees in a weird position that worked out just right. Numerous people slapped Bonnie and cheered us on as we got down to some serious public dickupuncture. We eventually had to call a time-out until we could retire to the Streak's place to finish. I never made it to the party.

Egg Nog Numbskull

For a couple of years during my first four years of college, I usually kept an iced-down cooler stocked full of various alcoholic beverages in my van. During the summer, I occasionally forgot to replace the warm stagnant water with ice. That is not a wise move during May in Oklahoma as temperatures begin rising to their blazing summer norms, especially if you keep a half-gallon jug of expired eggnog liquor left over from the holiday season in your overly warm Igloo.

L-Ron's older sister, K-Ron, graduated college our sophomore year. I hopped in with him for a road trip down to celebrate with her and her friends in Wichita Falls, TX. Stocking his cooler, I decided to grab my eggnog.

Already a Texas twelve-pack in at her place, I cracked my jug. It took more than a few pulls for me to figure out that extended exposure to heat had soured my eggy booze. I tossed it and switched back to beer and vodka for the duration of the night.

We rolled the windows down for the ride home the next afternoon. The antique, rancid eggnog had worked its way through my system and escaped my body in the form of the foulest gaseous explosions I have ever created. The stench was so bad that it still took nearly three minutes for the 70mph winds blowing through L-Ron's Jimmy to clear out each anal blast, of which I generated plenty.

An Inconvenient Store

Although Waterford sits on both I-40 and Route 66, our first 24-hour full-size gas station did not open until 1996. I worked nights there their first summer. The place opened with a Baskin Robbins and three low quality knockoff eateries: Smash Hit Subs - a fake Subway, a Mexican stand so bad it made Taco Bell look like gourmet grub and a cheap pizza place - the best of the trio.

Oklahoman summers are hot as balls during the day, but cool down rather nicely after sunset. Most nights, I bicycled to work, parking my trusty old Columbus Clipper in the basement. The night shifts were always a steaming hot mess of madness. Chaos ruled until the morning shift arrived.

A complete lack of security cameras ensured that a constant stream of petty theft and other wild transgressions took place. A Southern Baptist zealot coworker hated the Floyd, Zeppelin, Beatles, and Buffet I played on our boom box behind the counter. When I once commented that Jimmy Buffet was the "lord of the beach," she blew up at my blasphemy and informed me that, "there's only one true god." Friends of mine using the drive-thru often enticed me to lean out of my window to puff on their joints, pipes and/or bongs.

Some of my coworkers took to selling beer to their friends long past Oklahoma's 2 a.m. cutoff. They wrapped cases in garbage bags, hid them between the two Dumpsters sitting along the drive-thru. Friends in the know stopped to snare them on their way to the window where they were rung up as other items, if they were rung up at all.

I loved working the night shift, because it meant that I got to stock the walk-in cooler. None of my coworkers liked the cold, nor did they wish to spend two to three hours in there filling racks and stacking cases. I have always suffered from a high core temperature and indulge in every opportunity that I can get my hands on to get cold.

My stocking duties allowed me to grab my Discman and hide out from coworkers and customers alike for at least a quarter of my shift every night. I delighted in frightening drunk and stoned patrons reaching for cold beverages. Even better, stocking came at the end of the night, just before the morning crew arrived. The best part was getting drunk.

Convenient stores have to pull every tall boy, six-pack, 12-pack, and case of beer that gets dented, ripped or loses a single sudsy soldier. These we returned to our distributors. I made sure that every package of beer which had lost one can or bottle also lost a second or third. It was rare that I didn't pound at least a six-pack during these sessions.

Each night ended with the morning shift arriving late and selling my 19-year-old butt a 12-pack of Red Dog, our cheapest piss. Beer safely stored and iced down in my backpack, I rode to a park to drink six on the merry-go-round while watching people drive to work.

One of my roomies at the time, Tex, worked nights for an oil rig service, and we often arrived home at the same time. Many a morning I continued on home to find him sitting on the front porch. We'd finish off what remained of the dozen, burn a jay and retire to our bedrooms to sleep off the worst of the day's heat.

I'm a Joker and a Toker

I love the Steve Miller Band and was lucky for many years when they came through Oklahoma City at the end of every summer to wrap up the concert season and get us back to class. With the exception of the Clowns, there is no group I've seen as many times as I have Miller. My birthday also falls at the end of summer vacation. Miller always arrived within a week of the anniversary of me not dying for another year and once on the actual day itself. Mom and Dad accompanied me to my first Miller show at the Zoo Amphitheater. As I mentioned earlier, Mom had expressed her dislike of Miller's "The Joker" as we painted the Seventh Street Lighthouse nine months previous. At that moment, I decided that I would test her theory that she didn't like the song while stoned.

Still too young to drink, my friends happily traded my cash for drinks when they went on runs of their own to the Zoo's various beer stands. I wandered around visiting the various gaggles of my people who made the summer pilgrimage to see Steve and his crew.

The band hit the opening notes of "The Joker," and scrambled back to my parents. As Mom stood there, beer in hand, I whipped out a tightly rolled doobie from the breast pocket of my favorite sleeveless plaid flannel shirt. Mom stared at it.

"What is that?" she asked incredulously.

"You told me that you didn't like this song while stoned, and I don't believe you. So let's spark this puppy up!" I replied.

"You shouldn't have that," she said as she snatched my joint and stuck it into her pocket.

I never learned the fate of that joint, but I'm fairly certain Mom and Dad made it disappear later that night one they got home.

Wahoo's Small Apartment and Big Balls

My inner circle generally maintained an open-door policy at our apartments, trailers and houses. I loved Wahoo's comfy one-bedroom apartment partly because it sat half a block from campus. That created real convenience for the lazy stoner in each of us. We got too drunk to finish games of *Pass Out* there on many nights.

Drinking at Wahoo's ramped up upon our discovery of Coors Light's party balls. Golden Colorado's beer king had the wise idea to stuff five gallons of its beer into plastic, non-returnable balls in the mid-nineties. A long-stemmed tap stabbed through its rubber top to access the golden goodness inside.

As great as they were, the real fun didn't begin until we got creative with their semi-transparent corpses. I began cutting the tops off and dubbing them "smoke domes." Taking turns donning them, we exhaled clouds of smoke into our makeshift helmets, obscuring our vision and getting us really, really high. Being that stoned came in very handy when we got drunk enough to take cheap pot shots at whomever happened to be wearing the dome at the time.

Spankers

I had the pleasure of working with an adorable blond girl, Katy, for nearly a year while we were in college. She graduated high school a couple years behind me.

While we never dated, we gobbled genitals in my van a few times when she and her boyfriend, Mark, faced yet another break in their on-again, off-again relationship. But this story isn't about Katy and myself - it's about Mark and six other guys.

A year before we ever hooked up, she came into work laughing her ass off. She had a story to tell me about her weekend. Fresh out of high school, the parents of one of Mark's friends had left town for the weekend. Mark and six friends informed their respective girlfriends that they were taking a "boys' night out" on Saturday. An equal number of their female counterparts decided to have a "girls' night."

The girls' night didn't last much longer than a few drags up and down the length of Main Street. They didn't have any drinkers in their crew, leaving little choices for a small town on a Saturday night. Without any other obvious options, they decided to surprise their men folk.

They found the door unlocked at the house they knew the boys to be hanging out at and entered. Sneaking into the living room, they discovered a grisly scene: The television blared porn as the boys sat around the room, each with a towel over his lap and a hand beneath it.

This raised several questions for me, none of which ever received answers. Did the six visiting friends bring their own wank towels, or did their gracious host toss around his parents' linens? What did the guy who came quickest do while waiting for his friends to finish? If any of them blew their load unreasonably fast, did he call it quits or pretend to continue until a more desirable time? How did this idea come about?

While I'm quite happy not having been in the room when the girls interrupted their circle jerk, I do wish I could've heard the conversation that sparked this penis night out.

I'd Like to Introduce You to My Grandmother From Hell
Every life is a works in progress story. Most of us freely criticize each other's stories while we are living. Death ultimately writes the final sentence for each of us. No epilogue. No hope for a sequel (unless you believe in reincarnation). It also ushers in a mysterious partial editing of many of our tales. Except for people widely recognized as completely evil entities like Hitler, Celine Dion and mimes, a person's passing wipes much of his/her slate clean. We alter our opinions of people as a reward for meeting the fate destiny forces all of us to face. Most past transgressions and minor crimes are generally forgotten if not forgiven.

I have never understood this concept. I will die someday, but that won't make me any more or less of a saint than I already am or am not (leaning towards the latter). I hate to tell you this, but if I don't like or respect you now, dying today won't alter my opinion of you. I refuse to let anyone off the hook that easily. We should all forgive those who wrong us, but that doesn't mean we have to like them or give them a clean slate simply for becoming worm food.

A comedian my family once caught on a late night comedy showcase described the two grandmothers that most of us have. She accurately described the attributes of the wonderful, frail little old lady type of grandmother who seemed perfect in every way but lived far off and passed away when you were still a child. That was Dad's mother, my Grandma Mary.

She went on to tell the story of your other grandmother: A malevolent and evil beast of a human being, her family members believed she had achieved immortality by feasting upon the deluge of misery she poured onto others. She is the "Grandma from Hell." In that moment, Mom's mother's nickname was forged.

The Grandma from Hell entered the world on September 26, 1922, but nobody called her "Grandma" anything back then. It would be another five-and-a-half decades before people began calling her that and seven decades before we stopped calling her that. Slightly less than twenty-two years passed before she gave birth to Mom and began her reign of terror. But that's Mom's tale to tell, not mine.

Let's fast forward three decades to the birth of Goober and I.

Earning Our Lack of Love and Respect

The Grandmother from Hell officially became a grandmother in 1976 the moment I popped out of the womb and once again when Goober joined our clan sixteen months later. I came out resembling Mom's father, the first of Grandma's five husbands, while Goober received his looks from the men on the paternal branches of the tree. Grandma projected the ocean of ill will she harbored towards Mom's father onto me for merely sharing one of her ex's faces. She had no problem displaying this favoritism even when we were babies. Mom and Dad recount tales of her cradling Goober in her arms and shoving me away with her foot. She had no qualms about doing this in front of other relatives or even my own parents.

I received a bible as a birthday present from her one year while in middle school. Her chicken scratch dedication inked in the front page was as far as I'd ever gotten, although years later I would read the New Testament translated from an early Greek version. I never got rid of hers, probably as a result of my pack-rat tendencies, one of the very few attributes I inherited from her. It sat among the various shelves my books called home throughout my college years.

One day, one of my oldest friends, Dude, noticed it sticking out among my Hunter S. Thompsons, Stephen Kings, Dean Koontzs,

Ray Bradburys, Isaac Asimovs, and military surplus explosives manuals. I explained how it had found itself in my eclectic collection. He plucked it off the shelf, unzipped its cover and flipped through it. A $20 bill fluttered out and down to my dusty hardwood floor. She had stuck Mr. Jackson in towards the back in hopes that I would find it as I neared the end of my religious reading odyssey. It went back into the book where it still calls home today somewhere in a box in the depths of my parents' attic.

The Grandma from Hell handed me an envelope containing a card and a $50 bill for my sixteenth birthday. She handed Goober the keys to a car for his much sweeter sixteenth, sixteen months later.

Her old Chevy Celebrity sedan would serve him well until he rolled it while driving home smashed out of his mind on Route 66 late one night. His lone passenger sustained the only injury among them when he jammed his right thumb. He didn't even wake up until Goob shook him awake as they hung upside down, suspended by their seat belts.

Goober ran down to the large truck stop and restaurant in full view of the site of his accident. He called Mom who in turn called our favorite towing outfit. Their flatbed truck arrived to haul off the wreck without any law enforcement agency ever the wiser. The tower accepted the totaled car as payment for towing it away.

Grandma's car made one final ironic public appearance that spring at the local high school. The towing company dragged it and another wreck out to the parking lot to use in the annual anti-drinking and driving campaign. If only they'd known the truth…

The Grandma from Hell turned the death of Grandpa Charles (her fourth husband, and the only man Goober and I ever knew as "Grandpa" on that side of the family) into a spectacle to feed her insatiable ego. I wrote a story about the experience for my high school Creative Writing class which found its way into the school paper. She did not agree with my less than flattering opinion, but refused to be straightforward about the matter. It was far easier for her to complain to the rest of the world about it instead of discussing her issues about me with me.

Grandpa Charles
Reprinted from the *Waterford Claw*

Grandpa Charles should have survived his operation, but now humidity and relatives surrounded and engulfed me. The relatives were the worst. I had only a passing knowledge of most of them, but they hugged me and said how sorry they were and that they knew just how bad I felt. They didn't, couldn't and shouldn't know. Instead of looking them in the eye and screaming that their load of B.S. wasn't doing me any good, I gave them my "jeepers thanks" smile and thanked them to put their minds at ease. This carried on for an hour.

The time for the funeral came. Ushers led us into rows of pews, family in front. I thought that this was so we could get a great view of the action. A withered preacher stood before us, reminding us what a great man "Charlie" had been. I wanted to yell out that his name was Charles, not "Charlie," but it made no difference.

The preacher's ramblings about "Charlie" were nothing more than unproven facts to him. He did not know how great Grandpa Charles had been. Charles had never shown him how to bait a hook and cast his line at Cousin Wyatt's catfish pond. He had never watched birds with Charles. After some time had passed, we lined up to look at what had been my grandpa. My grandmother wept as she told me how nice he looked in his tuxedo. Grandpa Charles didn't wear tuxes. My grandma had always been as loony as a toon.

First, she had insisted on having an open casket. Her money paid for the shindig, so why not? It made no sense to me why she or anyone would want to look at the corpse of my grandpa. I believed that it was for the same reason that people slowed down at wrecks or went to amusement parks. Somewhere in their minds, they were getting a thrill out of this. Except you would never see a t-shirt exclaiming: "MY PARENTS SAW THE BODY OF 'CHARLIE' CHASTAIN, AND ALL I GOT WAS THIS LOUSY T-SHIRT," because even we fun-loving, sick-minded humans have limitations. My grandmother had said that he looked handsome. Looking at him made me sick. He was grossly pale. His eyes had retreated into his skull. His arms were loosely sheathed spaghetti. This wasn't my Grandpa Charles. Suddenly I realized I would never see my grandpa again. Tears rolled down my cheeks. We would never again cast lines for catfish or watch robins. Already, I missed him.

I endured a half-hour of loneliness on our road trip to the burial. My fellow mourners and I formed a semi-circle around the open grave, which waited to swallow what was no longer my grandpa. No dramatic rain or fog brightened our already joyous day. I looked around at the other graves while the preacher rambled. I thought about all the other grieving families and the lives that their people had lived. My spine turned to ice. A grass fire of sorrow spread throughout my body. I spent the rest of the sermon staring blindly at my Grandpa Charles' coffin.

Reeling in the Years

The powers of the universe granted me the powers of invisibility for years beginning in high school. Even though we coexisted in the same city of a mere 12,000 people, I could walk ten feet in front of her in Wal-Mart, and she would be clueless as to my presence, even after making eye contact with me. I wasn't about to remove this cloak of invisibility worn long before Rowling thought of giving one to Potter and his crew.

Rather than joy and glad tidings, the holidays brought dread, agitation and short tempers to our quartet. I doubt any child ever spent so many birthdays, Christmases, Thanksgivings, and other "special" days wishing we were in school as Goober and I did. Her visits were heralded with blankets of uneasy silences from us met by reproach and calls for pity from her.

Lasagna Lollygagging

We usually treated our homes with respect in college, but we had a lot of fun at and made an exception of Jizzball and L-Ron's Main Street house.

As much as I despised the Grandmother from Hell, I loved her lasagna. I had a gut full of her stab at Italian cuisine one evening while drinking on Main Street. Pounding booze while deciding what to do for the night, we figured out one thing we didn't want to do. Once in a while, Goober was too much to handle once he entered Dick Mode, so we played a game of avoidance.

That was the nature of our relationship until after we'd entered university. Running in the same circle of ninjas, we spent a lot more time together than we would have had either of us left Waterford for college. His Grotto and my Lighthouse stood a few blocks from each other. We often partied and sometimes crashed at each other's pad.

Any time that I went to a concert, I plied one or two of my female friends with booze and/or weed until they got drunk enough to put my ass-length hair into tight little braids. A couple of my friends could get them tight enough that they lasted for several days or even a week after the show, depending on how much of a toll it took on me. One of these braiding sessions led me to give Goober the silent treatment for a month.

After a typical night of booze and bud at Goober's, I passed out on his couch. I woke the next morning, walked home and emptied my pockets only to find that Goober had cut off one of my braids as I slept, rubber banded the cut end so that it would stay together and shoved it into my pocket. The little shit!

While we've long suffered from a rocky relationship, the smooth patches have always more than made up for the rough waves we've battled along the way.

This was one of those nights of rough patches.

Being the mid-nineties, college kids in Western Oklahoma didn't have cell phones, and only drug dealers had beepers, so it took little effort to evade people. Of course, we refused to exert even that small amount of effort. Goober came by while I was there. Even though my car sat in the driveway, we still decided to make it look as though the two men of the house were going to spend a quiet evening in, studying or some such nonsense. To this end, I hid in the bathtub, pulling the shower curtain shut. We would have gotten away with it, if I hadn't begun ralphing up vodka and grandma's lasagna in the tub.

My Wet Pussy

A stray female cat began showing up around my property a few years into living at the Lighthouse. Some scandalous neighborhood cat had knocked her up and didn't respect her enough to wear a condom or to push her down a flight of stairs after conception. We never named her, but she became our outdoor pregnant pussy. I placed a cardboard box with a towel in it in the 12-inch gap between my back porch and the sunroom off my bedroom. She ejected four bastard kittens from her uterus into that box.

One stormy night a couple of weeks later, a few of us decided to munch more acid. Oklahoma's spring storms can be violently vicious. Driving rain and hail shatter shingles while the winds strip trees. Hours of hard rain that night restarted Waterford's notorious temporary Seventh Street River. Water rose within inches of my front porch's steps. The drainage problems along my street gave occasion for some good ol' boys to go for a cruise down the road on their plastic bass boats and inflatables. We partied on throughout the storm until I began to realize that at least one of the numerous noises in my head was real.

I ventured outside to see what the mewling was all about. Four kittens floated in the cardboard box's swollen walls. I plucked them out to dry them. Felines provide much entertainment to people rocked out of their gourds.

I kept one of the kittens, a cute little brownish tiger. He looked like an underwear stain, so I dubbed him Streak. I had to leave him with my parents when I moved to Korea years later. Liking his name, but not its origin, they lied to people by explaining that he'd earned his name because he looked like a brown streak when he ran. I preferred the truth. Three years later, a neighbor's unattended pit bulls roamed our hood until they mangled all three of the cats at my parents' house. I'd still like to mangle the white trash-hole owners of those malicious mutts.

Old Paint

Wally also attended SWOSU, and we shared the random adventure every now and then. My meaty friend hailed from Sayre, a minuscule Oklahoma town so far west it might as well be in Texas. We got plowed one night while driving around in his old boat of a Monte Carlo, and he shared the story of Old Paint, a local legend.

The tale went that some guys a couple years ahead of Wally in high school got hammered one night and stole a life-size fiberglass horse from the front of a paint store, hence the horse's name. The guys passed Old Paint around for a couple of years like a homecoming queen runner-up on prom night. Paint later went off the grid. As he spun his tale, he drove farther and farther out of town, eventually pulling over at a seemingly random spot beside a field. I thought we had stopped to piss, but I couldn't have been more wrong.

Wally walked off into the grass and hopped a barbed-wire fence, far too much effort for a simple drunken bladder evacuation. Old Paint leapt over the fence at me! Wally had known the location of Old Paint all along and had decided to bring the stallion in from the wild at long last.

He popped the trunk. We tossed in the horse and took off with his head, tail and legs sticking out. Barely one hundred yards down the road, a loud clatter arose behind us as Old Paint tumbled out of the trunk. This time we tied him down and got him safely and secretly into my yard.

Old Paint spent years in my garage as a fun party decoration and interactive stoner toy until I decapitated him for a long since forgotten and never completed project. When I moved to Dallas after college, Old Paint went into the small shed/dog house off to the side of a dog pen next to the garage.

His next great adventure took place a year after my move to Korea while I was renting out the Lighthouse. A lightening strike caught Paint's shed on fire. Firemen axed into the flimsy wooden structure upon one of them seeing a horse inside through the burning wood. They worked hard to save my "horse" until they realized the fiberglass truth. He stayed in the charred remains of that shed until I dismembered him for a final drive to Altuna, L-Ron's farm, where he became target practice for our collection of more or less legal armaments. Rest in pieces, old friend.

Christmas Hell and Jesus

My parents liked, if not loved, the majority of friends Goober and I made throughout high school and university. Especially university. For our friends who couldn't make it home for the holidays, my parents opened their home to a series of Christmas Eve parties. Mom set out plates of her Xmas cookies and brewed batches of her heavily boozed crock pot punch. We drank in the house and smoked in the garage or the backyard, weather permitting.

One of these had a more mellow beginning and a crazier conclusion. Not many of my friends stuck around town for the 1996 holiday season. The faithful few of them who came to that year's party left earlier than usual, leaving me with my parents and several of their friends. Our sextet played board games and drank heavily into the first hour or two of Christmas. They let me drive home, despite one of the friend's close ties to local law enforcement.

Mom called to wake me up at 10 a.m. to come over to open gifts, eat lunch and spend time with Goober and the Grandma from Hell. My shower nearly knocked me down. I drove over in a condition only slightly better than I'd been in the night before, which I venture to claim as the drunkest I've ever sat behind the wheel.

Horribly hungover and passed out beneath our Christmas tree among the presents, one of our cats, Mickey, passed the day ripping long gashes into my scalp with his claws as he played in my long, flowing hair. Incapacitated, my only defense was to raise an arm above my head and to let gravity bring it down near the feisty feline.

I only left my spot on the floor to orally void my stomach in the hall bathroom. My final explosion came at 4:30 p.m. It was the first and only Christmas in my life where I didn't and couldn't eat before 6 p.m. When the Grandma from Hell inquired as to my condition, Mom and Dad covered my ass by selling her a story about me having the flu. It was the best "flu" ever! Throughout the day, she never once attempted to communicate with me.

Worn out from throwing up all day as part of the worst hangover in my life, I drove home to a thankfully empty Lighthouse for some much needed rest. This was not to last.

No sooner had I crawled into bed, then I heard my then-basement roomie, the Dude, and some of our high school friends enter the casa. They came up to see what I was up to on this Christmas night and to tempt me into some frivolities.

Ben had some Jesus Christ. For the few of you who haven't had the pleasure of taking LSD yet, it most famously comes in paper form as a small sheet consisting of one hundred tabs in a ten-by-ten grid, with ten sheets comprising a "book." The sheets usually have some sort of artwork on them for identification purposes. Blotter sheets often have logos from different rock bands, pop art or any craziness a chemist can concoct. Ben's tabs originated from a sheet with a drawing of Christ on his cross.

I was in no kind of condition to drop acid, but Ben convinced me that it was no coincidence that he had Christ on Christ's birthday. A person can't argue with that level of logic. I ate the square he handed me.

The Seventh Street Lighthouse, requires even further explanation at this point. A craptacular assortment of miscellany always adorned my walls and filled my home. Friends of mine once gave me the sun-dried broken corpse of a large bird they'd found while stoned near Ghost Mound, a camping and rappelling locale. I boiled it, reconstructed it, painted it black, and suspended it from the far corner of my bedroom's ceiling and walls by fishhooks attached to picture-hanging wire. It looked like a prop from an unreleased *Hellraiser* sequel.

An old yellow McDonald's table with attached fire-red booth seats I'd picked up at an auction served as our dining room table for several years. For a time, my entire 16mm film collection sat on gigantic metal racks at the west end of the living room. Old Paint stood watch in my garage. The Dude had flung capfuls of bleach all over the white walls of the basement's kitchen/dining room, creating amazing and trippy designs when subjected to the glow of a blacklight. Two full-size arcade games (*Centipede* and *Amidar*) served as strange night lights in the living room. An inflatable, ten-foot diameter UFO promoting the VHS release of *Independence Day* consumed the east end of the living room.

An ex-girlfriend worked for Wal-Mart and snagged the spaceship for me, because I really loved that crappy early Will Smith blockbuster. We used it as a strange piece of furniture and as a toy when tripping. The multitude of crisscrossing white lines sometimes glowed and reached out to my friends and I.

Five of us, The Dude, Ben, Aaron, Charlie, and I, tripped away the last few hours of Christmas '96. We played video games and bounced around on the balloon. It was the start of a good trip on an otherwise horrendous holiday.

Baby Mama, the mother of Aaron's baby, never approved of our experimentations. She had dropped Aaron off earlier in the evening and returned to hang out at his parents' house. Later that night, she called him to threaten him. He informed us that he had to go or else she would call the police. The idea that the law could intertwine itself with our evening was a harsh idea to handle and brought the fear down upon us. The Dude assured us that if we were worried about our drugs, he'd take them off our hands for us. Aaron ran out of the basement and disappeared into the night.

The fear dissipated as we rode the acid roller coaster. We felt concern for Aaron, but we lived on the edge of the era where everybody carries a cell phone, so there was little we could accomplish from the relative safety of the Lighthouse.

Baby Mama's Ford Probe pulled into the driveway an hour later. She stayed in the car while Aaron came to talk with us.

"So I had to go to mom's, because I didn't want Baby Mama calling the pigs," explained a flush Aaron. "I ran back to mom's. Everywhere I ran, I was in the past. I ran past the old Wag-A-Bag (a convenience store which had changed owners and names several times since our childhood). Everything was just like it was in middle school. I got home and went upstairs without talking to anybody, but everybody was looking at me. Baby Mama went up, and we decided to drive to see the sun rise in Corpus Christi. See you!"

Aaron ran out again this time to take the first shift behind the wheel for the long drive south and left us wondering what the hell had just taken place. We returned to riding out the remainder of our trip.

New Year's Lost

My work took me to a National Guard Armory in a tiny town outside of Oklahoma City for a teacher's New Year's Eve party going into 1997. The educators happily shared their booze with their DJ. They danced. We all drank. The curtain of a new year descended upon us. I repacked my gear into Bonnie's rear and left for the drive home.

It didn't go as planned. I got lost in that pre-GPS age and somehow ended up far north of OKC with no clue how to get home. Tired and discouraged, I made a drastic decision: I would stop at the next intersection, pick a direction and head off in that direction until I discovered a recognizable landmark or town. The next intersection came. Putting my hearse in park, I jumped out, yanked a street sign out of the ground as proof of my lack of directional awareness and stowed it with my DJ gear. Luckily, my chosen direction proved to be the correct one, and I eventually made it home with an illegal souvenir of my discovery of the 235th block of OKC.

1997

Sex I Didn't Have

My most dysfunctional relationship in college involved a girl whose obsessive-compulsiveness put mine to shame. Krazy's cheeks flushed with rage when one of our crew would switch her salt and pepper shakers around in the house she and her sister rented across the street from mine.

Krazy and I met in a marketing course my junior year. DR. Feminist was our professor.

"I worked just as hard for my PhD. as any man. You WILL call me DOCTOR FEMINIST, not MISS FEMINIST or MRS. FEMINIST!" she said to start each semester.

She hated every man in her class. I loved the material in my marketing class, but my professor was a hard core, man-hating bitch.

I dated Krazy for a month. We never got past second base. That didn't bother me, but it's an important nugget of knowledge for what comes next.

A good friend of mine, Stan, ran around in our circle before transferring at the end of his freshman year to another school on a soccer scholarship (if you can believe that in America). I called over to Krazy's house one afternoon to see what she had planned for the evening.

"Hello," a groggy but contented male voice answered.

"Um...hello? Is Krazy there?"

"Richard? Is that you?"

"Holy shit!? Is this Stan?"

"Yeah, man I just got into town."

"What are you doing?"

"I just finished fucking Krazy."

"What the shit man?! That's my girlfriend!"

Stan hadn't visited since transferring.

"I'm sorry. I didn't know."

Right about that time, Krazy emerged from her bathroom. Her psychotic fit of rage traveled well through the phone line.

"Did you answer my goddamn phone!? Why the fuck did you do that!? What the fuck are you doing!? " she screamed at the poor boy.

"Richard, honestly, I didn't know you two were together," Stan pleaded over the barrage of her insanity.

"Brother, I know you didn't know."

"You want to get a beer?" he offered.

"Sure. Get dressed and get your ass over here."

Stan hung up as she continued scream at him. He walked across the street. We went to The Office, our favorite, and only, afternoon bar serving liquor, and got skunk drunk. Upon learning that Krazy and I had never soiled any sheets, he revealed that I really hadn't missed much.

I attended my next marketing class the following Monday morning. Krazy wasn't there, which I considered a good thing, since I didn't want to face her and her madness. In fact, I never saw her in class again.

From that morning on, DR. Feminist treated me like a sexist plague. I wonder what bullshit Krazy fed her favorite anti-penis professor to convince her to allow her to not have to attend class for the second half of the semester. Did Mrs. Feminist...I mean DR. Feminist believe me a rapist? What level of horror story would a woman have to concoct for a professor in order to be granted that kind of immunity? Considering that I never did more than touch her breasts a couple of times (consensually, I might add), and that Stan did bang her, I hope that DR. Feminist at least based Krazy's final grade in part on her creativity.

Krazy transferred to another school in the state the next semester where she eventually married, appropriately enough, her psychology professor.

Two Turntables and a Lot of LSD

I have had the privilege of seeing one of the most talented artists of my generation three times. I caught him at two festivals and while headlining his own *Odelay* tour in Oklahoma City. A large crew more than twenty strong of Buzzards and K-Town Mafia journeyed to the Oklahoma State Fairground's Travel and Transportation Building for the show. We thought we'd be smart and get to the building early, score great spots and pre-party in the parking lot for an hour or two. We planted our party of five cars next to the building. An hour passed without anyone outside of our group showing up. Knowing that the show would soon start, we walked around the building to see why we were alone - we had parked on the wrong side.

I dropped some acid and hit some whippets for my pregame action. The LSD began to take hold of me, and I got lost in the crowd before entering the building. The splitting of the crowd into two lines labeled "BOYS" and "GIRLS" further confused me as nobody was paying attention except for those of us under the influence of quality mind-altering substances.

Gaining entrance to the venue almost did me in. A truly shitactular and obnoxiously loud band, Atari Teenage Riot, had already taken the stage. My drug-addled brain couldn't make heads or tails of anything happening around me. Atari might have made a great video game system or two (I'm looking at you, 2600 and 5200), but it's a lousy band. They sang in German except for a song which had the band's name in its lyrics and when they asked us to riot. The fast, loud atrocities emanating from their instruments helped us appreciate the next band even more. I stumbled into a friend and stuck close to him for safety until we thankfully reached the intermission before The Roots came on. The Roots allowed me time to mellow out and enjoy some decent music.

Beck came out and rocked my universe. With Mixmaster Mike spinning wax for him, the pair turned my reality inside out. As magnificent as Beck was, Mike stole the show with his solo set. Wearing a bandanna over his face cowboy style, he flung vinyl over his shoulders and caught them behind his back, never skipping a beat in his mix.

The show ended like a supernova. I stood dazed as thousands filed past me on their way out of the building. My confusion served me well when The Roots' Questlove appeared for a few minutes to sign autographs, including my ticket stub.

Crazy Bitch Cut Off

One fine spring day in Western Oklahoma, I was driving eastbound through an intersection near the Lighthouse. North-south traffic had a stop sign. I did not. A woman in a nondescript sedan barreled northbound through the intersection, forcing me to swerve all the way into the oncoming lane to avoid a messy case of perpendicular car compaction.

I honked my horn, flipped the bird out of my window and got on with my life. Or tried to. That batty bitch devoted the next fifteen minutes of her life to chasing me around town, honking her horn and shaking her fist at me.

One of the town's four stoplights caught us. She exited her car to come give me a piece of her mind. Instead, I rolled up my window, shot her the double-bird and unleashed a thesaurus' page worth of synonyms for "crazy" at her. The light turned green, and off I went. She followed. At another light, she scribbled down my license plate number and pumped her fist in a misconceived notion of victory before finally driving off to harass some other poor soul.

A week or so later, a handful of police officers swung by the Lighthouse to evict the three hundred people who'd shown up for one of our Thursday night bashes. One of the officers took me aside for a little chat above and beyond our usual discussions about getting everyone out of my house and cleaning up my neighbors' yards (which was never an issue thanks to many years of Boy Scouts).

"Richard, did you have a confrontation on the road the other day?"

"Yeah, some insane woman ran a stop sign, almost hit me and then chased me all over town," I said, introducing the story you just read. He listened.

"She was definitely in the wrong, but you should be careful about who you flip off. It can be dangerous giving the bird to a state trooper's wife."

I think that it's far more dangerous to be a fucktard behind the wheel.

Funky Frankfurter Follies

As much weird shit as I ate when I was messed up, the D-Man put me to shame. Yet another P-ton amigo who once roomed with me at the Lighthouse, the D-Man was a chill, chain-smoking ninja with a severe sense humor you had to wait a long time to witness emerge from his serene shell. We pretty much had free run of Wahoo's apartment for a couple of years. Stoned out of his gourd one evening, the D-Man excavated an antique pack of hot dogs from the back of her fridge.

The D didn't bother to cook the five forgotten franks. Subsequently, he spent the next day in the hospital. Six of us paid him a visit, but not before getting totally ripped at Wahoo's. The cloud of herb enveloping us when we entered his room clung so strongly to our clothes that his nurse twice accused us of smoking something in his room after she'd stepped out. D-Man was pissed that we'd not only come to make fun of him but that we'd also gotten so high without him.

Forget Her Thrice

My roomies and I threw more than a few insane bashes at the Seventh Street Lighthouse. Many kegs perished at the mouths of my family, friends and strangers. As I explained earlier, some guests didn't have money for the beer barrels and instead paid by handing me random bits of drugs and pills. More than a few skipped my hand and deposited their "payments" directly into the 64oz glass beer mug from which I frequently swigged. Obviously, my memories of these affairs are sketchy at best. One party was especially fuzzy and had many "scene missing" fillers when I replayed the game film in my mind.

I woke late the next morning in my waterbed to find a pair of earrings on my headboard. This isn't as abnormal as it sounds, since those in my inner circle frequently used my room as a place to consume those substances they couldn't consume in front of others. Random bobbles often ended up in my room after a dozen or two people had spent the night partaking of a cornucopia of drugs. I thought nothing of it on this, or any other occasion, and tossed the earrings into a lost and found box I kept.

A month or so passed. Three friends came over with a request that I guide their mushroom adventure that night. The evening led to me driving them to a trailer house party on the north side of town. A cute girl on the front porch caught my eye.

"Good evening, my name's Richard. Who the hell are you?" I was not one known for his inspiring and/or effective pickup lines.

"My name is Ronnie, and we've met before," she shot off at me.

This brought a symphony of guffaws from my schroom-headed posse.

"Richard, don't you remember fucking her at your last party?" one of them blurted out. I had zero recollection of our horizontal mambo, nor did I land a second round with her that night.

Yet another month passed by, and I found myself at yet another party, where yet another cute girl caught my eye. I introduced myself. She spun around and stormed off with a, "hrmmph!" Your don't have to be a Rhodes Scholar to guess that I had met Ronnie for a third time. I do blame her for banging me while I was in such of an altered state of mind and then not sticking around until I woke the next morning/afternoon. Had I found her in my bed the next day, I would have asked her name one time and gotten it nailed. As it is, she never even came back for her earrings.

Everything Is Shittier in Texas

Some weekends were worse than others. Then there was my weekend in Texas. The Herpinator called me down to Dallas to do a series of shows in West Texas during prom season. I drove down to Plano to meet him at his house along with Rodney, another guy from our high school working for him.

In addition to his Hummer, Herps owned a trio of other trucks: a beat to shit Ford Ranger pickup, an older two-door Ford Explorer and a newer four-door Explorer. The older two were manuals, the latter an automatic. As you'll learn soon enough, I had not learned to drive a stick at this point in my life thanks to a hail storm.

The Herpinator instructed me to come to D-Town where I would pick up the new Explorer and drive on to my show. After making the four-and-a-half-hour drive south, he "suddenly remembered" that he had to take the new Explorer to pull a heavy trailer he somehow had forgotten about, sticking me with the older Explorer, a vehicle I didn't even know how to drive.

We hit the streets of Plano on Thursday evening where he gave me a crash course in using a stick. It did not go well, but I had done just well enough that, in his stoned eyes, he felt secure in sending me out in his old beater of a truck. We got high and had a couple of beers with dinner. I slept on his couch.

Our caravan rolled out early Friday afternoon, all of my gear crammed into the old Explorer alongside its hundreds of thousands of miles of history. Herps had told us that all three of us were to convoy south on Highway 75 until we were clear of Dallas. He called my cell just north of where a stretch of construction began to inform us that he had also magically remembered that both he and Rodney had to turn off onto I-30, leaving me to weave and crawl through the miles of construction solo. He had a talent for "forgetting" these crucial details until it was too late to react to them.

We split, and I entered one of the lower levels of hell for the next fifty-five hours.

The stop and start traffic did not bode well for my forty-five minutes of freshly minted manual driving skills. It didn't take long for things to fall apart. I had no problem with the stopping but began to experience increasing difficulty with the starting. US 75 narrowed to one lane with road cones blocking the passing lane, and construction crews occupying the shoulder. I completely blocked the lone lane on and off for two hours while covering a few measly miles. It got so bad that 18-wheelers began to plow through the traffic cones to get around me. Listening to a local rock station in an attempt to calm my increasingly frazzled nerves, I almost ejected my Slurpee when the DJ announced a traffic jam on South 75 with no known cause. Great, I'd made the news. The mostly Hispanic road crew laughed at me the whole time until I finally got my truck moving again.

My escape from Dallas proved a painful one. I got to a convenience store where I picked up a snack and then drove away with the emergency brake set for twenty minutes. The remainder of the afternoon passed quietly enough, considering my start. The show that night went off without a much of a hitch. My gear worked. The students in the tiny West Texas town danced. One guy in a cowboy-style tuxedo did approach me as I was setting up and instructed me to play both kinds of music: country and western. I stayed in a musty motel that night and got drunk alone on Lone Star.

If Friday's show took place in a tiny town, then Saturday's prom was held in a microscopic piece of nothing. I never found more than a few mobile homes clustered a mile away from a decrepit gas station shuttered since the formation of OPEC. The smallest gig throughout my career went as well as the previous night's had. Plenty of Garth Brooks, George Strait, Brooks & Dunn, and the usual selection of modern craptactular romantic ballads flowed from my 15" speakers that weekend.

The ride home was as crazy as the ride out had been. It would take me the whole night to return to D-Town. I reached the interstate and concocted my standard long haul go-to drink at a large truck stop. It starts with a cup meant for soda, 32oz or larger. Coffee, ice and plenty of sugar, along with any flavored creamer the store might happen to have, fill my deep cup of stay-awake-juice. It did its job for part of the night, but I soon found myself running low on energy.

I pulled off at a rest area to swallow a handful of ephedrine-heavy No Doz and to sleep. I conceived a plan based on my exhaustion guaranteeing a quick trip to sleepy town, and kick-starting my system after less than an hour's nap thanks to my cheap trucker speed.

It worked. I woke up behind the wheel with a jittery start and went to water the lilies before hitting the road again.

Waking to an alarm clock of gas station legal, low-grade meth skewed my senses. The bright fluorescent lights of the public toilet didn't help me any. I shuffled in and stood at the urinal closest to the door. It wasn't until a steady stream of processed coffee poured forth from me that I thought to look around my porcelain wonderland. Holy shit... Someone had Scotch-taped pages from man-on-man porno magazines all over the place. Everywhere I turned, homosexual men lustily glared at me from their various frozen positions of carnal pleasure.

It was then that I noticed the man standing at the farthest urinal. Topped by a black ball cap, he wore a black shirt over black pants with a black duffel bag draped over his left shoulder. This monochrome man looked over at me with a grin bordering between sheepish and malevolent. My mind began processing the situation. I quickly realized that there was not a snowball's chance in hell that your average homophobic Texan would have entered that restroom without tearing down or defacing at least one of the porn pages. I looked at the pristine pages in front of me and then at the man in black. While I had been dozing and waiting for my drugs to kick in, this guy had been papering the public pisser with pornographic penile pictorials.

Who knew what else he had in that duffel? I quickly re-holstered my meat pistol and made for the door. He maneuvered from where I had first spotted him to get between me and the door.

"What are you doing?" he asked in a serial killer's voice if ever I've heard one.

"Just going home."

He mumbled something that I couldn't understand. I made the mistake of asking him to repeat himself.

"What do you like to do for fun?"

"Umm..." was the best response I could concoct at the time.

"Would you like to have some fun?"

"What?" I stupidly asked.

"Can I suck your dick?"

"No. No thank you." I couldn't come up with an answer as to what I did for fun, but I sure was respectful when turning down a free gay BJ.

I got out to the truck on fast feet and pounded some pavement. I drove well above the speed limit for the next hour. I didn't even slow down when an armadillo exploded beneath my right front tire.

The sun had just broken over the horizon as I hit the outer edge of D-Town. I made a beeline for the Herps' place where I managed to spurt out this crazy tail before crumpling on the couch for some much needed recovery.

The Texas Chainsaw Farce-acre
Memorial Day Weekend

To date, the longest relationship I've had with a woman was with Bonnie, my hearse. As much as I loved her, I could not rely on her for many of the longer road trips I made. I used her strictly for my in-state DJ work and camping trips out to local lakes, usually Ft. Cobb. She accompanied me on exactly one trip across state lines. Scooby had grown up down the street from my family. We took her to Texas on a historical/hysterical fact-finding mission.

Long a fan of the old slasher flicks, I convinced Scooby to head south with me to research the "real" story behind *The Texas Chainsaw Massacre*. The movie begins with a then unknown John Larroquette's now infamous introduction:

The film which you are about to see is an account of the tragedy which befell a group of five youths…The events of that day were to lead to the discovery of one of the most bizarre crimes in the annals of American history, *The Texas Chain Saw Massacre*.

We were quite certain that some element of truth to the classic splatter film existed but were unsure as to exactly how much truth it held. We were determined to find out. In case you have yet to view this low budget masterpiece, its sequels or its reboot, the original movie very loosely based itself upon the crimes of Ed Gein. Ed Gein only murdered two women. More a digger than a killer, he was a creative grave robber/interior designer who fashioned human remains into skin lampshades and seat covers, a belt of nipples and skull bowls. Hollywood has used elements of his story to inspire such horror classics as *Psycho, Silence of the Lambs* and *Titanic*. Gein operated out of Wisconsin. Not Texas. We didn't have the Evilnet in those days to guide us and provide us with porn.

We met with the Herpinator in Dallas for a night of heavy weed toking to either pick up or drop off some piece of equipment that has long since slipped the craggy recesses of my cranium. Before we left town, Herps led us to a restaurant recently cobbled together by an acquaintance of his. Not yet open for business, he offered us a sampling of his mostly fried fare: fish, gator and sides. He also brought out a plate of raw oysters, a creature I had yet to allow access to my gullet.

My first and only raw oyster to date didn't call my body home for long. It took longer to get it down than it did to get it back up. Luckily, we had plenty of beer to stabilize my stomach. Our restaurateur didn't have a liquor license, nor had he any intention of obtaining one. He figured that it wasn't against the law to give draft beer away. I never returned to his restaurant and have no idea how it turned out for him. Our bellies and bladders filled, Scooby and I made our way north.

Our expedition took us into the southeastern parts of the Texan Panhandle to the small town of Childress. I chose this as it was the only town to receive a mention in the movie.

Everyone we questioned in the town gave us the cold shoulder. We took this to mean that we had caught the trail. In retrospect, I believe that they were more likely frustrated with uninformed stoners pestering them with questions about a horrific Hollywood-created tragedy which never took place based on a terrible true tragedy with very little in common between the two. We did find a little museum of creepy art and a few rundown and/or abandoned buildings.

To console our lack of findings, we picked up a few cases of six-point beer, a common Texas goal for Okies doomed to 3.2 piss outside of liquor stores. Hoping to camp out at a lake, we discovered the gate shut and no way onto the grounds after dark. This left us pulling off of the highway at a random exit to slam beers, get stoned and pass out for the night. A few hours slipped by without incident.

Well into the bag, I suddenly freaked out. We had taken care to cover the windows, but could still see out through a few slots. The flashing lights of a highway patrolman's car slipped through a couple of the cracks in our shell.

We stashed our herb and open containers. Considering the nature of my Bonnie, this was easier done than said. We had two cases chilling in one particularly deep storage compartment lined with Hefty trash sacks to get us through the evening. I told Scooby to wait and stepped outside before the bubblegum machine had rolled to a complete stop.

The patrolman threw open his door and told me to halt. I'd had the forethought to stick my empty hands out in front of me to indicate my lack of intentions and weapons.

"Stop there, son," he warned me. "What're yew doin' out in these pahts?" He drawled as though he would have been more at home atop a horse on a ranch a century before.

"I'm just traveling back to Oklahoma and pulled over to sleep for the night," I said through a cottonmouth spewing alcohol vapors.

"Uh'd feel a might better if yew wuh to drive on up the road a few miles. There's a rest stop there. It's got lights in the lot and there's a toilet. Yew'll be safer."

"Okay, officer. I appreciate the help," I said, turning back to my Bonnie, happy that we never got closer than fifteen feet to each other.

Hoping that I was walking a straight enough line, I got behind the wheel and started my old girl up.

"What did he say?" asked Scooby, wondering whether or not we'd be making a detour to the local hoosegow.

"He suggested a place up the road with a toilet where we can get drunker and more stoned!"

The few miles passed quickly enough as we settled into our patrolman-approved spot for the night. A pair of hitchhikers wandered by an hour later. We shared our beers, and they sparked a joint before heading back out onto the road, leaving us to our own devices.

D.U.I.:
Drinking Under the Intelligence

Dad bought a 1964 Chevy pickup to rebuild and use to teach Goober and myself how to drive. Our parents wanted us well acquainted with the fundamentals of driving a stick before we moved on to lazier automatic transmissions. It took him a few years, but it was worth the wait and effort.

Plush red interior with a flat black paint job outside, she was a thing of beauty. Goober and I couldn't wait to get our hands on her, but alas, it was not meant to be.

While most non-Okies tend to only associate our state with tornadoes, meth labs and racism, we do get our fair share of hail. Frozen balls of ice, wooden roofing shingles and an antique wooden chest kept me from learning to drive stick for many years.

For some mysterious reason, many Oklahomans used to cover their homes in cedar shake shingles. These particular shingles didn't completely cover the roofs they're meant to protect. Standing in an Oklahoma attic on a sunny afternoon, shafts of light spilled over forgotten possessions throughout the dusty space. The first few drops of rain to hit caused them to expand so that their edges pressed together, creating a watertight seal.

A massive hail storm struck Western Oklahoma in the spring of 1989. It hit without any rain preceding it. Fast falling ice chunks shattered more than ninety percent of the shingled roofs in my town. This brought about a flood of roofers to replace and correct the errors of our ways.

This all went down as Mom was putting the finishing touches on a wooden trunk we'd brought back to Oklahoma from her aunt in Mississippi. Dad usually kept the Chevy in the garage but put it out on the street for a night, so Mom could stain the trunk.

The re-roofing of our little burg had necessitated the influx of a small army of contractors of various levels of trustworthiness. Several of the more unscrupulous of the bunch had no issue hiring labor of questionable legal status. The truck didn't last a single night on the street.

Waking at 4 a.m. for his job driving a semi-truck to haul an MRI machine he operated and maintained to smaller hospitals around the state, he took a look outside the kitchen window and noticed a vacant spot where his truck should have been. We never again saw the truck he had spent so many hours lovingly restoring. If you ever come across a 1964 Chevy truck with a softball-sized dent on its front left fender, give me a shout and claim a reward. From that point on, Mom's trunk earned the sarcastic title of "Mom's $5,000 Trunk." I wouldn't learn to drive a stick until a strange evening in Dallas in my early twenties.

I never took a driver's education course. I never even so much as started a car before the morning of my sixteenth birthday. I had, however, played a lot of *Mario Cart*. Mom, Goober and I piled into her old station wagon for my first lesson on the mostly empty roads north of town. Clueless didn't begin to describe me.

I pulled the steering wheel back and forth in comically dangerous arcs. My foot couldn't decide whether to pound or tap the gas. All it knew for sure was that it never wished to apply any sort of consistent pressure. By the time we returned home, Mom was ready to French kiss the ground and take up smoking again. My skills behind the wheel would improve over the years, although not by much.

My first driving test didn't go well. I aced the written exam, only missing the four questions about motorcycles which I hadn't known would appear on my paper. When it came to the actual driving test, I didn't even manage to finish it.

High schoolers in my area feared taking this test. We had a notorious examiner who smoked cigars in his testers' vehicles, whether they liked it or not. Most didn't. By the time my people came of testing age, he had quit the stogie. He also quit me.

I bumped around town without driving too erratically. When it came to parallel parking, I was quite perpendicular. Mom and Dad taught me little more than the basics. The instructor pointed to a car parked curbside in the middle of an otherwise empty block and told me to pretend another car sat behind it and to park parallel between them. I pulled up alongside the real car and swung in behind it, reversing nearly back to the intersection before moving forward again. He informed me that I had driven completely through the imaginary car. Twice.

"Return to the station now," he commanded.

Back at the police station, he reviewed my results or lack thereof. I had failed. I had failed embarrassingly, miserably even. He gave me a list of the areas I needed to work on, which pretty much included everything but putting on my seatbelt.

Oklahoma law states that if a person fails his driving examination, then he must wait another three months before he can retest. Having a late August birthday, I was already the second-youngest in my class and one of only two without a license at the start of our junior year. Now I would have to wait until November to try again. For reasons I never deduced, nearly no extra practice took place during the following quarter year.

November crept around at such a maddeningly slow pace that I would have sworn it had been riding shotgun with me. I retook the test. He didn't ask me to parallel park this time. Nervously, I returned to the station. The examiner once again reviewed my results. He began by giving me a nearly identical rundown of my previous laundry list of mistakes. I knew what was coming: Another ninety days of a learner's permit loomed heavily on my horizon.

"I totaled your score twice. You received a seventy. Sixty-nine is a failing grade. You really must work on…" The rest of his speech was drowned out by rounds of applause from the sold-out crowd in the stadium of my mind.

I never did learn to parallel park.

Doin' the Crime
Not Tryin' to Do the Time

If you haven't gathered by now that I tend to drink heavily, then you have been reading this book in as drunkenly of a state as I was in when I lived and then wrote it. Through all of those years of hard drinking, I have had numerous close encounters with the law. The law of averages dictates that I would eventually get caught, and I did…

Most of my non-high school-related DJing gigs involved alcohol. SWOSU didn't have many Greek organizations. Our campus' largest sorority claimed several of my friends among its members, including Val Hollar. They called upon me to play their Spring Formal for a second time in 1997. I would turn 21 that

August. I loaded my gear into my van and pointed it in the direction of their hotel in OKC.

I'd gotten a friend to scare me up a few bottles of Mad Dog 20/20, my early liquid weakness. I knocked these bottles of homeless juice back along with all of the alcohol the girls and their dates supplied me with in our hotel banquet room.

The party drew to a close. My playing a lot of Jimi Hendrix didn't help draw the festivities out further. I loaded my equipment and received an envelope of cash and a six-pack of mismatched beers.

Knowing that I was in no condition to make even the straight one-hour drive west to Waterford, I opted to instead drive into the heart of OKC to crash at Boozer's, my Mom's closest friend from nursing school. I made a wrong turn on my way up to her house south of the Penn Square Mall and ended up on Lake Hefner Drive.

I killed the six-pack and attempted to pull into the driveway of a house on a side road off of Hefner. In my fucktarded state, I managed to completely miss the driveway, popping the curb while pulling up under the branches of a tall tree set off to the right of the drive. Thank goodness for the high clearance of a full-size Chevy van.

My swerving bulky vehicle had attracted the attention of a pair of undercover detectives some time before. They watched me stop beneath the tree and arrested me.

My first, and so far only full night in the clink (knock on wood), was traumatic as an experience but not as traumatic as an ass-rape. Oklahoma County Jail performed an *Alice's Restaurant* on me by removing my shoelaces and belt so I couldn't hang myself over my DWI and by taking my wallet so I wouldn't have any cash to spend on the myriad of items not available in their drunk tank.

I shared their tank with two other people, both already in residence when I arrived. Mario happened to have a daughter working as a maid at the hotel I'd spun at. He was drunk, friendly and talkative. The third member of our trio, a man I dubbed "Ace," was a muscle-bound black man with a tattoo of an ace of spades playing card on his upper shoulder visible thanks to his stained wife beater.

Ace spent the night sleeping on his left side, facing the wall. He didn't stir until the guards roused us the next morning for "breakfast." They gave us each a cheap cafeteria tray with a slice of un-toasted Texas toast, a slice of what (for the first time in my life) I hoped was Spam and a scoop of somewhat still-powdered eggs. Not that there exists an awards ceremony for jail food, but I pray that OK County would never rank anywhere above the dankest bottom of those awards... If that's the food they give to folks convicted of nothing yet, I feared what people in proper lockup were forced to get down their gullets.

Officers herded our trio out that morning for processing. Although I can't recall what it was, no less than a few of the guards knew Ace by his real name. I would say that it usually pays to be a repeat customer at most places of business, but I had just spent the night at the one exception to this rule. It didn't help that he was a grumpy, argumentative wanker. They shot our mugs, took our fingerprints and gave us our phone calls.

My parents had a long-standing rule that when and/or if Goober or I were ever arrested, they were the last people we should call. They were more than happy to pick us up at any time, day or night, if we were too fudged to drive, but if we had gotten our asses arrested, we should consider them persona non grata. Unlike Goober, I took this to heart.

I considered calling the Boozer, the woman on whose couch I'd originally intended on crashing the previous evening. Instead, I sweet-talked the operator into tracking down Ben's new number. A friend of mine from high school and the provider of my Xmas Jesus five months previous, he'd just moved to OKC with his wife, Leslie.

They agreed to blow off their Sunday to bail me out and assist me in rescuing my van from impound. We spent the day bouncing between far North and South OKC in this effort. If you've never been, then you don't understand exactly the amount of effort involved in this undertaking. OKC was not too long ago listed as the nation's largest city in terms of land mass, until Anchorage annexed some land and took that title.

We put some serious miles on Ben's truck until we got to the point where I was finally ready to un-impound my van. The yard required the pink slip which my parents kept at home. Late afternoon had come. I had done everything I could the past seven horribly hungover hours to keep this from Mom and Dad until I had believed that I could drive up to their house and explain what had gone down in the comfort of their living room. Instead, Mom had to drive out with the pink slip and pick me up from Ben and Leslie's.

A day as strange as that would be far from complete without a bit more oddness occurring. We bought the van's freedom, which I was able to drive thanks to the 8x11 sheet of paper the police had given me to serve as my license until I'd resolved my case one way or another. Mom and I caravanned, ironically enough, to Boozer's place. I dropped off the van and rode with Mom and Boozer to more irony. The Lighthouse was a bar on near Boozer's house. Nearly recovered at long last from one of those drawn out hangovers resulting from the most unfortunate of self-inflicted circumstances, the bartendress asked for my ID.

"He is my son. Do you really believe that I would bring my own son in here if he wasn't old enough to buy himself a drink?" asked Mom, challenging the bartender.

To this day, her and Boozer's actions remain a mystery to me. I still can't believe that they rewarded my failed attempted to cover up my DWI by getting me slightly drunk and letting me drive the hour home on I-40.

Deconstruction

Advanced Development provided me with my strangest summer. The Dude, also landed a job with this absurd construction outfit. We embarked on a summer adventure neither of us fully understands to this day. AD had been hired to build a nursing home on the east side of town. Most of the building's structure already stood by the time we joined their crew. AD's people from Eastern Oklahoma lived in RV trailers on the site. None of them spoke English. Or Spanish. Or any other discernible language. They all sounded like *King of the Hill*'s Boomhower. We understood but two or three words from them any time they gave us a task.

"Mmmaourf soffta doun blazer you damn boys," they often informed/ordered us. Or maybe questioned us. We were never certain. Sometimes they referred to us as, "you goddamn boys," for a little variety, and we could understand it when they said, "fuck." They dropped F-bombs on us like real bombs on Cambodia and Laos.

The Dude and I had to guess at the nature of each job assigned to us. We spent one week on the nursing home's considerable lot raking dirt for eight hours a day. We weren't seeding the lot, nor were we redistributing fresh soil. We simply made rake marks on the ground for a week in the sun.

In one of our more concrete tasks, we assisted in pouring concrete for the home's circular driveway. They later moved us inside to clean and do odd jobs as it neared completion.

Willie, a wiry-haired, pot-bellied Hispanic-looking guy, usually had the job of giving us our daily instructions. An angry, incomprehensible beast of a man, he resembled Wolverine's clawless, schizophrenic fourth cousin loaded on PCP. He took joy in screaming at us. The Dude had had his fill of it one day and jumped into his car, a little grey thing affectionately nicknamed, "the Flintstone," and peeled out as best as he could waving a middle finger out the window at AD's mush-mouthed morons.

I stayed on against my better judgment, as only a few weeks in the summer remained. I showed up day to day to complete seemingly meaningless tasks. AD maintained a large hole on the northern side of the property they used to dump empty and nearly empty containers of oil, paint and assorted chemicals. They later filled in the hole. Waterford City Hall didn't give a shit when I reported this to them.

Waiting for the Axe to Fall

The following year brought little joy as I learned my lesson. My 21st birthday fell two months later, forcing me to bounce around bars displaying my 8x11 sheet of paper in lieu of a plastic-coated license.

I have had plenty of automotive accidents, but only two were my fault. On the afternoon of my 21st, I pulled out of the infamously accident-prone entrance to our old Wal-Mart and a Pontiac Grand Prix tagged the rear driver's side corner panel of my hearse hard enough to spin me around in a complete circle. I got out of that one only because she was speeding and was an illegal alien. It totaled her car and broke my bumper in half. Dad and I later dug a big piece of metal from her car out of my fender as though it were a hunk of meat stuck in my Bonnie's teeth after a plate of ribs. Dad kept it and always talked of framing it.

My little side trip to the hospital wasn't going to put the brakes on my birthday. I went to my parents' for a surprise party which I screwed up by having to return to the Lighthouse shortly after leaving to pick up my camera, only to find my home suddenly vacated. The party still rocked the house until we had to move on to round two.

The Herpinator was DJing a party in the courtyard in front of Waterford's lone sports bar (it served beer and food I wouldn't toss on the floor alongside the shells of the joint's complimentary peanuts) and had convinced a friend working at a Dallas radio station to "borrow" his employer's promotional gas-guzzling monster for the weekend. I consumed my first "official" beer at midnight on top of the back of that truck. We'd parked it in the bar's courtyard to use as a prop. The evening concluded with me puking all over the door of the semi-stolen Hummer as it sat parked in the lot of our honky-tonk bar for round three. I would throw up on one more Hummer, but that wouldn't come for another year in another state.

Not having had any experience with legal entanglements, I decided to seek the counsel of an attorney to see whether or not I had any options. I hired Jed Clampet. Mr. Clampet, Esq. was listed as the numero uno DUI attorney in OKC. Not quite what I had expected of a high-end lawyer, he certainly earned his nickname. My attorney could pass for Jed Clampet from *The Beverly Hillbillys* twin, albeit in a much nicer suit.

His office, however, was no room the real Mr. Clampet would ever set one of his worn boots in. *Star Trek* memorabilia coated most every square inch of the hardwood. Plates, action figures and models ranging across the *Star Trek* television and movie franchises gave me the idea that anybody this weird was probably a good lawyer or had a basement filled with women chained to the walls wearing Lt. Uhura and Seven of Nine uniforms.

For two grand he offered to take my case under the belief that he could get me off. I weighed blowing the cash against not being able to drive for six months when one of my two jobs was <u>mobile</u> DJing. Losing my license would remove the "mobile" from my business, and I doubted that any Oklahoma high school had any desire to hold its prom in my living room.

I gave a deposition, and the case went to court. Mr. Clampet didn't require my presence for this. We won on a technicality concerning the calibration of the breathalyzer. I had blown a 0.18, nine times the legal limit for a minor behind the wheel. Having grown up playing Atari 2600 and Nintendo, I couldn't help but feel a small amount of pride at scoring so high, even if I didn't get to put my initials on any scoreboard.

Not desiring a loss on its record and having deep coffers of tax payer money to burn through rather than using to improve our low-ranked public schools, the state appealed. This made Mr. Clampet mad, fightin' mad. He agreed to handle the appeal against those polecats for free. I couldn't say no to this deal.

We lost.

Mr. Clampet explained that he could not take my case to the Oklahoma State Supreme Court for free. It would cost upwards of 20 grand. That was most definitely not worth six months of not walking. I paid him, thanked him and threw in the beer-soaked towel.

Last Call for Driving

Nearly one year had passed since my original arrest. I rode with Mom to OKC's Department of Public Safety one last time. I had to give a final deposition in a cramped basement room with a court reporter and my pair of arresting detectives. Mom stayed in the van to read a John Grisham paperback.

I entered the building for my 2 p.m. appointment knowing full well that in less than an hour's time, I would at last have to face the inevitable repercussions of my drunken mistake made a year previous. Detective #1 sat in the cafeteria waiting for us to begin. I took a seat at his table. Through my various meetings along this process, I had gotten to know my captors. They were nice guys, and I'm not one to be a dick to them just because they were doing their job. I was the one who broke the law and was stupid enough to get caught. It was a quarter to two.

With the hour hand precisely accusing the cafeteria clock's two, the court reporter stepped into the cafeteria and approached us.

"Where is Detective #2?" she asked.

"In court," replied Detective #1.

"Okay. I'll see you in fifteen minutes." She walked out.

Detective #1 and I continued chatting for another quarter of an hour until the reporter returned.

"Has Detective #2 arrived yet?"

"No, he's still in court."

"Okay. Mr. Lichman, you're free to go," she said, leaving without giving me an opportunity to respond.

"Detective #1, what was that? What does she mean, I'm 'free to go,'" I asked, more than slightly puzzled.

"My partner is at a trail right now and couldn't be here."

"So when do I come back?"

"You don't. You're free to go."

"What...?"

"Because both of your arresting officers couldn't be here for the deposition, the state has to drop the case."

I dropped my jaw.

It turned out that Detective #2 had been first on the scene at an OKC honky tonk homicide months before. A man had found his ex-wife at the bar with another man. He took his ex's new man out to the parking lot and boot-stomped his skull in. It turns out that a murder trial ranks somewhat above a DWI deposition on most detectives' lists of priorities.

I had gotten off. I could neither believe nor understand it. I walked outside to the van in a daze cloudier than the drunken state in which I'd originally been arrested a year ago.

"Richard, are you okay?" asked Mom upon seeing my drawn, pale face.

"I won."

"What?"

"A man got stomped to death. I can drive again."

It didn't make any sense, but it had worked.

Shitilogue

My family and I have a strange relationship with death. Anytime death comes into our lives, it comes in triplicate like office paperwork from the sixties. Within two hours of leaving the DPS building, we'd learned that my parents' best friend's father had dropped dead, and that my girlfriend's best friend's father had died in a tractor rollover.

I'd like to say that I learned a lesson from all of this, and that I never again got behind the wheel after drinking, but that wouldn't exactly be honest. I did, however, become more careful about it and never drove anywhere nearly that drunk again. I can now say that I don't do it all anymore, but that's mostly due to living in Korea where owning a car is rather unintelligent for a person who has no family and spends as much time out of the country as I do. The amount of breathalyzer checkpoints here also helps combat this plague. I have since turned paranoid enough that I no longer do it when I return to WLOTUS for a visit. I guess that is some sort of progress.

I fought the law, and I got off on a technicality.

Boscoe's Loosest Lodge

Waterford, Oklahoma once had a bar. It was one of the greatest bars on the planet. Known loosely as "the Loose," it was a biker bar on the outskirts of town. It had one drawback: Oklahoma's puritanical booze laws. Okie establishments have three licensing options: 3.2 percent (low-point) beer; high-point beer; and wine and full-on liquor. The Loose more than made up for its watery beer with its backyard beer garden where patrons partook of numerous high-point self-supplied alternatives when they thought the bartenders weren't looking.

The Loose began its life as a beer bar in Waterford's downtown. It backed up to and shared an alley with the D.U.I. Bar. The Loose moved into a new building outside of town decades ago. Somebody torched the popular biker bar.

Alanis, the owner, was determined not to let her haven perish. Still holding her beer license, she hauled out coolers filled with iced-down brewskis to sell from the bar's bare concrete slab. She began each day by taking the previous day's proceeds to a local hardware store to invest in supplies. She then lugged whatever random construction materials she'd procured to the slab to install in a drawn-out reconstruction process. She managed to rebuild the bar one 2x4 and concrete cinder block at a time. Bikers stood exposed to the elements as the business slowly rebuilt around them like a scene out of the original *The Time Machine* film.

I worked at the Loose for almost three years in total. Before I started, part of its charm was that minors could occasionally score some beers, depending on the bartender. I managed this feat more than a few times before my 21st birthday. A complication leading up to my legalization almost screwed this up completely.

Some friends of mine and I journeyed out to the Loose late one night. Classic rock blared from the jukebox as we threw darts and shot pool. Sandy the bartender, a late 40-something blond stereotype, asked us for IDs. All in our troop but I could produce one, perpetually being the youngest in my crew. She didn't bother to boot me, telling me instead not to drink. That lasted almost five minutes.

Sandy nailed me on the second beer I tried to covertly chug. Logic would dictate that she should've thrown my underaged ass out. Instead, she scolded me and let us stay as long as I didn't drink again.

I snatched my third cup a couple minutes later and was immediately caught. "That's it! You are banned for life!" Sandy screamed at me. She didn't bother to kick me out. She just felt obliged to inform me that I was banned for life as the bar came within forty minutes of closing time. We stuck around a few more minutes, went out to our cars for some more booze and then went to a party, thinking nothing more of the incident.

Less than two months later, I returned to the Loose to report for my first day of work. Mom knew Alanis and her daughter very well. This resulted in me having been done a solid.

I strolled in at a quarter 'til 8 p.m. for my first night shift. Sandy manned the bar waiting to leave after a usually uneventful afternoon shift.

"What are you doing here? I banned you for life! You can never come in here ever again!" Sandy roared.

"Shut up. That's Richard. He works here now," said Alanis from behind her bottle of Bud Light.

A befuddled Sandy showed me the ropes and left with the quickness. Thus began a wild ride.

The Loose was a magnificent den of debauchery. The day and night shifts were as different as…well as different as night and day or weed and meth.

Day shifts involved arriving before 2 p.m. and not doing much besides some light cleaning and occasional heavy drug use until the 8 p.m. changeover. The Loose had a foul jar of pickled eggs and a rack of snack-sized bags of off-brand potato chips. The afternoon shift also had happy hour. A short parade of drunks celebrating dollar Buds and Coors changes the way people see the universe. Mostly, it confirms a few stereotypes.

Some conversations became repetitive at the Loose, especially during the afternoon shift.

"Hey man, I don't have any money for a tip today. I've just got enough for a few beers, so here's a (insert drug here)," said many patrons who followed this up by slipping a joint or pill into one of my tip jars.

"There's no ATM here, and I don't have cash for a tip. You wanna do a line in the storeroom?"

"Can I smoke this here?

"You wanna smoke this with me?"

"Have you ever had one of these?"

I miss the Loose.

Smart bartenders at the Loose didn't drink too much on the job, because they often had to drive home carrying more drugs than they had shown up to work with.

Irregulars

We had some wild regulars. Being in a small Western Oklahoma college town, we had a healthy mix of college kids, townies, meth heads, Indians, and bikers.

Two large 40-something Indian women hated each other with extreme, drunken passion. It didn't matter which one entered first, the second to arrive would charge screaming like an Indian on the warpath from a semi-racist John Wayne western and attack the other woman. Beer always flew, tables upended and we herded the buffalo out until they would return a week or two later to repeat their performance.

The Loose saw its fair share of morons as well. I had to refuse service one night to a young idiot sporting his high school graduation class t-shirt...from five months previous!

My favorite second-hand Loose story came from a part-time regular who opened up to me one late afternoon when we were alone and stoned. Boscoe's regulars had the greatest stories to share after they'd properly lubricated themselves.

"The best five bucks I ever spent was in '69. A fiver got me into Zeppelin's first Chicago concert, the best hit of acid I ever dropped and the best blow job I ever had," one of the regulars told me one lovely liquefied afternoon. As much I love the Zep and LSD, I wondered as to what kind of blow jobs the guy received during the subsequent twenty-seven years. This is the same guy who once confided in me that he was blasted out of his gourd on LSD when he made his first parachute jump after getting drafted and sent to Vietnam.

115

Among our pool tables, dart boards, pinball machines, and various video games, we had two video poker machines. They were not for gambling…unless you knew somebody. A small notebook behind the bar tracked the payouts. Some guys waited outside for us to open at 2 p.m. when we arrived to get on the machine and would still be with the night bartender when he tried to close at 2 a.m. Sometimes they stayed later. As long as it was someone in cahoots with the owner, we didn't have to close, only lock the door at closing time. As long as whoever was forcing me to stay bought me beers, I didn't mind leaving until after the sun had risen.

Larry was one of our poker players. Larry, since passed on, was a little stick figure of man with a friendly laugh always cut short by his debilitating emphysema or lung cancer or something. He drove a beautiful beast of an old Cadillac and dragged an oxygen tank behind him. He spent all of his many hours at the Loose switching back and forth between sucking on a Camel, a bottle of Coors Light and his oxygen mask.

Of course it wasn't just the regulars who made an impression. One guy showed up with a stack of cash right before happy hour while I was working a quiet day shift.

"Hey there, I'm getting divorced. That bitch is going to get everything, so I want to make sure there's nothing to get. I'm going around to every bar I can find and dropping a hundred bucks. Let your people drink this 'til it's gone." And he left. And we drank. Thank you, mysterious, broke, divorced man.

Alanis would allow her bartenders to close up the bar a couple of hours early on the rare nights when we had no customers. I accomplished this once in my years I there. I almost managed a second early closing one night. So certain was I that I was going to get to close, that I munched some mushrooms I had on me. I was shutting the doors when a half-dozen cars pulled into the parking lot. A group of my friends wanted to come out and play for the night. I had to work the following four hours through a curtain of fungus-induced haze. Except for not always being able to distinguish different beer labels, I did well, all things considered.

I nearly came to live at the Loose one time. Alanis built a quaint, one-bedroom apartment into the bar's A-frame roof. With an entrance in the rear, it would have been comfortable for anyone who wished to be outside of town and close to beer.

She later rented it to a local the authorities suspected of having gone on a robbery spree. She let the county mounties, including Deputy Dicks, into the apartment to search for evidence. When they turned up nothing, Alanis asked if she could have a shot at it. Their search ended once she reached the closet wall. It was not the wall she'd built - this one made the room way too shallow. With the cops watching, she Chuck Norris-kicked in the fake wall the guy had slapped into place to conceal his large collection of stolen goods.

Bathroom Conquested

Many great sex tales involve drugs, bars and booze. This one just happens to take place in a bar known for the consumption of drugs...after a bit of boozing.

The Catholic Schoolgirl was my first long-term girlfriend and remains one of the best. One drunken night during one of my shifts at Boscoe's Loose Lodge, some of the sisters in our group got it into their heads that it would be a lark to try to have sex with their respective boyfriends in the girls' room. They had to inscribe the details of their conquests on a stall wall for all to bear witness to after defiling the foul room. They didn't let the boys in on their master plan, declaring it more sporting if they had to lure them in without knowing it was a competition.

"Richard, there's something wrong with one of the toilets in the girls' room," said the Schoolgirl, knowing full well how craptactular Boscoe's plumbing was.

"What's the problem," I asked looking around once inside.

The bathroom door swung shut as the Schoolgirl yanked away the chair propping it open. I turned. She grabbed me, kissed me passionately and forced me down onto the chair. She wore a skirt that night (probably as much because she knew how much I liked her legs as much as for ease of access) and straddled me. The deed completed, we cleaned up as much as the rustic bar's bathroom allowed and rejoined our compatriots.

The story didn't come out for a long time. By then I had an idea due to the amount of time I spent each week cleaning the women's room and noticing the fresh graffiti. Most of the sisters managed to accomplish their missions, but the Schoolgirl finished hers first.

Blow Jobs for Beer

I only drove drunk so often in college, because I was so often drunk. Jizzball and I tended to maintain the same level of un-sobriety in those days. For a while, he dated the Uzi Floozi, a girl who worked at a wild cowboy clothing store that also displayed and sold her namesake among other semi-automatic weapons straight out of your basic mid-eighties action movie. Like many of his girlfriends back then, she was a skinny little thing who couldn't begin to hold her alcohol even if she'd had a bucket.

The three of us spent a night cruising the farm roads outside of town in Jizz' two-door Chevy pickup. We had to listen to the radio, because a copy of KISS' *Destroyer* had gotten stuck in the CD player and would only play "Beth." The official cut-off for shitty, underpowered beer sales in Oklahoma, 2 a.m., had long since come and gone. Our last beer rightfully belonged to me. The Uzi Floozi coveted my beer.

"Jizz, tell Richard to give me his beer," the Uzi Floozi pleaded.

Jizz chuckled in the way he did when something was funny to him and likely insulting or infuriating to someone else. "Sorry hon, but it's Richard's."

"Richard, give me your beer!"

"No can do, darlin'. It's my last," I replied. Therefore, no incentive existed to compel me to give up my beer. She wasn't my girlfriend, and I correctly doubted she'd be his much longer.

"Jizz. Tell. Him. To. Give. Me. That. Beer," she spat, as she started to sweat crazy.

"I can't."

"Richard. I'll suck your dick for that beer," she offered.

"Is that cool with you Jizz?" I checked.

"It's your beer," he got out between laughs.

"Hold on. Jizz, what will you give me for the beer, so she'll give you the blow job?" I countered.

"Nothing. I've had her blow jobs before."

I kept the beer.

K-Town Harvest

Joining more than seventy percent of the Americans willing to admit it, the majority of my people and I smoked a lot of ganja during our university years. Western Oklahoma's weed once all came from the

118

lower quality Mexican bud smuggled north. Kind, hydro, Northern Lights, and all of the fancy buds that have since become commonplace in most of America were relatively unknown to us. We were always on the hunt for alternatives. One of those fell into our laps.

A couple of the K-Town Mafia Boys discovered a large patch of wild marijuana growing on a farm outside of their town. Our crew decided to assist the farmer by alleviating him of some of his accidental but still illegal plants. The harvest was on like Donkey Kong in the Viet Cong!

Seven us of piled into L-Ron's GMC Jimmy putting the rear seats down so we could all cram in to sit on the floor. We left Lolla in the truck to drive away for thirty minutes and left Gokey with her to entertain/torture her. Those two didn't always get along too well. They dropped the rest of us off at the edge of the property.

Outfitted in black as though about to knock over a bank for one last haul before retirement, we stuffed Hefty bags for the next half-hour. We looked like we were kids who'd won one of the old Nickelodeon Kay Bee Toy Hobby toy spree contests. The truck returned at the appropriate time to perform our extraction. Jubilant celebration was the theme for our triumphant return trip. That's not to say that it was a completely relaxed trip, either. We had a half-dozen garbage bags overflowing with cannabis stuffed into the back of the Jimmy. Despite the air of joviality, we still faced a very serious victory ride back to Waterford.

Some of our spoils went towards cooking, some towards smoking. Hours were spent cleaning our plants so that we could dry them for later usage. This was not our greatest moment.

The herb used for cooking emitted a wet stench in every pot of spaghetti and pan of brownies. The herb used for smoking forced us to blaze an unholy amount to simply cop a buzz. When it came time to attempt to get stoned, we had to roll a regular-sized joint for each person partaking and one super-sized Cheech and Chong zeppelin to share. The harsh smoke hurt our lungs, but we had accomplished something few people get to do: plan and execute a clandestine midnight raid on an unknown and unguarded accidental patch of pot.

Quitter

I never took up the noxious habit of smoking cigarettes, although I did try to quit once. Lolla had just moved into a new apartment. The crew came over for a party to welcome her into her crib true to our style. Her furniture hadn't arrived yet, so we sat around on the floor playing drinking games. L-Ron often tried to give up the coffin nails. Every day.

"This is my last pack. I swear." He wasn't lying. That was his last pack...until he bought his next pack, that is.

On this particular occasion, he was semi-serious about his desire to be smoke-free. He had gone so far as to buy nicotine patches. Someone decided it would be funny to see what would happen if I wore one. I rolled up my right sleeve and slapped it on my arm. Nothing happened, and we soon forgot about it.

I drove home, got into bed and realized I couldn't sleep. Or move. Lying on my back with my head turned facing the solid state stare of my alarm clock's digital red lights, I found myself immobilized. I was trapped within my own body as though I was living out Stephen King's incredible "Autopsy Room Four." The numbers silently changed for more than an hour as I watched, helpless.

It took every bit of energy and concentration I could muster to lift my left arm and drop my hand onto my right shoulder. I ripped the patch off and flung it towards the wall. Freed from the yellowing yolk of nicotine, I immediately passed out for eight straight well-deserved hours.

False Expectations and My Favorite Homo...sapian

Many of the Buzzards loved the Wreck Room, an 18 and up rave club in OKC. I wasn't such a big fan. Club music was created for people on club drugs by people on club drugs. Rational people don't go around listening to club music when not under the influence of the appropriate drugs. I only went to the Wreck when I had a line on some trip or 'schrooms. The best night I had at the Wreck came under a number of false expectations.

I had decided to go to the Wreck based on three assumptions, all three of which turned out to be incorrect.

1. I would eat a square of LSD and fry my balls off.

2..The only people I would know there were the people in my car.

3. I would be stuck listening to mindless club music for eight hours.

The acid turned out to be bunk. I waited all night just on the verge of tripping without ever doing so. Imagine a roller coaster clanking up to the peak of its run and then never dropping.

Over the course of the night, I think I saw half of Waterford at the club.

Not only did the Wreck do a hip-hop night, which made me extremely happy, but Del the Funky Homosapien performed, which made me ecstatic. Ice Cube's cousin, and one of the three people behind one of the greatest albums of all time, *3030*, Del rocked the house and then walked around to hang out with us after his set.

The wildest aspect of the Wreck was its location and the post-2 a.m. action. It sat just down the alley from the Banana Inn, a cheap hotel with the city's most famous/infamous gay bar in its lobby. A regular bar serving alcohol, the Banana closed at 2 a.m. to satisfy the state's liquor laws. Immediately thereafter, the Wreck floods with drunken older gay men checking out younger, tripping raver boys. The Buzzards and I always had a blast there from this point on. Stepping out to some self-professed queen's late-seventies pimp Caddy for a conversation, smoke and a pull or two from bottles of vodka and whiskey or a beer always provided a nice distraction from the driving club music we'd been subjected to the previous four hours.

Eventually all strange things must come to an end. The rising sun always met groups of discombobulated, drowsy and sweat-soaked trippers and covering their eyes as they made that ever so brief temporary transition into the real world before they could escape into a plate of greasy breakfast nosh or the seclusion of their bedrooms.

Ski Bums

I was introduced to the magical world of skiing my senior year of university. It served as a harsh introduction at best. We put together our crew: L-Ron, Tex, Mex, the Gambler, Lottie, Mom, and myself. Thus assembled, we set a crude plan in motion: Drive to Crested Butte, Colorado for their free ski Thanksgiving Weekend, with a

121

slight detour in Texas along the way to pick up Mex, Tex's twin brother. The simplicity of our plan guaranteed failure on a catastrophic scale.

Mom volunteered to drive us into the mountains more, I believe, out of her inability to sit comfortably as a passenger than out of a lack of confidence in our collective skills behind the wheel. We took off the night before Turkey Day '97 to maximize our ski time. Being the only one in our '89 Chevy van who didn't smoke tobacco in those days, my people of course had me ask Mom to stop for a smoke break. I wanted to smoke, just not cigarettes.

"Mom, can we pull over at the next rest stop for a quick smoke?"

"But Richard, you don't smoke."

I looked to my friends for strength as I admitted something to Mom I had only ineffectively brought up twice before.

"Not that kind of smoke..."

"Umm...okay."

Mom pulled over, and we unleashed a joint. All but Mom got high under the big Texan night sky and all of its stars before returning to the road. Picking up Mex in P-Town with a buzz, we had at last rounded out our crew.

The miles spun away beneath us as we rolled towards Colorado. Clear skies greeted us until we left Texas. Clouds darkened the night as we ascended into the mountain passes which would bring us into the Highest State. A snowstorm soon pounded us worse than the Columbian snowstorm that hit WLOTUS in the late 1970s. The powder only got thicker as we crawled north. At one point a 15-passenger church van pulling a trailer passed us as its high school devotees pushed it.

We called it quits somewhere over the border at a stop with little more than a gas station and an old motel. Scoring the last room, the receptionist disappointed us with the news that it was too late to purchase alcohol in his county. Instead, we passed around the pints of Peppermint Schnapps and Hot Damn I had brought for the slopes. Mom called Dad who informed us that, according to the Weather Channel, the skies across WLOTUS were completely clear with the exception of the blizzard spot directly above us.

We gave Mom and Lottie one of the two beds. I grabbed a piece of floor on which to crash. My gas station dinner didn't sit well with me. I pulled out my lighter and lit the most explosive fart of my life. The light flash burned my friends' images onto the walls Nagasaki-style.

Day 2

We got an early but useless start the next morning. Colorado's interstate system has some painfully designed rest area entrances and exits. The one we stopped at that morning didn't have an entrance or exit ramp. The area had a tiny 90 degree turn off of the interstate servicing all comers and goers. An eighteen-wheeler had slid off of the entrance/exit, blocking half of the minuscule two-way access point. A full-size RV later got stuck next to the truck, cutting off all entry and escape for the next four hours.

The boys smoked and urinated in the snow to pass the time. Two hours passed before one of the girls ventured out to their restroom. Their heated restroom. We had spent hours shivering in the van only to learn that free heat lay less than thirty feet away in both restrooms.

A wrecker finally cleared the RV out of our way. We didn't achieve much distance before a state patrolman met us on the road. The authorities had shut down the interstate north of us. They only allowed people to go back south if they had chains on their tires. We had none which earned us a mandatory detour west to the nearby town of Walsenburg. In retrospect, I wish we'd had chains.

At noon, Mom parked in front of one of the small town's four bars servicing its 4,000 residents. Throughout the course of the day and night, we would have at least one member of our crew kicked out of each bar.

The interstate shutdown had filled the town and its hotels with stranded people. The bars offered up free snacks. The town opened the high school to the displaced masses. We ate chili and got drunk. And high. One of our number had brought some meth for us and bundled it into single-ply squares of toilet paper for us to swallow. We took turns going to the van to consume magical powder packets of fun.

Nine hours of booze, weed and meth took their toll on me, forcing me to be the first to drop. I remember a repeat of *E.R.* playing on a bar television as an older Mexican guy with a trucker hat hit on Mom. With great difficulty, I got out to the front passenger seat of the van. Mom later unrolled a sleeping bag, so she could sleep on the van's foldout bed.

"If you're going to throw up, make sure you don't do it in the van. Not. In. The. Van," Mom warned me.

Obviously, I puked in the van. I managed to get the door open, but failed to get my head all the way out and coated the step and runner below the door. The fates of my people were revealed to me at 3 a.m. when L-Ron and the Gambler came knocking at my window. They invited me out for a late night smoke break and to fill me in on the remainder of the night's adventures. The entire town had long since retired for the night. We sauntered down Main Street passing a tightly rolled doobie.

Bartenders booted L-Ron out of a bar after he took a stool next to a woman, looked her square in the eyes and, without pretense or foreplay, slurred at her, "Hey baby, you wanna fuck?" The Gambler stole a mug from the same bar, sliding it under his coat. Too drunk to remember his theft, he opened his coat upon entering the next bar, dropping and shattering the glassware.

High as hell, we entered the high school and claimed a spot on a stairwell landing between the first and second floors. Sleep did not come easily. Many of our fellow strandees got caught on their way to a dog show in Denver. Barks, yaps and yips from overly pampered squeaky-ass micro-mutts evolution has fought to forget echoed through the hallways long into the morning.

Day 3

The school cooked up a free breakfast for us the next morning. Our little trio entered the cafeteria to find the rest of our crew already seated at the far side of the room. They looked across the dog lovers as I unzipped my jacket. Their jaws dropped as Mom waved me off. I glanced down to discover that I had coated the front of my shirt during my earlier vomit session. I re-zipped.

We learned of a ski resort not too far away and decided to try to salvage the final day of our trip with some actual skiing. My oral expulsions of the night before mandated a brief break at a car wash so that I could hose off the chili, beer, whiskey, vodka, toilet paper, and lord knows what else I'd consumed the afternoon and early evening before.

Never having skied before, I thought it prudent to take a lesson. Not having arrived until the early afternoon, Tex took it upon himself to give me a literal crash course. Tex's School of Ski turned me into a professional fall guy in less than five minutes. Not knowing any better, I slid on my ass and rolled down red and blue runs for the remainder of the afternoon. I did pause to vomit behind the periodic pine tree.

State workers cleared the roads during our debauchery in Walsenburg, granting us a safe, if not mellow, ride home.

1998

Getting My Nut on Thanks to the Nut

One of my many reasons for loving the Nut took place at the Woodward branch. Stopping in to score some greasy tacos while on my way to DJ a dance in Oklahoma's panhandle, I scored a phone number. I gave Amanda a call two months later on Super Bowl Sunday. Not hosting a party that year at the Lighthouse, a shot at sex and a definite taco score sounded like a good idea. I piloted Bonnie up to Woodward and found Amanda's place in spite of the directions she'd given me.

Her father welcomed me into his home and asked if I wanted to get high with him. He was a one-legged, leather-clad biker sitting on a couch in one of the filthiest homes I've ever entered. He smoked out his daughter and myself. His house could absolutely find itself on one of TLC's programs depicting examples of the shitactular state of random American homes. I took Amanda out for a drive and picked up some beers. We talked a little, when the reefer allowed, and went back to her place.

We dodged empty beer cans as she led me past her passed-out father to her bedroom. She was kind enough not to turn on the lights as we got down to business. I woke the next morning on a soiled mattress tossed askew on the floor. I found myself next to her beneath an ancient *Smurfs* bed sheet.

I picked my way through her landmine field of clothing, beer bottles and miscellaneous clutter to get to the bathroom where I discovered my previously white boxers had acquired a large patch of blood on the front. I hadn't taken them off when he had done the dirty among her flithies. Women, warn your men when you're having your period, especially if you're having a one-night stand. I never talked to her again, and I had to throw out my Hard Rock Cafe boxers. At least the non-bloody tacos I ate on the drive home were great!

You Can Get Anything You Want

Most Americans know of Woody Guthrie, the legendary folksinger who gave us "This Land Is Your Land." He also gave us a son, Arlo. Arlo gave us *Alice's Restaurant*. His debut album introduced the world to greatest Thanksgiving song ever. An 18-minute, 23-second monologue, sung in five-part harmony, "Alice's Restaurant Massacre" comically chronicles what happened to Arlo and his friends on Thanksgiving Day 1965 and the subsequent fallout. It evolves into an anti-Vietnam War protest tale as we learn all about "blind justice."

Entering the final few months of our relationship, the Catholic Schoolgirl and I met up with my parents for this astounding show. The Boar's Head was one of the Oklahoma City's greatest taverns. Before its closing and conversion into a fucking Men's Warehouse, it boasted a happy hour buffet, pool tables, arcade games, pinball machines, and a small concert hall.

Like most quality folk singers, Arlo is a storyteller. Every song he played had an amusing or poignant anecdote to accompany it. He recalled his childhood and the friendship between his father and Bob Dylan when Dylan would stop by his house just to hang out.

The small setting of the venue made it seem as though he was sharing stories with us at a comfortable house party. He was kind enough to sign my vinyl copy of *Alice's Restaurant* after the show.

Low Water Rave-vival

I had a vision one day while not paying attention during a Promotional Strategies class my senior year of college. I saw myself organizing a benefit concert near Waterford.

I sketched out a raw plan. I tried to make it as legitimate as possible by getting a charity that shall remain unnamed which grants wishes to children on board as my beneficiary. I convinced the Herpinator into donating sound and lighting equipment for the weekend as a tax write-off for Hiroshima, not realizing that he didn't file taxes. Unfortunately, he couldn't/wouldn't do it the weekend I had asked for, resulting in us missing a beautiful weekend and holding the event on a weekend where daytime temperatures rose slightly above freezing.

We managed to get the event promoted by the OKC's big rock radio station and local media including radio stations and the city and college papers. This tide of good will and advertising was unfortunately not enough to defeat the two obstacles we would face the weekend of the show: the weather and our town's only bar of size and influence.

The idea behind the event was simple enough: I wanted to throw a massive concert/party to support my chosen charity and the local music scene. I thought I could do our culturally-starved backwoods half of the state some good. I would cover what supplies weren't donated. After costs were covered, all the profits were to be passed on to the charity.

A farmer donated a piece of land just northwest of town for the weekend. I secured a flatbed trailer to serve as the stage for the dozen or so bands I'd lined up. Generators, lighting and Porta-Potties helped round out the logistics. Alanis of the Loose picked up a temporary license to sell beer at the event. A friend of hers came out to do henna tattoos.

The owner of the local shit-kicker bar feared even one weekend of competition and did what she could to shut us down or at least make us as ineffective as possible. She contacted the charity's people and warned them that the Rave-vival would be promoting drug use and selling lord only knows what. They immediately penned a letter, after we'd already established our relationship, informing me that they couldn't be bothered to be a part of whatever debauchery it was that I had planned.

The bar I was supposedly in competition with was a 21-to-enter joint. Our show was for those 18-and-up, with 21-year-olds receiving a special wristband to identify them as such. Nobody was going to sling drugs on my watch, although I'm sure folks would bring some for personal consumption as they do at any concert.

The honky-tonk's proprietor also decided to call in some favors with the local highway patrolmen. These men in brown spent their weekend and our tax dollars patrolling roads around the farm. They pulled over almost every person they encountered on those two lonely stretches of road that weekend.

My parents, eternally my best friends and biggest supporters all my half-cocked schemes, spent the weekend out on this piece of land working the gate, checking ID's, collecting signatures on responsibility waivers, and taking entrance fees. They also took turns making supply runs into town. The brown shirts pulled my Dad over three times. I can't help but wonder what quantity of drugs and how many illegals passed through our part of Western Oklahoma thanks to the highway patrolmen's diligent focus on me and all of our "illegal" activities throughout the weekend which failed to produce a single no drug bust or arrest.

With the exception of the lack of attendance due to the weather and the KGB-esque presence of the local highwaymen, the weekend went off without a hitch. A small group of dedicated people showed up to camp out and party for the weekend. Without exception, each and every band rocked the field despite the challenges inherent that weekend. The guitarist from Two Ded Flyz had a pilot friend who delivered him to the field in a helicopter. I drove around in my 1984 Chevy van to the various campsites giving people blasts of high-octane screwdrivers from my Super Soaker 100.

While the weekend itself was a financial disaster, costing me over $600 out of pocket (a large figure in those minimum wage days), it was a major learning experience for me and a good time for most everyone involved.

Altuna and Larry the Methy Rig Pig

In the pre-Evilnet age (and even for a good long while after), Western Oklahoma offered little to do in the way of entertainment besides random forms of outdoor recreation, guns and drugs. Sometimes we combined the three. We often mixed them at L-Ron's farm, Altuna.

Altuna was our favorite camping location. Altuna has a couple of fishing ponds with turtles to pop .22s at when the fishing slows. He and his brothers once cleared out a camping spot in a grove of trees and built a fire pit just above his grandfather's old trash canyon with its seasonal crick. They even set up an old cowboy camper to crash in during times when a tent fails to protect against Oklahoma's stronger gales.

A dozen of us decided to camp out under the stars one night during the passage of a comet. For reasons still unclear to me more than a decade later, I took Methy, a girl who once pissed on Goober's floor and tried to cover it with a Rollerblade. The rest of us dropped acid, while Methy lived up to her namesake. A large bonfire warmed us on that chilly night.

129

The fire served as a beacon to Larry, a rig pig working an oil derrick on the next farm. He correctly deduced that a fire on a farm at night meant people were partying. He came over to see what brand of mischief we were getting up to. We attempted to contain our internal insanity. He shared some of his meth and made Methy's night.

I passed out in the early morning on the ground next to the fire in my Marlboro Miles ski jacket I had worn for the first time that night. A colossal coal leapt from the pit early in the morning and smoldered a hole through my collar. I awoke to find Larry gone, little more than a lone hazy memory from a night filled with more of the same. Methy had kept a not-so-diligent, twitchy watch over our fire throughout the night.

Finishing Moves

I entered university in the fall of 1994 with little clue as to my purpose there. Once I knocked out my core classes, I enrolled in some business courses for the simple reason that I had long thought that I might have a head for business. Three-and-a-half-years into school, I had a strange conversation with my advisor, Dr. Farmer, which altered my course by providing me with direction.

Dr. Farmer reviewed my transcript and realized that I was one semester away from completing a bachelor's in Business Administration. This came as a surprise to both of us, seeing as how much I had bounced around in my coursework. Every single credit I had taken would count towards that sheepskin if I'd just enroll in the correct final fifteen hours. My transcript listed such oddities as SCUBA, bowling and medical terminology. I walked across the stage they'd set up in our embarrassingly bad football team's stadium with a flask of rum under my gown and an ICP *Riddlebox* sticker on my mortar board in May 1998.

A group of us ventured out to the Hole (also known as Paradise), a local swimming hole at the corner of two farmers' properties. One farmer never cared that we went out there to drink, party, smoke, and swim as long as we cleaned up after ourselves. He sometimes rode his horse out and sat a distance away from us just drinking a couple cans of Coors Original as he watched our shenanigans. The other was a major cock who called the police every opportunity he got. That graduation day, only the cock saw us.

The sheriff's department dispatched Deputy Dicks to end our fun. This was a well-matched choice. Particularly despised by the youth of Custer County, Dicks was notorious for taking delight in dispersing the outdoor activities of local youths. Overweight and under-brained, he really didn't like catching me snapping his photograph that warm afternoon. He lumbered his considerable heft over to me.

"I know you're making fun of me! And I don't like it. I could be at home right now with my wife and kids instead of coming out here to tell you people where you shouldn't be. I didn't have a problem with you then (pointing out towards where I'd held the Rave-vival), and I don't have a problem with you now," he warned me. I found it strange that, if he was on duty, then why did he have nothing better to do with my tax dollars than hang out with his family at the homestead?

Thus began three weeks of major change, most all of them quite unpleasant.

Not one hundred percent sure what my next move was, but feeling certain it wasn't in Waterford, I temporarily moved back in with my parents in order to rent out the Seventh Street Lighthouse and contemplate my future. The Catholic Schoolgirl, then my longest relationship, and I parted ways once we realized that we weren't meant to be. Then came the surgery.

For a couple of years, I had experienced a small recurring bulge above my waist. I would push it in, which usually made it go away for a few days, sometimes even a week or more. It rarely saved me from feeling anything other than a mild tingling. Finally getting around to telling Nurse Mom about it, our doctor later confirmed her diagnosis: I had a hernia. I guess they run in the family. I didn't inherit much from Dad's side of the family. However, I did score his weak abdominal wall.

The surgery put me in a month-long living hell. It wasn't until years later that I learned that Waterford's Civil War-era surgeons had performed such an antiquated hack job on me. My father's fifth and final hernia repair took place in the late 1970s. His doctors fixed it by placing a square polyurethane mesh patch over his tear and securing it with a single stitch in each corner. Over time, his abdominal muscles grew into the mesh, holding it securely in place. This is an incredibly logical solution. You would never try to fix a hole in a bicycle tire tube by pinching the sides of the hole together and sewing it like two pieces of fabric, but that's what they did to me.

Subsequently, their barbarism restricted me from straining myself or exercising in any way for months. I couldn't sit normally the first month. I had to lower myself down like a woman in the ninth month of an unwanted pregnancy. Our toilet, which sat at a normal level, suddenly sat too low for me to lower myself to, causing me to hover above it holding onto a cabinet for dear life every time I baked a batch of booty brownies. Due to the stress that pooping puts on your abs, I couldn't squeeze any Play-Doh from my Fun Factory. I had to literally wait for nature to take its course. What had long been a relaxing twenty minutes of reading time for me had transformed into a sweaty forty-minute daily endurance test.

I finally learned just how badly I'd been screwed when I had a second hernia fixed in Korea. It took moving to a country that still allowed booze and cigarettes in its hospitals and elementary schools until 2009 in order to have surgery performed using more modern methods, but that's a story for another book.

I was single, graduated and in pain with no real idea of where my path was taking me. I moved to Dallas to DJ while I studied funeral science.

Roomies

Having roommates allows us the chance to learn how to live with people and to learn about them. No less than a dozen people shared the Seventh Street Lighthouse with me during the six years I resided within its aging plaster walls. I had some powerful experiences - some good, some not-so-good and some downright wretched.

L-Ron lived with me for six months, although he only slept two nights in the house. A good looking lad, he was rarely single and usually crashed at his girlfriend's while keeping a place of his own as a fallback. Somewhere along the way, he picked up a cardboard refrigerator box. This box signaled where he was staying. If it was at his home, we knew he was on the splits with his girl, otherwise he was at her place.

L-Ron also had the unfortunate luck to have a couple of run-ins with the Grandmother from Hell. Goober and I always dreaded having to visit the Grandma from Hell, but sometimes we ran errands for Mom to alleviate her suffering. I can't recall the exact mission necessitating a visit to grandma's house, but I dragged L-Ron with me to prove that she was as crazy as our family claimed.

We walked in, and I introduced my friend.

"It's nice to meet you L-Ron. What church does your family go to?" she incredulously asked right off to bat-shit insane.

"We're Catholics," he responded, unsure of the direction or purpose of her awkward greeting.

"Oh…well… I guess that's okay," she slowly spilled, dumbfounding the both of us. He still laughs about it, while I still apologize for it.

The next time she saw L-Ron, he was a woman and Goober was having an affair with him.

Goober and I were members, for almost a decade, of our local Boy Scout troop, the third-longest consecutively charted troop in the nation. Our troop holds an annual chili fundraiser. It is one of our biggest moneymakers and one heck of a meal for a $5 donation. Our family never missed one, even after Goober and I had grown too old for the program and left town, the troop remained yet another branch of our extended family. Mom stayed on the troop committee for fifteen years after we'd turned 18 and still lends a hand when they need it.

One year Goober took L-Ron with him. My brother was working at a local burger grill owned by a married couple. A head of straight, shoulder-length hair topped L-Ron's slight, tan frame. When the Grandma from Hell saw Goober walk in with L-Ron, who had his hair pulled back in a bandanna, she immediately convinced herself that L-Ron was in fact the wife of Goober's boss, and that the burgers weren't the only meat he was playing with at work. She had to call Mom to alert her to her child's sinful ways. We all laughed at Goober's "adultery."

Jesus (of meth-lab-in-the-trunk fame) moved into the Lighthouse for a semester. An ideal roomie while in the house, he was a dick once he stepped outside. He had the balls to go to the apartment of the Catholic Schoolgirl right after we started dating. He wasted the better part of an hour explaining to her why she shouldn't date me. Luckily for me, she ignored him and dated me for nine outstanding months, a record for me.

On to the Lighthouse ladies.

I loved the Seventh Street Lighthouse, even if it did cause me a headache or two now and then. Roommates leaving before the end of their lease always put me in a bit of a pickle, and I have always hated pickles of any sort. I had a quartet of female roomies during my years in mi casa including two ex-girlfriends, an old friend and a complete stranger. No more than one of them roomed with me at a time.

The first ex refused to clean a single dish until she'd dirtied every other dish and needed to use one herself. This took place during an Oklahoma summer with no air-conditioning in the kitchen.

The friend never cleaned her room. Mom actually came over one day and did it for her.

The second ex debated joining/selling her soul to the Mormon cult and frequently invited our local missionaries to drop by for discussions (she managed to avoid their enticements).

Then there was Mission Control.

After the second ex had unexpectedly moved out midway through a semester, I placed an ad for a replacement in the local paper I had thrown around town in my youth. Mission Control responded. We talked on the phone, and she sounded pretty cool. The decision to move in was made early one afternoon I had spent chugging 40oz bottles of Olde English. She lacked a set of wheels at the time, so I plowed over to the next tiny single stop sign town down Route 666 to pick up her and her possessions. However put off she might have been by meeting a long-haired drunken guy in a beat-up hearse, it didn't stop her from loading her gear and returning with me.

She sipped on my 40oz during the short hop to back Waterford. We got her set up in her new bedroom and then had sex for the first and only time during her six-month sojourn at the Lighthouse.

Mission Control was an interesting roomie. The size and weight of a dry twig, she always sported a big grin made shiny by the mass of metalworks in her mouth. She had an enlightened view on sex and even coined her own phrase for it. When she wanted to get laid, she referred to it as going out "on a mission."

"Richard, are you on a mission tonight?" she would ask on the five to eight nights a week we drank.

"Who do you know who isn't on a mission in this town?"

Mission Control also had a compulsion to number her conquests. I believe that I was number forty-two or maybe I'm asking the wrong question. She accomplished enough missions to put her well into her sixties before she moved out. During the course of her half-year at the Lighthouse, she only slept two or three nights in her own bed. She preferred the couches in the living room. Many Buzzards, K-Town Mafia and other assorted freaks and ninjas frequently overnighted at the Lighthouse. Many of them ended up completing missions with Mission Control. Each morning she'd give me a detailed mission debriefing. As time wore on, people stopped sleeping over. I never grew accustomed to seeing an empty living room in the morning or early afternoon.

L-Ron wasn't the last of my roommates to fall victim to Grandma's slights and delusions. She attacked Mission Control during one of her few surprise visits to my den of sin. I feared what ignorance would pour from her mouth as I introduced her to yet another of my friends. She never let me down in this respect.

"Where do you go to church?" she inquired with as much innocence as she could muster, which wasn't very much.

"I don't go to church," Mission Control said with as much disinterest as came natural to her after hearing the many tales of the Grandma from Hell.

"One of these days you are going to need God," she warned her.

"Well I don't today, and I don't think I will tomorrow either," Mission Control said with an undeniable coolness that undeniably displeased Grandma.

She never returned. That very well could have been our last conversation, despite it having occurred half a decade before she died. What a way to go out. Mission Control was a bit of a lightweight when it came to the booze, but that didn't stop her from trying. She was a regular at Phunky Jay's, the bar I would come to co-own, where she continually knocked over and/or dropped her beers. Mom picked up a child's sippy cup for her from Wal-Mart, Sharpied her name on it and kept it behind the bar for her. She took great pride in showing it off to many of our patrons.

Her Lighthouse missions came to an end when she met a carnie. I shit you not, she left town to run off with an honest-to-god dishonest carnie. He worked for one of those dingy, dinky outfits which came around to small towns like ours and set up shop in vacant lots for a few days, giving local marks just enough time to tire of their small selection of hastily slapped together antique rides and rigged games.

They lived together in the trailer he shared with five other people. It was not a communal trailer, but was instead divided into *Tetris*-like L-shaped pieces accessible from doors on the starboard side. Each room was the width of its door with an additional lower or upper bulge to one side housing that room's bunk, also about the same width as the door. The two of them shared that space. The only real advantage I saw to living in that metal box was that they used the vents connecting each room to pass joints and pipes. Talk about your hot-boxing.

Peyote Ugly

I have eaten peyote exactly once in my life, but it was one hell of a night. This particular journey began with me loading up a troupe of my ninjas for a trip to Altus, OK. The Cutitz sisters were living in a log cabin near Lake Altus and had invited us down to party for the night. We drank in my van throughout the ninety-minute trip south.

Peyote had not been my original goal for the night, but I happened to find a baggie of old caps a Native American buddy of mine had given me. A secluded cabin with some of my closest and most trusted friends seemed like the perfect place to pop those caps.

We drank. We smoked. I boiled a small pot of 'yote tea. It went down well. We played on through the night, climbing into the rafters of the cabin's interior. It went well until I had to make a quick trip outside to make a mandatory upchuck offering. In a mellow and trippy mood, the remainder of the night followed amazingly.

Rain poured down as we decided to go for a drive, with all but one of our crew piling back into my van. The most screwed up among us, I chauffeured us around roads I'd never before driven. The late hour and the downpour pretty much ensured clear roads for the night. Almost within sight of the cabin, the van hit a large puddle and hydroplaned off of the road into a ditch. The mud beneath my tires wouldn't give. We had to make a run for the cabin only to be met with laughter from our lone, dry friend who'd stayed behind.

With the sun out and burning the next morning, one of the sisters drove me out to see whether or not I could free my van from the mire and muck. Her Ford Probe didn't hold a lot of useful tools.

However, she did have the remnants of a cardboard box in her trunk. I proved her wrong when my tires were able to get enough purchase with that single chunk of a nearly forgotten box.

Road Hummer
Day 1

Before the summer had even really gotten underway, my time with the girlfriend to follow the Catholic Schoolgirl quickly came to an end. Two days later, the Herpinator, the Dude and I rolled out of Oklahoma bound for St. Louis. Herps owned a puss-yellow Hummer. When people asked about its cost, he always replied, "It's not about being able to buy a Hummer. It's about being able to afford to own a Hummer." While Schwarzenegger made owning a Hummer look cool, they were in fact horrifically uncomfortable machines prone to frequent breakdowns. You must understand that this is the civilian model upgraded for comfort, long before Chevy released the sad soccer mom H2 and H3.

Growing up in Western Oklahoma, not too many people owned foreign-made cars. They did this partly out of patriotism, but mostly because repairs had to be made in OKC. For Hummer owners in the Midwest, they had to decide between getting their gas-guzzlers to either Las Vegas or St. Louis. Herps made a road trip out of a journey he needed to make to have some maintenance work done.

The three of us struck out in the late afternoon of a sweltering Oklahoman summer day. We hadn't gone eight miles before Herps drove off of I-40, because he missed the off ramp. We had to pick up his Chevy Blazer to tow behind us, so that we'd have something to drive while the Hummer sat in the shop.

Day 2

We dropped off the Hummer and hit up Players' Island and Harrah's Casinos. We gambled a little, drank a lot and utilized the good folks at County Cab to get us back to our hotel room for some bedtime bud.

Day 3

Our Wednesday kicked off with a tour of the Anheuser-Busch Brewery. With a couple of free beers in us, we picked up the Hummer and left the Blazer at the dealership, intending to grab it

Saturday. We drove off into Illinois in search of some place to do some camping.

Day 4

We picked up some camping supplies and grabbed a room at a dingy motel in a dry county in Kentucky. Ingesting a couple handfuls of mushrooms at the parking lot of the Mammoth Caves National Park, we joined a guided tour of the longest known cave system in the world.

The Herpinator's paranoia paid off once in awhile. He had a set of Gen 2 night vision goggles. If you've never taken a cave tour, one of the highlights is going deep enough for the guide to kill the lights to let the people experience absolute darkness. We took turns with Herps' goggles, waving our hands about in front of the clueless peoples' faces around us. The mushrooms hitting us full throttle, we struck off on our own through some side passages. With only the one set of goggles between us, we had to hold on to each other's shirts as two-thirds of us stumbled along blindly at any given time. We rejoined the group before our absences were noted, or we got too lost to find our way back.

A couple of joints in our motel's parking lot calmed us down and gave us a chance to reflect on and laugh about our day's adventures before turning in for the night.

Day 5

Mammoth Cave National Park has some campgrounds, which we deemed a great place to establish our camp for the night. We hiked trails on the northern side of the park for a few hours to find a decent place to sleep. Taking a couple drops of liquid LSD didn't aid our navigational skills. During our trek, we had to return to the Hummer once and made the mistake of splitting up the second time out.

The Dude and I eventually found each other and almost instantly became completely lost. A lone small house stood in a field. The grizzled owner gave us directions the first time we showed up at his front door. I don't think he had much faith in us the second time we knocked on his door.

Somehow we met up with Herps, who showed us to the site he had picked out. We started what fire we could with the damp wood available and cooked some tasty pizza hot dogs. Bedding down didn't work so well. Herps turned in a little earlier than the Dude and I. A nefarious sound in the woods interrupted our fireside conversation. Still under Uncle Cid's persuasion, we concluded that a bear lurked nearby. It took us several minutes to realize that our "bear" was simply the Herpinator snoring like a monster.

Day 6

The walk out of the park proved far less confusing and daunting than our entrance. The idiots at the Hummer dealership had forgotten to park the Blazer outside their gates for us, since they're not open on Sundays. It took us no small amount of time to get someone out there to let us on the lot.

Getting lost on our way to find Harrah's Casino so that we could hit its buffet for lunch, we stumbled onto the H.O.R.D.E. Festival at the Riverport Amphitheatre. A large-scale festival served as icing on our weird weekend of a cake. We bought tickets and entered.

Sitting in the grassy outfield of the venue, we dosed multiple hits of liquid trip. I lost my shit enough at one point that I convinced myself that we were at Lilith Fair. Between the drugs and the large number of girls around us with short hair and overalls, I think it's possible to forgive some of my confusion. Thoroughly convinced all of the women in attendance were lesbians, I didn't believe the Dude when he tried to point out that one of the overall-clad women was hitting on me. I was far too discombobulated to make heads or tails of the situation or the conversation. The ability to formulate comprehensible sentences evaded me for well over an hour as I peaked.

This all took place after only consuming two hits of trip. I downed a second double dose in one of the stalls of either the men's or women's toilets. I honestly didn't know what was what at that point. We survived the show and the long, hard drive home.

Dallas Debacle

Some moves have no choice but to be doomed from the very beginning. The year was 1998. I was a recent university graduate and knew that the time had come for me to seek my fame and glory in the world. I didn't find fame or glory. Instead, I followed the devil to Dallas, where, for six months, I hung out with hookers, drug dealers and people who liked to dress up corpses. What ensued was utter balls-out chaos.

I spent the summer partying in Waterford. I had bought into Hiroshima Music. The Herpinator and I had quickly grown close during those early years. He had the idea for me to move closer to the center of his business' action, and I wanted to attend the Dallas Institute of Funeral Science (DIFS). He knew for certain that we'd be making a million dollars within a year. He had good ideas, which was part of his draw. Unfortunately, they rarely worked out as he planned, especially for those who went in with him. The move to Dallas itself in September was indicative of what was to come.

I loaded up my '89 Chevy van. I rented out the Seventh Street Lighthouse. I learned that the Beastie Boys were coming through Dallas for their "In the Round Tour" in support of *Hello Nasty* and invited Goober, the Dude and Jersey Josh to come down and see the show. They left Waterford just far enough behind me to ensure that they wouldn't have to help me unload the van. Smart thinking.

I found Herps' house in Allen, the northeastern-most suburb of Dallas back then, empty. Herps and I would rarely cross paths at the casa. I know that we didn't see each other there five times in my six months there. I traded Herps a piano I had for rent at this place he rarely used except for storage and later as a failed mushroom farm.

The boys pulled in as I had just begun to open some of the boxes from my now-empty van. We barely had enough time to exchange greetings before piling into Goober's car (the Oldsmobile in which I had suffered a rape attempt years earlier) to get to the show in time.

The parking lot gave us an opportunity for a quick pre-lube. With none of us too accustomed to driving in Dallas, this meant forgoing the usual beverage check and diving directly into the distribution of the LSD. Goober had a vial of liquid and gave us each a hit. Thus properly dosed, we headed in for what remains to this day one of the best shows I've had the privilege of losing my mind to. The show would have been mind-blowing even without the trip, but having Uncle Cid with us didn't hurt any.

For "In the Round," they toured with a circular island of a stage. They only played venues with 360-degree seating. The rotating stage guaranteed a great view for all.

Mix Master Mike kicked the show off with a mind-blowing remix of Rush's "Tom Sawyer." The Boys took over and rewrote the concert experience. Whether you quit listening after "Fight for Your Right," thought *Paul's Boutique* was their most under-appreciated album or got hooked on "So What'cha Want," there were Beastie songs a plenty. The story of "Paul Revere" flowed from the lips of the thousands present as the Beasties turned up the house lights and let us take over.

We thought we had had it in the parking lot after the show. After large concerts, there are always three types of people: The sober and straight alike which amass into one discombobulated throng in a sad attempt to be the first one out and on their way. The other two groups are both made up of drunks and druggies, but they vastly differ. The aggressive substance users battle with the sobers to get underway. We passives are content to sit in our cars and let the other fools clear out of our way as we enjoyed the fading effects of our ingested substances.

This move has always worked in the past, but we were in Dallas, the insane heart of Far Northern Mexico. Police officers patrolled the lot, eager to get us to move on and to bust people for committing the crimes one would expect to be committed in the parking lot after a Beastie Boys show. With a head full of crazy, Goober drove us home with mad skills. The boys passed out in the living room some time later. So ended my first night living in D-town.

Day 2

Mostly composed, we woke late the following day. The boys had to return to Waterford. I had to work a rave for Hiroshima that night, a racket in which we briefly dabbled. A couple hours after they departed, I left. I followed the Herpinator's directions to a venue somewhere in Dallas a little after dark. He stood outside looking disappointed as he held his cell phone aloft to me. This being 1998, a few more years would have to pass before everyone over the age of four possessed phones.

"Richard?" asked Mom.

"Is everything okay? Is Dad alright?" I asked, worried about my father and the sixteen years he had on Mom.

"We're fine. It's Goober."

Oh shit. They had had a wreck on the way home.

"He and the guys are okay, but they're in jail in Denton," said Mom, allaying my fears while creating new ones.

"What the hell?"

"Your Father and I are coming down in the morning, but we need you to get some money and meet us."

And just like that, my second night in Dallas, my first working night in Dallas, had come to a brutal conclusion. I hung up and returned Herps' phone along with an apology. I went home to get the rest that working a rave until 5 a.m. would not have allowed.

Day 3

Our Denton reunion was not a happy one. It was better than a three-hour drive for Mom and Dad. Goober was unhappy. I was unhappy.

Their story was one indicative of Texas madness.

The Dude piloted them out of Dallas. They stopped off in a wet county for a sixer of quality 6.0 percent beer to split between the three of them for the remainder of their four-hour drive home. A highway patrolman passed them on I-35 and didn't like the fact that the Dude had kept his kept his hands on the wheel and his eyes on the road in front of him instead of looking over and waving or signaling to him.

On their side of it, they didn't even bother to try to hide what few empties littered the rear floorboards of Goober's Olds. The patrolman saw the bottles and asked whether they had anything else on them. Goober immediately gave up his vial tossed into the center console for the trip home.

We bailed him out. I drove home.

With those three days serving as my introduction to Texas, I should have been smart enough to realize what it was going to snowball into later.

That first month passed quickly enough as I learned the lay of the land, worked a little and began classes at the Dallas Institute of Funeral Science.

DIFS

To understand why a person would consider becoming a funeral director ("mortician" in old-speak) requires another journey to the past: the early spring of 1998 to be precise.

I grew up around more death and medical situations than most people not residing in or fighting in war-torn, third-world countries such as the Congo, Iraq or Detroit. I grew up thinking it normal to see bloody injuries and/or the occasional corpse. This led me to believe I could be a funeral director.

I knew our town's lone director, Marvin, a DIFS graduate himself, with hair well past the length you'd expect of a man in a suit in most any other profession. I talked to Marvin, and we decided that it would be a good idea for me to watch and assist with the preparation of a body before I completed my bachelor's in business administration that May and moved down to Dallas only to freak out when I saw my first piece of meat on the slab.

The problem with living in a Western Oklahoma town of only 11,000 regular citizens (SWOSU raises the population by a few thousand two semesters each year) is that people rarely pass away at convenient times. Between my classes, my weekday part-time job and my weekends DJing, it took two months for someone to die at a convenient time so I could meet him. Although in retrospect, I shouldn't have.

Day of the Dead

The last Sunday in April brought a typically beautiful spring day to Oklahoma - just a touch on the warm side if you stood in the sun in the perfectly azure sky, but wondrously cool in the shade. Tex, still a roommate at this time, and I had spent the morning and afternoon doing yard work. Yard work for us meant clearing the corner lot of the Seventh Street Lighthouse of all the tossed alcohol receptacles, pulling a few weeds and mowing while we drank iced-down beers from a cooler on the back porch and smoked weed from Douglas, the one-hitter in my dugout. We were to have a couple of hours in the late afternoon to clean up and relax before we went to a Wal-Mart party.

Wal-Mart employees form large and weird cliques out of necessity. They work odd hours at an odd place with odd people. They may be offered stock options, but they are still forced to begin every morning with the "Wal-Mart Cheer." Don't ask.

My first ex to live at Lighthouse worked at Wal-Mart. Having gone to school with some other Wal-Marters and their children allowed my friends and I special outsider status to their alcoholic-induced throw-downs.

One was going down that night at Leo's place north of town. All Tex and I had to do was finish the lawn, clean up and not get so fucked up that neither of us could drive out there.

We mowed. We drank. We weeded. We weeded. I remembered a quarter bag of mushrooms I'd been sitting on for a while and decided that a Wal-Mart party would be the perfect place to unleash myself for an evening. I swallowed my schrooms and stripped to shower. The phone rang. Tex answered.

"Richard, it's for you."

"Hello?"

"Richard, this is Marvin. I've got a body, if you're not busy today."

I'd waited two months for this. I didn't have class. I didn't have to work. The timing was perfect. Almost. Except for the hallucinogenic drugs I'd ingested.

"I'm sorry to hear that, but that's great?" I answered with expectation, hesitation and awkwardness flooding my voice. "I can totally be there, but I just finished doing my yard and am in need of a shower before I can go anywhere."

"Don't worry about it. He's not going anywhere. Can you be here in thirty?"

"No problem."

"I need to tell you one thing, though. It's Sunday, so I don't have the front open."

"Okay…"

"You'll have to park in the side drive and knock. Walk around to the back of the building and knock on the embalming room's air-conditioner. I'll open the garage door for you."

"Not a problem. Thanks, and I'll see you in thirty," I said, hanging up.

Despite our shared stoned state of mind, Tex was able to cipher what I was getting myself into.

"You can't do this! You just ate a sack of schrooms!" he admonished.

"It's okay, brother. By the time I shower, I'll just begin to come up. I can handle the drive there (it was only seven blocks). From there, I'll play it by ear and have a wild story by the time I get back

144

here to pick you up for the Wally party," I said, probably more to encourage myself than him.

The Swirling Dead

Showered and hopefully ready for action, I slipped behind the wheel of my then 29-year-old Bonnie, cranked down the window and switched on her original single-speaker AM radio. Its crackle didn't aid my situation.

The fungus was just beginning to take me away as I pulled up to Marvin's place of business. I was under its spell enough to be confused as to how to knock on the air-conditioning unit of a funeral home. I gingerly tapped it a few times and then threw a few louder raps at it, hoping to overcome the roar of its fan as though I were Helen Keller visiting Jabba's palace at the beginning of *Jedi*.

The two-car garage door rumbled up revealing Marvin's Cadillac hearse, a stretch car and a galaxy of half-used and unused funeral home paraphernalia tossed about on heavy metal shelves. The shadows made it difficult to focus. Marvin greeted me and issued an edict that later made me realize that I was losing yet another type of virginity altogether to someone who has popped more than a few of these particular cherries. We faced the metal door to the embalming room.

"What you're going to see and do here today is unlike anything you've ever done before. What I do in there is completely natural and is a necessary part of the process of life. A lot of people think that they can handle what they see on their first try, and many do, but there's no shame if you can't. You shouldn't be worried or embarrassed if you feel the need to be sick. Just let me know if you're going to be, so we can handle it. Are you okay?"

I told him that I was, mustering all of the drug-fueled confidence I could. He opened the door, and I walked into a room that came close to driving me even crazier.

Slab

By this time the mushrooms were fully piloting my body's machine. To say that I was even a copilot in my own shell was to overestimate my role in the situation. The door opened to reveal a room of shining surgical steel and sharp distractions. In the midst of it all lay the body of a very shriveled, very dead and very naked man. Time morphed into an indecipherable enemy.

A dry-erase board next to the door conflicted with the sterility and scientific-ness of the rest of the room. Marvin told me that he used the board to record any accidental sticks or transfers of fluids. Funeral directors take regular HIV/AIDS tests after embalming room accidents and need to know the possible source of their diseases on the off chance that they one day contract one. I never knew a dry-erase board could be so morbid.

Gored out of my head, I watched and assisted Marvin with his work. An embalmer's consists of tricking a piece of meat into looking and smelling not too unfresh for several days. This mostly involves the removal of the quantities of bodily fluids which, left unchecked, would hasten decay but begins with cleaning the body's outer husk. I had to Head & Shoulder the man's anus.

What's the first thing you'll do when you die? Piss and shit yourself. Death brings about the release of all of your muscles currently and subconsciously tightened as you read this. I ensured that he slipped off of this mortal coil with a dandruff-free asshole. You're welcome, mysterious geezer.

Morticians replace your bodily fluids with highly toxic chemicals which stave off natural deterioration for a short duration until internment or cremation. This fluid removal requires an 18-inch needle attached to a rubber hose running up to a vacuum device hidden in the ceiling. Marvin jammed that metal monster into the man's chest well below his left ribs. The needle has to hit all of the major areas containing fluid: lungs, stomach, kidneys, and heart. To get into all of those areas, he has to jab in and out and swivel the needle around. It doesn't make for pleasant viewing.

I held out well through this torture until ripples began emanating from the center of the man's chest and flowed out to the ends of his toes, fingers and head. The fungus had me by the balls and this was not the place to lose my shit. Marvin had many surgical weapons I was sure he wouldn't hesitate to use to put down this giant raving beast I rapidly found myself devolving into. Control and order must be maintained at all times. The more I focused, the more I lost it.

"Richard, are you feeling OK?" Marvin broke my foul concentration. A cold piece of man meat stared up at me. Nothing more, nothing less. No permanent damage had taken place. I would survive.

"No, I'm fine. Just got a little weirded out for a second," I replied, tossing out the single biggest understatement of my life.

"Really, it's okay if you feel the need to be sick."

"No, it's passed. Thank you, though." Thankfully, he had mistaken my inability to divert my eyes from the hallucination taking place on his client as the onset of a bout of illness. I've never vomited on mushrooms without aggressive help from alcohol, and I wasn't about to start in this lonely cold room.

Facial

Embalmers begin their work outside to take care of the most pressing issues regarding hygiene. They then move inside in their attempt to stave off the effects of death for as long as necessary. Finally, return to the outside to work on aesthetics. Shampooed and filled with toxic chemicals, we now had to focus on putting his face in order. Marvin told me we'd cover the basics that day. He'd take care of the cosmetics later. What followed surely would have damaged my soul, even if I hadn't been two dimensions removed from our own parcel of time and space.

There are certain basics to cover. Their complexities rise in difficulty with age. To do the job properly, the deceased's lips and eyes must be shut, although, according to movies, this is incorrect. In reality, your bowels release, and your mouth and your eyelids suddenly fail to respond as you would assume upon your demise. Old movies indicating that the first action of a dead person is to shut their eyes lie to the public and ignore the evacuating bowels and open eyes (not to mention the bloodless gunshot wounds in some of my favorite classic westerns).

The confusion and displeasure lay in how morticians accomplish these feats.

Closing the eyes of the dead looked simple enough on the surface. Marvin has special contact lenses that could very well have been cut off of the end of condoms dotted for her pleasure. The bumps supposedly hold the eyelids shut. They didn't that day. Marvin whipped out a tiny, crusty bottle of Super Glue to fix the lids to the lenses. It took a spurt or two, but he finally got that poor old guy's eyes shut for the last time.

The man's mouth turned out to be a different story altogether. It refused to stay closed on its own accord and even defied Marvin's strongest adhesives which once claimed to attach construction workers' helmets beneath high-rise I-beams at death-defying heights. The man had not a single tooth left in his head, so Marvin resorted to a magical mortician tool which shoots spiked anchors into the gums. A string tied around the tiny posts sticking out of the upper and lower gums holds the mouth shut.

The man's gums wouldn't take to the anchors. I had to watch while suppressing my freak-out as Marvin repeatedly jammed his gun-like device into the man's mouth in failed attempt after failed attempt to get an anchor to stick. Ka-chunk! Ka-chunk! Ka-chunk! It was a maddening, echoing sound in that little room.

On what may have been his tenth try, an anchor gripped his lower gums. He got the second in slightly quicker and twisted a string between them. A few drops of Super Glue permanently sealed his lips with a surety that would impress the CIA.

Thus ended my first professional, organized experience with a corpse. I thanked Marvin profusely, got into my car and sped home where Tex was waiting to hear the details or just to make sure I hadn't gotten myself locked up in the loony bin or jail.

After having survived the whole experience while so entirely out of my mind, I realized that if I could handle it under such extreme circumstances, then I could certainly handle it on a day-to-day basis when I'm less likely to be screwed up on hallucinogenic drugs. Therefore, I decided to move to Dallas and enroll at the Dallas Institute of Funeral Science once I graduated.

Juggalo Nation

The course of my life was forever altered by the Herpinator when he introduced me to the Insane Clown Posse's, *Riddle Box*, two weeks before they dropped *The Great Milenko*. I immediately counted myself a Juggalo, a fan of the Clowns. I had found a new source of music in a rapidly decaying art where Snoop Dogg had signed on to Master P's gold-plated ball of shit that was No Limit Records and where Hard Rock Cafés around the globe had begun hanging Backstreet Boys and old lady Madonna paraphernalia on their walls.

I listened to nothing but *Riddle Box* until I laid my hands upon a copy of *The Great Milenko*. As of this writing, I have ventured out no less than a dozen times to see the Clowns themselves or as part of one of the super groups from their homegrown independent label, Psychopathic Records. Three of those attempts have ended in catastrophic failures.

What Is a Juggalo?

Two weeks into my Dallas misadventures, I witnessed the Clowns devastate Fort Worth's Bronco Bowl on their *Juggalo Funhouse Tour*. Texas' asinine alcohol laws being what they were, I had to wait in a line at the venue to pay a dollar to join the Bowl's "club" so that I could drink during the show.

I ran out to Northeast Dallas with some younger Juggalos after the last blast of confetti and sprays of Faygo had hit the ground. The Dark Carnival spectacle involves Shaggy and J spraying Faygo on the soul-shells of all of us good and faithful Juggalos. For those of you who don't live in the Northern Midwest, Faygo is their Shasta, Fanta or any other ghetto-cheap soda from your neck of the woods. Due to a crazy onstage mishap early in their nearly three-decade career, spraying cheap Detroit-born soda on their fans evolved into an integral component of every ICP show. They have canceled and/or rescheduled shows at venues that wouldn't let them get their fans wet. The Clowns bounce two-liters off of mini-trampolines as they bust rhymes into their soda-proof microphones. Faygo's headquarters actually sends 18-wheelers out on tour with them. A proper Insane Clown Posse concert is an assault and challenge to all five senses:

Aural: Any Juggalo/Juggalette worth his/her salt knows the lyrics to almost every song in their extensive library and will sing along throughout most of the show, hugging one another when one of their personal favorites gets underway.

Olfactory: We Juggalos will never earn much praise for our collective personal hygiene regiments. I willingly join this stinky clan during Gatherings. No matter your level of hygiene or obsessive-compulsive scrubbing, a single show consisting of warm-up acts and an hour of moshing in a frothing sea of soda pop will bring the cleanest germaphobe down to our level.

Tactile: Faygo. Confetti. Sweat. Drugs. Titties. Buttholes. Hugs. Explained.

Taste: By the time the Clowns take the stage, they face a throng of hot, sweaty Juggalos surging towards the stage in an attempt to score a half-mouthful of sweet, sugary Faygo (Root Beer and Moon Mist top my preferences). As the two-liters begin launching, Juggalos grapple over the plastic rockets in attempts to drain the last bits of soda not expelled during their flights. Passing a particularly heavy two-liter to fellow Juggalos is considered a form of good conduct as you grab the fun bags of a crowd-surfing Juggalette passing overhead.

Visual: To only focus on the stage would be to miss half of the show, but looking anywhere else opens your world up to getting beamed in the head with a Faygo missile. Every Juggalo who maneuvers up to the front of a Clown show has seen at least one Juggalo (or been one himself) who failed to maintain a proper level of situational awareness of their surroundings and got dropped thanks to Shaggy or J railgunning a two-liter into their cranium.

The Family has gone to great lengths to remedy this situation. House lights occasionally go up in the middle of a show as the speakers announce a "Faygo break! Send yo momma straight down to tha store, an' tell that bitch to bring home some Faygo!" During these mini-intermissions, clown suit-clad ninjas wearing wicked clown masks flood the stage with water guns, water balloons and even five gallon buckets of Murder City's most infamous sugary concoction to douse the crowd.

Those were the good old days. Evolution is a bitch for Juggalos and Juggalettes who don't think towards the inevitable future and drop their phones, wallets and drugs into baggies before entering a manifestation of the "mystical, magical, great Dark Carnival." Converted firemen's hoses have since guaranteed that there will not be a dry eye, head of hair or article of clothing in the house or on the field.

My new Jugga-homies had a spoonful of enlightenment for me concerning the local drug scene during those dark days as we drank and smoked in an alley among the pristine dumpsters of this upper-middle class neighborhood.

For a time, Plano, TX had held the unsavory title of "America's heroin capital." This suburbanite neighborhood managed to earn this trophy thanks to a sordid complication of unfortunate coincidences. I moved down there just as the nation began to take notice. MTV kicked off its long-running *True Life* series in Plano focusing on their dragon-chasing problems.

All of them just out of high school that spring, they shared a handful of grisly stories of addiction and consequences among their friends and classmates. They all knew some of the more than a dozen kids who had overdosed from their town. Nearly as disturbing, they knew some of the kids who'd cheated death. One fellow Juggalo couldn't make it out to the show that night. Owing money he didn't have to his dealer, said dealer opted to take a few of the boy's fingers in lieu of payment. An hour of similar tales had sufficiently harshed my buzz to the point where I had to call it a night.

Seven Words You Can't Say in Waterford

South Waterford Oklahoma State University is not a very well known institute of higher learning, although we did score high marks in entertainment. Since 1991, the school's Panorama Series has brought a variety of events to our little school on the hill. From a play about what Martin Luther King Jr. and Malcolm X would have said to each other had they ever met and numerous musical groups from around the world to comedians like Jeff Dunham and Lewis Black, SWOSU's students rarely find themselves without a great opportunities for some surprising entertainment in a small town.

The closed-mindedness of some of the townsfolk created controversy on more than one occasion. Carrot Top and Dunham both drew letters from people dissatisfied with the choices we made in the university paper. The school never selected these acts. Each year, students were presented a list with different categories of events and were asked to vote for their favorites in each category to ensure a variety. The school compiled the lists by looking into which entertainers, acts and events would be out on the road the next school year falling within our price range. Events in our range were free to the public. Events slightly outside of the school's budget forced it to charge a small fee for tickets.

No act caused as much of an uproar as did George Carlin. Before I graduated, my fellow South Waterford students and I voted to bring one of the funniest men ever to live to Western Oklahoma. By the town's reaction, you would've thought that we had invited the Devil himself into the bedroom of every "decent" Christian citizen of the city.

The tickets to the 1,394-seat Fine Arts Center sold out with the quickness. No other event would produce as many letters to the university newspaper as did this one. The fallout even spilled onto the pages of the city's paper. Despite the facts that the student body had democratically chosen to bring Carlin to Waterford and that the school issued no shortage of warnings as to the mature nature of the subject matter, his impending gig enraged many morons. I couldn't score enough tickets for my family. Dad offered to sit it out so that Mom could go.

Trying out material for his then upcoming HBO special, *You Are All Diseased*, Carlin heard about the controversy surrounding his upcoming appearance in our backward little town. He walked out onto the stage, stepped up to the mic stand, looked around at the assembled crowd, and yelled, "Fuuuuuccccckkkk!" Dozens of assholes who'd paid good money for tickets immediately stood up and walked out of the building. One of those tickets could've gone to my Dad. Shitbags. Some people pulled the same dickbag move when Jeff Dunham paid us a visit. Of course, he managed to get out a few more words before he offended anyone badly enough to run away.

Supporting Single Moms

I have never been a fan of strip clubs. The idea of paying money to watch a bunch of girls I'm not going to hit on or sleep with dance around for strips of cloth paper featuring images of long dead hemp-growing slave owners has never appealed to me in the least. I did enjoy my first strip club experience, but this was more to do with the absurdity of the night than with the club itself.

As bad as Dallas was, I did meet some great A-Holes. No, seriously, A-Hole was the name of a heavy rock band on the Dallas scene for a couple of years. They had the greatest motto: "Your hole is our goal." This they centered on a flyer beneath a picture of the band standing shoulder to shoulder facing away from the camera bent over with their pants down and cheeks spread wide.

I once visited the Lone Star, a monstrous bar in Ft. Worth featuring volleyball courts, blackjack tables and a dirty, black light lit room for bands. Here, I met the boys of A-Hole. We became friends, and I would catch them around the metroplex when I could.

A-Hole enjoyed freaking people out during their shows by tossing immense, inflatable genitalia at their audience.

They had a gig at the Diamondback Saloon in Medicine Park, Oklahoma one weekend in December 1998 and invited me to hang out with them, seeing as how I was an Okie. Medicine Park is a shitty little spot on the map just outside of Lawton, which is itself a much larger, shittier spot on the map.

I helped them set up at the large bar out in an area with nothing but three other buildings: Sidewinders, a Love's truck stop and an empty building. I drank with the band's girlfriends during their set and helped them stow their gear afterwards. I was to crash on the floor of one of the two motel rooms the Saloon had gotten them for coming up. We dropped off the gear in the room, got really high and drove back to Sidewinders.

Sidewinders provided me with a night of several firsts. It was a BYOB bar, which I had never heard of in Oklahoma. It was my first strip club. It was also my first experience with segregation since leaving Mississippi. A-Hole had brought a pair of 100-quart Igloos stuffed full of iced-down Texas beer. We carried them into the bar, which confused the hell out of me. A-Hole had played the dive bar next door and followed those gigs by taking their girlfriends to Sidewinders enough times that the doorman not only knew them by name but also didn't charge us a cover.

We set up our coolers around a table in the first of the Sidewinders' four rooms. We drank a few cans seated around a long, classy table with fold-out legs before the urge to explore overtook me. I should have stayed where I was. Our room held the people who didn't fit into the other three rooms: methed-out bikers, pseudo-hippies, preppy college kids, and my heavy metal friends with their tattoos, multiple piercings and black leather everything.

It wasn't difficult at all to distinguish the other three rooms: cowboy, black and Army (Fort Sill sits outside of the ghetto that is Lawton). Guys in each room momentarily took their eyes off of the girls to stare at me and to wonder what the hell I was doing in their respective spaces. The Wranglers, Fubus and crew-cuts only mingled in one place: the line for the bathroom. It created a very awkward vibe. I returned to the freaks' room and got drunker, interspersing it with bouts of rocking some Mary Jane, the only girl there who drew my interest, in the parking lot.

Color Blinded

The whitest girl I ever bedded was black. One of the few times I actually did any DJ work with Hiroshima once I moved to Dallas was for a weekly Monday night gig we had at John's Pub for its Service Industry Night. John's charged no cover for those in the service industry for whom Monday is often their Friday. Dallas was a pretty dry run for me, although I did hook up with Emily one of my last nights at John's.

The Herpinator was killing the show as usual. The drunken masses moved to the music. A cute girl with a respectable-sized afro began hitting on me. I've always had a thing for big 'fros. I don't know if it was watching all of those Blackspoitation movies or pulling my pud to the Lady of Rage, but afros are sexy. We started chatting, and everything below her fro turned out to be just as interesting. I had on more than one occasion turned away drunken sluts looking to hook up with anyone providing them entertainment. She wasn't one of them, nor did I turn her down.

Emily and I hit it off as the night wore on. She invited me back to her place. One hitch quickly arose: I was supposed to give MJ, a guy in our crew, a ride home or somewhere. She countered with the explanation that she lived in a two-story, one-bedroom apartment with a gay male roommate who slept on a foldout couch in the first floor living room. He had gone out for the weekend, so MJ could crash on the couch if he so desired.

MJ was the kind of guy who would do just about anything to help a friend get laid as long as he wasn't going to get laid or it didn't interfere with any chance that he may have had in getting laid. He had no prospects that night and agreed to crash at Emily's place after we finished the show.

MJ and I burned a joint as we followed Emily home. We stood behind her as she unlocked her door. Pulling the door open, she revealed her pale white male roommate getting his ass plowed by his boyfriend on the foldout. MJ and I were both too drunk and stoned to do anything at this point. Emily was shocked, not that she'd walked in on this scene, but that she'd walked in on it when he was meant to be somewhere else for the evening. She apologized to MJ and tossed a blanket on an armchair for him before pulling me upstairs.

Damn. For a moment, I thought I was the darkest thing in the room. While I am sure that there are more than a few black girls who have gone home with white guys to find themselves in bedrooms decorated with nothing but posters of black athletes and rappers, I had never considered landing in the mirror opposite position. Entering the room of 22-year-old Emily, posters of Andre Agassi, the Backstreet Boys, NSync, and 98 Degrees greeted/offended me. We had sex, but it was difficult to do so under the eyes of many douchey crackers.

MJ's night in the armchair left him with a mild case of PTSD. I thanked him for his service with a joint and lunch the next day.

Dallas Institute of What the Hell?

I didn't last a full quarter at the Dallas Institute of Funeral Science. It's not because the work was too difficult or disgusting. It was because it got too weird, even by my lax standards.

This all takes place when I had really long hair, almost down to my arse it was. The school informed me during enrollment that while they couldn't force me to cut it, they requested that I wore it above my shoulders for class. As I got to know some of my female classmates, they made a game of putting my hair up in the strangest manner possible each morning in the school's parking lot. Depending on what tools we had at our disposal, some days I donned a Princess Leia. Other days I walked into my first class with a sloppy pile of hair precariously mounted on the top of my head. We did a scorpion one day where a girl braided my hair and then flipped it forward, pinning it to the front of my head. It was a silly game for a silly school which trained people to do very serious work.

We composed a strange collection of students, one of the truer versions of America's idea of a melting pot. Aged 18 to 55 and a rainbow of colors, we were one of the most disturbed pools of individuals with which I've ever come into contact. Our classroom held more than fifty people, and we filled it. I quickly recognized the three groups into which they fell: people who had grown up in family funeral homes looking to become state certified, licensed people looking for a another credential or the minority I belonged to: people with no funeral home history looking to get into the game.

On one of my very first days of class, the administration felt the need to issue a twenty-minute warning about the neighborhood in which our institution was located. We were morticians in the hood.

They spent this time warning us about stereo burglaries, car-jackings and pistol-whippings but then had the gall to warn us against packing our own pieces in self-defense as a pistol, shotgun and SKS with a thirty-round clip sat beneath the captain's chair of my van during this insipid speech. Whoever heard of a Texan discouraging folks from arming themselves? Of course, as I write this, the state recently passed an open carry law.

Classes began in the morning and ran until lunch. Our teachers passed through our single classroom throughout the morning. Most were okay, if not a little on the boring side, as the first two quarters focused on the business aspects of running a funeral home. Coming in with a bachelor's under my belt, I was able to skip the first quarter's coursework.

Alan was the teacher nobody could stand. Lanky and pasty, he was responsible for implementing a seating chart, but that's not why we didn't like him. We required assigned seating in a bad way. Some of my female classmates (our student body was roughly 60/40 male/female) were bruisers.

A morning class would be progressing nicely enough as we fought to stay awake in the middle of a lecture, and then out of nowhere, BAM! Two of the women would start slugging it out in front of us and our teacher. They never explained the reasons for their mid-class explosive outbursts. The fights rarely involved the same two women. They were apparently all bat-shit crazy.

Ally McBeal was the reason we didn't like Alan. The show featuring a cast of anorexic women experiencing multiple dream sequences was in its second season. Robert Downey Jr. would spend the next decade trying to make up for this crap-fest of a show before he played Tony Stark for the first time. Alan loved it to the point that he based our classes on it. We quickly deduced what was going on and took turns buying *TV Guide* each week. If that Monday night's episode was new and good, then we had an easy day in class on Tuesday. If the show was a rerun, we could usually expect a rough day. We mainly worried about repeats of bad episodes which guaranteed difficult quizzes. He was a sad man.

I began hating my classes and the whole scene in general. I found myself working later and later into the night at a job that was not Hiroshima, missing more and more classes and stopping in at a bar next to a Texas Instruments plant for breakfast beers with increasing frequency.

I wasn't long for Dallas. The following story of my main source of income will shed more than enough light on my situation.

Dallas Pt. II
Disillusionment and an Unexpected Career

The month I had before school started was meant to be time to get things up and running with Hiroshima Music. That didn't and wouldn't pan out. I helped the Herpinator set up lights and speakers for a couple of raves and a few of the John's Pub shows. The job and partnership I had crossed state lines for ended up being as hollow as the man who had offered it to me. I needed additional work, because what I currently had going I could have made working a few hours a week at any of Dallas' frequently robbed gas stations.

MJ worked next door to us and helped out when we needed an extra roadie for shows. Herps' headquarters sat, appropriately enough, next to Force Entertainment in an industrial office complex Northeastern Dallas. Force claimed to be the largest personal escort company in the Dallas/Fort Worth Metroplex. Force provided everything from girls who danced nude for lonely husbands and crack dealers to dates for the Dallas Cowboys and high-end businessmen (think *Pretty Woman* without the pretty).

During one of the few nights I actually worked as a DJ in Dallas, MJ offered to get me on with him at Force. Being a person who enjoys all the little extras in life, like eating and paying my tuition, I agreed to check out Force out of desperation, seeing as how the Herps' grandiose idea of, "if you move to Dallas to help me, we'll be making a million in a year" was nowhere near to panning out. That night back at the office, he introduced me to Fillmore Dynamite, Force's owner, and David, one of the DMs (Driver Managers). I gave them my pager number, and they agreed to call me in some night when they needed extra help.

Dial-a-Girl

Force Entertainment placed hundreds of ads in phone books, newspapers and the free adult papers found at strip club entrances. These ads offered exotic dancing and/or sensual back rubs (local laws only permitted licensed masseuses to use the word "massage" in their advertising) while hinting at more. Desperate men called any one of our dozens of numbers from whichever particular ad appealed to them. All calls were routed to a central call room where crews of two to four girls manned the phones. The phone girls were paid hourly wages to cajole callers into agreeing to shell out a basic fee, usually $250/hour, to get a girl to their homes, hotel rooms or one of the half-dozen "in-house" hotel rooms Force kept rented out at all times across the metroplex.

We kept hotel rooms constantly rented at revolving locations to satisfy clients who didn't want neighbors to see a scantily-clad woman and her driver show up in the middle of the afternoon or night while the Mrs. was at work, away or non-existent.

The girls wrote down the clients' information and passed their notes on to that shift's DM. If located at a personal residence, the DM ran it through a database of addresses kept on file where previous financial, physical or legal transgressions had occurred. If the address was clean, then it went onto the board.

A dry-erase board listed the status of drivers and girls on call that shift. The DM then paired up the next available driver with the next available girl, unless the caller had made a request for a specific girl. Then we sent out the girl most closely matching the unrealistic description given in that particular ad, or the favorite girl of a frequent client, of which we had plenty.

At a typical show, a driver drove a girl to the show's location. She went in solo. She was responsible for determining the level of safety at her current situation and calling it in to the office. The DM relayed her message to the driver via a call to the driver's cell or to his pager using a numerical code system.

The relayed message alerted the driver to his ward's situation. The girls let us know whether everything was okay, whether or not we should sit next to the door and await further orders, or if we needed to kick the door in and perform an immediate extraction. Other codes contained information about the presence of extra guests, unexpected weapons, rapey fiends, and law enforcement.

Less sex transpired than most folks would believe. Force did not hire prostitutes. We had female escorts. The girls performed a sexy dance for their clients. The clients masturbated to the girls' shows. Sometimes they didn't even beat their meat. Some guys just wanted a paid, sympathetic ear for an expensive hour or two. However, towels covered in dried spank did fill bathtubs at our in-house hotel rooms.

A successful show involved a location with an easily located address (GPS still being an object of the future) in a well-lit area with plenty of parking. The girl entered and gave the code telling her driver that all was copasetic and that he should kick back and read a book for the next hour (the standard duration of a show regardless of what went down). She exited with the show fee and a large tip (of which the girls usually gave a minimum of ten percent to their drivers), and they both returned to the office obeying the posted speed limits. Regrettably, this was a rarely realized pipe dream.

The Making of a Pimp

For me, my time as a bodyguard/pimp (or sous-pimp, according to my friend, Jammies) began in the same way as most experiences in my life have gotten underway since I finished high school: with a couple of beers. I had had a few at a nearby bar one night when I got the call from MJ. If I was still interested and could get to the office in half an hour, I could enter the fast-paced career that had provided Kevin Costner, Whitney Houston, Richard Gere, and Julia Roberts with weak plots for miserable but commercially successful movies.

Quickly arriving at Force, David instructed me to jump into Jason's extended cab Ford F-250 to go to central Dallas with Danny and Beth for my first show. Jason was a short preppy non-cowboyish cowboy. Danny was a huge Mexican who worked security at Dallas' stabbiest Hispanic nightclub. He often bragged that the owner threw a party for his staff whenever they managed to pass a couple of weeks without a shooting or knifing. Beth was a religious nutter with equally insane justifications for taking this job.

The mood was light in the truck as Danny and Jason explained our job as drivers, and Beth laid out what the dancers expected from us. I learned that they were taking me out on a "burn" for my inaugural experience.

A burn worked like this: the caller asked for sex, which was illegal and usually turned down. If the phone girl didn't believe it was a police sting, we sent a girl anyway. The girl got the mark's money and ran off hoping that he wouldn't shoot her or call the police to tell them that he had tried to hire a hooker who refused to screw. It was a sketchy maneuver at best. Force Entertainment normally avoided burns, but sometimes the idea of fast cash is too much to pass up, especially on a slow night.

We arrived at a swank apartment complex in an upper class section of Dallas. My new coworkers assured me that we were in for little more than a quick in and out. The most important lesson I learned that night was that there was no such thing as "easy" in our business.

The complex's gate wouldn't budge. The lock was on the inside, far out of our reach. Danny sent Beth writhing under the gate to hit the release. The mechanical clunking swing of the lock's arm sounded, and we walked through. Anticipating a quick departure, Danny plucked a leaf from a bush and shoved it between the locking mechanisms as he shut the gate. He and I stashed ourselves behind two bushes on either side of the walk fifteen feet from the target's apartment door. Beth's heels clicked on the concrete as she walked past us to the door.

She knocked. He answered. She went in. He closed the door. She called the DM and passed him a code. The DM paged Danny and I to let us know to stay close. We waited. I had to pee. The door opened. One uncertain click after another of her heels echoed through the courtyard as she excused herself from the apartment. She used the typical burn cover story: she wanted to have sex with him, but she had left her condoms in her car and needed to get them before any lovin' for money could go down, because she couldn't afford to trust his genitals or his jimmy hats.

The door closed. The heels picked up their pace as if the door's closing had been the starter's pistol at a prostitute's track meet. Her ominous clicks blasted past us. Danny shot out one of the two tree stumps attached to his shoulders and removed me from the ground with all the effort it would take the weakest of winds to push around dried out leaves. Beth reached the gate and pulled it open without resistance thanks to Danny's leaf preventing the lock's arm from dropping back into the slot in the gate's catch.

Jason had backed his Ford up to the curb. By the time I caught my first sight of the truck, Beth was safely inside the cab with the door shut behind her. Danny's hulk barreled toward our escape as it pulled away from whatever danger we were fleeing. His deftness defied his girth. He leapt into the bed of the truck as it picked up speed with all the forethought that a kite allows its tale to follow. We landed sitting up with our backs towards the cab. Danny remedied this by dropping his left arm across my throat as though he had decided to show off his WWE skills. My head slammed against the truck's bed. Jason gunned the engine until the complex was but a distant flash of a nightmare behind us. I really wish he had shelled out the cash to rubberize his bed.

Back at the office, Beth filled us in on the details of what she had seen. Walking into the apartment, it had looked normal enough. Upon entering the bedroom, however, she described a shocking scene that would become common to me over the next several months. Semi and automatic assault rifles and enough stock of other weapons to outfit a small militia unit covered his bed. Detracting from her penchant to over exaggerate, we gathered that the guy had more weapons than the three of us could've been prepared to deal with. She had still collected the standard $250 fee for showing up, regardless of what was to go on or not afterwards, and ran out the door.

Thus began my short jaunt into the field of pimping.

Showdown at the Anything but OK Corral

I couldn't have picked a worse week to begin my short-lived career as a sous-pimp. I also can't think of another driver I worked with who commanded or deserved more respect than Peter. A lanky ex-Marine in his forties, his military service held clout when working with women constantly placing themselves in dangerous situations with horny, unpredictable men. While no other car drew less enthusiasm than my bulky Chevy van, his beat-up red compact Ford came close.

Peter drove Diamond out to Ft. Worth for a show on my third day with Force. The john's wife came home unexpectedly only a minute or two after Diamond had relieved him of his cash. Force's strict no-refund policy prevented her from returning the fee and tip. Madness ensued. The man tried to calm his wife while failing in his attempt to retrieve his $500.

Peter and Diamond fled. The man shook off his wife and hopped into his Ford Ranger to give chase across the entire Dallas/Fort Worth metropolex with a total disregard for every traffic sign and light in his path. Miraculously, both vehicles made it to our offices unscathed and without gaining the attention of even a single traffic cop, possibly because of the complete whiteness of all parties involved.

The pickup's driver flashed a pistol at Peter throughout the chase. Diamond's phone calls alerted the office to their imminent high speed arrival and to his pistol-packing, pickup-driving pursuer. Three of our drivers, Danny, Jason and Thomas, took up positions side-by-side in the parking lot as they waited for Peter to swerve into sight. I stood behind the opened side door of my van, Remington 20 gauge shotgun loaded alternately with buck shot and slugs in hand.

David made sure to call Fillmore, to handle the melee about to ensue. Fillmore called the police to the office. He had us stand down as Peter's car, the pickup and two squad cars thundered into the lot in the space of sixty seconds. The ripped-off mark decided that it really wasn't a story worth bothering the police with and left upon completing a brief discussion with the officers and Fillmore, who had swung into the parking lot in his new Corvette after everyone else had arrived.

Compensation

The DM and phone girls worked on salaries. Of Force's $250 standard fee, the dancers received $50 along with any tips they cajoled out of their clients. Drivers earned $20 per show, and each girl was expected to share ten percent or more of any tip received with her driver, although this was not written anywhere. The majority of each fee was split between the office rent, an expansive advertising bill and the retainer of a lawyer or two. Even after taxes, Fillmore claimed to take home $40,000 monthly.

Unfortunately, not all of our clients were always willing to pay for our time and the girls' services. That's when the looting began. Fillmore could have run his business out of a much smaller office space if he didn't have his people steal for him. Drivers were more than willing to confiscate items in lieu of payment. The rear half of the building was an open warehouse packed with stacks of furniture, electronics, exercise equipment, and an array of other items far too random to begin to list here.

Sometimes our people found themselves in a position where wanton destruction of property was easier and more amusing than trying to make off with anything. MJ once entered a third-floor apartment of a man who refused to cough up $250 upon learning that his girl wasn't going to do the horizontal mamba with him. MJ warned the guy and then began tossing components of the man's high-end entertainment system through his window. It was November, and the window wasn't open. Piece by piece, MJ almost tossed out an entire entertainment center before he received payment. All but the wannabe john's television took flight that night.

Night of the Burns

Of all the girls I worked with, none drew more contempt than Beth and the Gutter Slut. Gutter Slut was a white woman who spoke as though she were an extra in an obscene version of *Boyz n the Hood*. She averaged four curse words for every clean word her mouth mangled, most of these were the "N" word. She also had a rap sheet longer than those of the rest of Force Entertainment's staff combined.

Beth couldn't have been more different. As fanatically Christian as Osama bin Laden was fanatically Muslim, she never cursed, had sex (except for that one time with her husband, before they married, which gave her a son and the pressing need to get married, which not too much later resulted in divorce) and almost never danced. A born again Christian, she believed that while it was completely immoral to have sex or even dance for money, she felt perfectly justified in lying to people when she told them she would have sex with them and then absconding with their dough. Her misunderstood religious convictions allowed her to screw horny men out of thousands of dollars every week. In other words, she was a lazy bitch who used her sketchy belief system to cheat others.

On normal nights, the drivers went out with a girl for a show and then returned to the office to wait for another show and their next girl. The ratio of dancers to drivers never matched. Busier nights required drivers to do multiple shows with one dancer before returning to the office to drop off credit card receipts, cash and/or stolen goods.

On one such busy night, I ended up stuck with Beth, Queen of Burns.

Our first show that evening had no other prolific results other than to set the stage for the rest of the night. She walked into her venue, passed on the code alerting me to be prepared to run, and then sped out of the house. As wacky as this sounds, nobody was too eager to call the police to report that they had hired a hooker who won't put out.

We drove across town for our next show at the Hilton Hotel at the Dallas/Fort Worth International Airport. I hated hotel shows. They presented the highest risk of potential police stings. No matter how well or badly a hotel show went down, drivers still had to position themselves near the room. With Beth inside, I had to wait in the hallway and hope hotel security didn't kick me out for loitering or worse. This episode evolved into my second-worst hotel experience during my short stint at Force.

To get onto the airport grounds, I had to stop at a toll gate where digital cameras photographed my license plate. We continued on and parked at the hotel. Beth's "date" waited for her on the eighth floor. She entered the room as I did my best to nonchalantly meander around a Coke machine attempting to appear un-pimpish.

Her john was no dummy, and she had to dash out the door to escape him. Beth may have been a hypocrite, but she was also no dummy, at least in this regard. She made sure her marks were down to their birthday suits before bolting out on them. She suggested we run, because she thought he might be a chaser. The staff at upscale hotels don't take kindly to people zipping through their halls and lobby. We managed to escape to the van without incident. The hotel didn't present much of a challenge, because we had the element of surprise on our side. I feared that the toll gate stood as the highest likelihood of becoming our Little Big Horn. One phone call from the hotel could lock us in tight. Sweating as Beth paid our ticket (drivers never paid for tolls or parking), the call never came.

Our third show brought us nearly back to our office. Our target lived in one of the pricey neighborhoods near the Southern Methodist University campus. His two-story place sat at the far end of two rows of facing townhouses with a single-lane drive between them. Covered parking flanked the drive which ended in a brick wall at the end of the property. The parking spaces were small, not that it mattered - the largest cars there were three late model plastic Mustangs. Porsches, BMWs and Jaguars squeezed into the other slots. The lone open slot sat at the far end of the strip, directly in front of our target's townhouse. Beth went inside, leaving me to wait in my van. Five minutes later, I received a page to be on guard.

Even though the page consisted of nothing more than a pair of digits, my mind didn't have sufficient time to register their meaning before Beth flew out of the front door. I threw my ride into gear and undertook the painful process of backing my full-size van out of a space meant for a vehicle I could've stash behind my captain's chair. Running away proved more difficult than sneaking in. No car occupied the space next to me. Somebody's 16ft Bayliner speedboat sat in that space awaiting its next venture out to Lewisville Lake in the coming spring. I couldn't cut my maneuvers tight enough. People tend to move faster when they have been more or less robbed of $450, forcing pimps to respond accordingly.

The concrete block propping up the boat's trailer hitch placed it at a height matching that of my bumper. I knocked it off its block and sent it careening into the Porsche 911 on the other side. My Chevy's 355 horsepower pushed us as hard as it could, distancing us from the underwear-clad Samoan I saw in my rearview mirror run into the street after us and his money. The Porsche's alarm followed us out of the neighborhood, but Beth's newest enemy didn't. If it hadn't been for the insurance fraud she later offered me, I would have so hated her at that moment.

Gravediggaz

Beth had had a husband at one point. She also had had an insured Ford Explorer that was free of dents. Nothing lasts forever. The divorce was ugly. Part of their agreement had been for him to pay child support and car insurance. He lied. She slid into a metal highway divider during a rainstorm not knowing she wasn't insured. The Explorer suffered enough body damage for her mechanic to declare it totaled, although it still ran perfectly. This was also the moment when she learned that she lacked proper insurance to repair, let alone replace, her SUV. She gave her religious beliefs a short vacation and made me an offer I didn't want to refuse.

Her grandfather owned an expansive farm outside of Dallas. She offered to pay me $500 to drive her gas-guzzling beat-up beast out to a remote section of the farm and use his backhoe to bury her rollover machine from Detroit. The plan faltered after she subjected her truck to a second and properly crippling wreck.

Wax On, Wax Off and the Sting

The most important aspect of the phone girls' work was to determine whether the call came from a real mark or a police officer setting up a sting. To protect everyone, they almost never told a caller that they would have sex with him. This maintained Force's status as a legitimate escort company. Anything/anyone else the dancers did upon arrival was their own business, and Force received not a single dime from these sex shenanigans. That didn't necessarily mean that our filtering process was perfect. Our people still got caught up in the occasional dragnet.

Not every girl was as bad as Beth. Some were worse. And then there was Melissa. Out of the two dozen or so girls that worked at Force, there was no girl I enjoyed working with as much I did with Mel. Spending a good portion of every day or night driving someone around could drag out painfully if the person sitting in the passenger seat didn't have anything to say, or worse, didn't have anything to say but still refused to shut up. Mel didn't have either of those issues, as she was a thoughtful and well-spoken young lady. She was a tall brunette with a pair of kids from a pair of baby daddies. She possessed a wry humor and quirky disposition.

Mel trusted me, and I liked her. She was a refreshing alternative to most of our skank-tacular colleagues. We even hung out together outside of work on a couple of occasions. Once I took her and her kids somewhere, but scared the shit out of everyone by going the wrong way down a one-way street.

In her mid-twenties, she was the cutest girl there despite the shotgun blast wound across her abdomen, or perhaps because of it. One of her baby daddies had tried to cut her model-tall and slim body in half with a load of 12 gauge buckshot. Failing in his original intention, he did manage to force the removal of several yards of intestines and left her with an abdomen-wide montage of scar tissue making her look like Freddy Krueger's hot younger sister. She always sprung for a beer or tacos after each of our shows.

I enjoyed every show we did together. Even the bad ones. Especially the bad ones. One man, upon learning of Mel's refusal to not bang for cash, managed to pull a large Bowie knife from a sheath hidden in some unseen alternate reality, blocking me from gaining access to my van and, subsequently, my firearms.

"That fuckingslutwhorebitch stole my money and won't suck my dick! I'mma cut'er!" he raved.

I didn't have enough distance between us to grab one of my weapons to intimidate him with, and neither of us had a phone to call for backup. His neighbors weren't home, didn't care or had grown accustomed to this type of conflict at our new enemy's house.

I played the negotiator and talked him into getting rid of his blade. It took twenty minutes to convince him to focus on me in order to get Melissa into the safety of the van. She didn't know about the guns. I wedged my way into my ride using all the diplomacy I could muster. No wait, I just screamed nonsense at him.

The man acted leery of me the whole time. I didn't understand why until Melissa and I were busy ignoring traffic signs on the way back to the office. As her show degraded inside the house, and the guy began tossing threats, she had warned him to ,"back the fuck off, because my hippie has a black belt in kung-fu." To be fair, it was not a complete fib as I had taken exactly seven Taekwondo lessons over the previous two months. Master Kim had not taught me any defense against bladed weapons, only to kick at teenagers. Luckily, it was enough to intimidate our douchebag enough into believing his knife was no match for my lethal Hippy Hair of Furry! In the end, he fell for her ruse and let us go, having no desire to have the police dispatched to the home he shared with his wife. This episode earned me a couple of rounds on Mel at the nearest bar, even though it was all thanks to her quick thinking.

Our second challenging episode together involved a hotel show. Again, I loathed hotel shows. Especially after this one. The set up was par for the course. She went in ahead of me to ensure that her target didn't see us together. The girl who took the call warned us that it might be a sting, but off we went regardless. We took the proper precautions. This included checking the halls for cameras and people lounging about that looked even more suspicious than we did. Nothing jumped out at us as being out of place. I took up my position at the far end of the hall in the stairwell and waited for Melissa to phone in her status to the office.

The coded message never came. Something spooked her at the door forcing her to high-tail it out of there. She burst through the door, nearly knocking me down. She screamed that the cops were coming. We booked it out of there. Weaving through two floors to outdoor staircases, we landed at the rear of the building. We saw nothing out of the ordinary. Still, we wasted no time in getting back to the van. Nobody hassled us as we peeled out of the parking lot. I never found out whether or not we had almost walked into a trap. The guy never called back to wonder why his girl was a no-show, so I figured we had escaped the noose. Even if the police had busted us, Force kept a few knowledgeable attorneys on retainer for just this scenario.

Destiny's Porn

Force Entertainment kept one other driver named Richard in its employ. This other Richard dated one of the dancers, Kat. My second week at Force had yet to wrap up. I was between shows at the office when they came in with a surprise like no other.

Their shared love for watching pornography was no secret among their coworkers. They frequented a 24-hour porn shop less than a mile from our office. On this particular evening, they strode in glowing as though they had found a tape of Jesus banging his favorite whore, Mary Magdalene.

Another of our girls used the name "Destiny" during her shows. One rumor circulating the office went that she had "acted" in a porn eleven months previous. She vehemently denied the accusation. Her denial made it all the sweeter when Richard and Kat walked in with a copy of one of the *Freshmen Fantasies* series.

David, that night's DM, shut down the office for half an hour, so the whole crew could watch Destiny get boned.

It opened on a young man dressed in his southern gentleman formal-casual best sitting in a white wicker chair on the porch of a Southern plantation-style home. In turn, he questioned each girl about her fantasy before her clip began. They each replied with some line of bull cocky concerning the wheres and hows of their getting-nailed dreams. The interview then switched to that girl receiving the opportunity to live out her scripted sexual dream.

Destiny's fantasy revolved around the "fact" that she had never had sex on a baseball diamond. The movie cut from her in a breezy summer dress on the porch to her standing on a pitcher's mound in a baseball shirt cut to a halter top and shorts that barely covered her own pitcher's mound.

Before this, my knowledge of pornography was fairly limited at the time until I began spending copious amounts of time with the K-Town Mafia. Like horror movies of the 70s and 80s, decent porn (talk about a paradox) has some rules. One of them is that it's okay if the male star has the face of a donkey, so long as he's hung like a horse. Look at Ron Jeremy: he is by no means what most women would consider a handsome man, but he sports a piece of timber that makes elephants blush. Destiny's "coach" only managed to possess one of these qualities: he had a horse face but no other equine qualities.

Coach summoned Destiny to the dugout. He proceeded to run faster than Rickey Henderson through first, second and third bases while sliding into her home, crotch-first, to complete a grand slam with a piece of lumber barely meant for bunts.

The fantasies to follow in the movie continued with the same lackluster formula of an uninterested woman with a less-than-qualified man completing her naked dreams.

We watched. We laughed. We mocked. We rewound. We watched again. We laughed again. She cried. She quit. She returned a month later.

It took some time, but the full story eventually surfaced. Destiny had, in fact, done the movie (difficult to deny it when we're watching it in the office's stolen VCR) for the immediate cash. She earned $2,000 for spending a Sunday with her legs wide open the previous November on a cold, abandoned high school baseball diamond. She had refused to do it until the producers promised to only release it internationally, never hitting shelves in the States.

The moral to the story is not to trust porn people. Not only did they lie about distribution, but they went so far as to paste Destiny's face on the cover of the domestically released video.

*If anybody out there can find I copy, I would pay handsomely to own porn costarring someone I once worked with!

Tranny-Mission

I didn't have the best of starts at what was not the best of jobs. A couple of weeks into my time at Force, my transmission died en route to a show. I called the closest repair shop. They sent a truck out to tow me in. The owner had a surprise for me. Easily 50-years-old, a shabby white summer dress covered his protruding pot belly. A half-pound of makeup applied with all the skill of a five-year-old girl who finds her mother's cosmetics for the first time or of a $3 crack whore fixing her face in a dingy unlit alley after sucking cock for blow coated his. He was not a pretty woman. He drummed his fake claws on his desk as he told me that it was going to cost a smooth grand to fix my literal pimp ride. I slapped down my Discover Card and let him get to work.

My van was ready five days later. I picked her up, went to work and had to call in for a tow less than a hundred miles later when my tranny-repaired tranny crapped out on me again. We coasted into the far end of a Taco Bell parking lot before we ran out of momentum. My dancer called in our situation to the office, while I called a tow truck. Not ten minutes passed before two police cruisers swept into the lot with their lights blazing. Four officers brandishing four pistols emerged from their rides. We quickly learned that a gunmen had held up our Bell and killed somebody the previous month. I allayed their fears, and they drove off once our tow arrived.

The next morning, I had to argue with the modern day Klinger knockoff for an hour to get him to repair his repair. Rupaul's honky uncle caved to what was right and got me straightened out after another week. The moral: Never trust a tranny auto repairman with clean hands.

Companionship and Drugs

With everything that went crazy on so many of these shows, we still managed to hold down some steady customers, although they were some of our most unbelievable clients. I referred to my favorite as, "Mr. Powder."

Mr. Powder called for a girl once every two weeks or so. He refused to pay cash, which was okay with us. Force kept a small fleet of the most horrendous portable credit card machines, laughably large by today's standards. They were the credit card equivalent of the clunky old bag-style portable phones.

Mr. Powder didn't trust cash or our chatty credit card machines. Extremely paranoid, he wouldn't allow his girl to ring up his bill at his place. Whomever he talked to at the office had to run his number over the phone. Whoever visited him used a crayon to rub out a copy of his plastic. Nobody at the office could say "no" to his eccentricities, because few of our clients tipped like he did.

The calls always came between 3 a.m. and 4 a.m., and he paid for a two-hour show. Powder's paranoia ran so deep, he didn't want the drivers to park anywhere near him. He had us park in a small shopping mall parking lot almost a mile from his apartment complex. The girls trusted him, so nothing was ever said about it, in spite of the complete oddness of the situation. Police cars constantly patrolled his neighborhood. He resided in an infamous spot for high-level drug transactions.

Powder had a job in order to support the $15-20,000 he blew monthly on call girls (not all of them ours), none of whom blew or banged him. He watched a bush outside of his front door for a living. More specifically, he watched for the rotation of two briefcases two people hid in a bush outside of his front door two or three times a week. He had to sit at his window and watch it from the time the first case arrived and someone exchanged it for another until a third person picked up the second case. He spent his days watching large-scale, low-key drug transactions.

That's not all he did. Mr. Powder used his drug money to pay for his apartment and utilities. He had other means to pay for the girls. A contact of his in Canadia created American birth certificates complete with social security numbers. The names on the certificates didn't exist, but their SSNs were completely legitimate. In addition, each "person" had excellent credit. Powder signed up for credit cards in the names of his made-up people. He maxed out the cards and then had a friend in Mexico draw up equally legitimate illegitimate death certificates for these people who had never lived. Thus, with the circle of imaginary life completed, and the girls were paid, and paid well.

1999

Casino Whore-al

Force Entertainment's owner had visited a casino for the first time in his life less than six months before he took me on as a driver. In half a year, he had amassed $250,000 shooting craps. He used forty large of that cheddar to purchase a new full-size Chevy van with every extra imaginable. He outfitted his white beast with leather seats, a television/VCR, radar detector, and a gun safe. Few of these items were quite what they seemed. The rear bench seat folded out into a queen-size bed automatically with the push of a dashboard button. The television featured ports built under the windows next to the passenger seats to plug in PlayStation and N64 controllers. His radar detector defied detection. Front and rear sensors covertly built into the bumpers had an indicator unit which exposed only a pair of LED lights from behind a thin, unremarkable plastic strip installed in the dash beneath the radio. His small gun safe was bolted onto the floorboard between the front captain's chairs. The safe's combination key pad had four finger-shaped depressions. This way, he could slide his hand into the grooves without diverting his attention from the road and gain access to the safe's contents.

Fillmore bought this van with his gambling winnings for the sole purpose of making more casino excursions for himself and his employees. At the time, my casino history consisted of a trip to the Blue Chip Casino in northern Indiana for Goober's twenty-first birthday, to Shreveport a month before for my first visit there and to the major letdown alcohol-free, video poker Indian casinos across Oklahoma. Visits to the gambling dens of Detroit, St. Louis, Seoul, Pusan, Ho Chi Minh, Shanghai, and Las Vegas were all still a long time away.

When Fillmore decided to run off for a short weekend, he invited along all of his off-duty drivers and dancers to come along. It was easy enough for drivers to go, because we were the only ones at the office who didn't have set schedules. We basically showed up and left at our leisure unless they were shorthanded on a particular shift. We had the option of doing one show a night or for working several days in a row. Josh, Tony, Sapphire, and I hitched a ride south. Fillmore's wife never went. Somebody had to stay home with the kids, and this was his private time.

Josh, Tony and I began the ride by splitting a six-pack and viewing the one video Fillmore kept in his leather-clad love machine: a how-to video on the finer points of shooting craps. He blew through Southeastern Texas without incident. The only amusement we received came when Fillmore popped open his safe at 88mph. He whipped out a 9mm Glock and ten $10,000 bundles of $100 bills. He regularly carries a hundred grand as his walking around money when he visits Harrah's Shreveport Casino & Hotel. This time, he owed Harrah's $10,000 from his last trip which hadn't panned out so well.

Going with Fillmore was like getting a preview of NBC's audacious and long dead *Las Vegas*. Everyone from the parking valet to the pit bosses knew Fillmore, or Mr. Dynamite, as the highly professional and tip-hungry staff referred to him. The hotel had set up two complimentary rooms for us in the time it took to walk from the van to the check-in counter. Fillmore stayed in a penthouse suit on a floor not listed in the elevator. Access could only be gained by inserting the key card into a special slot below the buttons for the other floors. It featured a sitting room, one-and-a-half baths and a glass shower off of the king-size bedroom. The rest of us shared a room on the seventeenth floor that was not too shabby, either.

Outside, the sun had done her thing for the day and began to let the moon party the night away, but you would never know it beneath the eternal fluorescent and neon retinal overload inside of Harrah's. We had thirty-six hours to gamble away any chance of our future offspring having a college funds or inheritances. We also had thirty-six hours to see how serious Harrah's about its free drink policy. I accepted it as a personal challenge.

That first night, Fillmore turned in early but not alone thanks to an agreement he had with a friend of his in Shreveport. As it turns out, this friend had introduced him to the wonderful world of gambling and owned escort agencies across Louisiana. When they visited each other, the host provided free bedroom entertainment for his guest.

Tony and Sapphire were dating and ran off for some private time in our room before Josh and I fell down for good. By 2 a.m., my liver's superpowers had already astonished Josh enough that he retired to the room. My body decided to take a ninety-minute nap at 4:30 a.m.

Five years would pass before I would eat a stranger breakfast than the one I ate with my crew that morning. We sat down at the casino's 24-hour restaurant. When I think of 24-hour restaurants, greasy spoons like IHOP and The Waffle House come to mind. The most obvious drunken late night meals consist of soggy bacon, stiff pancakes and coffee so strong you have to have the strength of King Arthur to withdraw your spoon from the depths of its murky lake, all accompanied by the sounds of people puking or porking in the toilet. That morning, I devoured a filet mignon and a lobster tail with a half-dozen bottles of Coors Light (a phase between my Milwaukee's Best Ice and Pabst Blue Ribbon stages). A pit boss happened by at the end of our meal. He greeted Fillmore, who introduced us. The boss signed off on the ticket and walked away.

The attacks on our wallets and sobriety rambled on.

The remainder of the morning passed quietly enough, or as quietly as it could amid the din of screaming slot machines. We gambled. We drank. We got crazy.

Fillmore gave us the spare key to his room. The four of us went up to play. Sapphire wanted to clean off and get filthy in the glass shower with Tony while I took pictures with my camera. I didn't know them that well. Not that it mattered if I had, I possessed zero desire to see either of them nude, wet or nude and wet. He managed to sneak my camera away from me. I can't believe that Wal-Mart printed my nude photos of Sapphires ashen cellulite pressed up against the shower wall. Thankfully, she didn't get around to taking any of him.

Sapphire napped after her dirty shower. Tony and I rejoined the retirees, bachelor party participants and addicts downstairs. He had had sex less than thirty minutes before, but he was already checking the scene to see if he could find any women he could bag during this brief reprieve from his girlfriend. He decided that the cocktail waitress who had brought our last three rounds of drinks was cute, available and making eyes at him. We joked around with her as much as her position allowed. We moved on, only to see her walk out through an employee exit an hour later with Sapphire. By the time the door shut, their tongues were racing to see whose could get down the throat of the other faster. Tony thought that this might turn into a ménage a trios. It turned out that she was only getting her bisexual jollies with the girl, leaving Tony dry.

The day passed, not that any of us could have known having spent it in the confines of Harrah's. I cleaned up to meet my people for dinner at the casino's formal restaurant.

The last to walk in, I couldn't believe what awaited me. The wait staff wore fancier clothes than I currently owned, would ever own or would ever want to own. I took the fifth seat at our table and ordered a screwdriver as an appetizer, the first of four to find their way to me. I sat across from the bar. I watched the female penguin drop ice into a glass and follow it with a healthy but not overwhelming shot of Absolut and enough Tropicana to color the vodka. The importance of this process will make itself apparent at the end of the meal.

The four males among our number each went for the Jack's T-Bone Steak, a $45 chunk of cow. Our lone female ordered a no less tasty filet mignon. I alternated between screwdrivers and Coors Lights. I watched the bartender extract frosty 12oz bottles of the Silver Bullet, use a church key to pop them open and then pour them into a chilled vessel six times. Again, this has meaning later.

Five frosted, layered or ice cream-covered, but all scrumptious, desserts capped off the meal. Then the bill came, delivered by another penguin. The total for our five meals ran well over my food budget for three months. The number leaped off the tab and permanently melted itself into my cranium: $698.43. We had eaten and drunk enough food and booze to come just shy of the $700 mark.

Astonished, we scanned the breakdown of this ghoulish tab:
Coors Light: $12.50
Screwdriver: $24.50

This is where you should pay attention to the fact that neither of what I just listed are in their plural forms. My drinks alone accounted for $160.50 of the ticket. Again, a manager came over, introductions were made, and we didn't pay. We each dropped a Jackson on the table for the tip and partied the night away.

Our group separated for the evening. Later, all but Fillmore had resurfaced and rejoined the fray. We thought he might be in his room and went up to wake his lazy butt out of bed. He wasn't sleeping nor was he alone. The hooker didn't care that we had walked in on them.

Everyone was quite inebriated and thought a picture was in order. She had already departed by the time I had run down to my room, grabbed my camera and returned. Josh said that she had paused to make out with Sapphire on her way out.

The next morning, Fillmore secured his remaining $90,000 in his safe beside his pistol and sped us back to D-Town, so we could return to making him money to fund his next trip south.

Gettin' Outta Da Game

I owe my leaving the business to Stacy. I had my suspicions that some of the girls might have been doing more than dancing for their clients, but it wasn't something that was discussed in the office. As I've said, the girls who negotiated the naughty at their gigs did so independently of Force Entertainment. For me, proof of independent dealings came on what ended as one of my final nights after a show with Stacy in Northeast Dallas. The show went off without a hitch. She went in and gave the signal to let me know all was calm on the exotic dancer front. When she returned forty-five minutes later, she propped one of her cowboy boots upon my dashboard and yanked out a ten-strip of assorted rainbow-colored condoms. "I'm so glad I didn't need these this time," she said.

That was all the confirmation I needed. Five months of doubt had culminated in one woman sitting in my van, grateful that she hadn't had to have sex for money that time. Her next show might have gone, and probably did go, differently. I wouldn't learn the outcome: that was the last show we shared and nearly my last show altogether.

I did work for a few days after my revelation but only with girls I knew didn't hook. Confused and morally upset, I jetted off to Shreveport for the weekend to collect my thoughts, contemplate my situation and formulate a new life plan. Instead, I drank and gambled away a day.

I had moved to Dallas for two reasons. My primary mission had been to attend the Dallas Institute of Funeral Science. The second involved my gullibility in allowing a diseased beast of a man to convince me to join him as his business partner.

No inner peace came to me in the Big D. Of course, I could attribute a large part of that to my crazy jobs and school. I found it increasingly difficult to stick around. I was working 24-hour shifts four or five days in a row most weeks. I did this more from a lack of anything else to do. I slept between shows on a sweaty stolen sofa in the employee lounge. For longer naps and showers, I took advantage of the in-house hotel rooms we kept. I was tired of sleeping with hookers (you know what I mean), eating ramen noodles cooked on a camp stove in my van and returning to the Herpinator's house every two weeks to do laundry. A particularly ugly case of Bell's palsy consumed the right half of my face.

My departure from Shreveport wasn't pretty, either. After bouncing between a few joints during the day, I transitioned into the evening at Harrah's. Plenty of screwdrivers over many craps tables in several casinos made me illiterate, but I persevered. When I returned later in the morning for a final drink and round of dice, a dealer near the end of his shift called me over to his table to give me almost $200 in chips. He explained that I'd left for the bathroom and not returned while a shooter was in the middle of a good run. He'd let my wager ride and held the chips for me. He earned one hell of a tip that morning.

Hours of vodka-fueled meditation at the craps tables resulted in me breaking my right hand the next morning while clambering around on a riverbank to take a picture that didn't turn out well. I slipped on some loose gravel and sturdy booze. Falling, I had to decide whether to protect my body or my not-so-trusty $3.50 Pentax AE. My camera survived, but I broke my hand and started the long drive back to Dallas and then Oklahoma with it wrapped up for days before I got around to seeing my doctor. That sealed the deal. I was finished with Dallas. Dallas was finished with me. I decided to return to Waterford and start my MBA.

Even that exit strategy didn't go as planned. I hadn't gotten far from the river before a tapping noise woke me. I lifted my head to find myself stopped in a left-hand turn lane at a stoplight. While waiting for the light to change, I had passed out cold with my foot on the brake. I don't know how long I had sat there.

The man wore a uniform, but luckily, it was that of a paramedic. He told me that he and his partner had pulled up behind me and had become suspicious after watching me sit through two light cycles. He inquired as to my condition. I lied and said that I was on a road trip and had driven all night on my way back to Oklahoma (I had never gotten Texas tags) and had simply fallen asleep while searching for a non-casino hotel. He couldn't smell my booze over the stench of the river. He provided me with some quickly forgotten directions to a Motel 8 and left me to my own devices. I got the hell out of there, packed up my shit in Dallas and returned to Oklahoma. Fuck Dallas.

My Dallas experiment was obviously a bust. I returned to Western Oklahoma to do my MBA, which also turned out to be a bust. To top it off, my right hand was busted, literally. My tumble down that Shreveport riverbank at the end of my hellish half-year in D-Town hurt the hell out of my right hand badly enough that I had to make the return drive to Dallas, and Oklahoma days later, with my hand propped up on a pillow on my lap.

Our wonderful and trustworthy family doctor of the past two decades has a nickname in our town: Dr. Malpractice. Breaking my hand helped cement this diagnosis. Dr. Mal played with my hand and took an X-ray, which he didn't show me. Studying the picture, he concluded that I had merely sprained my hand and instructed me to visit my chiropractor for a few sessions to get it straightened out.

This led to four weeks of paying a man to twist and torture my hand. I possess a high tolerance for non-dental related pain. I've walked around on a broken foot for days. I was once shot in the shoulder by a Roman Candlestick. I patted the spot for a minute believing I'd been bitten by one hell of a mosquito until a friend pointed out the embers surrounding the hole in my shirt's collar. This hand business was not fun.

After putting me through daily sessions of hell with zero improvement, Dr. Twistnshout decided to shoot his own X-ray film and share it with me.

"What do you see, Richard?"

"Well, Dr. Twistnshout, I see a break on a little bone there below my thumb," I responded knowing that it didn't take a doctorate or having seen a season of *E.R.* to see that I had gone around for the past month with a broken hand protected by little more than the occasional Ace Bandage. I might not have known the scaphoid's name at the time, but I sure as hell was quick enough to recognize a break in a bone when I saw one.

Dr. Twist asked to see Dr. Malpractice's film. He called me in to take a gander. Wow, did Dr. M. ever earn his name that day. Dr. Twist showed me a beautiful picture of the bones showing no problems with my hand. The shot of my middle finger to my pinkie only told us that I had nothing wrong with the half of my hand which felt no pain.

Dr. Twist sent me to a hand specialist in OKC, which was strange, because I'd thought that I was quite the specialist in my hands, especially my right. My hand guy informed me that letting the break go untouched and yet so mistakenly manhandled for so long had done damage to the bone.

I had two options:
1. Put a cast on it and hope for the best over the next month, and then maybe give it another cast.
2. Go under the knife to let a surgeon scrape away the growth that had taken place in my body's attempt to mend the tiny but bothersome chasm between the bone's halves. This would also entail the insertion of a screw and a pin into the cashew-sized bone.

Either way, he told me that I would likely develop arthritis in my hand in later years. I went with the cast. Two casts and nearly four months after the original break, my hand didn't heal exactly right. It gets weird sometimes when it rains or when I write, bowl, masturbate, or take acid for too long.

Returning to Waterford in mid-March, I'd have to wait until August to start my Master's. I needed to find work in the meantime. A life-changing project soon landed in my lap.

When I was DJing, the high school proms and homecomings paid the bills, but it was the random college parties and even some of the weddings that I enjoyed most. I found myself occasionally working for a couple of Waterford bars trying to cater to the college kids.

Winners was an unspectacular and short-lived sports bar next to the Loose outside of town. Their biggest draw was serving to minors, including me, throughout my duration as their DJ. The building's subsequent owners converted it into a church.

The Hot Spot was another local dive bar which had been quite the party barn in the 1980s when it was known as AJ's (and at other times as Clyde's and The Moose). A fire and a theft transformed the joint into a decrepit shell of its former selves, although that shell is rather interesting and sits at the epicenter of this drawn out dollop of drama.

Originally built as an RV sales and repair complex in Oklahoma's oil boom days, the setup consisted of a smaller building containing the offices and a sales floor attached to a cavernous room with a large pit sunk into the center to aid in repairs and maintenance projects. Together, they totaled 99,999 square feet to slide beneath the state's sprinkler regulations. A fire back in the late eighties proved this to be a mistake.

While doing shows for the Redneck, a farmer who had fallen into possession of the building, we developed a decent working relationship. He often called on me to come out to the Hot Spot when he opened the side room for larger bashes. I happily brought my equipment out, the three-minute drive easily the shortest I ever traveled for a show during my five-year tenure behind tape decks and CD players. It was easy money, and I got to drink for free, regardless of my age.

The parties themselves were usually only one or two steps above some highly white trash bash actions. The Redneck invariably forced me to emcee wet t-shirt contests which almost always elicited more jeers than cheers from the crowds. Methed out, yet still overweight, women aren't the biggest draws. Fights were not optional when the Redneck opened the side room. Some racist hillbilly would say some shit to piss off an equally racist Master P wannabe, and shit would pop off. In Western Oklahoma it is difficult to get five hundred or more people together without at least two closed minded white and black guys coming into contact with each other after liberal applications of alcohol, even if it was only the 3.2 percent OK piss the Redneck was licensed to sell and whatever liquor they'd either snuck in or had shot-gunned in the parking lot. Ironically, I believed that if these freaks had ever had the opportunity to consume their pre-party substances together, they would probably have preemptively squashed any beef to arise later.

The Offer

The Redneck heard that I'd returned to Waterford. His ability to piss off all of the city and county law enforcement had put him in a position where running a bar of questionable legality was no longer an option within the confines of our county. He approached me with an offer. Knowing the scale of the parties I had thrown at the

Seventh Street Lighthouse and the success of most of the events I'd done for him, he asked if I was interested in renting the bar from him.

I was interested and smart enough to know that I couldn't do it alone, but dumb enough to choose the only and worst partner I could have selected. Despite so many situations having gone south for one reason or another with the Herpinator, I asked him if he wanted to co-own a bar in his hometown. He tossed me a quick and solid affirmative.

Herps would DJ and work on promotions, while I would manage the daily business of the bar. Mom and Dad said they'd help out however they could until we got on our feet. My parent's unwavering support of any venture I dive into has long been a wonderful constant in my life. We had less than four weeks to get the place in shape.

Herps moved up from Dallas and stayed with my parents for free for a few months until he moved into the Lighthouse's basement. We dubbed the bar, "Phunky Jay's" after the nickname he used on scorecards when bowling.

Phunky's evolved into a work in progress over the next few months. The bar became a hodgepodge of decorations as cluttered as my mind. A fresh coat of sky blue paint on the Route 66-facing side of the building and a plywood Phunky Jay's sign Herps and Jackoff (an artistic bartender far more skilled at art than bartending) made the outside presentable. I covered the wall above the men's room urinals with CD covers from some of the 1,200 discs I had amassed during my DJing days. The bar's counter occupied the far left corner of the smaller room, a raised stage at the right corner. A fish pond ran in front of the stage as though it were a moldy moat protecting a shanty castle.

An April Fool

Phunky Jay's opened its doors on April Fool's Day, 1999, our first in a long list of follies. The first four weeks saw few customers.

Once the glow of owning a temporarily unsuccessful bar began to wear off, the next high came from a short-lived but very fun sexual tryst with Firecrotch, the best friend of our head bartender, Ronnie. While my brother had a perpetual redhead fetish for many years, I broke in numerous places at Phunky's with this young lady and her fiery mane.

181

Opening a college bar in a small Western Oklahoma town just before the end of the spring semester was piss-poor planning. Just two months after opening, we already found ourselves forced to resort to booking strippers. It gave us a small, but much-needed, cash infusion. Our summer business was typical of an Oklahoman summer: long, hot and dry. I drank heavily and spent the summer with a sweaty cast on my arm. We set it on fire a few times while I pretended to be a movie stunt man and sometimes just because I was passed out. A flood of five-dollar tabs of white blotter acid provided the majority of entertainment and optimism I would experience that summer.

Refusing to Punch My Train Ticket

I met the Train and her husband, the Conductor, during my first round of university. They were a fun, outgoing couple, and I enjoyed the few chances we had to hang together. A long period of time passed where I didn't see them. One weekday night the Train showed up at the bar. She asked to speak to me in private in the side room.

"Richard, I want to fuck you. I want you to fuck me," she fired off for her opening salvo.

"What? Train, you're married. You're married to the Conductor. Your husband is my friend," I reasoned.

"It's okay. The Conductor likes you."

"That doesn't make any sense."

"No, he's working in D.C. right now, and he doesn't care. I'll call him right now," she said, Nokia already out, scrolling for his number with one hand whilst grabbing my junk with the other.

I detached my privates from her penis pincher and escaped. We never did do the dirty, despite a few future attempts she made on my genitalia. She did, however, allow three of my friends to run a train on her a few months later, thus earning her nickname. I even believe that a participant might have videotaped the affair. What I wouldn't give to continue not knowing the fate of that tape.

Take II

After trudging through the summer, Phunky Jay's exploded in the fall. The Herpinator had some kick-ass equipment we used to produce what remain some of the best party fliers I've ever seen. He printed them on clear plastic sheets that blew away anything the clubs in OKC were handing out. We made laminated business cards/coupons/calendars that doubled as souvenirs for many people. We started putting together radio ads and getting them airplay on local radio stations. This wasn't the best idea, since most of SWOSU's student body (our target market) ignored the local country and pop-40 stations. I also doubt that the few mentions we managed to score on one of the bigger OKC stations sent too many people our way out west.

In the end, I think it was word-of-mouth from the first couple of parties that began to bring the masses through our doors. Herps got his hands on a foam machine through an associate of his. In 1999, we didn't know anybody who had heard of a foam party taking place outside of the more popular spring break destinations down in Mexico. To this day, I still believe we brought foam to Oklahoma first.

If you have never gotten funky in the foam, let me explain. For the party goers, it was a blast - for the club operators, a stinking pain in the ass. We used plastic sheeting to wall off the sunken pit in Phunky's party room. A homemade box housed fans and sprayers which pumped a foam solution out of 50-gallon buckets and oozed foam into the pit. Our party people watched multi-colored light beams shine through an eight-foot-tall pool of bubbles.

People danced in it. People did drugs in it. People got freaky in it. People had sex in it.

The foam sprayed until it got too cold for people to run around in bikinis (or less) and get soaking wet. Strangely enough, that was the only time I really had wished we had still done it.

Cleaning the mess made me envy adult video store wank-booth jizz moppers and whomever is tasked with cleaning up after porno shoots. This job fell to some of the bar's staff, Mom and I, but never the Herpinator.

By the next morning, the foam aftermath had reverted back to liquid in a two-foot-deep pit the size of a tennis court with no drain. We had to go in with buckets to scoop and a shop-vac to suck out the unreal pool of miasma. It always stank and filled the room with a level of humidity worthy of any jungle. We always found items we wish we hadn't. A common haul included random articles of clothing (including bikini tops or bottoms, but never a set), the odd piece of jewelry to go into the bar's ignored lost and found box, a used condom or two, and the ultimate Cracker Jack prize: a used tampon.

I loved the foam parties that semester, because they gave me hope for Phunky Jay's sustainability, but I *hated* cleaning up after them.

Bananas and Blow

Listening to Goober's copy of *Chocolate and Cheese* provided me with my first Gene and Dean Ween experience. That funky album forever hooked me into their weird experimental college sound.

My first Ween show wrapped up a perfect day. It started with a boat ride on a local dirty lake filled with plenty of drinking and smoking. Goober and a couple of our friends met us at the dock to roll to the show together.

Ween took requests from the audience at the Will Rogers Theatre. I drank more beer and smoked more weed. The ancient, single-screen theater was revamped long ago for small venue concerts. An island in the rear middle provided cheap beverages and saved thirsty people from missing an incredible show.

Changing Majors and Priorities

I quickly learned that I had little interest in graduate-level business classes. What saved me was that a couple friends of mine knew how much I enjoyed writing convinced me to take a couple of journalism courses when I started the MBA. These I loved and continued until I'd knocked out a second bachelor's degree. Some of the stories to follow I pulled from my portfolio, making a few necessary repairs as needed.

Breakdown

Barely a month into our first full semester, the Herpinator invited me out to lunch to announce a change to our previous arrangement of a 50/50 split on the door proceeds to an 80/20 for the Thursday night parties thanks to the success of the foam. He hadn't wasted any time in altering our terms.

By the end of September, my life had hit a three-lane rut with only one positive part to it. I spent my days and night in class or at the bar, but I went home each day to U-Kay, my British girlfriend who had moved in with me as opposed to crashing on the couch of my high school classmate who had introduced us. As much as I liked U-Kay, she did provide another source of drama when we first started dating, although it was through no fault of her own. Herps, who claims that women are nothing but "dick koozies," wanted to bone her when they first met. Choosing me over him created animosity between us. Like so many women (although not nearly enough), she did not care for him or his advances. I, on the other hand, really liked this woman, so much so that she was my first girlfriend with whom I ever cohabitated, even if it was short-lived (she had to return to England when her work visa expired at the end of October).

The bar happily fired the artistically inclined Jackoff from his bartending duties in October, but Herps kept him on for a short, awkward while longer with Hiroshima Music.

Stress from Phunky's took a heavy toll on my constitution that first fall semester. Herps and I decided to shut the bar down for Fall Break. At the last minute, he decided we should host a party that week and then took off to South Texas, leaving me to work his impromptu event. Not enough people turned out to make it anywhere near worth the effort, although it did piss off our staff who had been looking forward to a week off.

Mom and Dad opened their home one Wednesday for an employee appreciation party for the staff and some of our closer friends. A spat erupted between the girl for whom I'd originally returned to Oklahoma and U-Kay. L-Ron, Jizzball and Tex-Mex put in appearances. The latter two of the trio and I climbed onto Mom and Dad's roof. L-Ron brought the Jimmy around so we could jump off onto his truck, slink in through the windows and escape out to Cowball's. We closed the bar down and then went out to Phunky's to play some late night N64 *GoldenEye*. We later drove around the countryside to cause mischief until I crashed on their sofa well away from the feuding women.

Queenly King

I almost ran for SWOSU's Homecoming Queen during my second round of college. That's no typo. I wanted to run for queen. SWOSU didn't have a king back then. I tried completing the paperwork but hit a stumbling block when I came to a space asking which

185

university club I represented. Although I had been known to attend the occasional meeting of a few different clubs, I had never formally joined any of them and couldn't talk any of them to sponsor my bid for glory and equal rights. I convinced fellow students in several clubs to back my bid but failed to get any of their faculty advisers on board.

A week before the deadline, the Young Republicans' staff adviser agreed to sponsor me. I wasted the better part of the week tracking her down to get her to sign the form. I finally got hold of her less than an hour before the deadline to file. She had changed her mind but hadn't gotten around to informing me. The time had long since passed for me to talk someone else into doing it. I stand sure she did it on purpose to calm the waves I was making at the school. In the end, cancer killed her, although the two were probably unrelated.

I didn't get to run, but the school did add a Homecoming King the next year. You're welcome, SWOSU gentlemen.

Nude Introduction

Most of the people who held college parties along Washington Street did so in a number of apartments in a V-shaped complex which shared a very convenient courtyard between them. While there are many things in this world that I love, clothes are generally not one of them. I used to get naked every chance I had (and some I didn't have) in college…and beyond.

The only time I convinced someone to join me came at one of the North Washington parties. Even better, it was a girl. Immensely better, it was the Streak. I ditched my clothes with a friend, did a loop around the courtyard, and then, with the girl in tow, circled the southern side of the V. It wouldn't have been such a strange streaking, but at the moment I turned around to the back of the building, Kryle and Tone were pulling in to the back lot.

Kryle and Tone were people whom I had recently met and was fast becoming friends with around that same time. Kryle had brought Tone over to convince him to be his roomie. Both semi-mellow people at that point, Kryle was explaining how, while there was a little party going on that night, the complex was normally pretty quiet. At that exact moment, I ran buck-ass naked in front of Kryle's Ford Explorer. Just as they were getting over the shock of my nudity, the Streak's headlights came bouncing up and down in the glow of his headlights. Although I don't know to what extent my apprentice and I played in the decision, Tone did move in with Kryle.

Wisdomless Teeth

While I have experimented with my fair share of substances (and yours, and his, and hers...), I have never been a fan of prescription pills. Of course, I have rather enjoyed them when they were actually prescribed to me.

I've mentioned my rather high tolerance for pain. That being said, I am an uber-pussy when it comes to my chompers.

My teeth are a bit of a train wreck. I made one pediadontic dentist in Mississippi very unhappy. After a few visits at our county's lone dentist in the "Hospitality (Except to Blacks) State," with whom Mom worked, he pulled her aside and said, "Richard's Mom, you know I love you and your family, but don't ever bring that child back here."

My oral experiences changed when we moved to Oklahoma. We met the Hunter at the little church Mom forced the family to attend for a few years. Mom talked to him about bringing Goober and I to him. Being an honest person, she warned him about my severe odontophobia. He advised her to simply wait to bring me until I had a toothache.

In today's pussy pandering parenting world, this move would have likely ended with a visit from Child Services. As it was, his tough love succeeded. To his credit, his methods varied greatly from anyone else I'd experienced once he got me settled into the most frightening chair our species ever built.

Apparently this runs in the family, as the Grandma from Hell had to dose Mom with a Valium before every visit in her youth. For once, I wish Mom had taken a cue from her mother.

Mom and Dad had me wear a retainer when I was younger, but I refused to let anyone install braces into my mouth.

Wisdom teeth. What a lie. Two months ago, while having a filling replaced, the Hunter informed me that I should have my impacted molars (fancy term for wisdom teeth) removed my junior year of college for no reason clear to anyone but he and his accountant. They caused me no pain, and had yet to push around any of the nearby teeth. We decided to do it anyway.. I thought, "hey, no big deal." I was wrong.

Living in Waterford, my options were limited to going to Oklahoma City or to seeing the traveling oral surgeon that comes to town one day each week and be at his mercy. Having no desire to spend two hours on the road to have a complete stranger put knives in my mouth, I opted to go down the street to have a complete stranger put knives in my mouth.

I had to wake up at 7:30 a.m. on a Thursday morning after not being allowed to eat or drink anything after midnight the night before. One of those was a bigger problem than the other.

Since the traveling tooth man doesn't visit my dentist's office, I had to fill out one of those first-time patient forms in an office I'd never before visited. An assistant led me into a room and sat me in the big dental chair. She brought in a TV/VCR combo so I could watch "the video."

"The video" was a complement to the increasingly impersonal and lawsuit-happy times in which we live. It opens friendly enough. An older, mortician-like oral surgeon explains how and why a person's third molar can become impacted. At this time, everything was fine. We have all known people who've had this done, and what they said later: After a day or two of pain and a healthy dose of pain medication, they return to whatever passed for normal for them.

Then comes the part where your fingers begin squeezing the cushy padding a bit more tightly.

Complications MAY arise. The video told me that my surgeon might accidentally break off a piece of the tooth next to the wisdom tooth during the process, or might puncture, or cause an infection in my sinus cavity, or might have to break my jaw to get the teeth out. To top it all off, I may DIE.

At this point, I still hadn't met the man who would soon drug me beyond coherence in a cramped room filled with numerous stainless steel pliers, knives and various pointy tools. The time for him to make an appearance came.

He ambled in, introduced himself and promptly started me on nitrous. An assistant popped a vein in my arm, and I woke up thirty minutes later. I never saw my surgeon again. I left with Dad, my driving privileges having been suspended for twenty-four hours.

Nine years in the Boy Scouts of America taught me to "Be Prepared." Post-op preparation consisted of me whipping up three batches of vodka Jell-O shots the night before my surgery.

Dad dropped me at the Seventh Street Lighthouse. I popped *Star Fox* into my Super Nintendo and plopped down onto my beanbag chair. An hour later, the time came to change out my gauze and pop a Lortab. The bloody padding came out easily enough, but damned if I could shove the fresh one in. Blood gushed from my mouth, forbidding me from replacing the gauze or swallowing a pain pill to curb my increasing level of agony. It took a good ten minutes, but I finally stemmed the flow on my heaviest day. After a drawn out battle, I won, went numb and passed out.

That was the first and last pill I popped from that bottle. The remainder of my recovery involved my beanbag, plenty of shots and lots of SNES. The pills would sit in their bottle until the Four Days of 4/20.

Snow Job

I got sucked into a ski trip out to Angel Fire with Dewey's family, because the Herpinator declared that he wouldn't go unless I went, and he was determined to go. For the first time since signs of the end appeared, I didn't want to leave the bar as much as I wanted to leave the bar. Thanks to some piss-poor planning, we had to stay a night in Eagle's Nest, NM. I spoke less than fifty words during the first twelve hours of the trip. The fact that five of us (Herps, Mom, Goober, Goob's girlfriend, and I) rode out in his Hummer, of the most uncomfortable trucks ever constructed and only meant to carry four, didn't help mend our situation one iota.

Before Herps and Dewey's polite request turned into some jagged trip which hinged on my attendance, I had briefly entertained the notion that this trip could possibly patch the rift which had begun to open between Herps and me. A case of the flu infiltrated our ranks and knocked most of our numbers down during our five days in the mountains. I escaped with a mild fever on our second night out and more doubt than ever about Phunky Jay's future...

The Spitter

Running a bar often means dealing with assholes. Most of it involves dealing with people too stupid or ill-mannered to obey the "no drinks or cigarettes on the pool table" rule, folks too inbred to comprehend "last call for alcohol," or the number of people who sneak outside booze inside and don't bother hiding it. I'm in no way trying to say that I have never broken any of these rules, but at least I almost always made a small attempt to not get caught. I tried to kill the worst offender at Phunky Jay's but instead ended up smashing a Camero like Ryu in a *Street Fighter II* bonus round.

Mom often worked the door for our bigger parties. One night, a young man entered, flashed his driver's license and received the stamp from Mom identifying him as being under 21. He walked to the table nearest Mom and took a beer from it. Mom saw him and motioned to one of our bouncers to bounce him. Having been in the bar less than two minutes and being escorted out, he spilled the beer on Mom, cursed at her and spat in her face.

It didn't take but a few seconds for the news to reach me at the bar. I sprinted to the door, leaping across four tables Super Mario-style to get around the crowds. Checking that Mom was okay, I ran out in time to see the punk back out of his parking spot in one of those door wedge-shaped Chevy Cameros with New Mexico tags reading, "SHY-N." I blocked the front of his car, wondering what he would do when a half-dozen of my friends and security guards joined the scene. Half took up position in front and half behind the cheap plastic knockoff of one of America's greatest muscle cars.

Standing at the driver's side door, I yelled for the piece of shit to get out of his piece of shit.

"Fuck you! Let me go!" he responded.

"You fucking spat on my Mom, so I'm gonna beat your ass!" I don't know why, but that didn't entice him to get out of the car.

"Fuck you! I'll pop a cap in your ass, nigga!" he threatened me with wildly inaccurate racial slurs as he made to reach into the center console. I don't know how many times he dropped the N-bomb on me, but the little idiot made his two favorite words clear to me that night.

"Yeah! Pull your fucking gun and see what happens you little bitch!" I said, kicking and kneeing dents in the door.

"I'll fucking shoot you!" he warned me again but grammatically correct this time with his hand still concealed in the console.

"Shoot me and see what the fuck happens! Pull your god-damned piece and see what happens!" I said, through with formalities and brought my left hand down onto and slightly into the windshield, shattering a star pattern across to the passenger side.

By this time, a crowd had gathered. Someone had gone in to tell Mom that our new best friend was threatening me with a gun. A quick phone call from Mom to her friends at 911 brought out every on-duty officer from the station a whole two minutes away. Lights and sirens blazed as they screamed into the parking lot, Waterford's finest leapt from their cars, guns drawn, telling me by name to step away from the car, because, "We've got this." They dragged the kid out, who didn't actually have a piece on him, and towed the Camero once they realized that it wasn't even his car.

You don't mess with my family.

Floaties

The Illinois River crosses the northeastern corner of Oklahoma near tiny Tahlequah. Thousands flock to the area every non-drought summer to float rafts, canoes and kayaks down a six or twelve-mile section of the river. I had the privilege to accompany the K-Town Mafia on two of their excursions. They both began with some madness and had several parallels flow between them.

On both trips, we met up, stocked up and rolled out. They also involved getting drunk and high before we had left Oklahoma City's far-flung city limits.

Our troupe got underway later than planned on my first trip. Our octet pulled into a dive of an older hotel well after dark. Wasting no time, I immediately stripped and jumped into the pool as the guys checked us into our two rooms. It took less than five minutes before half of our posse had trashed one of the rooms. Knocking the television off its stand, flipping chairs and ripping the smoke detector off the wall, the guys who had instigated this just as quickly claimed the other unmolested room as their own leaving the rest of us to set right their quick carnage.

While the majority of my second float trip mostly mirrored my first experience, it had a startlingly different beginning. Our two-car caravan had not yet passed through northeastern Oklahoma City, giving us just enough time to crack the first round (or second round for the more dedicated of our crew) of beers and to pass around the Gambler's one-hitter, when Hand Job's SUV popped a tire. He had the misfortune of having this go down on a ramp with no shoulder.

191

Removing the tire proved a more difficult task than it should have. Not a one of us could crack the lug nuts. Luckily, I had way over-packed and brought along a tire kit I'd scored with Marlboro Miles. The kit included a cigarette lighter socket-powered impact driver. We plugged it in, and the lug nuts fell right off. Those fiends at Philip Morris might be cancer-causing cunts, but they did get us moving along that hot afternoon.

We slapped the doughnut on and limped to the nearest Hibbdon's Tire Center.

Our little party milled about the reception area in various states of disrepair. Some of us thumbed through the obligatory collection of outdated magazines. I found a devastating article in *Time* announcing Japan's erroneous decision to outlaw the sales of hallucinogenic mushrooms in convenience stores and vending machines. The rest of us watched the television sitting atop a small refrigerator. We would have survived without incident had it not been for Billy.

A pair of parents popped in to set their seven-year-old boy on a chair. They wisely left the room. "TV Billy," as we dubbed him, had some mental issues we couldn't handle in our discombobulated states of minds. TV Billy didn't care for having the television on and ran up to slap its power button the moment his parents left the room. Jackrabbit quick, he retreated back to his seat to stare at the powerless idiot box.

We didn't know how to react, so we responded the only way we knew how. Hand Job snagged the remote and slid it under the tattered magazine he'd been thumbing through before he'd found this newer, greater source of entertainment. He gave TV Billy a minute or so before he slyly clicked the tube back on. TV Billy jumped out of his seat faster than if it had had a car battery hooked up to his undescended testicles.

This routine repeated for roughly five minutes. I don't know how any of us kept our shit together. It was just about the funniest, albeit cruelest, shit I'd ever seen.

Thankfully, TV Billy's parents retrieved him at long last. They finished Hand Job 's truck at the same time. TV Billy's parents' BMW pulled out ahead of us. He turned around in the back seat (why he wasn't strapped down, I will never know) and shook his hands at us while making noises we couldn't hear. Our vehicle responded with a few middle fingers and possibly one anus before we sped on ahead to continue drinking and smoking on our river quest.

We arrived late in the morning on the second trip and secured more beer, a couple of rooms at one of the cheaper lodges along with our two rafts and a canoe. For nine to twelve people, this is the best configuration.

No matter how much forethought you invest in your drinking, you invariably run out of beer. The drunker your crew becomes, the more spillage you can expect. You can then use the canoe to send a team ahead to score another case or two of overpriced river beer. We started out with more than 100 beers for the eight of us the first year and still managed to run out long before we reached the end.

If you've never floated a river before, it used to be a day of total obscene drunkenness, dotted with potheads sneaking off into the woods to smoke. For the more daring of us, it was a day of drunkenness spotted with a hit of LSD and/or the random line of coke or meth if you had had enough foresight to purchase decent waterproof containers. A random Ziploc baggy stashed in your cooler protects nothing by the end of this sort of escapade.

Rafters spend their river floats leaping into the water whenever they find a deep enough spot, swinging from ropes on trees and sharing booze and drugs with other groups. Fraternities and sororities were my favorite groups to come upon during our drifts. Greek groups from the larger universities usually provided us with endless entertainment. They often tied their rafts together into massive flotillas weighted down with kegs and girls in bikinis. Taking turns trying to run/bounce across a flotilla produced results ranging from the insane to the incredible. I spent most of my trips wearing a life jacket upside down, letting the raft drag me and my beverage of choice in its lazy wake.

My favorite party shirt is a white t-shirt with a giant marijuana leaf on it. Its caption reads, "Keep off the Grass!" I bought it in high school during my one shot at rebellion more than a full year before I would ever partake of the sweet, sweet cheeba.

Any time I find myself in water, I feel the compulsion to get naked. During the course of both trips, I removed my swim trunks at some drug-induced point and lost them as my bare ass bumped and scraped along rocks in the shallow waters. On both occasions, I had to fish my soaked "Grass!" shirt out of one of the rafts and squeeze my legs through the short sleeves. My genitals inevitably hung down through the inverted neck hole, much to the dismay of the guys collecting the rafts and canoes at the end. We always arrived among the last vessels in each day and therefore more wasted and noticeable than had we pulled ashore with the bulk of the crowd.

Each full day of drinking, drugging and dunking under Oklahoma's unrelenting summer sun meant that we had a mellow night in store for us. The following day began with generous applications of lotion to combat the sun damage received and ignored the previous day. A breakfast at Braum's, the best fast food breakfast the Southwest has to offer, wrapped up our time in the northeast. A ride much longer than the one the day before awaited us.

Faygo Failure

No one ever accomplishes every goal they lay out for themselves. The amount of goals I have failed to accomplish involving me operating a motor vehicle un-proportionally outnumber my failures in any other area.

Cars and I have a long history of not getting along. People have hit me a few times, but most of my troubles stem from mechanical failures and my inability to deal with them. Over the years, I have burned up no fewer than three engines, four or five transmissions and a whole host of various, but critical, automotive components (most all of this between the ages of 16 and 25). Not a single one of these ever came about during the normal course of my daily life. Some ended better (or stranger) than others.

A friend from Dallas' main rock station hooked me up with a pair of tickets to the Insane Clown Posse's *Amazing Jeckel Brothers Tour*. I couldn't find a single taker in all of Western Oklahoma for the second ticket.

My '89 Chevy van's radiator hose blew south of Oklahoma City. I had to jog a few miles to the nearest truck stop to replace it, but I got underway without losing too much time, having factored in some pre-party action into my schedule.

I was actually pretty happy with the whole situation. Most of my automotive issues end with a tow truck, so the fact that I had conquered this hiccup on my own surely meant that I could expect smooth sailing for the remainder of the weekend. Usually a staunch realist, my short foray into optimism failed faster than my van.

Less than thirty miles down the road from the scene of my triumphant feat of man over machine (overcoming my mechanical ineptitude made the victory all the sweeter), my van dropped its transmission. I coasted into a shuttered weigh station. A heavy drizzle began falling on me as I began to walk down I-35 South towards Ardmore to find a pay phone. I believe the rain helped me to hitch a ride faster than I might have otherwise.

I called Mom who called Albert's Towing (the best towing service in Oklahoma if not anywhere). It was cheaper to have one of Albert's guys make the five-hour round-trip than to have somebody from Ardmore run me back to his city a few miles down the road.

Walking north along the interstate through what had intensified into a steady shower, I bent down to pick up a small crucifix pendant I had noticed at my feet through the rain and darkness. No sooner had I stood up than a car pulled over for me. The world works in mysterious ways, and mine is sometimes downright crazy. We got to talking, and I learned that Stoney and Angie, a stripper in OKC, had met Herps at a party a few months previous. What a small, weird world.

Having bid Stoney and Angie a safe trip, I ran across the four lanes of traffic back to the weigh station. Pausing under the overhang of the rear of the building to piss, I saw that a working pay phone had been sitting no less than twenty yards from my van the whole soggy time. Long hours stretched out before me as I waited for a steady but slow-moving truck from Albert's fleet to retrieve me and my ride. Ever the inventive young Juggalo, I knew just how to fill that time.

Among the crates of camping gear I kept in my vehicles, I also usually stowed an emergency supply of booze. During this trip, I had a half-case of Andre's Cold Duck Champagne. A small bag of mushrooms accompanied me to enhance the concert I was now going to miss. I would miss the Wicked Clowns show but not the enhancement. Hooking up my SNES to the four-inch portable television mounted to the van's ceiling, I fought through the mental fog of the schrooms and lack of definition on the tiny screen to play *Street Fighter II* for an hour as rain drummed down on my rooftop.

Albert's truck arrived as I had neared the end of my third bottle of bubbly. Understandably, the driver had me chug the remains of the bottle before allowing me to climb into the cab of his truck. The Andre's served a dual purpose that night. First, it got me a little buzzed, which is always a welcomed occurrence. Second, seeing me throw away three empty bottles hopefully fooled the driver into believing that any weirdness I displayed on the ride back was due to the alcohol and not the head full of fungus I kept secret from him.

2000

Stinky Hayes
-or-
"Shut Your Hole, Squirrel"

I ushered in the brand spanking new millennium at Phunky Jay's with family and some friends. Things at Phunky's hadn't turned completely sour yet, so there was still some joy to be had. The next morning, L-Ron, Gokey, Jizzball, and Tex woke me with a call from Goober's Grotto at 10 a.m. to come over and kick January 1st off with a liquid breakfast. How can a man decline an invitation like that?

I jumped in Bonnie with my final four bottles of the nearly four cases of Andre's Cold Duck Champagne I had stockpiled for the End of the World/New Year's Eve and hustled my butt over there. The five of us spent the morning chugging cheap champagne and trading our stories of the previous evening. We'd all greeted the new year in different cities.

The champagne killed and the stories spilled, we stumbled back to the Lighthouse for more booze and piled in Bonnie. Tex drove us out to Phunky's to play pool. Jizz and I sat in the back. Jizz felt a sudden urge to toss cookies on the way there, but instead of rolling down his window, he threw open the jump seat door next to me and let loose as we turned into the parking lot. Mom was in the parking lot and watched the spewage unfold. That day easily went down as one the best in my life, as it was one of the last times our six-year-old crew was able to all come together.

The fun didn't end there. I picked up my pet dead squirrel that morning.

A cold spell hit Waterford the week before New Year's. For Western Oklahoma, that meant that the temperature spent weeks never hitting higher than 45°F. At about the same time the weather turned Western Oklahoma into an outdoor refrigerator, somebody's car had hit a squirrel, flinging it into my yard. We saw the squirrel lying in the yard and knew what we had to do.

197

A waist-high stone wall enclosed my backyard. We placed the cold corpse on the wall where it ended at the driveway, stuck a Camel butt in his mouth and propped him up against an empty Budweiser bottle. He looked obscenely drunk, clinging to a giant bottle for dear life.

I snapped a group picture with our *Weekend at Bernie's* rodent. We then set the furry stiff up in the old gas lamp post next to the driveway. A broken tombstone with the inscription, "Baby Hayes," went on top of the post. The tombstone was a leftover from a great haunted house we'd put together at the bar that Halloween. It was meant to be a real tombstone, but the mason broke it back in 1947 and tossed it onto his mistake mound where it sat for more than five decades until one of my security guards liberated it.

Stinky Hayes, as we christened the new, deceased member of our crew, remained at his post for three weeks sitting silent sentinel over my driveway and sidewalk. One day I received a call from Officer Sally. Several parents had lodged complaints with the police that Stinky was scaring their kids as they walked past him on their way to and from the elementary school three blocks down the street. I told her that someone had done it as a joke (yeah, us), and that I just hadn't gotten around to taking it down yet (nor would I ever have gotten around to it had she not called). Stinky abandoned his post that afternoon. He received a proper burial in the Dumpster in the alley.

To complete this madness, the whole episode even made its way into the "Police Notes" section of the *Waterford Daily News:* Police talked to someone about removing a dead squirrel displayed in the yard with a cigarette in its mouth and a beer nearby.

Waterford isn't the most exciting of cities most of the time, but thanks to Stinky, people had a confusing blurb in the paper to speculate on for a day. Long live Stinky Hayes, the best pet dead squirrel I ever had!

Years later, for reasons I'll never understand, Goober resurrected my pet dead squirrel by carrying around a squeaky stuffed dog toy he named for my squirrel. Stinky the Plush has since traveled the world. Not too shabby for a deceased rodent.

Losing Control

Ten months into the Phunky Jay's venture, and the Herpinator decided and declared that I should switch from being his partner who ran the bar to being Phunky Jay's manager, working for a pittance of a wage which would supposedly increase at an unspecified later date. This move essentially removed me from the decision-making process and gave him the control his personality desperately requires in every situation.

Communication, or a lack thereof, became a running standard operating problem between us. Our Mardi Gras party bombed completely and truly signaled the beginning of the end of Phunky Jay's as a viable commercial enterprise. It also served as a signpost as to how far he'd sunk into his own one-man cult of personality that would make North Korean dictators jealous.

Herps put together a contest where every person entering the club would receive a beaded necklace. The girl and guy who scored the most beads through whatever means by midnight would win a trip with Herps and Dewey to Mardi Gras. I was not to be included on this trip.

Walking in as the staff was prepping for the party, Herps served up one hell of a shit-cake by announcing that he was raising beer prices and lowering our bartenders' pay. An hour into the Mardi Gras party, he informed me that the first keg of the night was supposed to be free. Not knowing this, I didn't get it iced down until he told me to tap it. He argued that he had mentioned it in an ad he'd made for a local radio station and on flyers he'd printed up and had plastered in a few locations around town. I don't know how I could have missed them considering that I don't listen to that station (and only had an AM radio in the hearse) and hadn't seen any of the flyers.

The boiler blew when the Herpinator called up the guys and girls obviously sporting the most beads to have them counted. He chose a girl he wanted to bone over the obvious winner. The neglected woman came from a very tight knit circle of my female friends. They were rightfully pissed off about this shady move. When they complained, Herps wigged out and screamed at them in front of the assembled masses and left knowing that he had no friends there that night.

I wanted out. I was no longer a partner and yet had my assets intertwined in this failing project. I had credit card debt for the first time in my life and owed money to my parents. Each week, I was putting in more than forty hours at Phunky's, taking seventeen hours of class and working on my university's paper for another eight hours. Every license keeping the bar running was in my name, and somehow I'd lost any semblance of control to a sexually perverted megalomaniac.

I didn't mind how far I'd stretched myself when I had a vested interest in the bar. Now it had transformed into the lowest paying job of my adult life. My "friend" had declared himself my boss, and I was rapidly losing faith in and respect for him. This quickly disintegrating situation encouraged me to punch out, but I was strapped into this downward spiral until the bitter, somewhat bloody end.

Ending our partnership did, however, work to my advantage. I gave my two weeks' notice and then still got talked into sticking around as an employee until we got out of debt. I was neither very smart nor assertive during this period in my life.

Our personal and professional lives were too intertwined not to cross paths on an almost daily basis. While Herps almost always had someone who considered herself to be his girlfriend, it never stopped him from having unprotected sex with as many other girls as he could con into riding his blistered bologna pony. He took the Innocent as his special female friend when he came to start up Phunky Jay's with me. A sweet girl and friend to this day, she didn't deserve the shitty treatment she received from him.

A stunning example of how well he took care of her took place one night at Gary's, Waterford's first and only 24-hour greasy spoon diner where you have to fail a breathalyzer to be served after 1:00 a.m. The Herpinator, the Innocent and a few of our friends had gone out for a late dinner after closing Phunky's one night. Herps and a girl there who had a crush on him went to the bathroom at the same time, screwed and returned to the Innocent and the rest of our people.

The Innocent came to talk to me at the Lighthouse the first time she had finally had enough of his shit. I listened to her, dried her tears and tried to comfort her for nearly three hours one March evening. The Herpinator even came upstairs during this but refused to even acknowledge her presence. As if the bar and school weren't enough, I now found myself having to look after the women he emotionally destroyed and/or physically infected.

The highlight that spring came in the form of a surprise that showed up at the front door of the bar. Boondoggle was an incredible band of young neo-hippies tooling around the country in an old yellow school bus they'd converted into an RV. At the time, I had described them as "4 Non-Blondes with a college jazz influence on acid." They played one of the best shows our club ever hosted and then crashed at the Lighthouse after partying away a good chunk of the night with us. I still have and listen to their 1998 *Songs that Sell Beer* cassette.

April Showers...

Phunky Jay's survived its first year by the skin of its teeth. Its second year kicked off with a controversy when a classmate and fellow newspaper staffer shat on my doorstep. This bible-beater published an opinion piece in a March edition of our paper. She wrote her column with all of the forethought and research of anyone destined to anchor FOX News. She lamented that "every issue is plastered with Phunky Jay's ads," despite the fact that we had only run two ads since the previous September.

The fanatical rant complained that Christians had no voice in the paper (we paid to place our two ads, and Christians were welcome to do the same) and that the club promoted getting "wasted." Not only did we not promote getting wasted, my parents and I used a lot of our time and gas to drive people home who had had too much to drink. My favorite line from her misguided attack: "Bars will not get you into heaven!" I was impressed with her bravado in damning my customers and me to an eternity in hell and wrote a column in response.

Thanks to some of the less intelligent drunks at our school, I had to write a second column two weeks later to defend her right to say what I had disagreed with. People placed obscene phone calls to her at all hours of the night. This made an unfortunate amount of sense, considering that most drunks aren't going to get up to that kind of tomfoolery until after the bars close. I still believe she had the right to speak her mind. Throughout the years I knew her, we never clashed outside of the Features pages of our paper.

Phunky Jay's first, and (spoiler alert) last, anniversary party had four local bands rocking the side room: Sub Seven, Stone Relic, Great Big, and Shagbone. While I still didn't have any desire to be a part of the club anymore, I loved hosting live music. Taking Ecstasy for the first time that night didn't hurt any either.

A week passed, and the Herpinator devised yet another scheme on how to run/ruin Phunky Jay's. This one would magically generate $64,000…a week! He was a little too discombobulated during this period to make his plan clear, but this nonsense never came to fruition. Neither did his plan to drop my hours at the bar back to twenty-five a week once I was no longer a partner. His plan to train me in cutting the commercials we were putting out on the radio also failed to pan out to nobody's surprise.

Four days later, Herps sat me down and told me that he wanted out. As with every business arrangement he's ever been a party to, everyone had sold him out, including me, Mom, Dewey, and a laundry list of others. On the heels of expressing his desire to bail, he announced to me that our banker, my Scoutmaster and a man I considered to be my second father, had cleared him to borrow twenty large if he wanted to make improvements to the club. Not three more days passed before he reaffirmed his desire to bail.

Collaborate and Listen

A high school classmate of mine got into concert promotion for a short time. He brought the epitome of one-hit wonders, Vanilla Ice, to Western Oklahoma. I used my position on the university paper as a means of getting backstage with a friend who wanted to meet the legend. Ice signed her ass (okay, the back pocket of her pants). Other than the most obvious track, he also performed songs about pot and showing boobs. He let some people on stage to take a shot at free-styling for a few minutes.

The promoter had somehow set up the audio and lighting systems without having secured a fog machine. He asked me to run home to grab mine. I got to supply smoke for Ice.

Shirtless and Underpaid Muscles

My strangest 4/20 celebration saw me hanging out at Phunky Jay's as we hosted the Underground Hardcore Wrestling Association. This no-budget wrestling group from across the southwest set up a full-size ring in our party room. I have never cared for wrestling, with the exception of the hardcore acts. I was out once I learned that it was all scripted and staged. I do, however, love the JCW (Juggalo Championshit Wrestling) and any other group of weirdoes willing to roll around in or hit each other with objects wrapped in barbed wire, pierced with nails (or even thumbtacks) or made of glass (fluorescent tubes being my choice).

A really nice group of extremely un-pretty guys traveled a long way to put on a really energetic show for an extremely small crowd. The wrestlers outnumbered the crowd. As cheap as the tickets were, I still find it hard to believe that so few people were willing to check out something that crazy which had never before come to our town, at least we learned why.

The Herpinator and I weren't the only ones to leave and return. He fired Ronnie, our head bartender, who had worked for the Redneck for years before we took over the place. He then asked her back a day or two later. He had me fire Connor, our chief of security, only to bring him back in a demoted position.

Connor's demotion came about over the theft of two of Herps' high-tech lights and their controller when a mostly unused and unchecked rear employee door was left unlocked after our failed wrestling show. What I never understood is how the one night we happened to have a door susceptible to unhindered entry, somebody happened to use it. Furthermore, why didn't he/she/they take more than two lights? Of all the gear and alcohol in the joint, the offender(s) only took two lights which most people wouldn't know what to do with in the first place. They somehow knew to take the controller, despite of the fact that it wasn't near the lights.

A new semester and warmer weather brought about the return of the foam parties and the return of larger crowds, although attendance continually fell from its peak the previous fall. The worst aspect of this was that the warmer the weather got with each party we threw, the increasingly worse the day of cleaning that ensued. The amount of foam generated was the same for a hundred as for a thousand party-goers.

Bring May Shit-Storms...
Our thirteenth month provided the last fleeting bright moment between the Herpinator and I. He talked me into co-hosting a radio

show, *Block Rockin' Beats*, a title he lifted from the Chemical Brothers.

We recorded the three-hour show in the Seventh Street Lighthouse's basement. Herps mixed a mess of techno, while I sat around waiting to do voice-overs with him. This plan scored us free air time on a not-so-local pop 40 radio station down in Altus in exchange for mentions on all of our promotional materials and a small amount of cash we received from some sponsors.

We continuously plugged upcoming events and specials at Phunky's throughout each episode in what amounted to a weekly three-hour advertisement interspersed with electronica nonsense. *BRB* played from 10 p.m. to 1 a.m. on Friday nights across most of Southwestern Oklahoma for nearly two months. Herps got stoned, while I was usually drunk by the time we wrapped an episode in order to get through the ordeal.

School was coming to an end again. Herps decided that he wanted to scale back *BRB* to two hours and possibly put together a second show focusing on pop 40 filth. Like so many of his ideas, it never transpired. He unilaterally made a decision to shorten Phunky Jay's week to one night where we would host a large party which would receive all of our promotional efforts: flyers, *BRB* and paid radio spots. Even the idea of producing television ads was tossed about.

The Innocent wasn't the Herpinator's girlfriend. That wasn't his style. He might choose to practice his dickupuncture on one girl more than others for a while, but he didn't "date" women. The Innocent began to repeatedly come to me to bitch about Herps and how she couldn't stand anymore of him or his shit. Then she had a seizure.

I had gone over to a friend's house to play some N64. I returned to the Lighthouse at 1 a.m. to discover a message on my answering machine from the Innocent's friend, Lisa. The Innocent had had a seizure and been admitted to the hospital. I paged the Herpinator on the intercom I had installed in each of the Lighthouse's four bedrooms and received no response. This was odd as both of his vehicles were home, and he refuses to ride with anyone. It was way too early for him to be asleep, even taking into consideration the copious amounts of Everclear he had been drinking for the past month or two.

A few minutes later, the Innocent and Lisa showed up wondering where Herps was. They pounded on the basement door with no success. They drove around and returned an hour later. The Innocent sent Lisa home and took my bed for the night. She talked about moving to a suburb of OKC with her father, but decided that wasn't far enough away from Herps. She went to bed thinking of going to her mother's place on the far side of the state.

The next afternoon I ran into Herps at the bar. He had one hell of a tale to tell from his night.

He opened by asking my age. I told him I was still 23. "What happened to me last night would be like you fucking a 13-year-old." What the hell did he mean by that? He had met an 18-year-old named Michonne. He is a few years older than me and takes great delight in screwing younger (but legal) women.

She came by and picked him up so they could go have sex somewhere. According to him, she told him, "This must be what it's like for a 14-year-old boy with a poster of Pamela Anderson on his wall to have Pamela Anderson appear in his bed." She sure knew how to stroke his ego, among other things. I hope he never learns about what Southeast Asia has to offer on the cheap.

Michonne came by the house the following Monday as Herps, the Innocent, Ronnie, Firecrotch, and I sat on my porch discussing the bar. She wanted him to confirm or deny the rumors she'd recently heard about him:
1. He had boned her high school's Spanish teacher after DJing a dance there. This led to her school refusing to hire Hiroshima Music for another dance.
2. He got some kids drunk at a dance after showing up drunk himself.
3. He had an STD.

I never learned whether or not the first two had any truth to them.

It was around this time that the psychiatrist father of a friend offered to give Herps a free psych evaluation upon hearing just a small portion of his outrageous stories circulating.

Desperate to find new ways to replace the crowd Herps had run off, Phunky Jay's ended the merry month of May with an alcohol-free dance party for high schoolers. It managed to draw 150 youngins into the club.

With Herps focusing on the big parties, I looked to find alternative events for the days we were closed, which was now most of them, especially with school out for the summer. My first summer contribution came when I rented the bar out one night for a bachelor's party.

The day started with me ending a couple of drunken days on the shores of Ft. Cobb Lake, my favorite filthy lake locale. I cruised back into town for the beginning of the festivities. There wasn't much to it.

A dozen horny guys hired a pair of pretty hot girls to strip for them. One was married, but that didn't stop them from getting naked faster than I can chug a can of beer. They weren't really into dancing, but for a few bucks were willing to perform strange "tricks" with their vaginas, reminiscent of Bangkok's infamous Patpong Road.

They let guys take shots of beer from their coochies. They pulled out a small cooler packed with popsicles. They dubbed these "pussy pops" and sold them for five dollars. I'll let you guess just exactly what they did to them to make worth five bucks.

The party petered out, and the girls invited me back to the hotel room the guys had gotten for them. We smoked a joint. They decided to go ahead and drive back to OKC but not before removing everything in the cheap room that wasn't nailed down. I hope those boys paid cash.

June came and found the Herpinator devising new schemes in his perpetually altered state of mind. We met on the afternoon of the first, so he could question my dedication and inquire as to why he had to do all of the work. I'd yet to see him show up one time to clean up after a foam party or deal with anything on the bar side of the business except for firing and rehiring people, in spite of those duties supposedly falling under my purview. He told me that we should both split for a half hour to take care of whatever personal crap we had to knock out. We would then bunker down and hammer out a new radio ad, an episode of *Block Rockin' Beats* and a television spot.

I left for fifteen minutes and returned to find him gone. He didn't come back until midnight. Instead, some buddies of mine showed up for a little impromptu gathering to say farewell to a friend moving to Texas. Herps finally arrived as we heard a neighbor yelling, "No! Stop! You're hurting me!" I called the police. Four cars responded.

When one of the police officers I knew came over to talk to me, the Herpinator pulled him aside and informed him that he thought that, from "sources he'd rather not name," the guy was on "some form of meth." Watching him narc the guy out, I lost a lot of what little respect I had left for Herps that night. I wonder how high he was when he randomly ratted out our neighbor to the officer.

The Herpinator called me the following Tuesday night from south of OKC to tell me that he was on his way back. He instructed me to run out to the club to pick up some equipment, because *he* wanted to record the next *BRB* when *he* got home around midnight. I reluctantly followed his orders and took a nap, knowing that the show would eat up half of my night.

Word from him didn't arrive until I received a page at 5:30 p.m. the next afternoon saying to meet him at 7:00 p.m., so we could start at eight. In the end, he didn't lay down the opening tracks until 9:30 p.m., a full twenty-one hours later than he had originally commanded me to prepare for. This was how things had begun to work. We accomplished projects at his behest when he was damned good and ready.

Welcome to the Machine

Roger Waters of Pink Floyd fame came through Dallas, and I had to attend. My parents tricked me into going…or I should probably say that they tricked me into not canceling my plans that weekend.

It began one night with JeEcHuA and I hanging out at Mom and Dad's. Ronnie called to ask if Mom had cleaned out the post-foam party pit. Mom and Dad were always volunteering to help out, but everybody (except Herps by now) loved them and tried to dissuade them from doing the heavy lifting. He and his top aide, the Lackey, (meaning the Lackey alone) were supposed to have cleaned it for the first (and only).

The Lackey had done a piss-poor job of it. I love Ronnie. She is a biker chick with a degree in psychology and two sons, the oldest of which was then almost at the end of his teenage years. Ronnie is not the kind of person who holds back when letting you know how she feels about any subject, and screwing up at work was a subject about which she felt strongly.

We put the phone on speaker as she bitched Herps and the Lackey out up and down and left to right. She pulled no punches. It was all my parents, JeEcHuA and I could do to keep from exploding with laughter.

Dad decided to roll down to D-town with me for the weekend. Besides the Waters' show, I had to run through Hiroshima's Dallas office to grab the last of my possessions still there after my return to Oklahoma: a pile of 16mm educational films I was splicing for visual shows at the raves we had planned on putting on before I had left.

We had a great weekend! Dad and I hit John's Pub on Saturday night where Hiroshima did regular shows. Our friend (and Dallas' then-number two coke dealer), Escobar, was doing a show that night. Even better, some of my favorite Buzzards were down.

I got Escobar's new cell number so I could get the correct keys to the office from him, because the Herpinator had given me the wrong set. Hawaiian Sun Tropic was conducting its Model Search 2000. Dad and I got to hang out with a few sexy, but mostly brain dead, girls in bikinis. We closed down the bar, and I took Dad back to the hotel where I munched some herb and stymied out to *Superfly* until I passed out cold.

Let's take a minute to look at Escobar. He pushed a lot Columbian snow around Dallas, but he was a far cry from your regular drug dealer. He dealt as a job, not as a means of acquiring uselessly blinged-out trinkets. He lived a modest life.

An associate of Escobar's, Benny, a fellow coke salesman, sold Escobar out to the cops. Benny was the antithesis to Escobar. He encapsulated the ideals of the stereotypical wigger. This little cracker strove to live life as though he existed in a Master P music video. Around this time, the U.S. Department of the Treasury changed the face of the $100 bill by super-sizing Benjamin Franklin's head. Benny took that enlarged mug shot and had a full-scale platinum charm made to dangle around his neck from an oversized gold rope chain.

Benny reveled in his illicit lifestyle, whether it was the hip-hop wannabe clothes he wore, his iced-out bling or his chopped and lowered pimp ride complete with 24" triple-gold Daytons. Bright enough to move up a few rungs on the drug ladder, but idiotic enough to get caught, he turned snitch as quickly as he had sold his stepped-on bags of blow. Benny took this opportunity to grass out his closest/only reluctant friend, Escobar.

The reality of Benny's poor life decisions came home to Escobar and his girlfriend as they slept one morning. A team of heavily armed police officers stealthily broke into his apartment. He opened his eyes to find himself staring down the barrel of a 12 gauge shotgun. The police confiscated the thirty grand he kept in his safe.

Intelligent enough to hold down a semi-legitimate job to cover his more nefarious activities, he peppered his salary with his drug money without being ostentatious. He tried fighting his charges and the methods the police used when alleviating him of his ill-gotten gains. I lost contact with him before the matter ever came to a close. The one thing I do know is that Escobar faced his fate like a man and refused to narc out any of his compatriots crafty enough to not get caught through mistakes of their own devising.

I took Dad to see IMAX movie, *Mysteries of Egypt*. I dropped him back at the room and went on to the Coca-Cola Starplex to see the greatest concert of my life. I couldn't talk Dad into joining me. He'd seen *The Wall* in a theater filled with acid-laden people wigging out and felt that he'd maxed out his Pink Floyd points.

Mistaking the time of the beginning of the performance for the opening of the gates, I showed up thirty minutes late to the show. The Coca-Cola Starplex Amphitheatre hosted Dallas' night of his *In the Flesh Tour*.

Due to the co-founder's somewhat messy departure from Pink Floyd in 1985, I only expected to hear work from his five solo albums. I was horribly, yet wonderfully mistaken.

I exited my van to be welcomed by "Another Brick in the Wall Part II." I bought my ticket to the sound of "Vera."

Waters' had a simple but overly amazing stage setup. He had more than enough band members and singers to comprise a baseball team during their off nights. A gigantic screen behind his band provided the smoothest visual show ever produced. Every song or group of songs had its own accompanying anime.

He covered Floyd's catalog well and did it with album quality production. He comprised his two-set performance of songs from *A Saucerful of Secrets, Animals, Dark Side of the Moon,* and *Amused to Death* among others.

The crowd couldn't contain its excitement when the traditional rays of light and prisms projected onto the screen to signal the beginning of his *Dark Side* set. He completed the first five songs before switching over to some of his solo work. After a couple of those, he returned to knock out the final two tracks of *Dark Side*.

The visual show for "Money" was stunning. An unbelievably large turntable was projected on the rear screen. Slowly, the needle moved over to the equally large *Dark Side* logo spinning in the middle of the disc. Throughout the song, the album shifted shapes and designs.

During "Shine on You Crazy Diamond," the screen slowly zoomed in on the eye of Syd Barrett until a red cross consumed the entire screen.

A projected field of stars mirrored by thousands of cigarette lighters in the audience provided the perfect backdrop for "Wish You Were Here." This song was the highlight of my then-seven-year concert career, spanning over fifty shows.

The show ended, and I dropped down to Deep Ellum to find Escobar at a high-end strip club in the promotional Hummer of a local radio station. I followed him back to John's. A couple managers invited us to join them as VIPs at yet another tittie bar. We closed it down and returned to John's once more to do some serious after-hours drinking until somebody suggested pitting a manager's Land Rover against Escobar's borrowed Hummer in some off-road action. I declined and buzzed off to catch a few winks at the hotel. I later learned that Escobar bashed in the hood and had to take it to a guy who could bang it out that afternoon for him on the quick and the sly.

Escobar's brother was supposed to meet us at noon at the office to let us in. Of course, he never showed. Dad choked down his first Jack in the Crack meal before we watched the remake of *Gone in 60 Seconds*. The bartenders of an Irish pub near the office got us buzzed that afternoon. The bartenders at John's got us drunk that evening. I had to meet Escobar there to get the keys. We didn't roll into Waterford until 4 a.m.

Now for the scandalous shit:

Mom, Dad and Ronnie had conspired to keep a secret from me until Dad and I were safely in D-town, as they knew it would enrage me to the point where I would have cancelled my plans and stayed in

Waterford to handle some seriously shitactular business. It turned out that Ronnie's griping out of Herps and his Lackey was only the beginning of that episode.

The knocking of a police officer on Ronnie's door woke her Saturday morning before Dad and I had taken off for the south. The previous night, some asshole (or assholes) had slashed the tires of her Honda, her sons' motorcycles and the cars of her neighbors to either side of her. The vandal had been smart enough to stab all of these vehicles' tires as to make it look as though it were some sort of random, mass tire attack. The vandal wasn't smart enough to restrain himself from slashing six-inch gashes into all four of her Honda's tires. The bikes and the two other cars merely had all of their tires stabbed with a quick in and out. The Honda was the only one to get the Jack the Ripper treatment.

Ronnie suspected/knew the identity of the culprit(s). Her suspicions were confirmed that afternoon when her sons walked down to Sonic to grab a couple of Cokes. The Lackey happened to roll up beside them in a borrowed hoopty and asked quite sarcastically, "So, you boys need a ride, huh?"

That night at the bar, the Lackey's girlfriend asked Ronnie about the slashing. Ronnie had told her boys to keep their mouths shut about it. They had told nobody, including the Lackey, in the hopes that the person they suspected would be stupid enough to reveal himself.

Closing the bar that night, James, another of our security guys and a good friend of Ronnie's, asked the Lackey to step outside so he could ask him a few questions. The Lackey flew off the handle and began pushing him around. James tolerated a few pushes from the taller tire-stabber before dropping him with one solid punch. He proceeded to put the Lackey in a choke hold and bash his head against a wall until he tired of his whimpering.

The next day, the police came round as the Lackey tried to press charges after getting ten stitches. When they heard from multiple witnesses that James had taken several pushes before responding, they understandably dropped the matter.

Ronnie had not been one of those witnesses. She had worked her first shift at the D.U.I. Bar that night. Knowing who had done her tires and having long since tired of the bullshit at Phunky's, she quit Saturday morning and had found employment at our competition by the start of their evening shift the same day. Mom bartended at Phunky's that night in her stead. Had I known any of this, I would have immediately turned around and gone back. They all knew this, but kept it from me to give a temporary reprieve from the constantly rising shit-stream of drama flowing in my life.

D.U.I. Bar

Waterford had three, sometimes four, bars throughout my university years. We had a couple of restaurants serving alcohol, but none stayed opened late. Only one bar sat within the city limits, the D.U.I. Bar. The living room-sized, suds-only joint sits across the street from our local newspaper and next door to our bowling alley. It earned its name once I realized that it became the watering hole of choice by default for patrons of the Loose whenever they lost their license due to drunk driving convictions or because they wrecked their cars while drunk. It was the only bar within walking distance for most of Waterford's citizens.

I used to play a game with the D.U.I. Bar. Even though the bowling alley sold beer, I enjoyed running next door to see how much I could drain between frames. My scores and my liver suffered.

Our already awkward situation managed to get stranger a week after Ronnie had left us. My old friend, and sometimes follow Hiroshima DJ, Laser, came to town to talk to the Herpinator about quitting his job and returning to Waterford to work with Herps in his business ventures. I spent a day trying to talk him out of it. He had a kid to support and a real job with a large company that allowed him to accomplish this worthy goal. I didn't want to see him screw that up. He called the following Monday to say that he was coming down to join us.

I was truly concerned about him and his future. By this point, the Herpinator was so far gone he couldn't remember anything said to him from one day to the next, let alone what he had said to others. But just as I had thought only a year previously, Laser erroneously believed himself to be the one person who could get past Herps' hang-ups and get him to see an opportunity through to a successful conclusion.

Laser had filled me in on his talks with the Herpinator. Herps had yet to mention any of this to me a half-week later, even when I asked him what Laser was doing in town. It wasn't until I asked him outright the final weekend of June that he ambiguously told me that Laser was going to be "helping out."

For the first time since we had begun producing them, he failed to find the time to sit down and get an episode of *Block Rockin' Beats* nailed down by the deadline. He explained that this was due to his inability to squeeze any more money out of our main sponsor, a local CD store, and that he refused to put his own money into the project. It had nothing to do with the alcohol and drug abuse or sex addiction.

By now I had managed to divorce myself from the club as much as I possibly could with the exception of co-hosting *BRB*. With that in the crapper, I hoped I had found myself a loophole. I explained my position to him. He gave me permission to leave if that was what I truly desired. I answered by dropping off a box with all of the bar's paperwork later that day. I was free!

...I was not free...

Quadruple Threat

I survived three shows in six days and can only discuss them by comparing them.

I had the pleasure of checking out The Steve Miller Band, Ween and Bob Dylan/Phil Lesh. I'll begin with a brief outline of each show.

Security was relaxed at best allowing me to sneak in disposable cameras to each show. The hour spent at a friend's house passing around two giant punching balloons repeatedly filled with nitrous oxide from a full-size tank acquisitioned from his place of work before taking off to see Ween was far and away the best pre-game of the week.

The Steve Miller Band played the Zoo Amphitheater on July 1. Miller has been one of Oklahoma City's best annual concerts/parties for years. This was my fourth Steve Miller experience, and, at the time, I thought it would be my last. They decided to go back to their blues-rock roots (minus the psychedelics) to open the show. This strategy didn't go over too well with a crowd accustomed to a jukebox performance of their greatest hits. We go to see Miller perform two of their albums. We know almost every song they play. We see a large number of our friends. We have a great time. Not this year.

I like a little blues music, just not at a Steve Miller show. After they got that mess out of the way, they returned to the classics, and the audience rejoiced.

Ween put on the most diverse show by far four days later. Gene and Dean Ween - Aaron Freeman and Micky Melchiondo in reality - came to the Will Rogers Theater to support *White Pepper*. The smallest of the three shows also had the most loyal following. A few hundred fans sang along with them for most of their two-and-a-half-hour set. In addition to "Stroker Ace" and others from *Pepper*, they included "Voodoo Lady" and "Freedom of '76" from their classic *Chocolate and Cheese* record.

A depressingly hopeless lot of aging ex-hippies and younger neo/pseudo hippies scattered throughout the parking lot of the Dylan/Lesh show hawking a slew of wares including a menu of mostly vegetarian fare. Living up to their stereotype, they simply labeled their grub, "Yummy." I disagree. That much veggie nonsense brewed in the back of a van was going to be far from yummy. It being Oklahoma in 2000, they didn't even have the decency to offer more than a sprinkling of weed.

I saw Bob Dylan, one of the most respected musicians of our time, when he came to the Zoo Amphitheater to open for Phil Lesh. We all know Dylan, but unless you are a Deadhead, you might not recognize the Grateful Dead bassist. He's one of the ones who wasn't Jerry Garcia.

Dylan and Lesh each played for ninety minutes. Dylan's set highlights included "Tangled Up in Blues," "Rainy Day Women #12 & 35" and his tribute to Woody Guthrie, "Song to Woody." On the other hand, I didn't recognize a single Lesh song until he covered the Dead's "Casey Jones" for his single-song encore.

Steve Miller gave their audience the most impressive visual show. They filled the stage with a variety of curved, geometric screens. Intelligent lighting blasted a multitude of colored patterns onto the screens to play with our minds. Lesh placed second (Dylan played during the day) with a somewhat impressive grouping of lights and large projected, psychedelic images behind his band. Ween went for complexity through simplicity by only bringing along a few rows of colored spotlights.

Putting everyone else to shame, Ween gave its audience the strangest musical styling. Mellow, near-metal and *The Mollusk's* nautical ballads, Gene and Dean gave us a taste of everything. Dylan and Lesh both veered from their more traditional, known and liked material. I only recognized a total of four songs from the pair. Miller's keyboardist added a hip-hop flavor to "Fly Like an Eagle" with his extra rap verses, which he shouldn't have done.

Each group's demeanor and messages varied greatly. While Steve Miller asked us each to do our part to save the planet, Gene and Dean cracked jokes about the true source of the smoke on stage. Bob Dylan's group looked the most professional in their gray and black suits. They were also probably the most miserable considering the ninety degree heat. By far the strangest message I've ever heard at a concert came when Phil Lesh asked everyone to become an organ donor. I already have that box ticked on my license, but I thought it weird for a show request.

Bob Dylan was the most impressive to tell people I've seen, even if his set wasn't too impressive. This is partly due to the fact that he is the only one of the three I haven't seen before (we're not going to count a Dead-less Lesh in this contest), and that he has obtained a near God-like status in music. Nobody responds to a performance like Ween fans. Gene and Dean even played some of the requests screamed by their throng of fans. Steve Miller disappointed fans by not playing requests for their classics until they had churned out their blues set.

Gathering of the Juggalos I
Novi, Michigan

Mostly thanks to parodies on *Saturday Night Live* and the F.B.I. declaring their fans gang members in 2011, there are few people in WLOTUS who don't know who the Insane Clown Posse, or their fans, are. What many people may not understand is that the Gathering of the Juggalos is a real event where hedonism and insanity clash/rule for up to five days a year.

When people think about multiple-act and event festivals, they usually name Woodstock, Lollapalooza or Edgefest. After a weekend in Detroit, I feel proud to add the Gathering of the Juggalos to this prestigious list.

I would be remiss in my duties as a Juggalo if I had missed the first Gathering in August 2000 at the Novi Expo Center. The journey to Michigan was going to be difficult with my car having recently died. Luckily, a friend of mine had a solution. That summer, Dewey moved to Cleveland with her boyfriend, Underwear. Her convertible Mercury Capri's transmission died weeks before their big move. Her father had it rebuilt, but he needed to get it north to her.

Mom wanted to see our family and friends in Indiana. I formulated a plan to drive Dewey's car to the Clowns and then on to her place where I'd meet up with my Mom for a road trip back home, stopping at our favorite winery in Altus, Arkansas.

When she was in university, Dewey's car could have been featured on one of those foul hoarding shows on TLC. It was a good thing I was traveling alone in the little two-seater, as her trunk was crammed with old school papers, books and who knows what else.

I had thought that doing a bit of camping might not be totally out of the question for this Midwestern adventure and packed accordingly: machete, pocket knives and random gear. Mom is an RN, and both my parents had been EMTs. They long harbored a strong belief that a well-decked out first aid kit is essential to any member of our family when out on the open road. My canvas Wal-Mart fisherman's bag held all manner of gauze, tapes, blades, CPR masks, and pills…lots of pills. I had antibiotics and way more pain pills than a 22-year-old should be toting around the country.

After a pit stop in Indiana, I was on my way to see what Psychopathic Records had cooked up for more than seven thousand kids of all ages in evil clown face paint while under the influence of a maddening rainbow of mind-altering substances.

Day 1

My adventure began at 4:45 a.m. upon my arrival in the parking lot after two hours of sleep on the road. The original plan included finding the Novi Expo Center and then a place to sleep. The seventy-five people already in line helped convince me otherwise. By 11 a.m., I'd kicked my hacky sack around, taken a three-mile hike and heard Violent J and Shaggy 2 Dope's interview on the *Howard Stern Show*.

I walked a few miles to a gas station to get raped for a pair of disposable cameras. A local ninjette named Christy picked me up on the way back. We breakfasted at Big Boy and then bought beer at Rite Aid (from where she was skipping her day shift).

I managed to score front row parking. I dropped the Capri's top and chilled in the sun. Ben, the guy in the Jeep Cherokee next to me, invited me to an after-party. The weekend was already shaping up. His crew blasted older ICP on the Jeep's dual 15" speakers. The whole thing had the appearance of a creepy circus caravan on LSD.

We traded Clown stories. Christy won when she told us she'd met the Wicked Clowns before. Not only had she met them, but they had given her a lift to a show in Chicago. She even claimed to have taken them home to meet her mom.

Thanks to me throwing out a hacky sack, some of my fellow Juggalos dubbed me the "Hippie Juggalo." By 3 p.m., it looked as though the Faygo factory had exploded outside of the hall.

Juggalos had gathered from all over. My 1,300 miles from Oklahoma were smashed by those who had traveled from Florida, Austin, California, and Alaska. Security guards walked up and down the line letting ninjas chant and sing Clown lyrics on their bullhorns, beginning one of many odd Gathering traditions. My attempt to gain a press pass by bribing a guard with joint failed.

Psychopathic Records filled the hall with dozens of strange attractions to keep us occupied until the concert each night. Tattoo booths. Merchandise. Velcro wall jumps. Video games.

Mini-museums dedicated to each of the five Joker's Card albums explored the history of the Clowns' most well known endeavors.

The Blue Monkey Circus Sideshow allowed me the opportunity to view an eclectic collection of sword swallowers, contortionists and other human oddities.

The Insane Clown Posse's Juggalo ChampionshXt Wrestling is the third highest grossing wrestling organization in the country. I watched Vampiro, Big Flame and Hollywood Chuck Hogan beat each other senseless. Although not a fan of this "sport entertainment," I was impressed by the degree of violence and mutilation these people inflicted on one another.

The Neden Game gave contestants the chance to win dates with Detroit-area strippers in a perverted version of *The Dating Game*.

Myzery didn't go over well with the crowd. In the Juggalo world, this results in a half-ton of garbage being pelted at you. To their credit, they were skilled at dodging our refuse barrage.

The Kings, the only of the three I'd seen before, opened with "Suburban Life," a jaded commentary on contemporary American suburbs, which drove the crowd ape-shit. In addition to the Kings' five musicians, a masked, Adidas-clad, break-dancing friend accompanied them. He busted out some mad moves while chugging Heineken tallboys, smoking blunts and showing off his naked girl tattoo. They sang about legalization. Another song about the cops having a short leash encouraged us to flip them the bird whenever we see them.

Corporate America came out and kicked it with their buddies, the Kings.

Closing out the evening, the Rydas shot up their mics with their gang-banger flurry of hard core lyrics. The super group was then composed of Psychopathic Records' artists using alter-egos: Bullet (Violent J), Full Clip (Shaggy 2 Dope), Lil Shank (Jamie Madrox), Foe Foe (Monoxide), Cell Block (Blaze Ya Dead Homie), and Twin Gats (Myzery). Their bootlegged beats blasted the crowd as the sextet hopped around wearing bandannas covering their faces.

A curtain fell on the first night of the first Gathering. In the parking lot, I found David, one of those I'd met in the morning. His sister had left him, so I drove him back to the Doubletree Hotel. A handful of us had decided to after-party in the hotel.

A clutch of cops were there to bust up any thoughts of after-parties. The lobby filled with Juggalos. We decided to work on the Scavenger Hunt list we had picked up inside the Expo. A group of airline folk walked into the lobby. We convinced two of the stewardesses, a pilot and a cop to take a photo with us. We failed to track down a kitchen sink, autographed MC Hammer memorabilia, pictures of "Fuck Eminem" gang tags, Taco Bell applications, "Shoplifters will be prosecuted" signs, or a sex toy still sealed in its box.

Lack of sleep and excessive alcohol consumption finally forced me to fly back to the Capri for some much needed rest.

Day 2

Saturday began like any other day: I awoke in a hotel parking lot in the convertible I had driven across the country. Faygo and sweat clung to me like an airport panhandler.

After determining where I had slept, I drove back to hang out with the desperate die-hards standing in line until the doors opened at 11 a.m. Even after smoking, drinking and scavenger hunting the night away, hundreds of face-painted fans already stood in line.

218

The only dry piece of clothing I could find was my Marlboro Miles trench coat, so I donned it, my Vietnam-era combat boots and nothing else.

I popped open my warm breakfast can of PBR. A few cars down the row, the rear door of a maroon Dodge Caravan flipped up. A Juggalo my age in a full clown suit, the sort you'd expect to see at a children's party if you could get past the smeared grease paint he'd already lived in for days, emerged and took notice of my beerfast. We traded the traditional "Whoop! Whoop!" of our people.

"What up, ninja?" my clowny neighbor inquired.

"What up, clown?" I responded in kind.

"I'm outta water. You got another of those PBs?"

"Yeah, brother. No worries," and tossed him a can of America's best beer in 1893.

The clown cracked open his can and killed half of it. We traded tales and the clown changed gears by reaching into an oversized pocket.

"It's the last day. You up for a trip?" he asked, revealing a baggie of windowpane LSD.

"Does a Juggalo shit in the woods?" I replied.

"What?"

"Never mind. Hell's yeah, my ninja!"

Like inserting a coin into a video game, I swallowed a hit of pane and got locked into the kind of day-long game which rarely produces winners.

Waiting for our trips to begin, a trio of preteens approached us with the type of business proposal scribbled onto a piece of cardboard torn from a beer box common at Juggalo events: "FIREWORKS FOR ALCHOL." Wow, a modern day face-painted incarnation of the Little Rascals wanted my beer!

"Firecrackers for beer?" they offered.

Not really having come prepared to trip my balls off, I tossed them a can each. In return, they filled one of the deep pockets of my full-length duster with cheap Chinese and/or Mexican-made pyrotechnics.

The acid began to grab me by the balls, and I decided the time had come to enter the Novi Expo Center for the final day of the Gathering. An entire day of geeking out around face-painted Family freaks awaited me, and I wasn't about to waste any of it hanging out in a parking lot getting drunk with kids and one pretty cool clown in a minivan. Looking back on it, leaving three preteens with a clown in a minivan might not have been the best judgment call, but this would prove to be a day of nothing but a "best of" album of bad calls.

As I drunkenly pound this tale into my HP TouchSmart tx2 in a little clam and shrimp restaurant on a small island off of Korea's western coast in 2013, I can't help but reflect on the variety of events and time killers the Psychopathic Family has provided to Juggalos attending any of the fourteen Gatherings held thus far. Some events are successful enough to draw Juggalos each year, while some get dropped due to what is probably a combination of the incompatibility of the current venue to host those we used to have in the convention centers, a lack of response on our part and I can't help but think that some inspire anarchy on a level that even the Psychopathic Dons (the highest ranking members of the Family) could ever have imagined. For this last reason, I believe that I may have personally had a hand in eliminating the haunted house attraction from future Gatherings.

The more creative attractions have always had more pull over me than most of the meet-and-greets, seminars and autograph sessions that consume a large chunk of daily life at each Gathering. A haunted house in August in a Michigan convention center while zonked out on LSD was a surefire win in my book. They had set up the haunted house in the middle of the convention center, and, like everything else that weekend, a long line greeted participants.

As I neared the entrance to the flimsy structure, my rollercoaster began ratcheting up to that first high, insane hill every trip-head comes to expect. I distantly recalled my pocketful of pyrotechnics and began talking to people in line into taking some of my bottle rockets, Black Cats, M-80s, and other assorted explosives with the promise that they'd set them off somewhere inside the makeshift, somehow appropriate, off-season haunted house. In an environment such as the Gathering, finding accomplices for some shenanigans on this level is like shooting lesbians in a Lilith Fair barrel.

With the exception of an abandoned Indian hospital in Waterford where college kids once hosted a haunted house complete with fully chained and running chainsaws to scare this crap out of kids, most haunted houses are rarely anything but slight variations of the same theme: Create come crazy, gory scenes and have costumed people jump out at you.

Those costumed people don't expect to have handfuls of tiny bombs tossed their way. That's exactly what happened at the first Gathering of the Juggalos. My randomly recruited ninjas and I lit and hurled cheap fireworks at every turn in the joint, scaring the shit out of those costumed cunts for a change. I got out of there once the sparks literally started flying.

Where I utterly failed with this bit of tomfoolery was in forgetting that I was in Detroit. If you don't know, D-town has a multitude of nicknames. The classic, family-friendly name is Motor City. Decades of downfall have at times donned the home of Ted Nugent, Kid Rock, Andrew W., Eminem, and the Clowns: Murder City. It's not quite as catchy, but it's just as accurate considering the number of years of insanely high homicide rates, gang activity and unemployment-inducing Japanese robots.

Throwing explosive devices in the dark at its citizens turned out to be a rather unwise idea. Once a costumed monster realized he/she wasn't shot or being shot at, he/she quickly ushered us on to the next part of the house.

By the time I emerged from the darkness into the Expo Center's harsh artificial light, I had fully succumbed to the grips of the first wave of my neighbor's windowpane.

The day progressed in a trance. Or maybe that was just me. I met people. I smoked and snorted substances with people. I spazzed upon seeing some of the more demonic paint jobs and costumes my Family had donned for the big blowout.

The most interesting attraction offered was a ride on the Clowns' tour bus through their old hood. I had started to freak out a little bit and needed a place to chill for a while. I lucked out and managed to get a decent spot in line for this. A line seemed the perfect solution, so of course it moved faster than I had desired for the first time in my life.

Their bus had the owner/operator couple driving and a lone security guard to keep the dozen or so Juggalos in line throughout the one-hour trip through some nasty Murder City attractions. The guard sat up front with the driver and made him feel good…sorry, I'm digressing into old Sir Mix-a-Lot lyrics. But the driver did sit up front, and that made us feel good.

The bus' lounge section consisted of a horseshoe-shaped couch built into the bus about two-thirds of the way to the off-limit bedrooms in back. My drugs had granted me sight beyond sight, and I soon uncovered the secret booze cooler tucked away into the seatback of one section of the couch.

I offered an apology for my lack of clothing as I leaned across a few Juggalos and Juggalettes and pressed down on the top of the cover, revealing my bits and pieces in the process. A concealed lid popped up to expose a hidden stash of beer. We covertly passed the bus booze around and had a high old time as the drivers pointed out ICP graffiti with "K"s sprayed over them as an invitation for other gangs to kill the Inner City Posse as they were called before specters of the Dark Carnival visited Shaggy 2 Dope and Violent J to show them the light and inspire them to change their group's name and messages. This transformed them into the multi-platinum selling artists we know and love/hate today.

We emptied out the booze cache with the exception of a single bottle of non-alcoholic O'Doul's which I claimed as my own for having discovered the liquid loot. I also ended up shoving a small throw pillow under my trench (which until recently resided in my parents' attic). Our group left the bus a little lighter on our feet than when we had boarded.

Evening thankfully rolled around as did the time to assemble outside the center for the final night's concert. My cacophony of bad decisions worked towards a crescendo.

A day of hallucinogen and booze had tired me out a bit and filled my bladder. I worked my way up to the front and center of the stage. Those of us who had shown up early weren't about to leave our spots for bullshit reasons like the bodily burden of unburdening itself of toxins we had inserted into ourselves. A neighboring Juggalo proffered me an empty Faygo Moon Mist (Faygo's delicious Mountain Dew knockoff) bottle in which to relieve myself. I filled it, capped it and tossed it. We both watched its trajectory and the unfortunate Juggalo who soon after plucked it from the ground, uncapped it, chugged it, and spewed it over and onto the ninjas in front of him.

Would that have been the end of the evening, I would have felt satisfied, but the situation disintegrated further.

Twiztid took control of the stage at 9 p.m. Jamie Madrox and the Monoxide Child had the audience going crazy to tracks from their albums *Mostasteless* and *Freakshow*. Like every act before them, their stage setup simply consisted of the diabolical duo and a canvas backdrop featuring the band's logo.

Later, two days of anticipation erupted as the Insane Clown Posse's Violent J and Shaggy 2 Dope jumped onto the stage. Their brilliantly disturbing prop people designed a stage overloaded with demons and a canvas backdrop featuring evil spirits spiraling into the depths of hell. The Clowns like to dress their stages in apocalyptic visions of the hellscape that will engulf people who have pursued a lifetime of evil.

The Clowns filled their slot with a variety of songs from their then decade-long career. The crowd chanted and moshed itself into a frenzy. I handed out and shot off more fireworks.

When I first started hitting Clown shows, it was a common courtesy to rush the stage during the encore and/or last few songs. The first Gathering should have produced no surprises. Unfortunately, I was still well under the influence of the hardcore pane with which my clowny neighbor had supplied me. Standing so close to the front of the stage, I found myself in a great position to rush it.

The Clowns have other clowns constantly venturing out on stage to refill their Faygo receptacles. During regular shows, these may be as simple as 55-gallon drums on wheels, but they dress them up for big tours and the Gatherings. They weren't about to spare any expense for the first Gathering. Even the shallow Faygo basins were done up with stalactites hanging down from their sides.

Regardless of the weather, to leave a Clown show dry can be seen as an affront to the whole movement.

Stage-rushing used to be another integral part of any Clown show. I have made my way up to the stage under all sorts of conditions before, and this was to be my crowning achievement.

Still fudged out of my mind (many thanks to my mini-van Clown brother!), I tried to get on stage. A mob of people overtook me, and I spent five minutes bent over the security railing as people leaped off my back onto the stage. I finally slithered over the rail and landed in three inches of what I knowingly and mistakenly hoped was only sweat and stale Faygo.

I mounted the stage-right Faygo basin and gazed out upon the Juggalo masses. As my drug-addled mind tried to comprehend just exactly what the hell was going on, I noticed many Juggalos pointing up to me in what I believed for a brief moment to be awe.

"Hell yeah," I thought through the acidy mist of my mind. I made it to the stage, managed to precariously balance my 6'4" frame on a Faygo basin and looked out upon an ocean of my people at what was most certainly the first of a new generation of concerts.

A slight moment of clarity quickly followed once I realized that they weren't pointing at ME in all my glory. Instead, they were acknowledging the fact that throughout my long, hard day of tripping my testicles off, every button on my trench coat had either popped off or come undone. Atop my Faygo basin, I towered over the crowd with my sweaty balls to the sweaty wind, pointing to the attending Juggalo army with not my fingers.

I turned as I realized what the shit was happening only to look down to see Violent J staring up. He quickly motioned for security to come take care of me, which was the wisest path for him to take. I hopped down to the stage, knowing that my tall, braided-hair, trench coat-wearing, naked-ass could never hope to blend in with the two dozen or so ninjas wearing official Psychopathic gear. Instead, I darted behind the stage, breaking one of the small, two-inch horns from the set, which was acceptable behavior as the rest of my people tore the set to pieces, and emerged from stage left to leap out and crowd surf my way to the middle of the masses, animosity and freedom.

I survived the remainder of the show and passed out in the relative safety of my borrowed convertible.

Epilogue

Canadia sits slightly north of our border and remains one of America's fifty-four favorite states. And no, "Canadia" is not a typo. Canadia is my renaming of the giant pot-smoking, beer-drinking, gun-toting landmass to the north of What's Left of the United States, but that is a story you won't read until *Ninjalicious II: Crazy Corea*.

The first Gathering ended without the rain of hellfire and arrests I had begun to believe to be inevitable. I had nothing better to do the Sunday following the show, so I got the hell out of the country for the first time in my life.

To fully understand this situation, you have to visualize where I was at this point. I was four days drunk, un-showered (not counting Faygo), the braids a family friend had done my hair up in were frazzled and disintegrating, and I was rocking a fuzzy acid hangover. I did manage to put on a couple of articles of clothing beneath my trench this time.

I learned that a not-so-secret tunnel connected Murder City to Windsor, Canada and decided to explore the uncharted hinterlands for an afternoon.

Before I got a foothold into our second-largest state, you have to understand that this was the year 2000. Pissed off Middle Eastern extremists wouldn't show off their box-cutter and flying skills for another thirteen months. I drove underground to the Canuckistanian border with no clear intention of my intentions. This was to prove my undoing…

"How long are you going to be here?" asked the cute Canuckistanian border guard.

"I don't know."

"Where are you going?"

"I don't know."

"What brings you to Canadia?"

"I don't know."

"Sir, could you please pull over there."

A nearly middle-aged guard pointed to an area to pull over for inspections. My head was still cloudy from the previous day's trip, but what happened next will forever remain imprinted on my mind and my spank bank. Canadia might lag a decade or so behind the rest of the modern world, according to *How I Met Your Mother*, but they have got their border inspections down pat. What followed reminded me of the beginning of one of the heavily-edited, soft-core porn comedies the U.S.A. Network played on Friday and Saturday nights when I was in high school.

If you are ever forced to blow an hour of your life getting searched, the Murder City – Windsor border is the place to do it. Five women in their mid-twenties stepped out of an office, all in appetizingly fitting uniforms. The worst of the lot was only mildly hot. Looking back on this episode and knowing my nature, I'm now certain that it was a piece of a conspiracy plot to convince

Americans to like, or at the very least to acknowledge the existence of, our northern neighbor.

A concrete curb held up my sweaty body as they went through Dewey's car with great care and attention to details, especially for this pre-9/11 world. Every few minutes, their search turned up something which excited them.

"What are these for?" asked one inspector, pointing to the machete and hunting knife she'd placed on the ground.

"I plan on doing some camping."

One agent rummaging around behind the Capri's two seats withdrew a pint of Hennessey and set it down with my weapons. I'd bought the bottle first day of the show, didn't open it and promptly forgot about it once it had disappeared.

Another woman found Dewey's trash-crammed trunk too much of a challenge and gave up on it.

A fourth mystified herself for a quarter of an hour as she dug through my first aid kit. She failed to hide her surprise upon finding syringes, scalpels, surgical shears, and a small galaxy of pills. The latter she tossed on a pile of booze and blades.

"What're these pills for, eh?"

"They are part of my Mother's monster first aid kit you have rifled through. My parents had both done stints as EMTs, and my Mom later became a nurse. As I learned in my nine years as a Boy Scout, we believe in being prepared. So, yes, you do have a few bottles of pain killers there, but you'll also find antibiotics and other pills I don't quite know the uses of that are just as illegal as the fun ones."

The last woman, their supervisor I believe, looked at the pile her hottie underlings had amassed and then looked at my frazzled braids, my stained trench coat and my combination of a half week's worth of sweat, Faygo drenchings and alcohol abuse which coated my body and looked back to the pile.

"Canadia doesn't allow you to bring these weapons into our country, eh. You also can't bring those drugs or that alcohol in with you," the boss lady explained.

"Okay…" I was about to be kicked out of the entrance to Canadia, the country that allowed Celine Dion and Nickelback to not only be born in, but also to exist in, and to rise to inexplicable levels of fame. She was preparing to deny me entry to a barren wasteland

226

of a country whose national sport consists of playing shuffleboard on ice.

"So please repack your things and enjoy your stay in Canadia, eh."

Maybe the acid hadn't completely worn off yet. She watched me repack the car, get in and drive…into Canadia.

Windsor, Canadia is a shithole. I didn't really know what to do there except to locate a bar and drink myself back to reality in preparation for the long drive to Cleveland. I found a casino, but knew that even a ratty casino in a ghetto town would know better than to allow the likes of me onto their premises.

A little hole in the wall bar called out to me. I put back three hour's worth of booze and decided I was finally straight enough to return to America, but not before I experienced an epiphany.

As my second beer came close to making way for my third, I realized where the border babes had gone severely wrong. They had admonished me for all of the illegal items and substances they caught me "smuggling" into their country, but they had failed to inquire about the Capri.

I had watched as one of the girls opened the glove box and sorted through the mess of Dewey's fast food napkins and condiments to locate the car's registration. The registration showed that the car belonged to her father. Except for the fact that they both have vowels and consonants, Dewey's father's name and mine share nothing in common.

I guess the moral of the story is that Canadia will allow visitors to bring banned weapons, booze and drugs just so long as they do it in a stolen car.

Returning to the U. S. of A. drunk off my tits proved to be much easier than escaping it mostly sober. Our border guard asked me where I'd been and what I'd been doing.

"I had an afternoon to kill and had never visited Canadia before."

"Please step out of the vehicle and pop the trunk."

Thanks to a half week of sweat, Faygo and whatever else was floating around the Gathering, I saw no reason to fear him smelling the alcohol. His eyes shot open almost as wide as the trunk when he bore witness to Dewey's crap collection. He shut it and sent me on my way to get horrifically lost in one of the most dangerous sections of one of America's most dangerous cities.

In those lazy twilight hours, smoke rolled out from sewer vents and manhole covers. I failed in my attempt to find directions and food at a Burger King. The place locked its doors at night, only operating the drive-thru due to its nefarious location. A homeless guy in the bushes called out to me and informed me that they shut their doors at 8 p.m. He almost never saw any "honkies in these parts" and that I'd "best be gettin' back to where it's safe." I bought inaccurate directions from him for two bucks but finally found my way out of that war zone.

This story nearly ends with the return of Dewey's car. I wish it did end there. I found Mom at Dewey and Underwear's apartment. One of my oldest friends, Dewey convinced me that I should spend the rest of my summer in Cleveland with them and Greyhound back to Oklahoma in time for class the following semester. We got really drunk during this decision making process.

Mom had nothing better to do the next morning, so she read a novel in the car as I filled out paperwork and took various tests at a temp agency. I did fairly well considering how hung over I was. Decision making sometimes proves difficult. I let Mom drive us back to the apartment, but only after she stopped at the entrance to the agency's parking lot so I could throw the door open and fling my guts out onto the hot asphalt.

The idea of a summer in Cleveland appealed less and less to me as the day wore on. Mom and I drove home to Oklahoma the next day.

Racism up in Smoke

Goober and I drove down to Dallas in August for Dr. Dre's *Up In Smoke Tour.* The tour featured Ice Cube, Eminem, and Dr. Dre with Snoop Doggy Dogg at what was then the Coca-Cola Starplex Amphitheatre.

People living in homes around the Starplex open their driveways and yards to make a few extra bucks by providing some overflow parking during shows. My brother had to drive, because I had broken my right foot at the beginning of the month while drunkenly scaling an inverted portable climbing wall parked at a Cutitz's house during the D-Man's wedding reception.

A middle-aged black man waved us into his drive. He offered to let us leave our ride there and promised he'd keep an eye on it for five bucks. We sat in the truck and smoked a joint with him and discussed music and drugs. Goober had some liquid LSD on him. I had some paper tabs. He squeezed drops onto a couple of my squares. Our new friend declined our invitation to leave reality with us.

Ten minutes later a black, late-model Mercedes with nice rims arrived, and we soon got paranoid.

"Oh shit! You white boys need to hide for a minute. That's my brother, Larry, and he don't like honkies," he warned.

A thin, early thirty-something man emerged from the car sporting a full-length black leather trench coat and sunglasses in spite of the heat and darkness. Larry glanced in our direction and entered his home with the graceful strides of a very stylish movie villain. That was our cue to get the hell out of there and experience some rap.

Goober and I had cheap tickets which only allowed us access to the grassy ring around the outside of the covered seating area and stage. I hoped to use my crutches to gain us access to the some seats. We had to limp around to three different entrances but finally got into some seats almost dead center, twenty rows back. We also found ourselves seated next to the only other pair of white faces in a sea of dark skin.

Ice Cube kicked off his set, and shit got racist. I don't know how our two Caucasian neighbors ended up at the *Up In Smoke Tour*. They would have been better placed in a Klan rally. Cube hadn't gotten four songs into his set before these guys were repeatedly making comments that were all variations of "nigger this" and "nigger that." The only two white people we could see were dropping more "N" words than Cube and our other neighbors combined.

Being stoned out of our minds on acid didn't help us one iota. We tried our best to cringe away from these racist-ass crackers before murderous actions followed the murderous looks all four of us were receiving thanks to those two. We safely fled the freaks and were able to enjoy the remainder of the show in safety.

Ten Wasted Years Gone and Wasted

Towards the end of this madness, the Herpinator's class held its ten-year reunion at a local sports bar owned by a guy from his class. By this point, rarely was he not stoned or swallowing meth (only snorting, smoking or shooting meant you were an addict by his twisted logic). On this particular night, he got really drunk on top of whatever else he'd consumed. It had started with a breakfast of rum when he woke up late Friday afternoon.

Ever the classy guy, he took a pair of eighteen-year-olds he was boning with him. He stumbled around bragging to anyone who would listen that he owned a Hummer and a bar. His classmates witnessed him get more wasted before passing out with his head down on a table. It wouldn't have been so bad if it had ended there, but it didn't. A classmate of theirs had died a month or two before. The organizers put together a little slide show to commemorate his passing. The girls said that Herps rose from the dead to lose his shit when they played it.

"Fuck! Fuck! None of these fucking people liked him in high school!" he screamed in a slurry haze for his grand finale of the evening. His classmates lowered their heads for a moment of prayer as Herps repeated, "Fuck!" several more times. While this may have very well been true (our school was very clique-ish and the unpopular were treated quite badly), a memorial during their reunion was neither the time nor the place to go off the handle on the subject.

So sloshed was he that one of the girls had to drive his beloved Hummer. Nobody but he himself ever piloted his expensive, high-maintenance machine, quite possibly the only true love in his life besides himself. He demanded to be driven to Phunky Jay's. Luckily for the bar, he was far too gone to move from the passenger seat, although he did demand to be carried into the bar. The girls refused this request because they knew the bar was hosting another high school party that night, and he was far too large of a man, in spite of the meth, for those two little girls to lug him anywhere. No young kid or the few parents outside needed to see him blasted off of his rocker.

They took him to the Lighthouse. As they popped up over the curb to park next to the basement door, I happened to pull into the driveway. I assisted them in pouring him from his ride into the basement as he was entirely liquefied.

One of the Hummer's more impressive tricks is the ability to use a built-in pump to re-inflate flat tires or, with the use of a hose, to inflate any other device you see fit. He mostly used this to keep a two-man inflatable raft filled to play around with. While on the road, he used it as a portable bed. While having unprotected sex, he liked to toss it on his truck's roof rack and screw away in public. He took great pleasure in recounting a morning where he was pounding away at another eighteen-year-old on the roof in the wooded lot behind the bar. Folks on their way to work at 6 a.m. blasted their horns at him in disgust or support. That night in the basement, things got really strange.

The Herpinator whipped out a bank bag he always kept on hand stuffed with seven or eight grand of emergency money. Imbued with the knowledge that the world would soon fall apart around him and descend into a spiral of Mad Maxian chaos, he believed it wise to keep a supply of cash stashed at all times to escape whatever crisis would befall him. On this night, he unzipped the bag and poured greenbacks into the raft and went for an inebriated swim, a la Scrooge McDuck. He tried to coerce the girls to dive in with him. That's when they went topside to share with me all of the embarrassment he had caused everyone that night.

By 12:30 a.m., the Herpinator had recovered to a state of semi-consciousness. He ventured out to the porch where I was hanging with some friends. I asked him to please take care of the bank loan payment, as I had received two late notices - Herps was crafty enough to have ensured that everything at Phunky's was and had remained in my name. Licenses. Tax forms. Utilities. Lease. Loan. All on me. The only item without my name was our bank account. Herps had somehow convinced/cheated our bank to take my name off of our joint business account without my permission. I reminded him that it was my DJ equipment we had put up for collateral on the bar's loan and that I'd really rather not lose it and see my credit screwed up.

Phunky Jay's put me ten grand in the hole between the credit card debt I'd accumulated on supplies and the five grand in loans we took out in my name to keep the club afloat. The Herpinator had agreed to assume these debts when he took over the bar. In the first week of August, he changed his mind. Considering that everything was still my name, this was an easy thing for him to do. I was sunk.

I received a phone call on August 17 that permanently changed the game.

Changeover

The Herpinator's attitude, actions and abuse sent our bar on a downward spiral from which it couldn't recover. The point came when my best friends refused to step foot inside Phunky Jay's, because they couldn't stomach being around Herps.

The Herpinator is a polarizing man. Regrettably like Hitler, he possesses the ability to convince people to put in work for him, even if it goes against their normal ethical codes or if they don't entirely understand what sort of mission it is for which he has recruited them. This held true for the final four people who remained committed to him throughout this debacle.

The Redneck might not have been smart enough to treat the local law enforcement agencies with an iota respect, but he knew when his money was in trouble. It didn't take any sort of a genius to see how far we'd fallen. All of the high quality flyers and semi-innovative promotions in the world couldn't undo the damage Herps had done to his and Phunky Jay's reputations.

The Redneck called me on August 17 asking to meet me at a restaurant for lunch and a conversation. He introduced me to Johnny who went by Fredo. Fredo looked and talked like a slick 50-year-old extra in a straight-to-video mafia movie directed by someone whose mafia experience was limited to having watched other straight-to-video mafia movies. However, they did make me an offer I couldn't refuse.

The Redneck informed me that he would not be renewing our lease. This was an easy task since there was almost no paperwork on our month-to-month lease.

Phunky Jay's had been all but strangled to death. I was heavily indebted thanks to the single largest of my poor business decisions. This small crack of salvation smelled funny, but I was out of options.

Fredo came to us from parts unknown (we later discovered that he was from not so far off Oklahoma City) to run a bar in Western Oklahoma for reasons which never revealed themselves to us. That he came there to rape and pillage is obvious now, but the truth behind how he landed in our little town remains a mystery. We also never learned how Fredo came to know the Redneck.

Fredo claimed to have done some sort of research and had come to the decision that he would only rent out the bar if I would come back on board as the manager and the face of the business. He said that while Herps was toxic, I had the ability to get people through the doors again. Fredo would let Herps stay on as the DJ if he wanted, but I knew that he could never work for anyone but himself. I had no choice. Fredo clinched the deal by offering to repay my bar-related debts as payment for sticking around and to show that he truly believed in Phunky's viability.

Two nights later, I came home at 4 a.m. to find Herps in some girl's car at the Lighthouse. He ranted that he was going to sue Fredo. For what, I don't have a clue. Like most of his threats/ideas, it never got past verbalization. Recent events had totally pissed him off. After yet another weak party with very few people that night, he went out and ripped the "P" off of the Phunky Jay's sign after the bar closed for the night.

Much of what follows reads like an old 35mm print at a drive-in with numerous scenes missing.

Ocean's 3

It all came to a head the Saturday night after the Redneck and Fredo approached me. I was having a beer on my front porch when the Herpinator, Laser and the Innocent showed up. Herps had convinced them to join him on an anti-Fredo campaign. He wanted me to run down to the club with them and pull out everything belonging to either one of us. I listened to his propaganda for an hour before he at last realized he couldn't sell me his cart-load of horseshit.

Herps proceeded to share a story this night from when he used to spin tunes at our place back when it was known as Clyde's.

In a tale reminiscent of our own, he had once DJed at that previous incarnation of Phunky Jay's. Believing that the scene had turned sour and that he would not be able to retrieve his equipment among whatever other paranoia infected him at the time, he concocted a break-in. Knowing that the bar's cheap alarm system only covered the multiple doors around the building, he enlisted two accomplices to work as spotters for him. Walkie-talkies in hand, one took up position atop the eighty-foot disused oil derrick outside the bar's front door with the other stationed down the road where U.S. 54 splits south from U.S. 66.

The Herpinator scaled the building, no small task for someone in his shape. He entered through a vent in the roof to clean out his equipment. The break in went down without a hitch. He unlocked the doors from the inside after disengaging the flimsy alarm system and liberated his gear.

Although I understood the connection, I didn't understand why he chose that particular moment to confess this crime. He had broken into his place of employment, because he'd thought somebody was out to get him.

Years later, after leaving my porch with two different people convinced of his near god-hood (how he got the Innocent mixed up in this and back to not hating him anymore is beyond me) he re-robbed the joint. This time he not only liberated his equipment, he also removed all of the bar's beer stock with had been purchased with money from the loan taken out in my name.

Settling In

Realizing he had lost, despite the success of his caper, the Herpinator began packing up the next week to move to OKC. An extra dose of paranoia set in, and he spent the rest his time in Waterford answering his door with a shotgun in hand. He feared Fredo. It only got crazier from there.

It didn't take any of us long to learn that Phunky Jay's had merely exchanged one perv for another. Less than two weeks at the bar, Fredo tried kissing one of Goober's ex-girlfriends, not once but twice.

The next day, a sheriff's deputy pulled Fredo over for speeding outside of town. When he realized whom he had snared, he informed Fredo that he'd heard that Herps and his meth dealer/sometimes business partner had put out a hit on him. What the hell? As maniacal as he had become, I still believed that Herps was a do-it-yourself kind of guy. I wouldn't put this sort of thing past him, I just don't see him hiring it out…unless he could convince one of his minions to take on the task for free.

To wash away the stain the Herpinator had left on Phunky Jay's, Fredo chose to allow SWOSU's historically and horrifically unsuccessful football team, the Bullfrogs, to rename the bar, "The Frog House". He ignored my warning that it was a bad idea considering how un-beloved the team was. I knew that even some of

234

the players' girlfriends were too embarrassed to attend their boyfriends' Bad News Bears games. When Mom ran the town's ambulance service, she used manning a rig at college football games as the worst punishment she could inflict upon her people, while getting assigned high school games served as a reward.

As far as delusions of grandeur goes, Herps and Fredo could give each other a run for his money. Fredo sprinkled some of his more believable theories with dollops of implausible bullshit. As time wore on, Fredo informed me that Herps had been running drugs through the bar. I found this a little difficult to believe as he was a consumer, not a distributor. A man toting around his level of paranoia couldn't possibly sell drugs.

Fredo handed me a business card one day with F.B.I. letterhead on it. He claimed to work as a "sleeper agent" for the government who could be called in at any time. One minute he worked for the government, the next he was expounding on his mob ties. He had run an Italian restaurant in Oklahoma City. The only way any of this made any sense was if Fredo's government gig involved snitching, but even that failed to hold water.

Square Dance Rap

One day, over ten years ago, one of my Mom's co-workers stopped by our house. He was listening to a cassette that would forever change my life. Sir Mix-A-Lot's *Swass* was the first tape I ever bought. This and A Tribe Called Quest's "Scenario" began my addiction to rap and hip-hop.

Sanford and Son Promotions and Entertainment and Schreck's Ballroom brought Mix-A-Lot and his crew to Western Oklahoma in September.

I started my day at 10:30 a.m. with a 40oz of Olde English, shots of Jagermeister and two hours of "Perfect Dark" with Goober and JeEcHuA. My parents showed up for a couple of drinks. Back at my place, I took some wine to my roomie's hot tub before passing out for a de-pruning nap. I downed six cervezas at a barbecue and then a couple more during dinner with Mix-A-Lot.

I met up with Sir Mix-A-Lot at Buttwarmer's, a local restaurant for people who don't like food, for a pre-show interview on Wrong Wradio. He talked about his old music, his new album coming out next year and mocked me for sort of being a Notre Dame fan.

His tour bus broke down in Waterford. I went out to see if I could lend his roadies a hand. We had to convince the Auto-Zone manager to unlock the doors for us, but managed to accomplish our mission. We got back and passed around a blunt outside the bus. They got back on the road in time to get Mix and his posse out to the show.

Far too stoned to drive (and a little drunk to boot), I caught a ride to Schreck's. Between the then-high-tech Sony Mavica (with its 3.5" floppy disks) I had from the newspaper and my old flash-less Pentax AE 35mm I'd picked up at a Mennonite second-hand store for three dollars, I came out of the show with next to no usable photographs, despite being allowed on the stage for part of the performance.

He put together a phenomenal show. He played something for anyone who has ever been a Sir Mix-A-Lot fan. He let the audience taste a little of everything from his five albums. To get in touch with his fans, Mix-A-Lot invited a group of girls to dance on stage with him during "Baby Got Back."

Thoroughly trashed by show's end, Sanford got the bright idea to have me drive his truck back to town, towing a trailer full of high-end audio equipment. I should have turned him down, but couldn't. I got home safely but tossed that night down as the drunkest that I ever drove, but that's because I'm a hip-hop soldier. I also have a .44 Mag with blunt instructions.

Toga Perversions

A toga party at the Frog House in late September brought back some of the crowd we had lost the previous semester. It also gave Fredo the chance to introduce Waterford to "Fredo's Angels," three girls he brought in and dressed up like low-rent hookers to serve beer and endure his advances. I also met his corporation's attorney, J. Hunter.

Hunter waited until we had a crowd to come down to see the place. He gave off an aurora of stability which offset Fredo's peculiarities. Hunter also brought down a waitress from the restaurant. She traveled to Waterford even though Fredo demoted her at his OKC restaurant for not having sex with Fredo. He did mellow out a little after Hunter talked to him and advised him to tone down his inner pervert. She didn't last long out west.

I organized a benefit concert to support a friend's efforts to raise money to build a skate park. Mercury 1 and Far East, a couple of my favorite local bands, played as skaters rolled around the bar's big room practicing tricks on a couple lengths of rails someone had set up.

Rumors began circulating that Fredo was serving minors and passing bad checks to one of our beer distributors. I could never prove the former, and was disappointed to learn of the latter.

Less than two months after quitting his job and moving to Waterford to work for the Herpinator, Laser had had enough and left Herp's service.

In October, Fredo announced that he wished to change the Frog House from an 18-and-up beer bar to a 21-to-enter liquor bar. While the liquor option had the potential to generate stronger profits, the license is much more difficult to secure compared to Oklahoma's other two options.

The semester moved along nicely. We never achieved the massive numbers Phunky Jay's had in its early days, but we did manage to bring out four and five hundred people somewhat consistently for our bigger bashes.

Fredo's entry onto the scene by no means made everything perfect, but it did bring down the level of day to day madness for the time being.

Two months into the new regime, Herps broke his recent bout of radio silence after seeing me pull into my house as he drove by. He called my Mom.

The story he fed her was that he would never walk off and leave us hanging. I found this ironic seeing as how that's exactly what he'd done a few months back when he had told me that he was laying the bar debt on me after he had agreed to let me out of the bar and take it over so he could run it as his own. He didn't drop one dime on those outstanding debts or on the bills he racked up in my name after he took over.

He couldn't believe that I had let business come between our friendship. I couldn't believe that he would turn out to be a person I still can't believe I ever considered to be a member of my family.

Mom told him that my lawyer had advised me to cease communications with him. The situation had grown bad enough that I had sought legal counsel. He responded that we were the closest thing he had to a family. I can't begin to imagine how he treats whoever comes in second in this horrific contest. She hung up on him after he called Fredo a scumbag. This came from a man who calls women, "dick koozies," because they're just places to keep your cock warm. He swears that, "Everybody I've ever known has screwed me over at least once."

October came to a close with our "Trick or Freak Ball." We laid out eight kegs and five hundred free hot dogs in hopes of attracting people to our costume contest. Once again, we broke five hundred again on the head count.

Halloweenie

I can't imagine what Halloween is like in our fear-mongering, politically correct country these days. I can remember the 1980s and the fear adults instilled in their children with horror stories of razor blades in fruit and drugs in candy. What we did to each other was far worse than any crime I knew of perpetrated in my town on that most wicked of holidays (next to Columbus Day and Black Friday, of course).

Halloween tricks in Waterford ranged from the milder classics such as tee-peeing houses to more outrageous acts like flinging biscuit dough into girls' hair, forcing them to cut it out. We spread peanut butter under the car door handles of friends and enemies alike. The two Clydes rode around in an old farm pickup with a little more evil in mind. They trolled for elementary school trick-or-treaters alone or in pairs. One of the Clydes drove close as the other reached out from the truck bed and snatched up children. The unfortunate child went on a horrifying ride for a block or two before being deposited on the street, sans candy.

By the time I entered college, Halloween night had evolved into a raucous night of drinking with guys in poorly conceived costumes and gals dressed as slutty (fill in the blank).

Lesbian Trick-or-Treat

No telling of Halloweens in Oklahoma would be complete without the touching tale of L-Ron, Pocahontas and the lesbian. L-Ron is a good looking man and sometimes a sexy woman. His lithe body, well tanned from spending many summers of youth life-guarding, and straight, shoulder-length hair made it easy for his girlfriends to transform him into a rather attractive woman for a night.

During the early days of Phunky Jay's, when I had gone through a particularly long period of singleness, the girls in our crew told me that an old girlfriend of theirs was coming for a visit. They thought she'd be just right for me.

The girls built up this impending hook up for the better part of a week. I flogged the dolphin and threw on one of my favorite shirts before heading out to the bar on the day of her expected arrival. The girls walked in with L-Ron in drag. I didn't get laid that night and didn't mind it one bit.

Pocahontas dolled L-Ron up as a very fetching woman for the Halloween they were dating. If he had looked good in the past, he looked downright sexy that night. She had gone to no small effort to do him up as he'd never been done before. A sexy woman herself, Poca wore a slutty cat suit out to Cowball's.

The party drew the usual menagerie of characters from specially ordered costumes costing hundreds of dollars to drunks who had fashioned something together with a roll of duct tape and aluminum foil they found in the bottom of their junk drawer. Packed to the rafters with shit-kickers and Midwestern college kids, L-Ron took a huge risk showing up in drag. It worked. Too well. Elegantly dressed for a night out with his woman, L-Ron turned the heads of several closed-minded boys who would have stomped him had they known he was sashaying around "their" bar in drag.

A number of cowboys asked L-Ron and Poca for dances. They managed to deflect all of their advances without revealing his gender, the failure of which would surely have resulted in the insertion of boots into L-Ron's rectum. The night wore on.

The shining moment of the evening came later when a lone girl who had been staring most of the night approached them with misty eyes. She revealed that she too was a lesbian. She couldn't believe that L-Ron and Pocahontas had the balls to be "out" in public in a small town filled with so many small-minded and prejudiced people.

She went on to explain her main reason for interrupting their evening: almost a year ago to the day, her partner had died. She praised the girls for their bravery and asked one of them for a dance as tears streamed. Luckily, she took Poca for a spin, allowing our "lesbians" to keep their secret. I don't know to how much close inspection his outer deception could have stood up. Thankfully, we never found out.

While we're on the subject of Pocahontas, we should throw out another pair of her greatest hits:

Being in our circle of friends often meant helping each other deal with our casually crazy significant others. Pocahontas was especially dear to my heart, because it was the booze that drew out her demon. During one of their numerous separations, she drove over to Goober's Grotto, where L-Ron was living, to pound on his bedroom window. Demanding to be let in and unaware of her own drunken strength, the window shattered. He took her inside, cleaned her fists up and laid her down for the night.

One drunken night after another of their breakups, she had gotten it into her head that she should drive to his place after closing down Cowball's. Her arrival woke Goober and JeEcHuA and prompted them to take quick action. In her sodden state, she had taken a slight detour through the playground of the elementary school a few blocks down.

Her Camaro caught a twenty-foot length of chain-link fence and dragged it all the way to Goob's house where it now lay half in the street where she had popped the curb to finally stop her vehicular debacle. The boys ushered her inside and quickly stashed the evidence in the Grotto's spacious backyard.

"Mafia" Mishaps

November got weird. By the second week, Fredo had convinced me to come in on Thursday nights to DJ parties for a slight bump in pay.

Fredo introduced his son, Chaz, as a potential pub partner. He was a college student in OKC and a nice guy I would later come to feel sorry for as I learned more about his freakish father. Fredo never made his son's role clear, if he ever had one. Then came Mario and his girlfriend, the "Mafia Princess."

Fredo claimed that Mario was a grandson of none other than Carlo Gambino, the infamous mafia boss. Even better was when he claimed that he had met with John Gotti's son to see about raising five million dollars to open a restaurant in OKC. Mario was off the booze, but when he was on it, it turned him into an angry drunk. He had supposedly played hockey in a European league where some

Russians had gotten him hooked on steroids and vodka until his career had found itself in a permanent penalty box.

Fredo explained that while he had "family" ties, he didn't care to participate in the illegal aspects of their business. Luckily though, he could call on members of the family for capital to fund his ventures.

Mario served as the Princess' bodyguard to protect her from a man would had stalked her nation-wide for more than a year. This freak caught her once, tied her up and repeatedly raped her. Between the law and the "family," I couldn't understand how this rapetacular guy was still running around.

"Stripper Night" hadn't worked at Phunky Jay's, and it didn't work very well at the Frog House either. Star and the Yellow Rose of Texas popped in to go down to their panties and pasties. This pair and the others were barely better than what you'd expect to find a dive strip joint on a Sunday afternoon.

It was during mid-November that I could no longer believe that we were not selling beer to minors. A police officer who had been in the previous week to break up a fight told me that he had been too busy breaking up the melee to stop the minors he had seen drinking. The next day I was introduced to a friend of a friend who had been out that night and didn't even know that she'd been given a "21" stamp until a friend had pointed it out to her. She was 19.

With Fredo having brought out his own crew, Mom and Dad were thankfully spending less and less time out there. I greatly appreciated all of the help they gave me over the years, but it pleased me to distance them from that madness.

Fredo's first semester at the Frog House drew to a close. In a Hail Mary to try to draw the college girls out one last time before the winter break, he brought out some male strippers the week before finals. The local girls didn't show much interest in hired beefcakes Magic Miking in their underwear and 3.2 beer.

Christmas brought about my own adventure in Florida for a week. I returned in time to meet most of the first week of the New Year and the beginning of the last months of the bar. Fredo's bullshit had increased exponentially during my short absence. He put the Princess on a plane east to pick up a car. He sent Mario to Louisiana to pick up his $56,000 cut from a casino in which he had an interest. He decided that instead of reinvesting the wad in the casino, his

241

usual move, he would let Mario use the majority of his greenbacks to fix up Phunky's burned-out side room and put $8,500 of it towards paying off Phunky Jay's debt.

Stealing Our Savior

Our crew assembled at Goober's Grotto one December day not long before Christmas. A brain fart had instructed him to venture out into the couple feet of powder dumped by a rare heavy Oklahoma snowstorm and steal a baby Jesus from a holiday yard display. It couldn't be just any Jesus, he had to have a plastic Jesus glowing from an electric light within, though this didn't stop him from liberating a dozen other infant images from across town.

While my brother busied himself jacking Jesuses, I spent my afternoon with Sosa crushing a thirty-pack of Busch Light around town in Bonnie. We picked up a plastic orange construction safety barrel with a flashing light affixed to its top from a highway construction site we'd passed that evening. I dumped the barrel in Goober's kitchen for a little pre-Christmas party he and his roomies were hosting that night. We got drunker. We got higher. I wanted to see if I could fit in the barrel and got stuck. My friends took a little too much joy out of kicking the barrel around.

Sifting through Goober's new Jesus collection, we came upon a Jesus in the manger painted on a piece of plywood. Its backside had the name and address of this particular future winemaker's owner. We would have been remiss in our duty as young vandals if we had simply thrown it away with the rest of the evidence or even worse if we had secretly returned it. A wonderful third option made itself clear: we covered it with drawings in Sharpies and White Out. That night Jesus received no gold, frankincense or myrrh. He did, however, get a Juggalo face painting, a Nike Swoosh headband, a syringe in one arm, a 40oz bottle of Colt 45, and a variety of various tattoos and treats. My three favorite tattoos were:

What Would I Do?
$ = Salvation
STDs and Greed for All!

The thick layer of snow on the ground didn't stop one of the girls from overfilling her pickup truck's cab with party guests and driving us out into the white to complete our mission. Sosa and I hid in the snow-filled bed. We jumped out at Jesus' home, replanted him, and hopped back into the snowy bed for more booze and bud.

2001 and the End Times

Fredo started off the New Year by offering Mom, Goober and I jobs in his never-named "corporation." We still didn't totally comprehend what the hell his company consisted of. His stories were still too far out there for us to give them much credence. The only aspect of all of this I had much faith in was his actions which had continually spoken much louder than the Herpinator's words.

"The thick sweet-sour odor of sweaty vagina hangs in the air around me like poorly hung cheap prints of artists no one has ever heard of." This entry I found in my journal describing my first night of DJing for a half-dozen female strippers Fredo hired. Thanks to a wild day spent with Sosa, I was half-out of my mind on ephedrine tablets I had attempted to water down with draft beer. Later, I wrote, "We got hotties, hoes, old snatches, and ghetto bitches. Just a typical night at the Frog House."

The end times were near. We just didn't realize it yet.

Fredo fired Mario. Chaz occasionally drove out from OKC to visit. He came down on a wet t-shirt night in early January. The girlfriend of one of Chaz's friends won the contest. When she approached Mario to ask for the prize money, he hit her. As opposed to so many parts of the Frog House saga I only received second-hand, I was standing next to Mario when he assaulted the girl. Fredo, Chaz and Chaz's friend pounced.

Mario escaped. The police came by and searched around the grounds for him to no avail. The Princess lost her shit and yelled at everyone and no one. Fredo canned both of their asses on the spot. Fredo then chose this moment to reveal that the pair had embezzled thousands of dollars from the club. The next day, the pair broke into the side room of the bar by way of the one door they knew wasn't wired into the alarm system. Fredo refused to say what was taken or how he knew the identity of the culprits.

Rather than call the police, Fredo assembled a posse to storm the house he had rented for Mario and the Princess. He had spent the morning installing padlocks on the doors of the house. The couple broke in through a back window to get their furniture. The Princess showed up with a pair of police officers and the landlord. I refused to have any part of that nonsense and left the scene to get the bar ready to open.

We never learned what came from Fredo's attempts to bring Mario and the Princess to justice, but it didn't end there. Mario's rap sheet grew exponentially over the next week.

Fredo tried to have them arrested for forging his name on a handful of company checks.

Mario later used Fredo's name to purchase airline tickets to North Carolina and New Orleans. When the airline tried to collect from Fredo, he told them that they had the wrong guy. The airline canceled the tickets, but the agency Mario tricked was still liable for them according to the police notes in the local newspaper. Mario stole Fredo's car that was supposed to have been repossessed. He made off with close to four grand of the bar's deposits. The police finally got their man somewhere in Oklahoma the next week.

Pat Winning chose the Frog House to bartend one night as part of her quest to be the first person to tend bar in all fifty-four states. The Frog House provided her with her forty-third state.

"Stripper Night" became a weekly event with the final one going down on February 5. It bears mentioning for two reasons: First, I was happy to no longer DJ for those skanks anymore. Secondly, the cops came out to bust up a fight. The problem was that they couldn't find a fight. Somebody called it in just to screw with us, knowing full well that our business would die out for the night once people saw the police rushing the bar.

Fredo began to fall apart just as Herps had. The parallels amazed me. They both became big boozehounds towards the end of their time at the club. I fought with Fredo about him taking his mixed drinks out of his office and onto the bar floor. They both loved the ladies in all the wrong ways. Herps chose to insert his penis into any young girl he could impress with the size of his Hummer or his infected nipple ring. Fredo grabbed the asses of random girls at the bar.

It suddenly ended as fast as and as hard as a space shuttle explosion. Fredo took on another partner. The ink on the check hadn't dried before Fredo had skipped town with $11,000 from the bar's account. He left behind a letter explaining that he couldn't run the bar anymore because of an unnamed illness and was going to live out the rest of his life in seclusion in Catskill, NY.

A Very Bizaar Bizzar Tour

The Dark Carnival once again rolled through Dallas, and along with a thousand other Juggalos, I caught the freak show. For me, this Insane Clown Posse adventure began ninety minutes before the doors opened to Deep Ellum Live.

Not having had the sense to purchase a ticket beforehand, I had to submit to the whims of the only scalper standing outside of the sold-out building. One $17.50 ticket cost me $40 after I talked him down from $50.

While in line, the crowd was the most mellow I've ever seen before an ICP show. I shared ICP stories with those closest to me in line. The only outside excitement came when a man on the second floor of the loft apartments of the Adam Hats building mooned us. He and a few of his friends were bombarded with a barrage of homophobic insults and a few beer cans and bottles.

Minimal security greeted us at the door. Driver's licenses were checked to confirm who was and wasn't twenty-one. No body checks were performed, even though I was sporting the trench coat I wore at the Gathering this summer.

Once inside, I made a much needed restroom break only to find a man unloading a duffel bag filled with everything from bags of chips to foreign cigarettes. Inside the long building, Juggalos filed to the front of the stage or the bar areas on either side.

Insolence opened first. They did a great job. Two on vocals, two guitarists, a drummer, and a DJ made up the band. If Limp Bizkit could sound good, they would sound a lot like Insolence. They covered the basics of hard rock: alcoholism, smoking marijuana and threatening people's lives.

Marz took the stage next, and he never should have. The sound was terrible. I could rarely hear the vocals over the music. When I could make out the lyrics, I wished the sound would overtake them again. The only time the crowd made any amount of positive noise came when the lead singer asked if we were ready for the Clowns.

The opening bands had only a small portion of the stage on which to play.

Black plastic covered Insane Clown Posse props which easily occupied three-quarters of the stage. The plastic was dropped in the darkness before their set, granting us only a minimal view of the set up. It was enough.

A twenty-foot-tall cog-like wheel spun in the background. It featured a white and black spiral - part of the background art for their two new albums, *Bizaar* and *Bizzar*. Four other smaller spiraling cogs surrounded the main wheel. Two eight-foot posts supported rotating clown heads. One side of the nearly identical heads had a smiling clown face, and the other had a frowning clown.

Speakers began repeating "Bizaar, Bizzar" over and over. The crowd chanted along until the volume reached an unbelievable climax. Lights exploded to life, cutting through the smoke-filled void.

The repetitive chanting gave way to the beats of *Bizaar's* first track, "Take Me Away." Two clowns rushed out on stage. They each wore shining, silver full body suits decorated with eyes and question marks and freakishly evil clown masks. Each clown danced around twirling a red on black flag. The crowd went chaotic.

Violent J and Shaggy 2 Dope sauntered out onto the center of the stage. The don mega duo of Psychopathic Records covered a wide range of their then-eleven-year library. Of course the show featured the two new albums with instant clown classics like: "Mr. Happy," "My Axe" and their remake of "Let's Go All the Way." The self-proclaimed "most hated band in the world" couldn't do a show without covering favorites like: "Hokus Pokus," "Toy Box," "Fuck the World," "Chicken Huntin'" and "$50 Bucks." J and 2 Dope took time from the show for many Faygo breaks, soaking the audience in hundreds of gallons of the cheap Detroit soda.

They stopped the music to talk trash on someone all the Juggalos know and hate, and then welcomed onto the stage none other than Marshall Mathers and Eminem. Two guys came out dressed like Eminem. They gimped around acting as though they were butt-fucking each other while slapping asses. The second song they did during this perverse performance was "Eminem's a Bitch." A sexy Juggalette dressed as a cheerleader during "My Axe" came out with some dude sporting Psychopathic Records gear and two large signs. Every time the chorus came around, they opened the signs to reveal "BITCH."

The final insult came when J told us they wanted to slow things down for a while. 2 Dope found a guitar and sat down in a chair brought out for him. "Please Don't Hate Me" is J's confession to his best friend that he's been having sex with his friend's mother. In the final line, J apologizes, saying "sorry, Eminem." While I never bought into their beef, I did enjoy the shots fired from both camps.

Afterwards, they asked us to make noise for a very special guest who has been "down with the Clowns since day one." Vanilla Ice came out sporting a *Ringmaster* hockey jersey and spouted his own lyrics to one of the Clown's songs.

Violent J and Shaggy 2 Dope ended the show with "Down with the Clown," a song from *The Great Milenko*. The song questions the Juggalos' loyalty in a barrage of what ifs. During the song, the Clowns thanked the crowd and told us to rip down the barricade and join them on stage. Fifty-five-gallon Faygo barrels sailed off into the crowd. Speaker towers toppled like Saddam's statue.

This put me at three for three in getting on stage at the end of an ICP show. I later grabbed a tour-themed tee for $20.

Back out on the street, I walked around freezing my ass off, soaked from the sweat of moshing for two hours and the continuous showers of Faygo. I wandered into The Rock. A local band, Tornado Alley, tried to cover Rush, Metallica and Black Sabbath.

"The question is, where's the blow?" a well-dressed man my age surprised me as I stood at the bar drinking my vodka. What the fuck?

"I wish in my nasal cavity," I answered. He laughed and walked off.

At Loose Change, I grabbed a brew and went to take a leak. A mountain of a man blocked the bathroom door.

"Is this the men's room?" I queried.

"Yeah," the Hulkling grunted.

"Pardon me," I spat as I tried to squeeze around his mass.

"You can't go in there."

"Huh?"

"There's business going on in there."

"Ok. I'll just come back later."

"Cool."

It always astounds me when people aren't too particular about what they do or where they choose to do it. I never did get to make an appearance in that bathroom. Eventually, I dried out but was still very sticky. A taxi transported me to the hotel.

The Four Days of 4/20
and
SWOSUpalooza

My friends and I celebrated 4/20 with the same enthusiasm military families celebrate the Fourth of July. Even though pot and I often do not see eye-to-eye, I had no issue with coming out of my semi-retirement to burn down a few once a year. My first university, SWOSU, remains a conservative school in a conservative town with a liberal student body. One of the great concessions to arise from this arrangement was SWOSUpalooza.

In 2000, SWOSU decided to take a step towards becoming a more open-minded and youth-oriented school. They gave us a concert. The day-long event featured local bands and some smaller but better known acts from around the state. The student body broke out their hacky-sacks, old furniture and massive quantities of alcohol to gather on the south lawn of the student union. Their experiment succeeded, granting them a go-ahead to host a second, slightly larger show the next year.

My crew expanded the event into a four-day blowout. Close homies couch-surfed at the Seventh Street Lighthouse for a few days more than usual. I went to class or work, then woke my still snoozin' ninjas with a healthy dose of breakfast in a can, bottle or pipe. I have mentioned before the numerous pills people gave me at my parties. These I deposited into an old prescription bottle from a long since forgotten illness. I broke out the bottle for our annual celebration.

At various points throughout the four days, I dumped out the bottle onto my old McDonald's table. Everyone in attendance snatched a random pill. I'm still surprised we never overdosed. Thus each day began. The school held its concert around 4/20 the first couple of years, so it was an excellent precursor to the mad events of the favorite holiday of anybody who's ever kicked a hack or listened to *Dark Side of the Moon* synced to *The Wizard of Oz*.

I broke out my Mexican serape that Mom had fashioned for me from a $4.99 Mexican blanket Dad had bought for me from a truck stop gas station. Tossing on a Hawaiian shirt and my favorite brown hat, I mixed up a few half-gallons of vodka and cherry Kool-aid, threw them in my backpack and rode my banana yellow Cannondale to the show.

Much of the campus spent the day getting blitzed while listening to the best the local music scene had to offer. We tried to see how many people we could stuff onto an old couch or chair before crushing it, a modern day version of Beetle or phone booth-cramming. While in altered states of minds, the less fearless of the crowd avoided their professors they saw wandering around.

It seemed to me as though the whole ordeal was comprised of two parts. Somewhere during one of the afternoon breaks, people would stumble home for a "quick" nap. Many of them disappeared until Friday night (SWOSUpalooza goes down on Thursdays). I went home to refill my plastic juice jugs and prep myself for the madness which descended with the darkness.

The second SWOSUpalooza will always be the only one which truly mattered. My friends and I dubbed this 4/20 celebration, "The Four Days of 4/20."

Sosa, Squareman and I terrorized the town for four days. They showed up on my doorstep on the first night of 4/20 (I'm sure there's a song in this somewhere). We got screwed up in the ways in which we were experts. Sosa served as our DDD (Designated Drunk Driver) the first night. He took us to the north side of town where he slid his car across several lawns before backing up in a random person's driveway.

Laughter still spilled from us when Sosa turned and asked if we wanted to see "something really funny." Of course we did. "Do you want to see something funny?" had become a loaded question among our people.

This question always served as a prelude to a random and horrible/embarrassing act. The most common "something funny" came whenever we caught one of our crew talking up a woman at a bar. One of us would approach, posit the query to the girl, and then bitch slap the guy talking to her. Few women ever found it as amusing as we did.

Sosa gunned the engine and slammed his car in reverse. We blasted through the garage door. Luckily for us, there was no car in the garage. With his car half in and half out of the stranger's garage, he peeled out and got us the hell out of the neighborhood.

We were far from finished that night.

In a state where many people have tried their hands at cow-tipping, our attempt to tip a Geo Tracker failed.

Our adventures culminated a couple of days later in a trip out to Red Rock Canyon State Park. Formerly a wintering ground for Plains Indians, the park now serves as a playground for families, rappellers and local drunks. A group of Buzzards gathered to burn an unseemly amount of herb and to drink vast quantities of alcohol in honor of the holiday.

Sosa and I had already gotten a good head start on our mission's objectives. I offered to roll us out there in my hearse. He and I tossed some beers in a cooler and headed east. The park's single entry involves an extremely steep winding road not two lanes wide. We encountered a park ranger at the blind turn at the bottom of the entrance. I quickly stashed my tallboy can, upright, beneath the high bench seat of my Bonnie. We both nearly shat ourselves, knowing how much we'd had to drink, not just that day, but the previous three, too.

We charmed our way out of the ranger's scrutiny and made our way to the far end of the park to party the night away. Unfortunately for us, the night only lasted until 8 p.m. or so when we swerved back to Waterford.

Bachelor Party Boobies

I haven't attended many bachelor parties, especially those involving strip clubs or strippers. My first big bachelor party resulted in an equally big mess. By 2001, the last of my friends who hadn't had the urgency to marry thanks to broken or drunkenly forgotten condoms had begun to get hitched. The Deputy, a K-Town Mafia boy, had landed a job as a sheriff's deputy. This surprised us all and frightened a few. The Deputy was the first of several of my people to join the gun-toting ranks of America's more legitimate organizations.

His party kicked off at a pool hall in OKC which caters to the 9-5 crowd at 5:01. A dozen of us met up, knocked back a few beers and chose designated drunk drivers for the rest of the evening. I hopped into Tex's extended cab Chevy to hit the second stop for the night, but not before burning one in the parking lot.

Before the Indians more or less re-conquered Oklahoma with their hundred-plus casinos, Remington Park was where you went to gamble legally in the Sooner State. I put down less than $20 on the horses and more than $20 on the long necks. I personally believe that I left a winner that night. Remington Park may be a decent place to watch the ponies run, but I came for the dollar long neck special they ran on Friday nights. We pounded those dollar Bud and Coors like the ponies we failed to place wagers on pounded the track past the future glue and Jell-O products we had bet on. I did well for myself at the end. In the first race, I lost three dollars on a six-dollar ticket. I more than made up for it by winning $57 and $58 on the last two races. I was content with my first and, to date, only horse track experience.

I would have survived our third stop had Tex and I not celebrated my winnings by smoking once again in the parking lot of Night Trip's, one of OKC's classier strip clubs (for whatever that's worth). I shouldn't have done this, though. Throughout history, most of my heaviest drinking nights have ended badly once we introduced the sweet cheeba into the equation. Not only was this night not an exception to that rule, it evolved into one of the better examples of proof of this rule.

We joined the boys on Trips' horseshoe-shaped even smokier second-level overlooking the stage. Our stage left table butted against the railing. I looked down at the stage, vomited on our table and watched it waterfall over the edge, splashing onto the center of the occupied table and its occupants below.

Wrecked but still in control of some of my motor skills, I wiped my mouth on the sleeve of my Marlboro Miles trench coat and lumbered out to the bed of what I distantly hoped was Tex's truck. In Oklahoma, passing out shitfaced in the bed of the correct pickup truck is no small feat. I succeeded that night. I'm just thankful that the only law enforcement officer around that night was one of our guys.

Phunky Jay's Shitilogue

I neither saw nor spoke with Fredo again after he took flight. We later heard that he had gotten himself arrested and was wanted in several other states, but we never learned the outcome of this. All I do know is that he finally died a few years later.

The Herpinator and I talked on the phone one final afternoon in the post-Fredo era during the short time Fredo's last partner made a stab at running the Frog House. It was insane. He "knew" that I was recording our conversation. He believed that we had had no problems until Fredo had shown up on the scene. No problems?! I wonder what he thought to be a problem if it wasn't the shit hurricane our employees, our customers, my family, my friends, and I had suffered through. While my parents have always supported me in my life's adventures, they had long ago warned me about their suspicions involving him. My parents have a knack at being good judges of character.

Too much bad and weird crap had gone down at Phunky Jay's/the Frog House for the place to ever recover under any other name or proprietor.

The Herpinator tried to communicate with me on and off for a couple of months after Fredo had absconded. He claimed to want to patch things up between us but refused to pay off his half of the loan he'd stuck me with. As much as I had once loved the guy like a brother, it's difficult to make amends with a person when he refuses to pull his herpes-infested dick out of your metaphorical anus.

Due to the amount of people I knew who knew both Herps and Fredo, second-hand stories and rumors rolled in for years after the bar had finally died its painful death.

A weekly meeting of the Frog House's staff on May 8 brought about the announcement of the bar's closing within the next week. Later that same day, one of the people I have most admired during my time on this spinning mud ball slipped away after a six-month battle with a tumor his doctors had predicted would kill him within six weeks at best. I had witnessed the downfall of both the bar and of my mentor, but only cared about the latter. The bar would sit empty until a farm equipment sales company would come into the place for a few years only to shut down in 2011.

The Herpinator would later ramp up his insanity. Y2K didn't bring about the end times he had so fully bought into, but that didn't stop him from preparing for the next round of impending doom.

Herps' fear of the authorities and his creativity led him to concoct some crazy schemes to protect himself when the shit goes down. My favorite of his schemes involved a plan to outfit his Hummer with secret emplacements of explosive traps.

He showed me his designs for one such trap to cut down anyone who came to his driver-side door. His plan was to cut a hole into the front quarter panel and replace it with a piece of light-weight fiberglass painted to blend into its surroundings. Behind this, he would install a homemade device consisting of eight 12 gauge shotgun shells splayed out in a ring on a board. He would run a trigger mechanism from the dashboard to the base of his device. He'd trigger it whenever he felt threatened by someone at his door. I don't know whether not he ever got around to installing this literal kill switch, but I wouldn't take any chances with him.

Word has it that he took to burying shipping containers on some land well away from any of Western Oklahoma's small towns. He filled his containers with supplies and weapons so that he can become a warlord during the coming apocalypse.

One rumor went around that he had gone so far as to plant explosives on the bridges surrounding his little post-apocalyptic burial ground to blow when the Man comes to take him down. It sounds quite unbelievable until you see the foil-covered windows, solar panels and multitude of security cameras on his house in a quiet little residential neighborhood. Between never having paid taxes, a history of drug abuse and pissing off and/or cheating everyone he's ever known, his paranoia isn't so surprising. Everything points to an eventual David Koresh - Branch Davidian hail of exchanged bullets.

Another Very *Bizaar Bizzar* Tour

My summer concert season kicked off with my fourth visit to witness the spectacle of the Dark Carnival. On May 24, the Insane Clown Posse assembled a group of Juggalos and Juggalettes at the Diamond Ballroom in Oklahoma City. This stop was part of the small venue, second leg of their *Bizaar, Bizzar Tour*.

This was my second time to catch this tour, but my first time to visit the venue. I liked the Ballroom. It reminded me of Shreck's, but the beverages weren't as overpriced. Security was overly tight. There are inmates who haven't been patted down as completely as I was.

I still managed to get a disposable camera past them. Although I won that small battle, for once I lost the war. I purposely missed the first opening act, Marz, and didn't mind one bit. Blaze Ya Dead Homie and Anybody Killa took the stage shortly after I arrived. I managed to get two shots off before I had a security guard behind me demanding my camera. I shouldn't have used the flash.

This was my first encounter with Blaze as a solo artist. He impressed the crowd. "Maggot Face" was especially tight.

As with most who travel with the "Wicked Clownz from the dark side of town," Blaze has his own freakish back story. He died in 1989. Voodoo brought him back six years later, but mentally, he still exists in 1989. His music is an eerie combination of 1980's gangster rap and ICP's morbid sense of humor. He still sports a bloody, bullet-riddled Flavor Flav clock around his neck.

Blaze and ABK primed the crowd for Detroit's most infamous duo. Violent J and Shaggy 2 Dope brought the crowd to a frenzy with a set identical to the one I saw in February. They included all of their standards plus many tracks from the two new albums, *Bizaar* and *Bizzar*.

Gathering of the Juggalos II
Toledo, Ohio

Psychopathic Records rented out Toledo's Seagate Center to house three days' worth of activities and concerts for seven thousand Juggalos. The Second Gathering of the Juggalos Ohio's Seagate Center, went about the same for me as did the first Gathering: music, Faygo, booze, titties, and drugs.

I arrived the night before the show started to find a good place to park the van I would live out of for the next four nights. My finances barely allowed for the ticket, so a hotel was out of the question. The van provided adequate room for my cooler and Marlboro Miles air mattress (I don't smoke, but I do collect Miles. Call it payment for second-hand smoke). Besides, I enjoy camping out on the streets.

I had barely gotten settled into my van which would serve as my home for the next four nights when John, a Juggalo whom I'd met the year before, whipped his Jeep Cherokee into the slot in front of me. His crew and I took a hike around Toledo's downtown area to scope out the neighborhood. The Bottle Rocket was the only bar we could find worth a damn. Our face-painted, Faygo-spraying legions scared the "normal" people off the streets. We were the lead news story for four days on every local news station.

Fearing a flood of ferocious Juggalos, several bars posted signs with variations of the "proper dress required" rule to mean no Psychopathic gear for the weekend. A bicycle cop gave us tips on how to drink on the streets, where to find the best nudie bars in Toledo and which states had the lowest age of consent. According to him, Connecticut has the lowest age of sexual consent in the Union at 14. He also listed his favorite Clown tracks. Whoop, whoop indeed.

The Toledo PD mobilized foot patrols, paddy wagons, bike cops, and horse-mounted officers to protect Toledo from us. The Clowns opened the Seagate an hour earlier than planned to get us off of the streets and out of the public eye.

Once inside, we had the opportunity to meet the entire Psychopathic Records family, skateboard, watch movies or buy merchandise. They put together contests with prizes ranging from winning dates with Violent J or Shaggy 2 Dope, or an all expenses paid night on the town at a local strip club to a trip to Detroit to run Psychopathic for a day and backstage passes.

I did some shopping and went out for some afternoon beers in the van. Bands played across the street at some festival on the banks of the Maumee River. A small number of Juggalos ventured out to mingle with the normals.

I met Tittie, Mame, Evan, Eric, and Tim back at the Seagate. We quickly took to each other and pounded some cervezas until the time had come for Twiztid to take the stage that evening. The Seagate had room indoors for three days of hot, sweaty concerts. Twizitd rocked the center, with Blaze Ya Dead Homie, Anybody Killa, Violent J, and Shaggy 2 Dope all joining them for a couple of songs each.

I changed clothes in the van and went to meet Tittie, Mame, Evan, Eric, and Tim for some post-show party action. Tim's aunt lived nearby and was going to let us crash at her place for the night and clean up. On the way to get the remote to her garage door from Tim's car, we ran into Toledo Mayor Carleton S. "Carty" Finkbeiner giving a television interview. We approached the camera to give him hell and to get on the idiot box.

I explained that not only did I have a pair of bachelor's degrees, but that I was also an Eagle Scout. Toledo's bag of dicks mayor only asked whether my degrees were from two or four-year schools. I responded that I had gone to SWOSU to which he informed me that Toledo had some basketballers out there. We left to the local media sharks.

The bars along the Maumee held no attraction for us. We grabbed many 40ozs and went to Tim's aunt's crib for the night.

Day 2

We kicked off the second day with a breakfast served to us by decidedly unfriendly waitresses at a decidedly anti-Juggalo Big Boy. The second night's show gave us Marz, Blaze, Bone Thugs-n-Harmony, and the premiere appearance of that Psychopathic super group, Dark Lotus. Marz underwhelmed. Blaze impressed. Bone filled the stage with pot smoke from their members and entourage. Dark Lotus blew our minds with their occult-laced wicked shit.

I almost missed Lotus. I stepped out towards the end of Bone's set. The Center decided to close its doors without informing us. Nobody was getting back in. Luckily, one of the door guards had questioned me about my Bone on my way out and remembered me when I got back during intermission. He agreed that this was a screwy policy and let me back inside.

Lotus tossed out tracks from their first album, *Tales from the Lotus Pod*, along with some ICP and Twiztid tracks rarely heard live. J and Shaggy closed the show by inviting everyone to party with them at the Radisson Hotel next door. The end of the night found thousands of Juggalos throwing their DLs in the air and chanting, "Party at the Radisson," over and over again.

Pandemonium soon ensued as our throng erupted from the Seagate and invaded the Radisson/Ramada Plaza. With one sweaty message from the two messiahs that seven thousand freaks traveled across the country and/or oceans to see, the hotel lobby quickly filled past capacity.

Only minutes later, the scene turned heavy. Juggalos heaved objects at a wedding party in the lobby and asked the women to display their milk sacks. Garbage and Faygo rapidly transformed the hotel lobby into a small landfill. Our people punched holes in walls throughout the hotel. During the melee, a member from Myzery, an opening band from the first night, tried stabbing several people upstairs.

A wave of cops flooded into the already overcrowded lobby to disperse us and make arrests. They had to take the stairs, because our people had already rendered three of the four elevators out of service. Eventually, they threw us out onto the streets for the night.

Day 3

I killed the first half of the final day cruising around Toledo with new Jugga-homies, Bryan, Franklin, Majestic, and Mylissa, on a mission to score pot. We could have hung a "Mission Accomplished" banner if we hadn't gotten so stoned and drunk.

Some especially strong LSD gave me the most vivid hallucinations of my life. Vanilla Ice opened for Detroit's wickedest duo. My trip peaked when one entire wall of the Seagate disintegrated, revealing an impossibly huge sun setting just behind the building. When I tried to refocus on the Juggalos and Juggalettes around me, they all transmogrified into glorious stalks of corn wearing face paint waving in a breeze I couldn't feel.

A much deserved intermission brought us to the Violent J and Shaggy 2 Dope's Gathering-closing set.

The audience reached a fevered pitch. We'd spent three days meeting each other and becoming a family (even if it was more of a Manson family vibe). Now came our chance to screw it all up.

Toledo had been our bitch for four days. We had tormented shopkeepers, reporters and local law enforcement agencies. Empty Faygo bottles lined the streets. Inside the Seagate Center, seven thousand sweaty and tired Juggalos waited for the most important concert of the Insane Clown Posse's career. They planned on playing an extended set including many songs not played live in years. For a grand finale, they were going to present the ten-year-in-the-making, sixth and final Joker's Card album cover.

The lights dimmed, seven thousand screams joined as a single roar and everything went to hell. The intro music from *Bizzar* began as glowing cogs and gears spun in the background. Violent J and Shaggy 2 Dope sauntered out on stage, microphones in hand and started one of their shortest shows ever.

I had secured a spot fairly close to the stage. Everyone else wanted to be as close or closer. During the first and second songs, our people broke through the security barrier without effort. The tidal wave of people was far too strong to fight By the third song, I found myself shoved onto the stage. One of the highlights of a Wicked Clown show is almost always getting to go onstage during the last song, not one of the first. Juggalos swarmed the stage. Shit went to hell with the quickness.

Someone grabbed J's necklace and dove back into the crowd. J jumped after the thief and beat him down until he reclaimed his property. Marauders on stage tore apart the set along with its lighting and audio equipment. Juggalos Frisbee-tossed giant gears from the stage's background into the audience. Alex Abbiss, then-head of Psychopathic Records, had a van standing by to get the bands out to avoid any police charges of inciting a riot.

The music died and the house lights came on. I stood on the edge of the stage, staring at a massive sea of angry, disappointed and confused Juggalos. People began pointing towards the stage. I had flashbacks to last summer when I was on stage at the same show in Detroit, except then they were pointing at my nearly naked body. I turned around to see a cloud of tear gas rolling towards me. Tear gas is not as fun as it sounds. In my altered state, having my eyes water and my skin burn for two hours was not a welcomed experience.

Twenty minutes after the destruction began, the crew set up a mike and a speaker. Abbiss let us know how bad we'd fucked shit up that evening: They had lost the stage, most of the sound equipment and the mechanisms needed to reveal the face of the Sixth Joker's Card. A giant display of the artwork for the Card was meant to unfurl from above the stage. He thanked us for three incredible days and said that they'd see us next summer in Vegas. I couldn't fathom doing this in a town with casinos, free booze and prostitutes. It was not a proud night for Juggalos.

With the house lights up, we streamed out into the night. I saw more police and reporters than I had ever before witnessed in one place. Tear gas flew which does not mix well with acid. I drank at my van as Juggalos set off fireworks. Mounted police and cops in riot gear stuck around until 2 a.m. to clear most of our rabble out of their city.

A street cleaner passing my van woke me early in the morning. A quick walk around downtown the next morning showed that Toledo had quickly recovered overnight. By the time the first beams of daylight reached out over the river and into the city, almost all traces of our tribe's presence had disappeared. A pair of abused Port-a-Johns and an ICP sticker on a convenient store stood as the last evidence that the Dark Carnival had ever rolled through and over Toledo.

The only other thing I can really say about Toledo is how completely unhinged their nightlife is. The closest clubs didn't want Juggalos mingling with their Bricktown 54-esque preppy crowds. Other rock clubs wanted ten dollars a head for the privilege of listening to local bands. There were many strip clubs north of us, but you know me better than that. Unless you enjoy stiff joints with dress codes and overpriced drinks, you're better off an hour north in Detroit or even Windsor, Canadia.

Not surprisingly, we didn't make the greatest of impressions upon the locals. Channel 11 quoted Mayor Finkbeiner as saying, "We are extremely disappointed the Seagate booked the ICP and didn't provide adequate security." A mother who had driven her son down from New York had a better view of our shenanigans, "It's easier to get a fire hose and clean up Faygo than blood."

Memphis Memories
(Or Lack Thereof)

A trip eleven hours east to Memphis with Mom and Goober for her fortieth class reunion helps to highlight the chasm of the differences between the Goob and I.

Friday

We spent our first night just outside of Memphis in a Comfort Inn complete with cockroaches and thirteen channels to choose from on the television. They did have a waffle maker and biscuit and gravy on their continental breakfast. Ten years had passed since I last had ridden the short hour to Ashcan, Mississippi.

Ashcan is the kind of place where almost nothing changes, even though it should. My family left in 1986. I skipped second grade after my teacher saw that I was the only child who could read and write at any level in my class. My fourth grade teacher told Mom in no uncertain terms to get us out of that town and into schools with more literate educators.

Despite Mom's lineage, we did not find Northern Mississippi to be a difficult place to bid farewell to for various reasons. Mr. Black was (and hopefully no longer is) a second grade teacher in the Benton County Schools with a classroom just outside of the main office. Mr. Black was a gigantically obese black man with a well-known fondness for young boys. From the moment we arrived in

Ashland, our parents hand-selected every teacher we had in its impoverished school system to ensure we had literate, non-pedophile instructors.

A tank of a man, Mr. Black's classroom next to the head office was no mistake. Unfortunately, it was not so they could watch over him. In the early eighties, we bore little to no semblance to what passed even then as modern school systems. Black served a secondary function as school's our PA system. I learned of the *Challenger* explosion from him bellowing the announcement throughout our school's halls.

Our parents always warned us to keep our distance from Mr. Black and to immediately inform them if we had any contact with him. Every day, Mom or Dad would drive up to the end of one of the school's three long hallways to pick us up. I met Mom one day and waited with her for Goober. His second grade teacher had had something to discuss with him which had held him back a few crucial minutes. When we saw Goober leave her classroom, we saw him carve a wide path around Mr. Black who came out of his classroom and tried to cajole Goober into entering his room. Goober ran. We drove off. Dad later returned and told Black flatly that if he ever so much as looked at one of his sons again, he would us his 12-gauge to cut his rotund child-molesting ass in half.

Our favorite librarian somehow managed to secure better computers for her library serving a town of six hundred than the one I originally typed this story on in my university's journalism lab. Our few relatives left in town were just as we had left them. I have always marveled how that little twilight zone could have so many of the most wonderful people I have ever had the privilege to share parts of my life with surrounded by people who honestly believe that "the South shall rise again."

The Piggly Wiggly, the town's only grocery store, had become a "food salvage store," whatever the hell that is. Kudzu, an Asian vine that can grow a foot a day and starve trees of sunlight, still covered most of Ashcan's surroundings. Local law enforcement had converted an old dress factory across the street from the Grandma from Hell's old house into a place to store criminals.

Mrs. Blanche lived in Michigan City, a speck of a dot of a town that had a church, a couple of houses, a shuttered post office, and a dead-end road. We couldn't visit the state without seeing this amazing woman who had lived and worked around the world, first with her Air Force husband and then solo with the Peace Corps after his death. She puttered around in her immaculately kept original 1960s convertible Volkswagen Bug well into her nineties.

Unfortunately, the ten-minute drive to her house took an hour. A light rain dampened the pot-holed two-lane highways and created the perfect opportunity for chaos. We stopped sixth in line at a wreck. From my window, I could see a Dodge Dynasty with its hood popped up sitting in the marsh that lined both sides of the road. Someone with an umbrella stood near the driver's door. No ambulance or police had arrived yet.

It took little to convince Nurse Mom to go have a look. I grabbed my hat and a camera. Mom and I slipped down the five-foot slope into the ankle deep water. The driver looked fine with the exception of an obviously broken leg and suffering from obesity. She lay on her back in the murky water. Blood covered the open door. The entire front end had crunched back into the car. She had hit a small, extended cab truck head on.

The man in the truck had not worn his seat belt. The front end was twisted and gnarled. The impact of the hit launched him up and over the front seat onto the rear jump seat. We stayed until emergency services finally arrived on the scene.

Even though we had evacuated Mississippi fifteen years before, the patrolman recognized Mom from her ambulance days. Some small towns never change.

Saturday

Back in Memphis after our visit, Mom scored a hotel downtown near Beale Street. Most schools begin combining classes for reunions as the years go by. Mom's fortieth included W. W. Herenton, Memphis' mayor at the time. He rented out the Redbird's stadium, a local AAA team of the Cardinals, for his classmates.

Goober and I struck out on our own. Beale Street is a carnival midway for drunkards. Instead of games lining the street, it offers bars. Police erect barricades each weekend evening to close off four blocks of road in downtown Memphis. Most of the clubs there set up small, fully equipped bars on the sidewalk in front of their businesses.

Neighborhood children perform astounding acrobatics on the street for tips. One teenage boy launched himself over eight of his friends and two party-goers in one, perfectly executed leap. A half dozen street musicians take up spots along the strip and play all night long. Vendors sell corn on the cob, hot dogs and burgers to starved party animals. On Beale, you can listen to bands or DJs, have your palm read or buy overpriced camera film (although I bet that last one has probably since died out).

At 11 p.m., Beale Street features its own twisted "changing of the guard." Anyone under twenty-one is allowed to roam freely along the strip until this time. After the kids go home, the vagrants come out to play. A small army of unwashed men march out to panhandle. Some will try to sell you drugs. Others just want cash. For the most part, they are a friendly lot. I've had more than one conversation with a couple of them over the course of my visits. Their stories are varied and yet share similar pieces or a core destructive event in their lives which put them in their current position and they want out, or they just want to get high.

Looking for dinner, Goober and I wandered into a pizza joint for a pie and some brews. We settled on their Rainbow Pizza. They claimed that they dubbed it the Rainbow, because you had to be gay to put that much meat in your mouth. Our large pizza was a properly obscene meat-gasm. It had most of what you'd expect from a meat lover's pizza, but checking under the hood, we found quite the surprise. They had taken at least a pound of breakfast sausage and pounded it flat into a half-inch thick disk and placed it between the sauce and the cheese. Another butcher shop's worth of dead critters rode the cheese. It was a heavy way to begin the evening, although we would come to find out that we needed those calories to get us through our respective nights.

Alcohol flowed. We survived three or four bar hops together before our natures beckoned us on to separate adventures. Fifty dollars left my wallet in the dark end of an alley for a bag of coke which helped me party until after 4 a.m. I crept into our hotel room waking Mom.

"Where's Goober?" she groggily inquired.

"I don't know. We lost each other a while back," I answered. "He'll be back later."

"Okay…"

The sounds of my worried mother later brought me out of my slumber. I can't recall whether I awoke to her phone call to the police, a hospital or the highway patrol, but she made the rounds that morning. Goober put in an appearance two hours after I rolled out of bed and almost an hour before I would've gotten concerned. He offered a lame story about having gone off to a party without being able to secure a ride back to our hotel.

Goober later confided in me that he'd gone off to the far east side of Memphis with two girls for a threesome. He banged two girls. I inhaled lines of low-end cola on the backs of toilets at several Beale Street bars. Such is how we respectively roll.

No visit to Memphis would be complete without tucking in for a meal at the greatest barbeque restaurant in the state, Charles Vergos' Rendezvous. Down a dank alley, it offers Memphis style barbeque at its best. Old Cotton Festival posters, maps of United Airline's routes from Memphis and other local memories cover almost every square inch of the walls.

We spent the rest of the day strolling through downtown. Mom had worked for the cotton exchanges in the '60s and showed us her past. We saw some Civil War memorials (most of which were erected during the Nadir when the south wanted black people to know how they felt about the "War of Northern Aggression"), the first all-black radio station and the mighty Mississippi River.

Bongzilla

The majority of my adult Halloween costumes have been lazy triflings compared to the special effects efforts of my childhood. Growing up on sci-fi and horror movies from the days before computerized special effects, I had long harbored a dream of getting into the effects game thanks to the likes of *A Nightmare on Elm Street 3: Dream Warriors, Star Wars: Episode IV - A New Hope* and *Basket Case*. The takeover of computer generated imagery all but slaughtered that for me, putting it in the grave alongside other, less-realistic, dreams of mine like becoming a mafia boss or a brontosaurus.

Most of my adult costume attempts failed miserably. Some of the girls in college tried to turn my excessively long hair into a mohawk using several cans of hair spray, a can of mousse and a couple eggs in a sad attempt to go out as a punk rocker. Sipping beer through a straw for half an hour as the girls took turns blow drying my hair resulted in a sticky, tall 'hawk that invariably collapsed shortly after we unstuck it from the torn apart Budweiser box upon which they'd done their work.

Dressing as a homeless vet years later in Korea didn't go over well as I drank with my friends in the bar area outside of the country's second-largest U.S. Army base. Throwing a sheet over my head the next year to be a ghost had even worse results. Every black soldier I encountered that night accused me of being in the KKK. I find it strange that they'd never seen a ghost costume before.

My sheet had no pointy top. It only had eye holes, a mouth hole and a few sex stains. Although, I probably shouldn't have been toting a burning cross.

I scored one overwhelming success as an adult. It went down during my last Halloween in WLOTUS. Cowball's hosts the town's biggest Halloween party each year. Indecision loomed over me as I sat at my desk at work, the bar opening in a mere five hours. A wave of inspiration hit me as I began scratching hasty sketches on company stationery. I would transform myself into a bong - a bong the likes of which no one had ever seen before. My boss let me go a few minutes early.

Three hours until the bar opened.

A quick trip to Ace Hardware scored me the supplies I would need: a length of PVC pipe, a roll of chicken wire, a coil of bailing wire, and a small length of rope. These items, along with a few others I procured from Mom and Dad, I assembled on their garage floor.

T-minus two-and-a-half hours.

An hour later, I had assembled the bong's body by stacking three tubes fashioned from chicken wire and connecting them with bailing wire. At about crotch level, I cut a circular hole in one side of the seven-foot tubular structure and a square hole opposite it. The square returned later on hinges. For some reason, I had originally planned on dyeing a white sheet black until Mom pointed out my bad idea. I should point out that I'd already smoked a bit and had started drinking by then. An old black bed sheet wrapped around this frame gave it its color. Another rectangular slot cut two-thirds of the way up provided me with a viewing port.

A liberal application of an industrial glue affixed a plastic mixing bowl to one end of the PVC pipe after I'd cut the bottom out of it and slapped in a piece of mesh. This stem and bowl I painted a metallic gray. Before inserting the pipe into the hole of the bong, I Duct Taped a half-dozen of the longest, thickest incense sticks I could down into its interior. I secured a handful of dried, dead plant matter from Mom's garden to the mesh in the bowl to simulate marijuana.

I reattached the rear door. Tying two lengths of rope inside the bong's frame used as suspenders completed my costume. The bong tube's width offered plenty of wiggle room. The suspenders let the costume sit comfortably on my shoulders while allowing me to turn around in it so I could access the rear bathroom door.

I was half in the bag when I loaded my masterpiece into my Dodge Caravan after I'd folded the seats down. Donning my bong turned me into a nine-foot tall ode to potheads everywhere. I had failed to take into consideration the size of Cowball's entrance. My night would come to consist of numerous extreme limbo moves. Thankfully, the dance floor had a ceiling two-stories high. Unfortunately, I don't dance. Difficulties ensued every time I needed to refresh my drink, which was often, and when I needed to use the bathroom, not so often.

Hours later, they started the costume contest. Bongzilla scored second place and $150, which didn't quite cover that night's tab. I would have taken first, but this happened to be Halloween 2001. Blind patriotism led my fellow bar patrons to give my $500 to a portly guy in a suit pretending to be Dick Cheney, two other guys in suits serving as his body guards and another dressed as Osama bin Laden. "Osama" wore a white bathrobe and a cotton ball beard obviously stolen from an elementary school student's Santa Claus art project. A paper towel roll rocket painted red, white and blue protruded from his chest. He looked like an Osama made by kindergarteners for the most offensive school play in history.

Bongzilla would call the Seventh Street Lighthouse's garage home for years to come. Cleaning up the Lighthouse to sell it, I donned my favorite costume one final time before burying it in the Dumpster in the alley.

2002

Too Much Tunica Tonight

I love the K-Town Mafia boys, but they gamble like I drink: to excess. One of the boys once had a $50,000 swing during March Madness. He went down thirty large in the beginning of the season and ended with twenty grand in his pocket by the Final Four. They even went so far as to forego their usual end of summer trip floating the Illinois River to drive out to Tunica, Mississippi for an overnight gambling excursion.

Nine of us loaded into Ned's parents' van to make the ten-hour drive to Tunica, a tiny shithole of a gambling town in Northwestern Mississippi. Casinos came to Tunica in the early 1990s to take advantage of the cheap labor in this impoverished town. Now the hotels have the capacity to hold the population of the town itself many times over.

A cooler of beer wedged between the middle captain's chairs kept us company for the duration of the night. The group designated a few of us with heavy livers to drink the night away while keeping the driver company. It made for a wise division of labor between those of us who are good behind the wheel and those of us who excel at not passing out.

Checking into Harrah's late the next morning, my people began to scope out what games they would attack first. Never having been much of a gambler, I immediately looked to the craps tables and how much booze I could score for slapping some chips on the line. To get some padding in our guts before we set out to make our fortunes, we hit the buffet. Already/still wasted, Houston regaled us with loud tales of hookers and other debauchery from a trip to Amsterdam. By the time he had finished practically yelling his stories, the normals in our vicinity had moved away to give us a minimum two-table buffer zone, despite the high amount of traffic in the restaurant during the lunch hour.

I played a little and drank a lot throughout the afternoon. Most of us met up for a light dinner and then to take advantage of the hotel's pool and hot tub. The gambling, if not the drinking, had stopped for a time at least. Houston cannonballed into the tub, ensuring that we would have it to ourselves. Night fell, and we returned to the tables.

As the night burned on, I noticed an older blond woman catching my eye more than a few times. We happened to wind up at the same table for a few minutes where Angie and I exchanged pleasantries. The night ground down, and our crew slowly made its way back to our rooms.

While comparing our tales of the day, I mentioned Angie. The K-Town boys leapt on me for not having leapt on her. They reasoned that any random woman talking to a random guy at a casino was up for sex. Although twenty hours of drinking gave this line of thought credibility, I didn't quite agree nor did I feel like venturing out to get in. At least I didn't until about half-an-hour later, when one of the boys tossed me a Valium which I washed down with yet another can of beer.

I returned to the casino floor and armed myself with a Jack and Coke, my official casino drink of choice. It didn't take long to locate my target on the mostly deserted casino floor. We talked and drank. Then she invited herself to my room. I had to explain that while the four guys I shared my room with would probably enjoy watching us get our groove on, she might not be too inclined to be watched like animals at the sex zoo. She offered up her room but said that she had to remedy a minor "complication" first.

Left weaving and drinking for nearly thirty minutes, I had just about decided to bail and collapse. Angie returned. She had resolved the issue keeping us from her room and led me back. The 45-ish cougar explained that she had had to get a second room for her mother, with whom she was traveling. Highly drunken sex followed.

I awoke the next morning in a dastardly hungover haze to the aroma of steak and fried eggs. Angie had ordered room service for us and fed me in bed. To date, our twenty-plus year age difference remains a personal record as does the breakfast that followed the bumping of the uglies.

A few drinks sobered me back up to drunk and prepared me for yet another long ride home. Sadly, that was the second best casino experience I have had in America.

Wrong Wradio

I held one final job of note before leaving WLOTUS. I put in five months at Wrong Wradio, the Western Oklahoma version of a media empire. At the time, WW consisted of three FM stations and an AM station. I had recently finished my second round of college, which earned me a sheepskin in mass communication, and was excited for the chance to work at a radio station, even if it was at minimum wage.

Although my official title was "Assistant to the Sales Manager," I was the station's jack of all trades. I worked on creating sales packages while deflecting my sales manger's attempts to bed me.

I served as the second member of our news department. Not that much ever happened in Western Oklahoma, but we had to cover what little did go down. The news chief handled the legitimate stories. I suffered through city hall meetings and court proceedings. One would think that watching meth-heads getting handed their sentences would be slightly more interesting than watching toast mold, but it wasn't.

Another duty, by far the worst, had me running the boards during football games and a Sunday morning church service. They couldn't have been more diametrically opposed.

Running the boards for football was the most hectic job I will ever have. It required me to listen to Chance, the best sports announcer in Western Oklahoma, broadcast the game as I simultaneously phoned every other school hosting a game that night to get updates on their scores. I constantly cycled through a list of numbers while trying not to miss any timeout called or quarterly breaks in the Waterford High School game to which I had to listen with one ear.

Chance is a great guy when he's off the field. When he's working a game, he transforms into a tyrant. Despite the fact that all I did for three hours was make phone calls for him while listening to games I couldn't care less about, I could never satisfy him. Anytime a score hadn't changed for more than a few minutes, I believe to this day that he blamed me.

The end of each game was the only part of this gig I ever truly enjoyed. Our DJs prerecorded their night shifts. Most games ended before their "shift" got under way. This usually afforded me anywhere from ten to thirty minutes of free time on 96.9 The Rattler.

I had fun ignoring the modern, mostly shit-tacular country music we usually played. Anybody who stayed tuned after a game that fall heard Kenny Rogers, George Strait, Hank Williams Jr., Merle Haggard, and Waylon Jennings when I helmed the post-game boards.

While most of my time at the station had nothing to do with journalism, I did play a role in covering two stories of note during my brief stint at the news desk.

I loved storm-chasing before it devolved into the parade of douchebaggery we now have across Tornado Alley. A small tornado struck a small town southwest of Waterford. I arrived on the scene not but a few minutes after an F2 had torn off a few roofs, pushed a house slightly off of its foundation and shredded the obligatory number of trailer homes. I nailed down a few aspects of the story on-site before driving back to Waterford's Wal-Mart to cover and assist in relief efforts taking place there.

Dad was always an early riser and a big fan of watching news channels and Fox "News." It was from him busting into my childhood bedroom to wake me up to alert me that our nation was under attack on a certain Monday morning in September, 2001. Born during the Great Depression, Dad had lived through many of our nation's greatest tragedies: Pearl Harbor, WWII, Kennedy's assassination, 'Nam, the rise of disco, the failed assassination of Reagan, the Challenger explosion, and the birth of reality television.

American Airlines Flight 11 wasn't the first to strike a New York City skyscraper. A B-25 Mitchell bomber flew into the Empire State Building in 1945. While tragic, watching the breaking news of that first plane's damage in the North Tower of the World Trade Center wasn't enough of a shock to evoke thoughts of anything more heinous than of an accident in the minds of most folks Dad's age (except of course for those in Bush's administration who had read and promptly ignored intelligence reports indicating a coming attack on American soil).

Then United Airlines Flight 175 struck the World Trade Center's South Tower. All doubt evaporated. Dad wasn't going to let me sleep through whatever fresh batch of hell was being served up in the Big Apple.

Living in Oklahoma gave a lot of us a certain feeling of disconnection from 9/11. We lived too far away from the actual events to experience any immediate sense of impending doom. But many in the Bible-Belt felt self-important enough to start wondering when we were going to get ours, while others wanted to suit up for action.

Having grown up on the original *Red Dawn* and that quadrilogy of fantastic future documentaries, *Mad Max*, I began my 9/11 by cleaning and loading all of my pistols, shotguns and assault rifles as the world quickly went to shit around me.

Checking in at the station, I ventured out to take Waterford's temperature. I wasn't surprised by the confused, panicking lemmings forming snaking lines of cars at every gas station in town. Those fools may have secured thirteen gallons of go-juice, but I had over a dozen locked and loaded guns and a cache of food and water to see my family through at least a month of the catastrophe W. and his minions had all but invited onto our soil. All of our precautions and knee-jerk reactions proved unnecessary. The apocalypse never came…at least not on that day.

For smaller media outlets like ours, we focused on reactions from locals and tales from the small number of our people anywhere near to the events of the day. In the end, there was little for us to do than to other than play feeds from the big players in the game.

My second job behind the boards was every bit as boring and uninvolved as doing the games was hands-on and frantic. I unlocked the station at 5 a.m. on Sundays to switch the overnight systems on our AM station to broadcast a four-hour local church service. Unlike the games where I placed phone calls while listening attentively to Chance, on Sundays, I only had to remain awake once I'd gotten the whole shebang up and running.

The church services were hell on earth. I arrived before the sun clocked into work for the day. I sat alone all morning long atop of a little hill just west of Waterford. Being a mere twenty-four-years-old, it was a rare Saturday that I didn't close down one of the few local watering holes and party into the wee hours. Companies shouldn't force secular people to work religious gigs. I had to run through the station screaming my head off to stay awake some mornings when the words in my novels began blurring together.

I never really understood what purpose I served there, because the system never failed on my watch and required nothing from me once I'd switched the prerecorded DJs over to the live feed. I easily could have left after starting up each morning's broadcast and returned hours later to switch it back without anyone the wiser. The idea was sound, but on the off chance that something had gone wrong, or on the rare occasion when somebody phoned the station, I had to be present. I always wanted to have sex out there, but couldn't find any girl able to party that late or to get up that early.

The mornings were difficult, but I sometimes found relief in watching the sun rise while smoking a bowl on the station's back porch.

As interesting as this gig was, it wasn't going to provide me the future I needed. Western Oklahoma had failed me. Or maybe I had failed it. Either way, the downfall of Phunky's helped to usher in unpleasant times in our little backwater oasis. Friendships fractured. Folks fled town. An era had ended.

College is a time for people to figure out just who the hell they are. Graduating forces them to see how well they can mesh those new selves with the rest of the world. The time had come for me to mesh with the Ninjaverse.

EPILOGUE:

The time had come to make a major change in my life. I decided to buckle down and join the rat race. I hunted for work in the post-9/11 age. Even with a pair of degrees and my varied experience, my prospects looked slim.

My first opportunity came to me in the form of a depressing job opportunity. I landed a position in Oklahoma City that would lead me down a path far darker than any I had previously traveled. Against my better judgment, I agreed to go to work for a telemarketing company. I had no interest in becoming a member of one of the most hated professions in the world, but I saw no other options.

While I did

Deciding that I had not traveled far enough on the bad decision train, I found a place to stay in OKC. A couple friends of mine from university offered up a spot in their condo. They had a carpeted attic space I could look at. The center of the triangular room of the A-frame building was nearly tall enough for me to stand upright on my knees. The floor allowed enough room for me to squeeze in a small mattress.

I went up to stay a night with my friends and to check out the neighborhood. They busted out several lines of cocaine and informed me that they had become local suppliers of that wonderful white South American powder. They desired to share their good fortune with me and offered their attic to me for free.

They taught me that I'm a tequila snob. I'd long said that I hated tequila. They proved me wrong by showing me a shelf filled with bottles of Mexican urine, the cheapest of which cost $50 a pint. Quality tequila is tasty. I learned not to purchase jugs of bargain tequila.

We pounded several bottles of their quality booze, Hoovered many lines and watched *Pootie Tang* a couple of times.

I woke up on their couch the next day drove back to Waterford. I had resigned myself to multiple facts of my reality. My attempt to run a bar had been fraught with bad decisions from its conception. Several amazing women had come and gone in my life, but I lacked the skills to hold on to them. Add to that the fact that I had decided to move into the attic of drug dealers to cold call people in feeble and unwanted attempts to sell them garbage they didn't need.

I would leave my minimum wage radio job at the end of the year to make the move. Then my life changed one morning in December.

Reading through the classifieds in the Sunday paper in a desperate attempt to change my direction, I stumbled onto an ad which would do just that. The ad wanted someone to teach conversational English at a three-year foreign language high school in Seoul, South Korea, "four-year degree required, teaching experience preferred." I possessed no teaching experience, had hair down to my ass and spoke my own, odd dialectical mishmash of Juggalese, random slang ranging four decades, words I'd concocted over the years.

My application reached Dr. Mulberry the next week. After a few rounds of interviews, I had purchased my first flight ticket and secured a passport. I was off to South Korea.

###
To be continued...

Ninjalicious II: Crazy Corea

A Tricky Shot

The doc, nurse and cameraman entered. This would be a good place to backtrack and briefly touch on my endless fascination with the human body. We inhabit amazing machinery. I have always possessed a desire to keep all of my parts together (or relatively close at hand). The first manifestation of this arose when, upon having my tonsils removed in third grade, I was told that the hospital would not allow me to keep them afterward. Instead, I received a plush tiger from a crazy woman and the final installment of Marvel's four-part adaptation of *Return of the Jedi* from my parents. I have every one of my teeth, including the hunks of my lower wisdom teeth which had to be shattered to be removed. When I had my first hernia surgery in 1998, all I had to show for it was a four-inch scar and the memories of an agonizing month of recovery. Dr. Lee, the surgeon for my second hernia surgery (last November at

아주대학교 병원 - Ajou University Hospital) made a copy of the video he usually takes of his surgeries for review and possible protection and/or incrimination in the event of a malpractice suit.

Dr. Jeong doesn't tape his surgeries, but he did allow me to bring in a video camera and an accompanying cameraman. I was able to secure a camera quick enough from a coworker (thank you, P-Funk) during the two hours I had between placing the initial phone call that set up the appointment and leaving home to head up there. Tracking down someone willing to watch Jeong slice open my reproductive organ for an hour who wasn't still at work or on his/her way home from work at 6 p.m. on a Wednesday proved an insurmountable task.

Jeong actually went out during my prep time with the nurse and found a guy to tape the event for me. He obviously didn't work there, and for all I know was some random bum off the street who thought he'd get a kick out of staring at a foreigner's penis for thirty minutes through a viewfinder. Either way, he had phenomenal skills. I don't know how many crackers' ding-a-lings he's filmed before, but he captured mine perfectly. He had a steady hand and knew how to frame the shot (it has since racked up more than 370,000 hits on YouTube). Thank you, mysterious pervert.

The cameraman stood on a chair to my left. This simultaneously kept him out of the way of the nurse and her tools on my right and blocked the surgery's reflection on the wall behind him. The doc took up position at my left thigh.

It was an eerie event to be sure. Those of you who have gone under the knife before probably remember barely remembering the UFO light above the operating table you stared into as that sweet combination of inhaled gas and injected drugs carried you away to a dreamless, painless void. Besides cutting your vas deferens tubes, a vasectomy also cuts out this part of the surgical dance. Disturbing arrays of thoughts pass through your sober mind while you stare at those lights. Conditioning from past experiences and a slew of fade-to-black movie scenes cause an unending anticipatory expectation of a darkness that never comes.

The local anesthesia turned my groin to rubber. The doctor's fingers probing, pushing and pulling at my flesh in search of my left and right vas deferens did register in my head, but it registered in the same faint, imaginary way my face does when I play with it while still sitting in my dentist's chair seconds after his assistant turns off the gas and asks me to spit the last of the rinse water, blood and filling shavings out of my mouth. Or when I play with my face three hours after munching a gram or three of quality fungus.

It took a minute or two of fingering me to locate the vein stars of the show. I tried watching it all on the overhead reflection, but it was as blurry as my doctor and nurse's touch. The color of their gloved hands and my flesh melded into one fleshy not-quite human tone broken only by spotty amounts of my bright crimson blood and the barely discernible gleams of syringes and other stainless steel tools of the trade floating in and out of my limited field of vision.

We traded short bursts of conversation at the outset of the procedure over the drone of a radio in the background. The topics and languages bounced around the room. Bounced around until he extracted my first tube, that is. "Your vas is somewhat thick," said my slightly surprised doctor.

Confusion still remains as to whether his amazement at my size comes from a lack of experience with foreigners or from the possibility that I do actually have tubes that could have once been worthy of carrying the first trans-Atlantic telegraph message via semen. When asked whether my girth simplified or complicated matters, Jeong affirmed the latter. It enhanced the difficulty of using his electric cauterizing gun to seal the ends of the sliced tubes shut. The conversation died out as he went to work on my right vas.

The remainder of the surgery passed in a quiet, event-less stream. Dr. Jeong and his nurse had laid their hands on so many previous penises that they completed the second slicing and cauterizing without so much as a single word passing between themselves or I in any language. They threaded a single black stitch through either side of the 1/3-inch opening they had created on the underside base of my penal shaft. The doc gave a curt acknowledgment to the completion of the procedure and left the cleaning of my crotch to his nurse. My cameraman switched the machine off and returned it to its aluminum case.

Wiped down and adorned with a fresh waterproof band-aid, my nurse instructed me to redress and went about ignoring me as he reset the room for the next patient. I let my shirt fall, carefully pulled up my black Adidas wind pants and adjusted my Nut visor.

In the lobby again, I paid my bill of 250,000won. Dr. Jeong handed me a prescription for a five-day's supply of two capsules - one to stave off infections and one combination anti-inflammation and pain killer. He gave me little else. The nurse had told me to change the band-aid the next day. The doctor told me to take one pill after eating three times a day. He wanted me to come back in a week to remove the stitch.

A pharmacy sat conveniently across the hall from the clinic. I had to walk less than thirty feet to get from one counter to the other. The pharmacist also spoke English and explained that it didn't matter if I ate or not before taking my meds. Korean insurance doesn't cover vasectomies or the medication for them. The medication cost 23,460won, the most I have spent in Korea for legal drugs.

A mere fifty minutes after first walking into the clinic, I stepped out into the brisk Bundang night. My vasectomy had cost me a two-hour roundtrip, less than 275,000won, another scrotum shaving, and a case of slight indigestion from a sub-par Subway sandwich.

About the Author

G.S. NEARING is a novelist, educator, vagabond, Hasher, and Juggalo. He currently lives in South Korea with his far superior half, Chairman Wife.

Hunt down Ninjalicious on Facebook:
https://www.facebook.com/Ninjaliciousthebook

Follow Richard Lichman's mental maladies on Twitter:
https://twitter.com/RichardLichman

Favorite G.S. Nearing at Smashwords:
https://www.smashwords.com/profile/view/RichardLichman

Works by G.S. Nearing:
Ninjalicious: The Fictional Autobiography of Richard Lichman
Ninjalicious II: Crazy Corea (Dropping in late 2017!)
Ninjalicious III (Slated for a release in 2018ish!)

www.ingramcontent.com/pod-product-compliance
Lightning Source LLC
Chambersburg PA
CBHW061553170626
46811CB00001B/189

* 9 7 8 1 9 4 6 5 5 1 0 0 9 *